THE FLAG

ROBERT SHAW'S new novel is the first volume of a trilogy, *The Cure of Souls*, and makes use of certain extraordinary events which occurred at East Thaxted when the Rev Conrad Noel was Vicar there. The Vicar, Calvin – an ex-miner, a zealot, a Christian Socialist – explodes upon the little East Anglian town in 1925. He presents his parishioners with a revolutionary conception of their Faith: the Lady of the Manor and a retired General are won over, but Calvin has powerful enemies, and troubles at home too – although his three children are charming, his wife is neurotic. The climax comes when an old man and a pregnant girl, who have followed Calvin from the Northern parish where he first worked, reach Eastwold with their supporters and the Flag is unfurled.

By the same Author

*

THE HIDING PLACE
THE SUN DOCTOR

THE FLAG
FIRST PUBLISHED 1965
THIS EDITION PUBLISHED BY THE REPRINT SOCIETY LTD. 1966
BY ARRANGEMENT WITH CHATTO AND WINDUS LTD.
© ROBERT SHAW 1965

PRINTED IN GREAT BRITAIN BY
BUTLER AND TANNER LTD, FROME AND LONDON

THE FLAG

By

Robert Shaw

THE REPRINT SOCIETY LONDON

For Mary

The first part 'The Flag' of *The Cure of Souls* derives from the life of Conrad Noel, Vicar of Thaxted, who hoisted the flag.

He was remarkable – very different from my Vicar, being an Anglo Catholic, a friend of Chesterton's, an intellectual, and upper class.

Elizabeth Calvin's poems were written by my daughter, Deborah – except for 'The Swallow', written by my daughter Penelope.

The poem *To an Isle in the Water* from 'Collected Poems' of W. B. Yeats is quoted by permission of Mrs Yeats and Messrs Macmillan.

Chapter 1

THEIR new house stood on a cliff top in Suffolk, its front windows looked out to the disordered garden with a lily pond beneath a poplar tree, and its name was Eastwold Vicarage. Here, yesterday, May the second, nineteen hundred and twenty-five, John Calvin brought his family from a slum parish in Houghton. He had not wanted to leave that parish where the average family of eight lived in a single room—wet rooms with sinks and the houses so dark the lights burned all day long.

Calvin's angels of persuasion were his wife, his son, his two daughters, his Bishop, and that emancipated and militant young Christian, Lady Cleeve, the patron of the East Anglian living. Calvin was also persuaded by his faith.

On the morning of May the third, Eileen was the first of the Calvins to wake. She stared up at the strange ceiling, listened to the unfamiliar sounds, raised her thin body over her knees, put her elbows on the window sill. She was fifteen, she already had lines in her neck.

Imperceptibly a silhouette appeared in the sky. 'How did it get there?' the girl whispered. Even as she wondered an intense etched mass of light and dark shadow rose in the east so that in five minutes there was a pale glow above and behind the horizon. Straight lines of light fell on to the water, fell and pointed at the girl in Eastwold Vicarage. She had never seen the dawn.

Sleeping next to his unhappy wife in the cold bedroom below, Calvin was dreaming of his past: 'Let us pray,' he said distinctly. He was in a wooden hall, standing on a platform, trying to talk of Evolution to the Trade Unionists. After they had prayed the men walked out, only his wife remained in the hall, biting her lip, huddling herself on the front bench as she huddled in the bed beside him, drawing up her knees. 'Parsons must be reverenced,' said Calvin's Bishop. 'They were praying for *you*,' moaned his wife. Calvin breathed through his mouth, his tongue had dried, the northern wind blew slag about his head.

Out at sea Eileen saw a boat sliding towards the land, the wake higher than the boat, magical, bearing some great person. 'It's like the coming of Christ,' whispered the girl. Above the boat the cloud lines that had never moved, disappeared. Higher, on the left, colder, a glacier shaped itself, the sky thinned, and over the sea a huge half circle of light suddenly broke. Broke. It was dark to her right, dark in the walled garden, dark above the church steeple where the weathercock stood, and it was still dark in the centre: Eileen sighed.

'I am trying to make the Bible plainer, Bishop,' said Calvin. 'Very dangerous,' said the Bishop. 'A parson must be reverenced. You were wearing a soft collar, an open-necked shirt and plus fours. You are on the brink, you will topple.' 'You and your church can go to Hell, Bishop.' The Vicar of Eastwold turned on his side, opened his eyes, squinted at the cotton and the frills, unclenched his battered hands, whispered: 'Poor broken thing.' He touched his wife's damp shoulder, he moved to give her warmth, naked, he pressed himself against her back: in her sleep she drew away. Calvin buried his face, was shamed, and he tried to thrust himself down into the arms of God.

In the centre of the sky Eileen watched long openings wave like a bed of seaweed. Mountain top clouds swam from the east. The garden trees got up and shimmered. Now there was such a line of radiant gold that the girl's face melted: 'I

6

shall never see anything so beautiful again.' She stayed there, still, as the sun rose, peering through her fingers beneath it at that single point from which all this light had begun.

At the back of the house in the bedroom above the deserted hen run, the tall grass and the apple trees, lay Richard Calvin, mouth firmly closed, blond hair tidy, and with his latest and much amended poem on the table by his side. This poem read:

> 'The birds that stayed this year are cold
> Winter itself is growing old
> Our chimneys do not reach the sun.
> The Prophet's blood is black for fear
> They will not stay another year
> Will not stay for anyone.
>
> It is written in the sand:
> "When singing birds do leave the land
> Then the flesh will shed the bone."
> It is written: "On us all
> Sun and moon and stars will fall
> Time will come to take its own."
>
> The singing birds have flown away
> The Robin was not seen today
> Time is falling everywhere.
> And yet a madman cried tonight
> He dreamed the Robin Redbreast white
> Woke up and saw Redemption in the air.'

It was Richard's final version. He hoped his father would like it. Richard respected his father but wished he wouldn't walk naked into the bathroom; Richard wished his father would speak the King's English and conform. This sleeping boy was not effeminate, rather as his sister Eileen had

7

observed: 'Very good looking in the conventional English way.'

Eileen jumped off her bed to dress. She wrinkled her nose, shook her fair hair; an unsentimental expression set on her face. She pulled on woollen knickers, a skirt, a jersey, thick stockings and a brand new pair of black rubber boots. She thumped out of her room, whistling through her teeth, descended the stairs, hesitated, looked back at the attic where her sister Elizabeth slept, shook her head decisively, went on, and entered her brother's room. 'Wake up, Richard.' There was no answer. 'Wake up, Richard,' she said again, like a school mistress.

'Go away.'

'Wake up.'

'Leave me alone.'

'Let's go and pick mushrooms.'

Without opening his eyes Richard said politely: 'Eileen do leave me alone, you're waking me up.'

'Come on.' She pulled the clothes off his bed. Richard lay there. 'What time is it?'

'Don't know. Haven't got a watch have I. Nobody would buy *me* a watch. It's about six I think. I saw the dawn. It was beautiful. Simply beautiful.'

'It's the wrong time of the year for mushrooms.'

'What's that got to do with it? Please come. Please come with me, please. I know we'll find some if you come.'

'You're a flatterer.'

'Please. It's our first day.'

'All right. First I want to write something down.'

'Is that a new poem?'

'Yes.'

'Shall I read it to you later?'

'Yes.'

Richard took his pen to copy his poem on a clean sheet of paper.

8

'I'll wait for you in the garden,' said Eileen. 'If I'm not there, I'm in the fields. Be sure I'm not in the town.'

'I'll find you,' Richard said.

As Eileen passed her father's bedroom she thought she heard him mutter, but did not stop to listen. He was lost in 'the temptation of the books'—a temptation often re-enacted in the early hours of the mornings when he neither woke nor slept. On the printed papers before him was not one question about the Bible: they had realized he knew his Testament by heart. 'Your children are already middle class,' said his wife. The busts of the several Bishops of Lichfield gazed cynically down from the walls at his youthful head. Beside the sheaf of doctrinal questions was a pile of doctrinal books: Amen. He had only to reach out and open these books—there were the answers he needed: it was simply a matter of conscience. No one was actually watching but the laughter in the cloisters below reverberated, ran up and whined about his brain like dogs. 'Keep still,' said his wife as if she'd been awake all night. 'I'm sorry, Calvin,' said the private tutor, 'I can't give you any more time, I'm fully booked up, and besides I may as well be honest with you. I don't think we can make a silk purse out of a sow's ear.' 'I'm the first working man you've ever had.' 'You're your own worst enemy, you know. Very weak on doctrine. I realize you cannot think with logic but this is not an impulsive profession. Thought must be organized.' 'My wife married beneath her,' said Calvin, 'I was a lay reader but there's not one question about the Bible. The Labour Party needs the backing of the church.' 'Fat chance of that,' said the Bishop. 'As for the insane doctrine that being born in a country gives right to the possession of the soil of that country,' said the Bishop, 'such doctrine does not require notice. How did you get those blue scars on your nose?' 'All miners have them,' said Calvin. 'How is that?' 'We have them on our foreheads and our noses,' said Calvin. 'We will carry them to our deaths. The dust of the air underground enters every cut, the skin grows over, we are tattooed, it is our badge. My grandfather's forehead is veined like a foreign cheese. You cannot dismiss me Bishop unless you prove an immoral act or my neglect in the ministration of my parish.' 'I am aware of Ecclesiastical law,' said the Bishop. 'Your children are already middle class.'

Eileen opened the front door, hesitated on her threshold: the trees were drying like fishing nets, the dew that had glistened silver turned gold. She saw that it was a sea garden for although it was sheltered by trees and walls it stood on a cliff top, and here the waves were always sounding, and whatever the season there was always the smell of salt. She went into her garden like a shepherd.

In the dream Calvin said: 'I do not believe in doctrine. I believe in Spiritual Union. I believe in Holy Marriage, I believe in free giving, I believe in free love. The miners are religious.' 'Straight speaking at Houghton,' wrote the *Bolton Herald*. 'You have gone too far,' said the Bishop. 'There are ninety-seven per cent out of work,' said Calvin. He sat in a circle of student priests who were telling dirty jokes, who were speaking with depravity of sex. He walked out of the room and was sick. 'But it was a deliberate test,' said the Bishop, 'they were trying you out because of your background.' 'You tell me now.' 'The social life of the college is important to your future career, your general ordination has failed, you need five pounds for entertaining, you only had money for two years. Revenge is natural. They want revenge. I was impressed by your Rector's letter.' 'He's a good man,' said Calvin. 'I believe that God is still creating, I am prepared to re-marry in my church.' 'When will you have a church?' 'Who is to say God joined them, who sundered the Bigamists? God is the only one who knows.' 'To put it mildly, your ideas are confused,' said the Bishop. 'You have no intellect,' said the Bishop, and with extreme and vicious exasperation broke his staff on Calvin's head: Calvin woke, Calvin turned on his back in the bed, opened his eyes, stared at the cracks in the strange ceiling. 'I will marry them in my church,' Calvin said aloud, and got up.

Far to the north in Houghton, Alfred Rockingham also got up. The mill girls' clogs were not clumping over the cobbles this morning, it was not the factory whistles that woke the old man. There were four in the bedroom, two still asleep, and the dead man who lay in the bed under the heavy glass chandelier—as he had for three days. Rockingham took his shirt and trousers off the gilt chair with the burst seat, his jacket and overcoat from the carved sideboard, he sat on the horse hair to put on his clogs, he took up the flag from the corner. He wrapped the flag in a piece of sacking. He tied the sacking. He left the room. He descended the rotting stairs. He was a big man of sixty, grizzled hair, a clipped moustache, more like a sergeant than a miner. He passed by the room with the commercial travellers and the newspaper canvassers, sucked on his short empty pipe as their hot smell hit him in the face like a slap: 'Bloody ferrets,' he muttered. He put down the flag. In the kitchen, Mrs Ramsden lay in the dirty fly-blown blankets on the sofa by the larder door. She did not wake. Her face was as anxious and yellow as always. 'Fat bitch,' said Rockingham. The damp washing stood before the fire. On the layer of old newspapers covering the table was a bottle of Worcester sauce: Rockingham emptied the last of it over a piece of bread. 'I shan't never do that again,' he said. He swallowed the sandwich, picked up the flag, and went out into the street. It was cold. He pulled the collar of his overcoat about his ears, raised the furled flag on his shoulder, stuck out his chin in defiance of the back-to-back filth about him, and clumped along Ramsbottom Street for the road that led south-east to Suffolk.

Eileen kneeled on her skirt beside the lily pond, with her fingers traced her name in a mat of red-green leaves. Nobody had mentioned goldfish but there they were in the water; and quicker than the goldfish fled water beetles, tadpoles, newts. She thought to get a jar from the toolshed and bottle some of them up, changed her mind: no need now to take such living creatures home. 'I'll come here every morning even in winter and term-time,' she said. The shadows on the pond fell shorter, the sun rose high enough to warm her back and shine upon her hair, she saw her image in the water, it reached for her smiling face. Eileen laughed. Birds began to sing.

'Birds began to sing,' wrote Richard. 'Birds began to sing and woke me up.' He repeated these lines over and over again so that they turned into an incantation, and lost meaning. He got off his bed to look into the long wardrobe mirror, he stared at his image uneasily, comparing himself to Dorian Gray. He thought this morning that he was already on barren ground, he was frightened by his facility which he suspected might never mature. He frowned at the mirror. He walked away from it, decided his poems began well but did not develop. He returned to the mirror. 'It's like bad Blake,' he said. Abruptly, despairingly, he took his new poem, so tidily written on the clean white paper, and tore it up.

In the bathroom below Calvin too was taking stock in a mirror. He'd washed in cold water, he stood naked. A filler: a little man made of iron; the body hammered. The wide shoulders tapered to a slender waist; the tiny pronounced buttocks, the sinewy thighs, had no ounces of waste flesh. He pulled on thin drawers, but not his clogs and his knee-pads, and yet as he knelt forward in prayer he might have been about to drive his shovel under a pile of fallen coal. 'Oh, God, give me guidance.' Still wearing only his drawers he rose from his knees, threw more cold water on the back of his neck, left the bathroom, passed by his bedroom door, entered his study with the faded varnished paper upon the walls, surveyed it with ownership and pride, stepped carefully over the piles of unpacked books, took a quid of tobacco from the box on the mantelshelf, started to chew it, spat once into the fireplace, went over to the window, drew the lace curtains, opened the window, took a deep breath of the air, folded his arms across his chest, and gazed across the fields at his church.

In the bedroom behind him, Calvin's wife was staring at the ceiling wishing her father had not died. Hannah Calvin, *née* Duckworth, only daughter of a dead Houghton schoolmaster, had such a sadness this morning, such an apprehension of loneliness upon her that her eyes stood out in her face as if she were starved. When her husband's steps had approached her door, expecting him to enter, she had assumed indifference, but when those steps faded away she pressed her lips together so tightly a little muscle began to twitch in her left cheek.

Mrs Calvin got up to brush her husband's clothes.

In Monmouth Street in Houghton Alfred Rockingham stopped beside the stinking green canal behind the foundry and swore because he had forgotten his pigeons. How he could have planned the journey and not remembered his pigeons was a mystery to him. 'I can't get them down to Suffolk,' he thought, and gazing at the filthy slum house subsiding on his left he muttered: 'Distance to lavatory fifty-five yards. We can't even shit in comfort.' Hoisting his flag on to his other shoulder he tugged ferociously at his clipped moustache, turned about, and went back.

Eileen listened to the birds and saw herself old, forty, continually haunted by the innocent memory of the walled garden in whic h she stood. The dewed grass, the dewed leaves streamed away before her so cool, so watery, so green. The whole garden had such a mobility, that she alone seemed permanent—as if she were a statue under the sea. She breathed deep. She saw herself married, lying in bed beside a man, remembering this dawn garden. She heard her children running up the stairs to break in upon her and felt them snuggling into her warm bed, she felt them reach out their tiny hands and draw themselves into her arms. She felt her husband's hands reach out and touch her breasts. She smiled. She stood in wonder. Then she set off down the path to look into the potting shed and as she did so the overhanging branches brushed her hair and christened her politely on the forehead.

Above her little Elizabeth Calvin pressed a chubby face against the window pane. 'Pig,' she shouted. The insult had no force; it was plaintive. Elizabeth looked like her mother this morning having slept badly without the accustomed noises of Houghton. She pressed her nose enviously down at her elder sister. 'She might have taken me,' she grumbled, but as Eileen disappeared behind the potting shed to look in the far side, Elizabeth lost interest, shivered, got down from the window, took her book from the shelf beside her and began to read *Stories from King Arthur*. 'I'm not going to chase after her if she doesn't want me,' she muttered, trying to find her place, 'one day she'll be chasing after *me*.' She found her place but then was forced to get out of bed, put on her handed-down dressing-gown, pull out the Victorian chamber pot from beneath the bed with the picture of Disraeli gazing up from its bottom, sit on its cold rim nervously, jump up, take courage, settle, and once more begin to read. A starling peered in at the skylight but Elizabeth did not notice, she was absorbed in the story of the Black Knight and the Lady from Lyonesse.

As he fastened his tie Richard was still in inquiring mood. Demanding to know, 'who he was', his handsome features assumed an obsessive expression. There was no longer any vanity in the face, the boy was really asking the mirror: 'Who am I? Am I real? Which one of me is me?' The questions unanswerable, his thoughts turned to his father. He realized that in their relationship of late, as had happened long ago with his mother, he was beginning to impose a restraint and to reserve his judgements, if not his love. He would have liked to have called this feeling, 'disinterestedness'—a word Richard was growing increasingly fond of—but he knew it was not quite that as yet. He hoped one day it would be that. Richard was striving to find an identity; and also to remain his age. He had formed an aversion to those who grew up too quickly. In fact, this was one of his commonest criticisms, in those long talks with his father, of the working-class boys in Houghton. And yet also he did not want to close in upon himself. He knew he thought too much of thinking. Suddenly the boy smiled at himself in the mirror.

Rockingham walked over the waste ground by the banks of the miry Houghton canal, stumped his way through the rubbish heaps, blasphemed the rotting single-deckers propped up with stakes, but not the people inside, and decided to kill his pigeons. They might help old Booker get to his grave. There was no sun here in Houghton. 'Somebody's making a good thing out of these bloody caravans,' he shouted. Nobody had energy enough to take notice so early, the inmates slept on. 'It's time they were told about it,' he shouted, but really he was thinking of his pigeons. He'd kept those messy birds in back yards in Houghton for thirty-five years and he'd raced them every Sunday of his life. He'd not been out of Houghton, not even on the tram. When he reached the back yard of the house in Ramsbottom Street he went straight into the shed, put down his flag, and strangled every one of the cooing birds with his old cold hands. Not a tear fell. He took them round to the front of the house in a sack, woke up Mrs Ramsden still snoring in the dirty fly-blown blankets on the sofa by the larder door, and dumped them on the layer of old newspapers covering the table. 'Here,' he said. 'Here's something towards funeral, sell them while they're warm, and for God's sake get old Booker out of the house or Tyldersley will die as well. And by the way! By the way, I'm off for good.' He banged out of the door, re-hoisted the furled flag, and once more set off south.

Eileen opened the door in the wall and left the garden. Three paths were trodden out before her. The path to the east ran down a field until it reached the stile in the stone fence, then wandered on to the cliff and fell to the dunes, the shingle and the beach. The path to the south led through fields to her father's church. The path to the north dropped through the fields into a valley, lost itself in the woods and the bracken that merged into the sea-marsh. Which path should she take? Not to the church and the little market town, where the river running parallel beside the coast swung abruptly right and slid into the ocean. In the harbour there, beside the inn, the fishermen were putting out. She watched. She thought she heard them call. She wondered if they blessed themselves. She looked north to the marshes. They were vast. In the middle a solitary windmill turned its sails. 'Oh, that must be mine,' said Eileen. Far away, at least five miles beyond the mill, a herd of cattle jewelled by the mist, shone and sparkled as they moved. Over the town girl's head a flight of swans stretched their necks towards the sea. 'If only they could see this in Houghton,' she said. Dazed she followed the great white birds along the cliff path, and when she lost them in the sun, she sat upon the ground to rub her eyes.

Elizabeth finished the story, got off the chamber pot, pushed it under the bed. She rubbed the weal on her bottom and looked out of the window again: Richard was now in the garden. 'Why's everybody getting up so early?' she demanded. She watched her tall blond brother as he ambled down the path. 'I'm glad I'm not a boy,' she said. She blinked. 'I think I'm going to have to wear glasses,' she said, 'but I don't care. Beggars can't be choosers.' She got back into bed, snuggled herself happily beneath the thick blankets and the eiderdown, deliberately thought of her birthday, and all the presents she hoped to receive, and within minutes was asleep.

At the potting shed Richard hesitated in case Eileen was hiding there: 'I'm not having her jump out and frighten me,' he thought. The potting shed was filled with last year's apples, yellow, red and striped. He peered in at the shelves of apples, then opened the door because he saw in the shadows on the wall a 'dog-collar' hanging on a rusty nail, and over the collar a shelf of books. He entered the shed and tried on the collar. It was several sizes too large. 'Fat brethren,' he said. 'I am here to bring you the word of God. The Labour Party needs the backing of the Church. Cutting across all systems of morality, whatever claims they may make to an absolute and immutable validity—I repeat that—whatever claims they may make to an absolute and immutable validity, is the fact of the class struggle. Now look here, brethren, will the normal person willingly lie down in the road and drink from a puddle? No! What we need is the interest of the whole of society for its duty to the community. Communism does not involve or desire the abolition of marriage, marriage should be based on human relations and not on property rights.' Richard took off the faded old 'dog-collar' with the brown stains and put it back on the nail. He turned to the books. The first he got down was difficult to open and entitled *Life of the Bee*. He wrenched the stuck pages and began to read of the marriage flights of queen bees. Since it was cold in the shed he came out to read in the sunlight.

A mile away Lady Cleeve woke up in her four-poster bed in the manor, reached for the ivory holder, lit herself a cigarette. She could not bear sleeping alone. She did not inhale —rather she puffed away like a schoolboy, pleased by the taste of the tobacco in her mouth.

Lady Cleeve looked consumptive but was not. Her high cheekbones, taut skin and pale complexion gave her an air of fragility quite out of accord with her robust disposition. (In fact she could beat almost any man at tennis, being possessed of guile, an accurate lob, the most ferocious of forehand drives, and a nimbleness on the turn surprising in one of her sex.)

Puffing, and wondering whether she should marry again— her husband having drowned himself in Africa—she decided she would not . . . could not. 'Lord,' she thought, 'there are a lot of attractive women about, where in the hell are the men.' London, she hated. 'I hate London,' Lady Cleeve said aloud.

Her thoughts turned to Calvin. 'Well,' she concluded, 'he'll stir 'em up. I'll help but I must leave him to it. I must see Pearce very shortly and Ainley too. But not Richards . . . oh no, not Richards!'

Just for a moment she offered up the shortest of prayers for humility. And then a longer one for Calvin's success.

These prayers having put her into a contented mood Lady Cleeve turned to consideration of the churchwardens of Eastwold, and when this was done, to herself in her eau-de-nil pyjamas. 'I may be brittle,' she decided, 'I may be shallow, but from my father I get one or two ideas every now and again. I must revere his liberal soul. Miner Calvin will stir them up. You would have approved dear father.'

Lady Cleeve put out her cigarette, smiled at her cat on the end of her bed, went back to sleep.

Although 'Miner Calvin' still sat in his drawers in his study he did not notice the cold. He had taken pen and paper and sat where he could see his church. He was trying to formulate his ideas for his first article in his parish magazine—a difficult and unaccustomed task. 'Brothers,' he began, 'I don't know much about writing so I'll just try to write plainly, and as I speak, and seek to improve as I go along. My son, Richard, told me in the train yesterday the thing for me to do is to use short words, no Latin or anything foreign, to be brief, and to say what I really think. That seems sound advice to me. I've had very little education you see. I was a miner for years, and then the miners' clubs took me up and sent me to the college at Litchfield, and then I went to France in the war as a stretcher-bearer because they couldn't take me as a chaplain, and then I came home and was a curate first in Jarrow, and then in my own town, Houghton. You may wonder why I've come down south at all. This is because Lady Cleeve heard me speak at the Christian Socialists' gathering in Manchester when she went up there to see a musical play. I also came because I couldn't get a church of my own otherwise, and I wanted one very much. I've had a talk with Lady Cleeve and she agrees with most of my ideas and beliefs but not all. I don't expect anybody to agree with all my ideas, that would be silly—and you are sure to find many members of our church who won't like them at all. Bishops for a start! Still I believe I'm on the right track and if I have to be hard I'm going to be. Some of the things I'm going to go into may seem strange to some of you in this little seaside town, but we've got to start somewhere and create interest, otherwise our church will die and be no help to anyone. I want to have a living church here in Eastwold . . .' Calvin paused to read what he had written and now he was conscious of the extraordinary difference in the air: 'It don't taste like Houghton,' he said. For a moment the perfumed sweetness from all the flowers drifting in through the open window seemed insipid and sickly after the gas and the sulphur, and then a faint tang of the sea was borne in upon the north-east wind and he was a little reassured. Once again, he wondered if he had decided right. Had consideration for his children weighed too much? Had consideration for his wife? Well, he was committed. All the same, how were they going up there in Houghton? On the bench opposite were clustered primroses as big as saucers and daffodils were opening and bullfinches hopped along the top and nipped across to get at the first blossom on an apple tree. 'Aye, I must send them some flowers,' he said. He put his hands on his thighs, and stared across the fields and past the church as if he were trying to reach those chaotic slums, and those dank filthy kitchens, with the aged creeping in and out the back like cockroaches.

On the top of the cliff a tall pale boy watched Eileen descending the path to the beach. This boy had one of those faces born old; intellectual already, and stamped with the resolve: 'I think for myself.' Large hands with long flexible fingers rested on a carved stick. He was growing his first moustache and he took a little bottle of Cologne out of his jacket pocket and wet the moustache where it itched. A faint smile softened his face as the spirit bit and stopped the itching. The stranger on the beach below tore across it till she reached the sea, shouting out as she went, startling a flock of gulls so that they rose into the air, wheeled, and cried raucously above her fair head. 'What a funny girl,' thought Andrews. He looked at his watch: it was a quarter to seven. He put the bottle of cologne back into his jacket pocket and set off towards the railway line to the north-west where it emerged from the woods, ran down a steep gradient, and entered the tunnel to pass under the hill a mile or so before descending into East-wold. He walked with a long resolute stride. As he progressed an excitement and a nervousness came over him and he began to swing his stick from hand to hand and scythe off the tops of thistles. A hare started before him, he jumped. And then he too began to run, faster and faster, frightening rabbits and birds and soaking his legs up to his knees in the tall clusters of grass. Straight as the crow he went, straight for the tunnel on the railway line. In the woods above him a train whistled.

Eileen ran too far and the water came in over the tops of her rubber boots: she sat on the beach to take them off. The only sea she had seen before was at Southport on the Sunday School outing and there she had walked a mile into the water before it had come up to her knees. She was alone on the beach. She looked at the cliff: nobody up there either. A cargo boat climbed over the horizon, and, though it did not seem to be moving, presently she saw that it had a stern. She stood to see better. The beach was cold, the little stones pained her feet. She decided she would walk barefoot all summer and start to learn to swim tomorrow—she didn't think her mother would let her swim on a Sunday. She picked up her boots, emptied them, unhooked her stockings from her liberty bodice, squeezed the stockings out, tied the stockings into a knot and set off along the beach to gather shells and coloured stones. Soon she had so many she put them into her boots. Although it was only the third of May and so early she forgot about the

20

cold underfoot and she started to sing one of her father's favourite songs:

> *'There's nothing sure but*
> *The rich get richer and the poor*
> *Get children;*
> *In the meantime,*
> *In between time,*
> *Ain't we got fun?'*

It did not occur to her to wonder what had happened to her brother.

Somewhere a dog barked: Richard looked up from his book, then at his watch. 'I'd better go and find her,' he thought. He put the book in his pocket. He knew there was no one in the world he liked better than Eileen. A pump stood beside the path. He felt thirsty as soon as he saw it. He went to it, worked the handle up and down: instead of the pure country water he had imagined, on the soil before him spluttered a stinking brackish pool of flies, tiny beetles, spiders and bits of leaves. He was reminded of Houghton. This part of the garden was silent and shadowed by tall trees. He shivered. He left the pump and followed the path to the door in the garden wall. Outside the breeze freshened and blew straight into his face. All at once the importance of this move from Houghton made him open his eyes wide. 'Well, well,' he said. 'Well, well, well.' He looked at the three paths; which one would she have taken? Dear old thing! So moody and so impulsive but so sensible sometimes. She wasn't pretty; everybody else said she was, so what did it matter what *he* thought. He was only her brother. And he smiled again. She wouldn't have taken the path to the church. He looked out to sea. A boat was saunter-ing along like a child's toy on a piece of string. He took out his notebook and pencil. A wave broke. 'Tumbler-rimmed,' he decided and wrote it down. 'Blue sailed, tumbler-rimmed.' To his left a train whistled and he looked up towards the woods and the railway line. In the distance he saw a tiny figure rise to its feet and disappear out of sight into the cutting. 'That must be her,' he decided and set off towards the track.

Although he had quite made up his mind, Andrews sat thoughtfully under the beech tree beside the railway. He was too exhausted by his impetuous run to mind about the damp in the log beneath him. He knocked off a piece of fungus with his carved stick. He considered what vanity there was in his intention and how much was a necessary testing out—he knew how he regretted being too young for the war. When he heard the train leave Moreton Halt above him to continue its journey into Eastwold, and whistle as it approached the gradient, he took out the bottle of cologne again and rubbed some of it on to the back of his neck, then stood up to look about. No one was there to see or prevent, but far across the shining fields below someone came out of the wall around the vicarage garden, picked up the light, and sparkled. The train whistled. Andrews took a long look at his surroundings, at the little town, at his uncle's house, at the sea, at the marshes, and finally peered up at the sky through the branches of the beech tree above. Climbing over the wire fencing he descended on to the railway track. There was not the faintest breath of wind in the escarpment. He knelt down to put a hand on the rail, and laughed when he felt the vibration. He looked at the tunnel. There he knew neither the driver nor fireman would see him. He shook his head as if in wonder at his own nature, got up and walked into the darkness. It was cold here, he heard water dripping, some of it fell on his head, ran down his face and his back. He licked his upper lip, tasted the iron. He turned and looked back into the light. He blinked at it. As if no one had heard before, the whistle blew yet again—a thin scream, followed by three short blasts, that seemed to be drawn forward into the tunnel, to fly crazily past him—the rails began to ring and hammer, air blew against his head. When the train rattled monstrously around the bend and headed right for him this air pushed against his body so strongly he was forced to brace himself to keep on his feet. He stared at the racing iron mass, took a deep breath, smiled to himself, propped his carved stick against the curved brick wall, and lay down on the track between the rails. Carefully, he fitted his body exactly into the middle. He closed his eyes. Then he opened them again. On the black roof light and shadow struggled to get free and now his eardrums almost burst as an incredible mixture of noise and steam whirled and crashed into the enclosed space about him. 'If there's a loose chain,' he thought, 'it's the end of you, Robert.'

THOUGH confident that life was about to take an enormous turn, and for the better, though positive that he had done exactly what was required, Rockingham was mourning his pigeons. His mind tried to keep these two reactions apart so that they would not confuse and weaken the purpose. He would allow himself to grieve, not indulge. It was too cold to stop and weep over his champions and too early for a cup of tea. If he'd not sworn off drink he'd have gone to the Mayor and demanded Crabtree fill the old army flask with brandy to carry him on his way. Rockingham wet his lips. He'd been a boy with Mayor Crabtree. Pompous, fat old hypocritical chicken of a man! Besides the Mayor's house was behind him. Aye, the Mayor lived in comfort! No Socialist he. 'Oh, my lovely birds,' whispered Rockingham. He was back among the slag heaps, he passed between and below on the winding road, and even at this hour and on the day of rest a stumpy shawled woman in her sacking apron and ponderous black clogs knelt up there on the hillside in the cindery mud and the icy wind, searching for coal chips. Behind her a boy and a mongrel dog moved, together, tied by a piece of string. 'Kill the dog!' shouted Rockingham, and then shook his head reproaching himself. Anyway the wind was blowing down the rubble and none of them heard. 'Half a hundredweight, value ninepence,' grumbled Rockingham. 'Not one of these bloody collieries can sell all their coal. Not one, and Christ, in weather like this, we want it more than bread.' A paper girl ran past but did not stop or bid him good morning. Her face was as bitter as the cold. 'She isn't no animal,' thought the old man, 'she knows what her life is right enough, running down these slimy stones, these slum drains they call streets, on a freezing spring morning early, and if she's only half awake and don't see me it's because she don't want to wake. Spring! What the hell's that?

Spring's something you read about, if you can read.' He whistled upwards into his moustache, which he'd started so long ago, to hide his birth mark, once red, now purple. As far as he could see above the gaunt hideous blackened and backed-to-back houses immediately around him, rose hill after hill of refuse, chimney after chimney. 'Filthy bloody bastards,' he cried. Even the railway embankment was made entirely of slag. Sunday morning or not, when he approached the corner of the road, right there among the house rows, a brick funnel, buried in the earth like a wine bottle, decided to belch so that smoke whirled into a monstrous cloud and covered the old miner in dirt from head to foot. He strode through the cloud and when he emerged, waved the flag fiercely, then blew on it himself to try and get off some of the smut. As he reached the top of the rise he paused in doubt: he wondered if there could be any end to this black haze stretching out in front of him and whether he would have the strength in his old bones, would ever be able to walk right out of this seemingly interminable vista of colliery, heap, and chimney. Train out of it, yes perhaps, but not walk. 'It's a defilement,' he thought. 'Even with the snow on it, it looks as bleak as the moon.' He stood there on Houghton Rise and blasphemed. And now to put the whole tin lid on it, it began to rain. 'Oh, Jesus,' he said, 'fifty-seven years of it, come what may, I'll be well out of this. All right, Miner Calvin, I'm on my way.' Up went the flag again, high into the air, and extraordinary as it might have seemed to anyone who had overheard his profanities, he set his face against the misting rain and began to sing a hymn, as he proceeded south: 'Onward Christian Soldiers, Marching as to war . . .' By the time the sun managed to break through the clouds, and shine palely down the rain on to this desolation, Rockingham was well into the second chorus of 'Jerusalem'.

Unconscious of the aid that was on its way from the north, writing so innocently in his drawers in the new study, Miner Calvin raised his scarred head when he heard the first train of the day whistle somewhere behind him, hurrying down the slopes into Eastwold town. There was ink on his calloused fingers. 'I was only a curate in Houghton of course. Now I just want to write a few words on the Church of today in relation to the Church of the past, and by the past, I mean a long while back.' What did he want to write? He sucked away at the ink on his battered thumb. 'First: there was a great difference between the early Church and the civilization around it; second: they were expecting the Advent, preparing for it, and not trying to build a new social order. It's different now isn't it? What I want to say is that the Church can only lead the world if it's different from the world and if it hasn't any material policies. I say that God's judgement on capitalism is to destroy it, and every true Christian should try to help in this as long as he remembered that God's judgement, like His mercy, is over all His works.' Calvin got up and stretched himself while he considered the last sentence, then dropped into a miner's crouch: he could think better in this position—years ago there had been a sad occasion when he had unconsciously relapsed into it at one of his wife's tea parties. He would have liked a cup of tea in his hand now, he would go and make one but he didn't know yet where everything was in the new kitchen. Richard must help him learn to write properly! He wondered if he had done right by Richard and became distracted by the problem of what would happen if his son did indeed win that scholarship to Oxford next year and how this could only increase the gulf between them, and where the money should come from, and would the school in Lowestoft teach Richard as well as the one in Bolton had done? Squatting there on his haunches Calvin scratched his ankles and grunted: he couldn't believe for a moment that these southern teachers were as good as those in the north. There wouldn't be anyone as vigorous and up to date as Jack Oldfield with his car and his school holidays abroad in Germany, in Italy, and in France, his incisive denunciation of old-fashioned methods of education, his enthusiastic expositions of what he called 'exam technique'; there wouldn't be a man like Arthur Whistler talking and reading to Richard of the poets, taking the boy on the train into the country, and insisting always that a poem was meaningless until it was *grammatically* understood; there wouldn't be an emancipator like his wife Hannah's father, with his politics and his scientific periodicals—Calvin had missed Bill Duckworth all year— he could see the old schoolmaster now looking across the supper table at himself and Hannah. How pleased Hannah would be if Richard won the scholarship—if she prayed at all no doubt she prayed for that. Calvin clasped his hands across his knees, brooding about the English class system, considering again his wife's values and his own, puzzling away at the future of his family, the place they had come from, and the place they had arrived at. A flock of starlings wheeled and clamoured from nowhere, filled the air outside the open window, and the Vicar rose to watch them as they settled in the elms. The noise was extraordinary, was vast—there was never anything like this in Houghton. Calvin pushed his curly hair back off his forehead. Abruptly, though he could not discern the reason, the birds flew out of the elms, circled, darkened the air, disappeared. He rubbed his temples with his fingers, shook his head in be-wilderment and walked back to his writing to examine that last sentence which had flowed so glibly from his pen: 'I say that God's judgement on capitalism is to destroy it . . .' Yes, well, that was right enough . . . any Christian should try to help in this . . . 'yes, right enough again, but what about? . . .' as long as he always remember that God's judgement, like His mercy, is over all His works.' Now that was not good enough for what did it mean? And was it so? Was God's judgement always apparent? Of course not! What *is* my position? he asked himself, what do I want to try and tell, and have I the right? Certainly I have the right to *try*. Now God is the Creator, the Creator of man. Life as we know it cannot finally satisfy man because man is not content to be shut up in time and space. God, Himself, outside time and space—beyond it, rather—came into the world as Jesus, as His son, to try and get close to men and God's always trying to get close to man. The funny thing is that while eternity is always encroaching upon

27

time, man, who is totally dependent upon God, is always asserting his independence. What's more the kingdoms of the world are so totally different from the Kingdom of God that man's always ashamed of the world and longs for the proper Kingdom even if he won't admit it. And what's difficult for most of us is how much to take the Bible literally; and how to get some kind of picture of what the Everlasting and the Second Coming really would be like. Calvin rose, hitched up his cotton drawers, and fell back into his crouch. At this point he only knew what he sensed. He *felt* Eternity with God but could not put it into words. At best perhaps he could communicate something of the feeling to others by his *being*. Then the train whistled closer by and he was reminded of Houghton and went back to his desk and wrote what he knew was understandable and uncomplicated and true. He wrote: 'Brothers! If you Englishmen remain infatuated with nationalism and economic anarchy you'll bring disaster on your heads—you've simply got to get a lot nearer to God, and give a lot more, and love each other, like He said, and stop being so damned mean, and read His words every day, really read them and turn right about the evil tendencies of this world. The early Church was like that! We've got to have a world friendship based on religious faith, and this friendship has got to go over all ties of neighbourhood, class, kinship, race, nation, and party. If we're going to be colonizers let's colonize a colony of Heaven. If we don't let Christ rule—and he's shown the way plainly enough—it's the end of us for sure. Don't let yourself be dragged down by the world for anyone or anything. Look at everything in the light of devotion to Christ. The proper Church, and the Church I'm after, should contain the seeds of regeneration. They say it was at the time of Constantine the world got into the Church . . . it's been there ever since. Well, if the world's so indifferent to the Church it's because the Church is so little different from the world. And to digress, I know what the Catholics say about the low Church of England, they say: "That's honesty is the best policy set to music" . . . well, be that as it may—and of course

I refute it—it's not at all set to the right kind of music . . . there's too much brass in the pit . . . the right kind of music is austere and disinterested and passionately loving all at the same time. We've got to dissociate ourselves from all these prevailing assumptions and habits. People state that if you dissociate yourself you throw away opportunities for influence and you abandon the community to its fate. That's a convenient quibble! It's a get out! You've got to set an example. That's what the early Church did. Sometimes the example can be very positive indeed. Christ dissociated himself from the society around him, but he didn't dissociate himself from the community, did he? He dissociated himself from the material world, not from the people living in it. All we can do in our lives is set a good example in ourselves and that's the truth of it.' Once again Calvin looked up from his work, and then back at it, astonished at how much he had written so quickly. Whatever have I written now? he wondered. 'Disinterested'—ah yes that was the word Richard used; it wasn't quite clear yet—words were clumsy things, deceptive things, but Calvin continued smiling because it occurred to him that at least one bit was absolutely right—capitalism *was* bloody well evil. It was bloody well evil!

So Andrews pressed his hands on the steel, got up, and could see how steeply the tunnel sloped. Yellow fringes of light fell at both ends of the womb-like place in which he stood. He had felt himself to be some kitten, raised in a great damp sack, weighted down, twirled, and flung into the middle of waters. Although the ground stilled his head kept ringing and the backs of his legs continued to ache.

He bent to pick up his stick: when he did so it seemed that once again the train was passing overhead. He left the stick where it was, closed his eyes, leant against the wall, breathed deeply. Something flew in the shadows behind, he could not turn to look. Drops of water fell on to the back of his neck. He clenched his hands, forced his eyes open to concentrate on a particular brick. He watched a spider. Then he was sick.

As was common with him after unusual occasions, descriptions of what he was doing began to run through his brain: 'Eventually I was able to tidy myself up, retrieve my stick and leave the place. I saw a grey cat at the entrance. It looked surprised to see me and slid off. I realized I wasn't frightened when the train was above me, rather, intensely curious of the physical details. It was something I felt I had to do. I wasn't ashamed of it, I had no desire to tell anyone else about it, and I certainly wouldn't repeat the performance. I had not expected to be killed – it seemed to me so much against the laws of probability – mind you I had envisaged the possibility. The experience had a significance for me and I came out into the sunlight looking older. On the other hand I did not feel in any way that the preservation of my life was a sign of my peculiar worth, or guide to my future conduct. It was something else, something I had explored, and that was all. Yes, that was all.'

A few minutes later Andrews was walking up the track that scarred the earth like some old wound still stitched together by the great black sleepers.

'Good morning,' called Richard Calvin above him. 'Excuse me, have you seen my sister?'

'I don't know your sister,' said Andrews and went on.

'Excuse me,' said Richard. 'She's a fair girl. She's fifteen.' Andrews had stopped and was smiling faintly as he took in the accent and the clothes.

'You would be the preacher's son.'

'Yes that's who I am. I'm Richard Calvin.'

'An appropriate name.'

'Oh. Oh yes. I'm looking for my sister Eileen.'

'There's a girl on the beach.'

'Oh thank you.'

'She looked a bit mad.'

'Oh thank you. I expect that's her.'

There was a pause. Richard found himself anxious not to end the conversation: then he realized that this was because there was something in Andrews's manner at once patronizing and ironic.

'What was she doing that you thought that?'

'Thought what?'

'Thought my sister a bit mad.'

'Well if it *was* your sister, she ran round in circles and shrieked up at the gulls.'

'She's never been in a place like this before,' said Richard and smiled. 'Where are you going now?'

'What?'

'Why don't you come and help me look for her if you're not doing anything?'

Andrews was so surprised at this request that he couldn't think of an answer to it. He remembered his uncle had said how forward they were in the north. He didn't want to go with this ingenuous boy at all, and when he looked at him more closely he realized that despite the accent and the clothes Calvin was typical of one of those unfortunates at his own school, bullied and put upon from the day they arrived, always anxious to please, always weeping at night, always proclaiming publicly how much they enjoyed it, and sure to send their sons back to the place of torment.

'I'd be very, very pleased,' said Richard.

'Are you a day boy?'

'A day boy? Oh yes. But I'm going to a new school in Lowestoft.'

'Very wise,' said Andrews. 'Any good at games?'

'No,' said Richard.

'No,' said Andrews and laughed.

There was another pause.

'What did you laugh for?'

'Oh nothing,' said Andrews feeling embarrassed, and sensing even then that he was being snobbish.

'Are *you* good at games?'

'I don't play them. They're a waste of time.'

'Not even at school?'

'No.'

'Don't they make you?'

'They can't make *me* do anything like *that*.'

31

'Where do you go to school?'

'Eton.'

'Eton?'

'Yes.'

'*The* Eton? Eton College.'

'Yes, *the* Eton,' said Andrews and couldn't stop himself laughing again, and then, making up his mind that he really must be kinder to this stranger, he climbed up the bank to say: 'All right I'll come and help you look for your awful sister.' When he reached the top he couldn't resist adding cynically: 'Of course, I'm a scholarship boy.'

Mrs Calvin sat before her bedroom mirror unplaiting her hair, trying to shut out worries, trying to shut out images of unpleasantness and pain, and not succeeding. Her hair looked lifeless. She began to brush it in such a dispirited fashion that one might have expected the brush to fall from her hand at any moment, and presently it did. As she bent to pick it up she bumped her head on the dressing table. Tears came into her eyes. She sat up, leaving the brush where it was, and began to weep. There was no sound. Only the shoulders hunched and shaking, and the hands on the knees shaking, and the tears running down her sallow cheeks.

But she had not forgotten to clean her husband's shoes.

Andrews and Richard walked through a white blossomed orchard as they proceeded directly to the beach. Still intent on drawing Andrews out, Richard had tried such subjects as the beauty of the countryside around them, and the best time of the year for mushrooms, without success, and now he decided to revert: 'I felt you don't enjoy your school.' Andrews looked down at his stick, grimaced, did not answer.

Richard persisted: 'Please tell me what it's like. You hear so much about it.'

'From whom?'

'Oh I don't know. Everyone. It's so famous. My mother always wanted me to be able to go to a school like that.'

Andrews was about to mock when a burst of serious irritation swept over him and swinging his stick at a pile of nettles he began to talk very fast. 'I'd like to blow the ghastly place up,' he said. 'And all such places. Don't you know they're the snobbiest places on earth. Some of the things they've taught me there have gone so deep I'll never get rid of them. Don't you know I feel superior to you every time you open your mouth!' Richard blinked. 'Even I, who don't want to, can't help it. Look here,' Andrews raised his stick to point it at Richard like a bayonet, 'I've been learning Greek for ten years, and when I'm thirty I won't be able to repeat the alphabet you can be sure of that, and yet my snobbishness has been so deeply ingrained that I have to root it out like those weeds there, and what's more I shall have to be doing that till the day I die.'

'I don't mind you feeling superior,' said Richard. 'I expect you are.'

There was a pause. Then: 'There you are you see,' said Andrews, 'you're so disgustingly servile.'

After another pause and without any offence Richard said very slowly and gently: 'No as a matter of fact I'm not. It's just that I don't mind people getting on with things that they're good at. I've got my own worries so I'm not envious of others.'

'Well that's very good,' said Andrews with respect. He smiled, and then began to laugh.

They walked out of the orchard and climbed over the fence into the wood. A telegraph pole had already begun to drone. The boys put their ears to it and listened. 'How it sings,' said Richard. 'Messages from other worlds,' said Andrews. In the shadows the bluebells smoked like gas lamps lit from somewhere deep in the ground. In the sunlight the daffodils opened and stretched like a row of French horns. They went deeper into the woods, startling rabbits.

'You see,' said Andrews, 'I won a scholarship. Lower upper middle class that's me. Father's an official in India. Eton has *taught* me to cling to my gentility, to resent those boys whose parents are richer than mine and keep me aware of it of course, to despise those not describable as gentlemen, and to hate the newly rich. It has *formed* in me the desire to be of gentle birth with no money.' He paused and then said sadly: 'The thing is, it's all true. It's all so *true*.'

'Yes, I see that,' said Richard.

'And I hate old men. Old men in power are responsible for everything.'

'The war you mean?'

'Yes.'

'My father says that.'

They passed down into a hollow and the branches of the trees above formed an arch like the roof of a nave.

'You'd like my father,' said Richard.

'I don't expect so.'

'Why not?'

'I despise the Christian religion,' said Andrews. 'I think it's the most half-baked, awful and hindering lot of rubbish.'

'What do you believe in then?' asked Richard when he had recovered himself.

'I've yet to find out,' said Andrews. 'I've got a few bits and pieces. Mind you I'm not impugning the value of the morality of that Jewish gentleman known as Jesus Christ.'

Richard Calvin was shocked.

'But look what's been done in his name,' said Andrews banging away fiercely at another clump of nettles with that long carved stick. 'And worse than what's been done, is what's being, and *going* to be done.'

'How do you mean exactly?' said Richard who was now very nervous, and he added hurriedly before Andrews could reply: 'It is Sunday morning you know.'

'I don't care if it's crucifixion day,' said Andrews with all the sarcasm he could muster. 'Do learn to think for yourself!'

Mrs Calvin went to the window shading her eyes from the sunlight, drew the makeshift curtains even tighter, gazed protectively at the bedroom carpet. Much of her furniture was yet to arrive. She intended to fill the house, to crowd it with

34

the sideboards, tables, chests, wardrobes, desks, sofas and arm-chairs inherited from the deaths on her mother's side. She would stuff from top to bottom the bibelots, ornaments, and clocks, the bric-à-brac, china, and glasses, the copper, the pewter, and the brass. She would preserve her treasures under domes and behind the doors of cabinets, she would hang the portraits of her ancestors, and she would cover the windows with thick, thick lace.

Mrs Calvin went back to sit at the dressing table, began to make a list: there was the food, the furniture, the bills, the gardener to be kept on twice a week, and the starched maid-servant yet to be engaged. She shivered. The lines on her face grew tauter. Her waking nightmares tore in and ate her up. Rent and clothes and school-bills, and the insults of the 'common' people with their coarse faces, their coarse manners, the coarse accents and their smell. She stood up. 'I must do something nice for him,' she said. She opened her wardrobe. No service this first day, and yet it *was* Sunday morning! She put on her corset, her black stockings, her white blouse, her gaberdine costume. She pinned her hair. 'Something he'll like.' She put on her white tulle scarf, her black shoes, her cotton gloves, and her hat. She went to the window. 'I'll pick some flowers for his church,' she said. She stood there peering out and no one would have seen her from the garden.

'But I love him,' whispered Mrs Calvin at that curtained window. 'I still love him.' And Mrs Calvin wept.

Eileen sat high on the shore by a rock pool dipping her toes in water warmed by the sun. Below her feet the plants were breathing faster, already were using the light. The walls were pink, the little forests dark green. A strawberry anemone seized a fish. To celebrate the capture at the top of the waving column two minute sea-spiders stretched eight pairs of legs. In a crack in the base of the prison, from the thin covering sand, a delicately patterned disk spread its tentacles towards the spiders. Eileen put her fingers in the water, luminous prawns darted backward, she freed the fish. She sucked her thumb and she tasted salt. Unaccountably she began to think of men. She looked up—there was no one else to speak to on the long thin beach.

The boys had emerged from the bluebell woods and could gaze at the sparkling sea.

> *'When each gun*
> *From its adamantine lips*
> *Spread a death-shade round the ships*
> *Like a hurricane eclipse*
> *Of the sun.'*

quoted Richard, not expecting Andrews to know the source, and still half considering some of those damning utterances on the Christian Church.

'Best lines Campbell ever wrote,' said Andrews, 'nobody'll remember him.'

'Tennyson wrote "death-shade" was a very good image,' said Richard.

'Beware of good images, decorative adjectives, and humbug,' said Andrews.

'I agree with that,' said Richard.

'I expect *you* write poetry.'

'Yes, yes I do.'

Andrews giggled. They walked through tall grass towards a fallen hedge with a stream on the far side. 'Sh,' said Andrews and stopped. Richard crept up beside him, together they peered over the wall. A hedgehog walked to a pheasant's nest, cracked an egg in his paws, ate it, went to the water and washed.

'I never saw anything like that before,' said Richard.

'Keep still out here early and there's no telling what you'll see.'

The boys walked up to the nest—four eggs were left.

'He's been here before,' said Andrews kicking another cracked shell.

'What are you going to do then?'

'Nothing.'

'Can't we save the eggs?'

'You could take them to the gamekeeper.'

'Why don't we then?'

'I don't like the gamekeeper,' said Andrews. 'He'd boil them I expect.'

Andrews walked on. Richard looked helplessly at the nest, then followed.

'So you write poems?' said Andrews when Richard caught up with him.

'Yes.'

'Tell me one.'

There was a pause.

'What's the matter?'

'Well I don't know you all that well and it's a bit . . .'

'Embarrassing?'

'Yes.'

'Don't be,' said Andrews. 'If you're going to write you've got to be professional—it's the only shortcut to getting better. The poem's written down and finished isn't it?'

'Oh yes.'

'I did ask you didn't I?'

'Yes.'

'And I'm not the sort of person who'd mock am I?'

'I don't know,' said Richard. 'You might be. Sometimes people don't mean to mock and then later on they do.'

'I wouldn't I assure you,' said Andrews. 'Neither now nor later.'

They looked at each other and nodded their heads as in some sort of acknowledgement.

'Imagine you have stabbed a deer,' began Richard, coughed and started again.

> *Imagine you have stabbed a deer*
> *In any public park*
> *The couples would not notice if*
> *You stabbed her in the dark.*

37

Richard picked a piece of grass and stuck it in his mouth to chew.

> *'Imagine you have thrown your soul*
> *Into her wounded eyes*
> *You'd find you're staring at yourself*
> *With infinite surprise.'*

They walked on. Richard waited. Andrews said nothing.
'Well what d'you think then?' asked Richard.
'I'm not saying anything.'
'But you said . . .'
'I expect you learned more from telling me it than from anything I might say,' said Andrews.
'Yes I see,' said Richard doubtfully. They walked on. 'But . . .' Richard began.
'I like the first stanza,' said Andrews, 'I don't like the use of the word "soul" and the second stanza has quite a good idea but it's clumsy and the use of the adjective "wounded" is so pale that the idea is not pushed through strongly enough. And anyway is it true?'
'Is it true?' repeated Richard.
'Yes, is it true?' asked Andrews again.
There was another pause and then Richard demanded firmly: 'What do you mean by: "is it true?"'
'A good question,' said Andrews. Beating at the grass with his stick he began to talk very seriously indeed.

Calvin put down his pen, hitched up his drawers, bit on his tobacco, turned back the pages to read. He was worried about the inconclusiveness of what he had written. He did not expect to arrive at some overnight solution but he had hoped for something his parishioners could understand and practise. He knew well that without his surplice the preacher is only human and it crossed his mind that he should preach his first sermon in his church naked, or wearing only his drawers. He sat up straighter in his chair to give this inspiration serious consideration. Then he laughed. Yes, well, not now, one day

38

perhaps. There was *something* in this idea, there was something in it. He looked for a place to spit.

Calvin examined the empty fireplace, thought of his wife, went to the window. ' "There are *no* solutions," ' he quoted, "The contradiction between what is and what ought to be is an illusion arising from the limited nature of human knowledge. In fact there is neither good nor bad. Only, necessary stages." ' 'No that can't be right either,' he said, spitting into the ivy. Who did his writing help? What exactly was he about? Slag heaps, chimneys and railway lines still seemed a more normal landscape than the flowers, the grass, the hedges and the trees before him. Did they ever think, those starlings? And those aeroplanes these days, flying so high up there, might they not meet their Maker? Calvin watched the biplane climbing north over Eastwold as though even now it were being drawn to Heaven. He frowned. What sort of place might Heaven be when all was said and done. Although the sky was cloudless the plane disappeared.

He was gazing at a pine tree. Something was wrong with the tree—those around it were firm and strong but though it looked no older the pine was dying. He could see no reason for the dying: it stood in the same ground; no one had chopped at its roots. Calvin thought of his wife, spat once again into the ivy, went back to his desk to read.

He was unable to shut out his wife. He found himself glancing over his shoulder as though he heard her coming up the passageway to enter the room. Once he turned because he thought she was trying the handle of the door. 'I must be kinder to her,' he muttered. 'I must help her more, I must love her more. She don't owe me her body. She owes me nothing.'

Calvin dropped his head forward on his pages, overwhelmed: How could a man tear away at the welfare of the world and give no joy to his wife? Calvin raised his head aghast. For the first time in his life it had occurred to him that some other might have succeeded with Hannah where he failed. Now he was still. He tried to imagine a kind of a man. Calvin got down on his knees. 'Oh dear God,' he began, 'if there is anywhere another man who could fulfil my wife, who could help her as a woman, send him to us.'

There was silence in the Vicar's study and then the Vicar rose: he had perceived the inadequacy of his prayer. 'The fault is in me, or in Hannah, or in both. The only answer is love.' Calvin shook his head despairingly from side to side like a proud and impatient soldier with a wound, picked up his article and read with extreme irritation: 'Brothers! A distinction must be made between "communism" in the sense that the word's used now by the political parties, and the proper communism. Brothers, a distinction must be made between communism in the Marxist sense and the early Christian communism. There's no moral idea of communism in the abstract that applies to both forms, brothers! I want to tell you first about this modern communism, why it is, and what it is. I want to say something about its necessity, I want to state a few facts about the working class.'

Calvin ceased his declamation, picked up his pen to underline the next heading, which was: 'Why capitalism declines' —then continued: 'These are the main features of capitalism. One: the means of production is in the hands of a small group —industrialists, financiers and landlords. Two: goods are produced not for the individual but as commodities for sale on a market. Three: the driving force of society is not to try and satisfy its needs but to increase the profits of the small ruling class. Any time there's a crisis you can see that when a production becomes unprofitable, no matter how much society needs it, it's stopped at once. (N.B. Dumping of foodstuffs like wheat.)'

Calvin nodded his head, turned the page over, and proceeded as before—the voice grew confident: 'To make such a system possible there are two main reasons: money is in a very few hands; and the huge group of people (us) with no property, who only have their labour to sell, and therefore must hire themselves out to those with the money. Since the profits for capitalists come from the unpaid labour of the workers—I mean by that the labour they do over what's necessary for their own maintenance and the renewal of production—capitalism must find some way to dispose of surplus goods. It does so in three ways: its own luxury consumption (which is a small part); re-investment in extension of production; and most important, foreign markets. So! And here we come to the main point: capitalism must always expand.'

'It can't,' said Calvin and put down his pages on the desk. Then, as was common with him in the mornings, he was overcome by the *need* to be kind to Hannah. He went to the window, spat out the remainder of his tobacco into the ivy and set off to the kitchen to see if he might take his wife a cup of tea.

Before him the snow descended so fast that that black lunar landscape he had contemplated earlier in the rain was becoming reality. The slag mountains, streaked and running like the walls in the damp basements with the one thin coat of impoverished whitewash, grew consistently paler. The sleet hissed and melted on the sides of the smoke-stacks, choked and vanished in the plumes above. The mud froze on the canal paths, and the cinders were being criss-crossed by the marks of hundreds of clogs as the men hurried out of their houses, coughing, spitting, stumbling and swearing, caps over their brows, studs in their collar fronts, eyes turned down, going for the Sunday papers, or the milk, or the Woodbines, or a packet of sweeties and a new dummy to quieten the screaming kids. It was horribly cold. Rockingham sang. He walked where plants and grass were evicted, where the ice on the pools was dark brown, where the bargemen were covered in sacks, and the shallow rivers ran chemical yellow. He breathed deep on the sulphur, walked another hundred yards, breathed deep on the gas. He closed his mouth, stopped his song. Even in the snow storm he could count sixty-seven factory chimneys. Rockingham walked on with the flag.

Wild roses, butterflies, oak-trees, clear water, and the bleating of sheep.

'I will tell you the truth,' said Andrews gazing sombrely out to the sparkling sea and once again wetting that faint patch of ginger on his upper lip with the cologne: 'I have always known I will be a writer.'

'Ah,' murmured Richard.

'Paradoxically,' continued Andrews, putting away the cologne, and quite conscious of Richard's fascination with the proceeding even at the moment of revelation, 'I am trying to abandon the idea despite the realization that I am outraging my true nature.'

'Sooner or later you will have to settle down and write books,' said Richard.

'I fear so,' said Andrews.

The boys were sitting on a hedgerow. Above them the sky was huge.

'Do you know that verse of Landor's?' asked Richard.

'Go on.'

> *I strove with none, for none was worth my strife.*
> *Nature I loved and, next to Nature, Art:*
> *I warm'd both hands before the fire of Life;*
> *It sinks, and I am ready to depart.*

'A most improbable summary of that poet's life,' said Andrews. He stood up and put his hand in his pocket. He looked thoughtfully at the ground about him. 'I have been a somewhat lonely child. I used to hold interminable conversations with people who weren't there, creating a private world. I don't say it's uncommon. I know I have two talents—facility with words and an ability to face unpleasant facts. In my own mind I am certain that my literary ambitions are mixed up with this loneliness.'

'You mean you feel undervalued?'

'I *do* mean that.'

'Well I should think that's sure to make you write.'

'I *am* going to wait,' said Andrews. 'I am going to examine the world, and live in it, and learn discipline, and listen, and get at the facts. I wish . . . I wish to turn journalism into art . . yes, that's it.'

'I couldn't wait,' said Richard.

'I'm not asking you to,' said Andrews moving away from the hedgerow and staring at the soil like a water-diviner. 'It doesn't strike me that you have any political sense.'

'Oh no I haven't. I just want to describe things as they are and how they touch me. The sea and people and things. I only want to be a poet.'

'I want,' said Andrews, 'I want to push the world on. I want to help other people to live better. I want to take sides. I know that if I don't take sides it won't be any good. Of course I am using the word "political" in its widest sense. I want to make judgements. I want to state values.'

'I don't know anything about things like that.'

'Well I only know a bit,' said Andrews looking up and grinning. 'And that's the point.'

'Yes,' said Richard, 'well yes, but somehow we're very different.'

'Oh we are,' said Andrews, 'we are.' He paused for a deep and considering breath. 'My aim at seventy is to have written a book that deals with the problems of the world and not merely . . . not merely with the . . . the subjective suffering of individuals—a book that speaks seriously, and with life, of the true nature of reality and the terrors of power.'

'I don't want to get my own back on the grown-ups at all.'

'It is,' said Andrews, 'a great deal more complex than that. Grown-ups! Hm! You misunderstand me.'

'Please don't think I'm over simplifying—I was just making the point.'

'Of course. I expect your problem will be how to learn to live your own life to the end.'

'D'you mean I'm weak?'

'It would be presumptuous for me to say.'

'But what d'you think?'

Andrews took something out of his pocket and looked at it. 'I think you may be weaker than you realize and if not weak . . . unaware.'

43

'Unaware?'

'As a friend I would wish you to increase your awareness.'

'Then are we to be friends!'

'Why not?'

There was a pause. Andrews knelt and pressed something into the soil.

'My father's always seeking to get to know himself better and so am I,' said Richard with a hint of gratitude in his voice.

'From what I hear your father's an anachronism.'

'What d'you mean?'

'I don't know myself,' said Andrews straightening up. 'It just came out.'

The two boys gazed at each other thoughtfully.

'The funny thing is,' said Richard, 'it sounds right.' And he repeated softly: 'Father's an anachronism ... father's an anachronism ...'

'Don't turn it into a limerick.'

Richard stopped his refrain. 'What were you doing?' he asked, looking at the spot where Andrews had knelt.

'I was planting an acorn,' said Andrews. 'I always do it when I can.'

'I suppose if they all come up you could do a lot of good in your lifetime.'

Andrews smiled. 'You're not a fool, Calvin,' he said.

'First impressions are always suspect don't you think?' A mist was beginning to rise from the marsh. 'I think I misjudged you, Calvin,' said Andrews.

Elizabeth Calvin opened her eyes and sat up in bed, wide awake in an instant. She sniffed that morning air. 'It's quite different,' she said. Her voice was almost as deep and as Lancashire as her father's. 'If all of them can write poems I'm sure I can,' she said and jumped out to get her satchel. She returned to the bed, tucked herself comfortably in, propped up her pillow behind her, took pencil and paper and straightway began:

44

> '*The windmill blows*
> *As it chose*
> *To do all day.*'

She couldn't think how to go on so scratched it out.

> '*On a summer's day*
> *In the middle of May.*'

She scratched out the word 'summer' and wrote 'spring'. Once again she couldn't continue. She scratched her nose. She circled her thumbs and fingers in the shape of imaginary spectacles and gazed through them at her manuscript. Inspired, she wrote firmly: 'The Owl.' She underlined it, and underneath:

> '*The owl lies in bed at noon*
> *And wakes by the light of the silvery moon.*
>
> *When evening has gone*
> *She sings her song*
> *All the night long.*
>   *Twit-towhoo, Twit-towhoo.*'

At the bottom of the poem she added the signature: 'E. Calvin', underlined that also, and proceeded to read the poem aloud. When she had finished she nodded her head in satisfaction. 'It's just as good as any of theirs,' she said.

The sea-spiders, the strawberry anemones, the transparent prawns and the little fish held her interest no longer; no longer the sandy caves, the pink walls and the dark green forests: she had cupped her face in her hands and was studying it in the pool. What sort of woman would she become? All stilled in the water as though they too considered. Above them the image trembled for the girl was breathing on it. The little fish turned upside down the better to see.

She remembered her friend Evelyn in Houghton and how like herself she had thought Evelyn to be. Somehow Evelyn had kept her together, now Evelyn was lost, and Eileen didn't mind at all. 'I am myself now,' she whispered. She questioned the mirror whom she should love next and who would love her. How awful to love someone who didn't love you. She frowned and the fish vanished. How awful to be criticized—they were always doing that when they had no need. Richard wasn't too bad, and that was surprising from a brother, but sometimes they were all against her—especially Betty. 'Nobody loves me really,' said Eileen, 'not *loves* me.' And then she thought that *she* couldn't love anyone else all that much and felt lonely.

Eileen looked up and down the shingle: nobody there. Richard obviously wasn't coming to find her and he'd promised he would. How mean! The warm green wind ruffled the pool. She grew proud to be alone. The silver waves climbed higher on the long thin beach. What her family didn't seem to realize was that she understood some things so much better than they. 'I do need to love and be loved. I know I do,' thought Eileen. The North Sea curled up over, smothered the end of the rocks in spray. A tiny head like a baby's or a very old man's, broke through a foaming claw of water. She did not see it. She had jumped up and was running to look into the sand dunes. She was remembering all the boys she had ever admired and never spoken to. She was blushing at a curate in Houghton who had never put down his cup of tea and thrown himself at her feet. That would have shown her mother—who didn't want her to grow up. 'Poor mother,' Eileen shouted and the words were blown far ahead: 'Poor mother . . . poor mother . . . poor mother.' Eileen wasn't going to let herself get like that. Eileen was worth loving, she knew she was. She'd make a man proud. If only she had some great purpose in her life, some ideal for which she could live and could die . . . then she would sacrifice everything. 'Everything . . . everything . . . everything.' Perhaps she could enter the Church like father and become the first woman bishop. But the Church was as dead as a doornail. Perhaps together they could revive it; an intelligent woman might lead the people to the true face of

46

God. As she saw herself ascending the pulpit she climbed on to the highest sand-dune to preach.

He had come to a field. In the middle of defilement stood this solitary untrodden improbable field. 'Mind you,' he said, blowing upwards into his cold moustache, 'if I dug a fork in ground cans and bottles would come up. Aye I'd pull 'em up like I would out of the stinking green canals.' But he couldn't help pause and look at the meadow. 'Someone must keep a horse in it, I s'pose,' he said. And yet there was no horse.

The sun began to shine; the snowing stopped. 'Spring *is* coming,' said Rockingham. Since he was standing still he couldn't help thinking of his pigeons. At last a tear did fall. He brushed it away. 'Oh Christ,' he said, 'I'm sloppy.' So far from the backyard at Ramsbottom Street he held the living birds in his hands. Then he was helped: alone in the abomination, confident it was indeed spring, two rooks descended out of the sky on to the unspoiled snow to tread. Rockingham was astonished: he had thought they did it in trees. Years fell off his shoulders. 'That's a sign,' he cried, 'bloody good.' The wife stood unembarrassed with her beak open, the husband high-stepped round and seemed to feed her. 'Now that's courting for you,' said Rockingham, 'that's right and proper.' The birds gleamed big an ebony. 'Oho,' said Rockingham. He was much cheered. When they left he jumped over the fence and walked straight across the field to where they'd stood. 'I like their spirit,' said Rockingham, passing over, 'there's nothing like it is there?' He stood where they'd stood—after all it *was* the best way south. He shook the snow off the flag and took up his song again, for on top of everything, the sun was beginning to warm his ancient back. He did not notice the young woman pick up her belongings in the tram shelter and climb over the fence to follow. The wind began to moan again.

Not having been able to find a tray Calvin came up the uncarpeted stairs with the mugs of tea on the lid of a packing case. He had been pleased to discover the stove alight and two pints of rich creamy milk in a jug outside the back door. He walked to his bedroom, turned the handle, pushed open the door with his foot and entered—his wife wasn't there. He called her name—no one answered. The bed was made, his clothes were neatly laid upon it. He put them on and drank his mug of tea. Hannah would be with one of the children no doubt. For some reason as he pulled on his shoes he felt worried.

He picked up his wife's tea and went down the passageway to Richard's room. He knocked, no one answered, he went in. The bed was not made—pyjamas were on the floor. 'Does he expect his mam to do it for him then?' said Calvin, irritated. 'And no doubt she will.' He saw the torn poem beside the mirror, put down the tea, knelt and picked up the pieces. He tried to fit them together until he thought to himself that this was not a proper thing to do, shook his head, and threw them down again. He took up the tea, left the room, and went up to see Eileen. This bedroom too was empty. He was disappointed. He stood for a moment imagining the feminine changes his daughter could make here, remembering her cupboard room in Houghton. 'Aye,' he decided, 'she can spread her wings here if her mam don't clip 'em.' He put the tea on the window-sill to look out—no one was to be seen in the garden. He couldn't understand how everybody had got up and about without him hearing. Just for a moment he thought he was alone in a dreamed house—just for a moment he felt like a child in a dark room looking into a lighted street. He turned back from the empty garden and went to make his daughter's bed. He smoothed out the sheet, briefly he held her night-dress against his cheek, before folding it under the pillow. His eyes lingered affectionately over the room, then he left to go up the little stairway to Betty. Again he knocked.

'Come in my Dad.'

'Ah you're in then,' said Calvin, 'like this tea?'

'I would my Dad.'

Elizabeth took the tea in both fat hands and began to drink.

'It tastes different don't it?'

'That's the cream.'

'I'll get used to it I suppose.'

Calvin smiled. 'There's a lot to get used to,' he said. 'You don't mind sleeping so far away?'

'I don't have to mind do I.'

'Oh yes you do.'

'Well you know what I mean my Dad don 't you?'

'I think so,' said Calvin, beginning to laugh at his daughter.

'You think I'm funny don't you Dad?'

'Sometimes,' said Calvin, 'in a nice way.'

'Oh I know it's in a nice way. I don't mind you laughing at me. I know you like me.'

'I love you.'

'Yes I know you do Dad. Dad I'm going to have to wear glasses. Will you look to it for me?'

'Can't you see too well?'

'Things keep bumping me.'

'Well I'll speak to your mam about it.'

'Yes, and I'd like *you* to take me Dad.'

'All right I will,' said Calvin and was pleased. 'Where are they all then?'

'Is Mam out too?'

'I can't find her.'

'I expect she's gone to your church.'

'Church?' asked Calvin surprised.

'Yes I expect that's where she is.'

'Well I shouldn't think so,' said Calvin doubtfully.

'Oh well,' said Elizabeth, 'I do.'

There was a pause while Calvin considered. 'Wouldn't she have got the breakfast first?'

'She hasn't has she?'

'No.'

'No,' said Elizabeth.

'Do you want to come with me and have a look?'

'No I'll stay here—I'm going to write my diary. I'm

beginning one for the new house. I have to find somewhere safe to keep it or you know what.'

Calvin did know what.

'And I've just written a poem Dad that's very good.'

'It is very good,' said Calvin when Elizabeth had read it to him.

'I'm going to write some more.'

'Good,' said Calvin. 'All right give me the mug and I'll take it down.'

'They're all exploring you see Dad.'

'Why are you so sure your mam's in the church?'

'I just know she is.'

'I'll give you a kiss then.' Calvin leaned over and did so. 'All right my Bet I'll take you for your glasses.'

'Are you going to like it here Dad?'

'What do you think?'

'I think you'll get used to it Dad.'

It was the child's turn to reach up and give the adult a comforting hug. 'I do love you, Dad.'

'Why do you Bet?'

'Because you love *me*, Dad.'

Calvin kissed her again and left.

So speculating on the characters of his children, considering how unlike himself and each other they were, wondering if he could ever really know them, realizing, and not for the first time, that although he tried never to show it there was something in Eileen that made him extra protective and she his favourite, Calvin descended the bare staircases, to set off to the church, to see if indeed his youngest daughter's prediction of her mother's whereabouts might be true.

Outside the front door Calvin trod a few paces on to the grass watching the dew soak into his worn black shoes and then turned to look back at the house. Since his new starched collar was tight on his neck he prised away at it with his strong fingers.

Calvin saw that the house stood three storeys high, facing the sea and the south-east, with a conservatory on one side of the main block, and a one-level extension—that was now the kitchen—on the other. The vicarage had been very poorly maintained. The roofs that had once been tiled with clay were now covered also with slates and over these grew moss and ivy. There were no eaves. The timbers were carried by over-sailing courses at the tops of the walls, on which hung cast iron gutters. He could see these gutters required painting, and patches of damp showed on the walls where they leaked. He could see broken spigots and that the collar of a rain-pipe was missing. He could see that the walls were red stone and that someone had colour washed and now needed to do it again. He could see that the roof of the bothy at the end of the single storey was falling in. All this comforted him.

He walked around his house. How grand it was. The ivy must be torn down but he made up his mind to have no hand in that. On the north face there was a large crack in the rendering of the main chimney-stack—the four-potter. Two fractures extended through the aprons of the first floor window and thence upwards. The conservatory leaked. He scrubbed his shoes into the gravel drive—the shingle was too loose. 'Now that's something I'll do right away,' he decided. 'I'll scarify, I'll put hoggin down, I'll get stone from the beach and I'll re-lay.' He walked to the iron gate: 'And I'll paint this,' he said. He liked the design. Filled with an enormous sense of well-being at all the work he could do on this house with his own strong hands he vaulted the shabby gate and set off down the road to his church.

He did not look down at the black shoes, he looked ahead for parishioners. 'It's vast,' he shouted, thinking of the house. If he had had the spiritual choice he would have chosen to live in a 'two-upper' in Houghton, but all the same it was en-nobling to have a bit of space. Like some sparse, irregular paper chain there lay on the road before him a trail of flowers.

Round the narrow bend, reading a newspaper as he walked, came a tall man in a tweed cap, a Norfolk jacket and knicker-bockers. Calvin stood still, allowed the soldier to pass—then called out enthusiastically: 'Good morning brother.'

The soldier did not jump as Calvin had anticipated, had hoped, he simply lowered his paper and turned:

'Good morning to you sir. I cannot say I approve your mode of address.'

'I'm your new vicar.'

'And a humorist too.'

'Ah well,' began Calvin, feeling undignified, feeling shamed.

'Write for *Punch*,' said the soldier. 'Very good periodical. I don't believe in brotherhoods do you see. I *would* have jumped had it not been that I am a little deaf. It has its advantages now that I am a practising uncle . . . caused by shellfire on the Somme.'

'A practising uncle?'

'A practising uncle,' repeated Major-General Andrews with a sardonic smile.

'That presupposes a talkative nephew then,' said Calvin, after a moment's thought.

'It does indeed—who seeks to reform me. My name is Andrews sir and although I am retired I have a talkative nephew. I always converse in non-sequiturs myself.'

'You do?'

'I do. I find it easier. You'll catch my gist.'

'Oh. Aye.'

'What are these flowers doing, Padre?'

'It seems someone was in a hurry,' said Calvin looking down at the trail.

'It does, it does. And on their way to the cemetery. Not a place to hurry to. And out of the vicarage gate perhaps.' The General pointed with his newspaper. 'We have many idiots in Suffolk—more than our just proportion. Some village Ophelia has danced down this road to her grave strewing her obsequies behind her.'

'I have a daughter,' said Calvin, thinking of Eileen. 'She might . . .'

'And I have a nephew,' the General interrupted. 'Can't we marry them off? You could perform the ceremony sir and I could give them away.'

52

'You should write for *Punch* yourself,' said Calvin beginning to grin.

'I do. I do,' cried the General. 'I write and they pay me a guinea. Which reminds me Padre, I wish to be cremated. I don't want to lie down there in the earth and rot.' He waved his newspaper vigorously in the air, shouted: 'Don't you let them put me down there to rot.' The eyes clouded, the hands shook, and the General seemed to find some difficulty in getting his breath.

'I won't,' said Calvin.

'Good God,' said the General calming himself. 'You're a man of authority. I like your tone. Shake my hand.'

Calvin did so.

'General Andrews, sir.'

'Vicar Calvin.'

The two men had a long look at each other—the General as he were studying the Vicar for promotion, the Vicar as he were studying the General for conversion.

'I've seen too many rot, Padre,' said General Andrews. 'Far too many.'

'I was there,' said Calvin.

'Ah. It was all wrong. It was monstrous.' The General raised his head, he drew himself up. 'Let us honour the dead sir,' he said.

They stood in silence. A cyclist came round the bend, tinkled his bell, swerved to avoid them, continued, discomforted. Neither moved.

'I hear you're all on the left Vicar,' said the General, falling at ease. 'I am all on the right myself. But I have . . . I have seen good fellows from the left . . . coming in with wounded men on their backs don't you know . . . and poets . . . Lady Cleeve did mention you were all on the left . . . silly young girl . . . needs a good man, never got one.'

'She's strong General.'

'Yes sir she's strong, rides like a man, and is loyal. But it's not her true image she finds in the glass.'

'I see,' said Calvin, although he didn't.

'You don't,' said the General, 'but you will. You'll follow my drift.' The General sighed. 'All our best men are dead sir, and I'm not feeling too well myself.' And now the General laughed in such a high pitched and yet vigorous manner that Calvin was reminded of a young horse. 'For God's sake burn me Vicar . . . blow me up like a cartridge . . . set some powder under my bones and strew my pieces in the sea out there. Strew me like these damned mad flowers.'

'I will.'

'I know you will. You've said so. I trust your tone. I'd have made you a sergeant of course—I'd have had that dog collar off in a jiffy. Why are these flowers lying so dead?'

'No you wouldn't,' said Calvin mildly.

'I would!'

'No you wouldn't,' said Calvin again.

'No? No perhaps I wouldn't,' said the General. 'I'd have tried though.' He waved his newspaper towards the cliffs. 'Put me in the sea Padre and keep going when I'm gone. I'll be there keeping time, keeping time. I'll think of you. I've got a dicky heart you know—ventricle. I hate the French. What have you got to say about this May Day incident? Ring out your bells sir, I'll hear them down there.'

'You hate the French, I hate fascists,' said Calvin.

The General looked at Calvin very sharply.

'You think they're dangerous, eh?'

'I do.'

'Ah. Ah. You may be right.' The General opened his paper and read: ' "Mr Bird stated that on Friday afternoon he stood on the embankment watching a May Day procession. Some of the demonstrators observed the British Fascisti badge which he was wearing and jeered at him. The defendant broke out of the column and making a running charge at Bird caught him in the ribs with his elbow." ' The General looked quizzically at Calvin and proceeded: ' "The defendant then re-entered the ranks of the column and was promptly arrested. This was followed by a great commotion. Witnesses denied that Bird jeered at the procession. Police Constable Wallace, who

54

arrested the defendant, said, that as they were crossing the Strand the defendant called out to his supporters, 'Come on don't let them take me.' He kicked the officer on the leg and spat on his neck." That's no way to behave, sir !'

'Not very nice,' said Calvin. 'What's his sentence?'

'One month.'

'I must drop him a line,' said Calvin. There was a pause and then Calvin said firmly: 'You must realize General that this fascism is power politics in its most naked form.'

'But what?' asked the General, 'what of this Mussolini? Is he not giving those Eyetalians some back-bone?'

'I wish the angel of God would hang him from my church tower,' said Calvin.

'Well,' said the General. There was another pause while the General considered. 'Well,' he said, 'still . . . why yours? He's a long way off. Can't do us any harm. Mind you he's . . .'

'He's not,' said Calvin. 'He's bloody well evil.'

'You swear, Vicar?'

'On occasion,' said Calvin without embarrassment.

Once again the General laughed. He turned a page and read: ' "Speaking at Briton Ferry, Mr MacDonald said he never felt more happy regarding political prospects than he did when Mr Churchill produced his budget. It was indeed a rich man's budget." '

'He's right,' said Calvin.

A clock was heard to strike, so folding the paper the General said, 'Excuse me, Padre, but it's my turn to cook the breakfast.' The General set off, looked back, and called to Calvin: 'Me and the boy prefer to do our own cooking do you see.'

Calvin watched him until he was gone, then turned to follow the 'damned mad flowers'. And they did indeed go to the church these sad flowers, and taking the way through the fields, over the stiles, up the little side lane to the cemetery gate, through, and on between graves to a lych gate leading into the main square of ground where stood the House itself. 'I'm sure it's our Eileen,' Calvin decided. When he got to the cemetery he paused to study the inscriptions on the tombstones: Tennyson, Strickland, Tyrell and Lynton; Ginn, Cheston, Perkins and Pearce.

But Calvin did not linger: he was more interested in the living than the dead. In fact he was not at all interested in the dead for they were with God and his province no longer. Calvin had never been one for the past or the dead.

He raised his eyes from the tombs to that perpendicular epitome of Suffolk flushwork standing so substantial over the wall, one hundred and forty feet long, its tall tower imposing on near and far, and feeling a sense of awe that *this* was his he got down on his knees in the grass before it. 'Pray dear God let me not demean thy House.' The prayers finished, he lifted his head to peer through his fingers at what he had seen only in dusk, at a distance, or by postcard—the sun sparkled on his wedding ring. 'That she should be able to give me *this* to honour,' he muttered, thinking of Lady Cleeve. 'She's God's instrument and that's a fact ... or the Devil's,' he added as a seagull flew overhead and spattered the gravestone in front of him. And was that an omen? If so, of what? He shook his head, smiling, lowered his praying fingers, and gazed.

His west tower was in four; the base flushwork arches, the buttresses flushwork panels, and the parapet flushwork diamonds. No battlements, no pinnacles. His west doorway was decorated by fleurons. In the spandrels stood two dragons; above them a cresting with shields. He could not read the crowned letters over the elaborate niches by the west window, he knew them from the postcards, and he said: 'Sancte Edmunde ora pro nobis.' He looked to the south where stood his porch on two storeys—with its arcaded and quatrefoil parapets, its niches above the two two-light windows. He looked at his unbroken roof running so straight from the tower to the east except for the little flèche in the middle rebuilt not a hundred years before, but correctly, and making his long church look Dutch. He had counted his eighteen close-set windows with the grey stone shafts in the clerestory when the birds and the wind were quiet, and in that strange, unexpected quiet he heard a sound from the open doorway, the sound of somebody sweeping. As he looked toward the doorway the shadow of a crow fell on to the gravel before it, passed over another of those fallen flowers, and although the silence had ended, he knew who the sweeper must be.

All alone in the vicarage, spurred by her father's praise, the prophetic and ambitious Betty was writing another poem:

> '*It was night*
> *The moon shone bright*
> *The lights were out*
> *No one was about*
> *Only the fairies danced in the moonlight*
> *They danced in fairie ring all night.*
> *When the day came*
> *They went to sleep again.*'

As before she signed her name 'E. Calvin', as before she read her poem aloud in a satisfied tone, then she jumped out of bed, opened the door and peered down the corridor. 'Mam,' she shouted, 'Mam, where's my breakfast?' When she realized the house was empty she began to grumble. 'I suppose I'll have to get it myself,' she said.

'Mm . . . Mister,' she called. 'Hey, Mmister.' Rockingham stopped. 'I know you don't I Mmister?'

'No,' said Rockingham. It was the first time he had heard a woman stammer.

'Yes . . . yes I do. You're a friend of Mm . . . Miner Calvin's.' It was only after she had come up beside him in the snow and he had waited while she gained the strength to continue to speak that he realized she was young. 'I've been to see him . . . but he's gone.' She breathed so heavily, leaned towards him at such an odd angle that she might have been frozen in the act of collapse and the old man considered putting down the flag and giving her his hands to prevent her falling on to the cobbles. 'They say he's gg . . . gone . . . gone south . . .

gone for ggood.' She was not tall, and terribly thin, emaciated almost—the emaciation had a startling whiteness about it, the whiteness emphasized by the black, nearly raven hair above, and somehow giving him the impression that this condition was recent—as if she had been 'struck down'. 'Bb . . . but you're young,' said Rockingham stammering over the 'but' himself, a thing he could not remember having done in his life before. It really was the ghost of a smile that crossed the ivory face: 'I'm not always like this . . . I've . . . I've known better dd . . . ddd . . .'' 'Days,' he said, finishing the sentence for her and relieved that he had pronounced the word in his normal fashion lest he had seemed to her to mock. 'Oh aye, days,' she said, 'and nights too. It's a good country if you're not poor.'

Neither spoke for perhaps a minute.

'I've been to Paris,' she said. She repeated it again, proudly like a child showing off to a visiting aunt, 'I've been to Paris., Then conscious that her exhaustion was partly responsible for her remark and seeking to explain why she had made it she said: 'When I mm . . . mentioned our country I thought of the other . . . I mm . . . mean I've seen others. One other. Third class via Dunkirk and Tilbury . . . that's the cheapest. He took me. You have to pay extra for a cabin . . . there's a huge hotel on the waterside at Tilbury . . . stucco he said it was. It's got pinnacles. They don't have mm . . . mint sauce in Paris.'

'Are you a prostitute?' asked Rockingham, and although she reeked so sourly he found it hard to stand his ground, he had known worse, so he managed.

'No,' she said surprised, 'did you think I was? No I've never been that. I've only had one man and he's married, that's why he took me to France . . . last year. I lost mm . . . my virginity in Paris.' The last phrase was so unexpected, so startling to the old man—in fact he couldn't recall having heard the word 'virginity' before, although he had read it in the *News of the World*—and uttered in such a breathless innocence that for some reason or other he found himself warming towards the exhausted girl and wondering how things might have been if he and his dead wife had ever borne such a

58

daughter as this. He looked shyly at her now, somewhere above the thin nose and the black eyes, somewhere at the high forehead, and he repeated slowly: 'So you're not a prostitute?'

'Of course not,' she said, trying to smile.

Rockingham glanced around him because it had occurred to him how incongruous they must seem, standing so long together in the cold wind and the snow, and she, interpreting the look that he wanted to leave her, leaned even further to grasp him by the arm, leaned and held on to him like an anxious drunk and said quickly: 'I've only had one mm . . . man and he's mm . . . married and I'm pregnant and that's why I want to see Mmm . . . Mister Calvin.'

'Who's the father?' asked Rockingham.

'What's it to you?'

'We're off to see him—he's no business letting you go about like this.'

'He give me money, I give it him back.'

'Why?'

'I don't want nothing from him now.'

'Why?'

'I don't that's all.'

'Why?'

'Don't go on at me, asking me questions like this. You're not mm . . . my father!'

'Why don't you want nothing from him?'

'He don't love me and I thought he did.'

'How old are you?'

'How old?'

'How old are you?'

'Nineteen. I'm nineteen. I think . . . or twenty.'

In the narrow hole in the corner street, between the chlorotic houses, on the tops of the stained cobbles with the threads of dirty snow, below a boot-black sky, the old man considered what best to be done—he needed his money and he must get south with the flag. He must!

'Is your tale true?'

'Oh I'm no liar.'

59

'And what d'you expect of Vicar?'

'Work.'

'Work?'

'Aye, I've been sacked from mill. Got sick you see. I was bad for three months. Heaving up all the time. I've stopped now.'

'You know,' said the old man (and half to himself), 'if you took yourself in hand and cleaned up you'd look nice . . . you'd look quite nice.'

'I know that,' she said, 'I've no money.'

'It don't cost money to wash.'

'Of course it does.'

'It's a shame,' said the old man, 'it's a bloody shame. You're no fool you know. I suppose there's hundreds like you. You smell you know. You won't get nor keep no job like that.'

'Excuse me,' she said. She left him and hurried over to the gutter to be sick. Nobody else in the street took notice. After a moment Rockingham went over beside her, took her hand and held it. 'Don't pay no attention to me,' he said, 'you go on and when you've finished you come with me and I'll buy you a cup of tea and some bread and butter for your breakfast and then I'll give you a sixpence and then we'll get ourselves down to the public baths.' He continued to have to hold her hand. 'Have you thought of names for your baby?' he asked. The wind continued to moan.

No clouds in the sky but from the marshes the mist had been drawn by the sun, had spread over the fields as it thinned, and beyond and through, they saw the church and the town risen up, pale-blue, transparent.

'It looks like fairy land,' said Richard. 'We are ghosts.'

'Well you've got a halo,' said Andrews, 'for there's dew on your head. It won't last much longer. It's going to be so hot. "The hottest day of the year," they'll say tomorrow in the papers.'

As they approached the edge of the cliff they turned their heads from the town and back to the sea. In the mist the breaking of the waves below was muffled, they thudded upon the shore like logs. Everything in the air about them was soft.

'You can feel the sea,' said Andrews, 'I mean the cliff seems to be moving under our feet.'

'What if it's eaten its way underneath and we both fall in and are drowned?' asked Richard.

'As good a way to go as any,' said Andrews.

'Do you think of death much?'

'I do.'

'So do I.'

'I don't want to die.'

'Nor do I,' said Richard. 'I hate thinking about it. Sometimes I wake up thinking about it.'

'There's so much to do.'

'There is! There is!'

'Mind you I'm not ever going to let it dominate me.'

'How do you mean?'

'Well if it comes to giving up my life for something I really believe in, I want to think I would.'

'I don't think I could do that,' said Richard. 'Not yet at any rate.'

'I don't know that I can,' said Andrews, 'but I want to be able.'

'Father could,' said Richard.

'And my uncle could,' said Andrews, 'that's what's so confusing.'

'Perhaps it's easier when you get old.'

'Of course my family always thought it their bounden duty to go and get killed,' said Andrews, 'they've never forgiven me for being too young for the war.'

'Really?'

'Oh yes,' said Andrews, 'oh yes. Very puritanical all my lot. It's going to be very hard for me to get rid of.'

'Really?' said Richard.

'Oh yes, oh yes.'

Blue, like periwinkle flowers, lay the sea below. Blue waves, green waves, swept in and foamed, behind the foam a thin black line, behind the tangled sea-weeds shallow pools of light in the sand. The wind freshened; the sea sang hoarser. Further out a single white sail flamed upon it. They stood as if they too were sails, breathing deep, giving themselves to the wind. High over their heads, a wisp, not a cloud, but part of the haze from the marshes had become pink, and was sailing up and along so slowly it looked as though the sky itself was turning over, on some gigantic spit.

'Beautiful as the day is, delighted as I am to have made your acquaintance, I must go and have my breakfast,' said Andrews.

'You can't,' said Richard, pointing to the sand-dunes, 'there's Eileen.'

'I must. Uncle will have it ready.'

'Please meet Eileen first. You'll like her.'

'I don't expect so,' said Andrews, 'and Uncle's a disciplinarian.'

'Please.'

'The food will spoil.'

'Please.'

'He'll nag me.'

'Please.'

'I don't like it when *he's* late.'

'Oh please. Just once. It's our first morning. There's lots of breakfasts.'

'There's lots of Eileens.'

'Oh no there aren't,' said Richard seriously. 'There's no one quite like Eileen. You *will* like her. Please.' He put his hand on Andrews's arm. 'You can blame your lateness on me.'

Andrews looked down at the hand as if he disliked being touched: embarrassed, Richard took it away, and yet still managed to look hopefully up at his tall friend. Something in that ingenuous face made Andrews give in. 'All right,' he said, 'just once I'll wait for your awful sister. However I'm not going to blame it on you, I shall tell Uncle the truth.'

'Thank you,' said Richard. 'She's not awful you know, not

62

Eileen.' He was happy, he waved, he shouted: 'Eileen, Eileen.'

Down on the sand dunes Eileen raised her head, looked up and saw. In her hair all those jewels sparkled, those blue, green, and yellow sparks of fire. The wide-opened eyes gazed upwards, saw the watchers on the clifftop not smaller but larger than life.

'You mustn't be shy of girls,' said Richard. 'I expect it's your school that's done that.'

Eileen began to move towards them, realized it was a young man with her brother, seemed to hesitate, seemed to grow awkward, to walk slower.

'She should have glasses you know,' said Richard, 'she just won't wear them.'

Eileen walked even slower, looking everywhere but at the boys, with her hands she tidied her glittering hair.

'You see you've got the advantage,' said Richard with a beaming smile.

'I don't suppose I'll have it for long,' said Andrews, and taking out the inevitab le cologne he started to wet the pale moustache.

For the second time that morning John Calvin stood, as one who feels a premonition. It was nothing in the attitude of the massive church, not the pink web from the marshes floating over the tower, nothing in the circling of the crow by the tombs, made him stand so still, with his scarred head bowed forward, feet pigeon-toed, and the palms of his hands pressed tight against his thighs: it was something in the sound of the sweeping. He stood before the great west door, before the crowned letters, before the 'Sancte Edmunde ora pro nobis'. If there had been a ladder to climb to the stained glass window he would have ascended and looked into the church with the rising sun.

There came upon him a series of physical images of the woman he had lived with so long: her feet, the backs of her hands, her elbows, her breath, the sound of her footsteps, her corset, her hat-pins and the smell of her hair. At first each

63

image led naturally to another, and then they mixed themselves up, and in the end what he realized was that he was standing apart, he was watching the intimate actions of some stranger, someone he had not spoken to, nor touched, nor kissed, someone who was beyond his understanding; and yet, throughout, not only did he know that this wasn't true, he knew also that what he wanted most was to feel, and touch, and smell, and kiss her.

Cows mooed, a dog barked: the foreboding went from him; he made up his mind to move, shaking his head. He was about to walk towards the door when he heard the footsteps within hurry towards it: was she coming out? The palms of his hands grew moist, he rubbed them on the shiny trousers. The door of the church was closed; the footsteps receded. He went to the door to try the handle. It was locked. It was such a heavy door for her, and since she could not have heard, or known it was he, he did not understand why she had barred his church. All his anxiety disappeared, irritation swept over him. His church should never be barred. He ran round the side to look for the choir door, and yet when he had found it and tried the handle he could not help entering on tiptoe. 'After all,' he said to himself, 'what is the nature of these women we live with?' However, he decided there and then he would have all locks and bars removed from his church. In the chancel he went on tiptoe to the corner of the screen and there he stopped, and stood in wonder. She had filled his church with flowers.

'Hannah,' he said gently so as not to frighten her, 'Hannah dear.' She was down on her knees brushing up the dust in the aisle, and he did frighten her. 'You made me jump,' she said. 'Yes,' he said, 'yes,' and not moving from where he stood. 'I locked the door,' she said, standing up with the dustpan. 'I didn't want anyone to come in till I finished. There's much to do. It's so very dirty.'

He could only stand there before this thin woman with the tulle scarf, the white blouse, the gaberdine costume, the black shoes, the cotton gloves, the hat—this woman taller than himself; got up in the splendour of her flowers, lit by the sunlight through the stained glass, drenched by the risen dust. She looked to him like some gaunt sad angel—some angel who had seen and suffered too much. He knew this woman, had lain naked beside her. He knew her as well as he could. And struggling through all his knowledge was some kind of apprehension that now was the turning point with Hannah, right here, was the instant when pain or joy would be snatched for ever.

She too stood still. She seemed intensely alive. Her eyes were so bright looking down the dark avenue between. Calvin thought the church was growing larger; it turned itself into a cathedral.

'There's tulips,' she said, 'and daffodils and primroses. I didn't pick the bluebells because they don't live long.' But that wasn't what she was saying. 'I do love you,' she was saying. 'Aye,' he said aloud. 'Aye. I know. I love you too.' He stepped down from the chancel. She seemed to tremble. He was so nervous. 'I can't have these Bible boxes,' he said, 'it's not right for the poor. The owners are pushing the labouring men to the back.' She seemed to whisper something but he couldn't make it out 'What?' he asked. 'What?' She whispered again but still he couldn't hear and as he moved nearer he saw her tremble and behind her the rising sun kept coming in at the window, touching her flowers, bringing out their glory in a way nothing else ever could. The pews loomed up at her back and as he drew closer he was forced to look away from those incredibly anxious eyes so that although he realized the pews were separate they seemed inextricably involved, and some of her host of flowers doubled up in their vases, stood together, two by two, one real, one phantom. 'I suppose there'll be trouble about these pew rents,' he said. Then he rushed towards her down the aisle, through the sharp wedges of light, he took her face in his hands, he kissed her full on the lips and before the kiss was begun he knew he had done the wrong thing. He heard her cry out and at first he thought it was himself. She pushed him aside and she sobbed all the way to the door. He could only watch as she struggled to open it and leave him alone in the church.

Eileen had joined the boys on the cliff top. The mist had gone, the sun had risen, the waves were sweeping the beach as regularly as a machine. The high light fell on cornfields and woods, turning the streams blue and the grass greener. The birds sang wildly as if it were their last. They sang with such passion that Andrews remarked: 'An they were bullfrogs they'd burst.' Eileen laughed. The birds swooped into the air, swept and soared, rested in the upper branches, looked down pityingly on everything beneath, and never stopped singing. They sang as if they must wake up the whole earth—a great busy choir dropped from the sun. The land grew militant, the white blossom streamed like banners, the corn raised its head like lances and plumes. 'Hurrah,' shouted Richard embarrassing no one. The sea drummed. Then, then, over all, rang the bell. Everyone heard it, everyone listened.

'It's the church bell,' said Eileen.

'It's a tenor bell,' said Richard.

'It's the custom for the incoming Vicar to toll,' said Andrews. 'To toll himself in.'

Everyone had begun to count.

'I wonder how long he'll last,' said Eileen.

'I never thought he'd do so many,' said Andrews after they'd listened to twenty. 'I never thought that. I never thought anyone could.'

On went the bell.

'Perhaps he's got help,' said Andrews.

'Not Dad,' said his son.

'Twenty-eight, twenty-nine, thirty, thirty-one, thirty-two.'

'He must be absolutely exhausted,' said Andrews. 'How big's your father?'

'Oh he's little,' said Eileen.

And Richard added: 'He's not as tall as Mum.'

'You know,' said Andrews. 'You know I couldn't do . . .' he stopped and blushed.

'It's all right,' said Eileen, 'he was a miner, Robert.'

Thirty-six, thirty-seven and thirty-eight, thirty-nine, forty.

'Well that,' said Robert Andrews, 'means nineteen sixty-ive.'

They waited: the bell had definitely stopped.

'How old a man is your father?' asked Andrews.

'He rang for two years more than his life,' said Richard.

'He's a young man then. Quite young.'

'Oh yes,' said Richard. 'Quite young.'

'He's younger than Mother,' said Eileen. 'I love Father. I love him.'

The birds began to sing again but their singing was not as before.

In the bell tower Calvin had fallen from the rope and lay on the floor. As Richard had informed Robert Andrews, Calvin was only thirty-eight. Halfway he was, halfway.

Chapter 3

'WE'LL be having to look for our beds,' said the old man.
With an obvious moment of disgust a well-dressed woman
shuddered away from them, going up on the pavement with
her husband to some middle-class palace on the slopes. The
old man lifted the flag higher on his shoulder. 'Thinks we're
dead cats,' he said. 'It's not as though you're dirty now.'
'Clothes are very im . . . im . . . important,' said Jean. They
went on descending. 'Eastward Ho,' said the old man. 'How
do you always know your way?' she asked. 'Learned map in
station. Follow the road signs.' 'Bb . . . bb . . . bbut in the
towns.' 'Strong sense of direction,' said Rockingham. 'Practised
it in the pit. The uneasy minds of the privileged.' 'What?' 'The
uneasy minds of the privileged,' said Rockingham, 'it's a
telling phrase.' 'What does it tell?' she asked and laughed.
'Ha! Ha!' said the old man. 'I don't know as it's true though,'
she smiled at him, 'they're no more than anyone else.' 'It is
true, it's especially true,' said Rockingham. 'It is a true and a
useful phrase.' 'I don't know as it is,' she repeated.

In the evening, because they could not exactly see the
graceless shapes of the houses, because the night was so black,
Sheffield achieved a brutal magnificence. The vast sky of
smoke was red with sulphur; uncinated flames flared and
bellowed up to the moon from out the great chimneys, squeezed
and screamed from the little ones. The scarlet boys in the open
doors hauled out the snakes of iron, and under the steam
hammers these snakes they hissed, they writhed, and they
wept. 'So the wind has taste in it again,' said the old
man, sniffing. 'It's not just like Houghton . . . bb . . . bbut
it does taste.' 'That country air had no taste,' said the old
man.

At the corner near the bottom of the hill, eating chips and
reading the end of the wrapping paper under the gas was a

68

navvy. 'Where's our cheapest bed if you don't mind please?' asked Rockingham, feeling this man would know. 'It's early yet.' 'Aye but she's tired and all,' said Rockingham. 'No, I'm not,' said Jean. 'Yes, she would be,' said the man looking more closely at Jean. 'Go further down, turn left into Lonsdale, see a sign "Good Beds"—there's others but not near and I've been there myself and it's cheap.' 'Clean?' asked Rockingham. 'Cheap and clean,' said the man. 'A representative house.' 'Thank you,' said Jean. 'Thank you,' said Rockingham. 'A representative house.'

They went on descending into the city. 'I hope there's a library in Eastwold,' said the old man. 'I do like a good read.' 'I hope so too. What do you read Mm . . . Mmister Rocking-ham?' 'Politics and men's lives and such like.' 'I think,' said the girl, 'I think I could be very intelligent if I read mm . . . mm . . .' 'More?' 'Yes mm . . . mmore.' 'Intelligence isn't a matter of reading.' 'It would be with me. I've a good mm . . . mind . . . but I don't know enough.' 'We'll investigate that,' said Rockingham.

They turned into Lonsdale Avenue (which being no avenue belied its name entirely) and saw the 'Good Beds' sign at the end over an exhausted house with pale lights in all the windows and most brown paper patched. Rockingham stopped under the gas to feel in his trouser pocket. 'I'm getting short,' he said. 'I've got to watch my reserve.'

Up the steps and down a stone passage. 'About a fivepence each I suppose,' said Rockingham. At the end of the way and by a table an etiolated woman ate cheese and pickles. 'You'll want a kip,' said she. 'Aye,' said Rockingham. 'One shilling single, one and three if it's man and wife sharing a bed.' 'One shilling!' 'You won't get better in Sheffield.' She squeezed the end of her nose like a boil, she bit on the cheese, she pinched up another onion out of the swimming saucer. Deciding he must confer Rockingham drew his companion away. Unmoved the woman swallowed her onion like a turkey, reached again into the vinegar. 'I'm getting short now, Jean,' said Rocking-ham. 'I don't see as we can afford this place. I must keep a bit in hand.' Below them in the cellar was laughter and singing, a warm smell blew itself up through the closed door. 'I mean we'll want a bite,' he continued, 'and there's the rest of the week.' 'You have a bed. I'll find somewhere.' 'You will not,' he answered, 'I will and *you'll* have the comfort.' 'Please.' 'Oh no, and it's not only you I think of.' 'I won't forget it,' she said. She touched him on his arm, she nodded at him.

Now there was a pause. 'Why don't . . . why don't we go down and have a bite while we think what?' She smiled in agreement. He returned that smile.

The cellar was crowded with navvies drinking tea from mugs as big as their boots; the day's menu chalked on a slate. On the counter the notice read: 'Stealing sugar from benches not allowed.' 'Two large teas and four slices,' said Rockingham.

They sat beside a Jew, eating bacon very quickly. 'He that takes away the sugar, shall be called a dirty bugger,' said Jean. The Jew looked up, Rockingham away: Jean blushed. Consequently she had more colour in her face than Rockingham had yet seen, which made him smile again when he noticed. 'Ah then that's something,' he thought. Now the Jew ate even quicker—half a minute and he was off. 'You shouldn't say things like that,' said Rockingham. 'I thought you'd laugh,' said Jean. 'It makes me uncomfortable when women swear.' 'That's silly if you like them.' 'You're right there,' said the old man. 'Yes it's all right if you like them.' 'I don't swear often,' said Jean, 'I thought as I'd make you laugh.' 'It was a nice thought,' said Rockingham.

They ate slowly through their second slices of bread and marg—not wishing to get to the end. They gazed away from each other at the ragged washing drooped on the strings from the ceiling before the great clinker fire. They realized the only light in the room came from that fire. In the shadows Jean thought the clothes to be poor children climbed up high to hang themselves. When she shivered Rockingham asked if she were cold but she only shook her head. 'Someone must have crossed over your grave,' he said. They watched. They watched the man whose turn it was to tend the clinkers. They watched 'poor Smith' come in through the door and dole out a pail of winkles. They thanked him for their portion. 'Poor Smith' was taken with Jean.

'It is going to be difficult together,' said the old man when they were alone again. 'It is rare together. I mean many a man and wife must split for the night. I understand so. It's hard for women to find a cheap bed.' 'I've heard that.' 'We can't spend another night out. You feel the cold, and I feel the cold. We'll have to split. You keep my money and I'll go to one of the Houses. It's too cold for out and we'll get no sleep. I don't suppose there *is* cheaper in Sheffield. No, I'll go to one of the Spikes. You'll have to keep my money as they don't allow you with money do you see.' 'Have you been before?' 'No, but I've heard.' 'I want us to be together,' she said. 'Can't we share? I want us to be together.'

Rockingham did not answer that question. After a while she whispered, and even shyer than before: 'Can't we share a bed on the one and threepence?' This time, looking at her directly, and with concern, he replied: 'I don't know as that's right, is it?' 'I don't mind.' 'Well . . . well, we're not family.' Again there was a pause. 'Mm . . . Mm . . . Mmister Rockingham I won't touch you.' 'It's not that. You see I don't know as it's right and you see . . . you see . . . ' 'Yes?' said Jean. 'You see I've never shared but with my wife.'

A tear came into the girl's eyes. 'Ah,' she said, 'you make me cry.' 'I'll think of her all night I expect,' said Rockingham. 'It's lonely without her do you know.' 'I'll keep you warm, Mm . . . Mmister Rockingham.' 'I think as I'll pretend to myself I'm the grandfather,' said the old man.

They finished their tea. Rockingham picked up the flag. Hesitantly they stood. 'But is it right if we're not family?' repeated the old man. 'It's all right for us,' said Jean, and nodded her head.

They left the warm cellar and went up the stairs to the cold hall. 'Poor Smith' had begun to sing:

'Her step was light and her heart was gay,
But she had no sense, and one fine day
She got herself put in the family way
By a wicked, heartless, cruel deceiver.'

'That's me,' said Jean. 'It is,' said Rockingham. And they laughed. 'What about the woman?' 'What d'you mean?' 'Will she believe us?' 'Oh her,' said the old man with contempt, 'the gobbler . . . the old turkey . . . I'm not bothered with her.' 'We *are* family,' said Jean.

Having paid the one and threepence a son was summoned by the etiolate to lead them up the bare unlighted stairway to their cubicle. Their cubicle had no door. It smelt of disinfectant and dirty sheets. The boy lit the candle on the saucer. Already in the dormitory many were in bed and Rockingham and Jean could see that these sleepers had piled their clothes on top of themselves, even their boots and their shoes. 'Regulars,' said the spotted boy by way of information and seemed to be knowing and amused for he laughed back at Jean and spat on the floor as he went away. 'I'll kick his arse,' said Rockingham.

They examined the bed—hard as a board, not six feet, and narrow. 'We'll have to hold on not to fall out, Mm . . . Mmister Rockingham. These sheets stink so mm . . . much I can't have them near my nose.' 'Shall we put them under the bed?' 'Yes.' When they lifted them up to do so they found "Stolen from Lonsdale Avenue" writ large across. And under the bed was a chamber pot cracked and stained: Jean began to giggle. She took the sheets from Rockingham and she stuffed them into the pot, she held the pot away at arm's length, tiptoed out of the cubicle, and like a thief slid it under the snoring couple two doors down. The old man watched aghast. When she returned: 'You'll be getting me into trouble,' he said. They had one of their pauses. Then one of their smiles. 'I suppose it's all right,' said Rockingham, 'you weren't seen' and we'll be off early. I think we'd best sleep in our clothes. 'Yes, there's only the counterpane.' 'It's not going to be hot.

72

'No, it's no oven,' she said. 'Is there somewhere to wash and all that?' 'Aye you look,' he answered, 'and I'll go last.'

Alone Rockingham sat on the bed and considered. He fell to wondering about this Jean—embroidering on what little he'd been told. He hoped he wouldn't have to get up in the night. When he heard her coming back he propped the flag between the mattress and the wall and tucked around the rag of cotton. He saw with pride that somewhere she'd washed herself as well as she could.

'Shall I get in?' 'Yes love.' 'Thank you, Mm . . . Mmister Rockingham.'

All the way down the dark corridor to the grimy sink, throughout the washing on the stove with the scraps of carbolic, all the way back to the ward, the old man wondered about her. He forgot his dead wife, he forgot his pigeons, he forgot the flag and he forgot the Vicar of Eastwold. When he reached the cubicle and the narrow bed he found she had blown out the candle and pushed herself to the wall. He took his boots off his bare feet, stuffed his socks into the boots, slid the boots under the bed. He dried his damp feet again with his muffler, put the muffler over the boots, took off his coat and wrapped it around the girl in the bed. 'Thank you, Mm . . . Mmister Rockingham.' He took off his jacket and put it over her feet. 'Thank you, Mm . . . Mmister Rockingham.' He took a deep breath and climbed into bed with his back against her. Almost without his noticing it she adjusted herself into the most comfortable position for him. 'Good night Mm . . . Mmister Rockingham.' 'Good night Jean.' Very soon he began to feel her warmth. She did not speak again and in the darkness this place he lay in began to grow: the shadows from the gas lamps thrown in at the brown paper windows took on such life that it was they who coughed, swore, used their chamber pots and lit their cigarettes, who called at each other in desperation and in anger: 'Shut up. Shut up for Christ sake. For Jesus sake shut up.' Time passed. People came, people went. Only the silent girl was real, silent and warm beside him. Still he did not sleep. About one, when the old lady opposite struck a match, he saw she'd pulled her knickers over her head for a nightcap and he gained the impression that the feet beside her, sticking out towards him, were black as a negro's.

He did not change position for fear of disturbing the girl, and he was forced to hold out his left arm over his head because of the pins and needles in the fingers. About two there was a horrid moment when he thought she had stopped breathing. He realized all was well, he found himself trembling, and he prayed for her.

At three there was a drunken jabbering and a man began to speak of the damnation of his soul in a public school voice, and another, beside him, to sing: 'Tipperary'. In the storm that followed either they or someone else produced a bottle, for the sufferers desisted and were heard to swallow and to suck. At four a woman sobbed quietly to herself for perhaps a quarter of an hour. At five, a cripple was seized by a spasm, woke under fire, and screamed of corpses. This time the old man felt the girl beside him stiffen. The cripple did not sound old. He seemed to be watching a man called Wienskowski burn up his gun crew, he cried out 'Oh! La, mon Dieu,' as if he were French, he kissed his dead sergeant on the hole in the temple, he locked the door in case they should rush him where only the door remained. This time no one cried abuse, this time all waited for the cripple to finish. 'Don't rush me. Don't rush me,' shouted the cripple. And other young voices joined in as though the cripple had switched them on. They shouted of blood and guts and shit; of two hundred and ten millimetre shells; of spewed up tree trunks, of the rails of marshalling yards standing up in the air like dead thistles; of stomachs on the ground so tiny, so red, and so wet; of arms and legs disappearing below the ground with monotonous regularity; of eruptions so steady; of noise so vast. And always, always, of human beings, torn up like dolls, torn up, splintered, spitted, ripped and thrust and stuck. For the first time the old man changed his position, he put his hand on the girl's shoulder. And now the hot smell of urine filled the ward. Everyone took

74

small shallow breaths, everyone breathed through their mouths. The night continued.

Towards light the old man heard her whisper. She whispered, 'Mm . . . Mmister Rockingham.' 'Yes love.' 'Would you like to feel my baby?' He could not answer. 'Don't you want to?' He sighed. 'Put your hand on my tummy Mm . . . Mmister Rockingham. Lower. Lower. That's it. Just there. There Mister Rockingham.' He rested his hand where she bade him but he couldn't feel life. 'Oh he's stopped,' said Jean, 'just when I didn't want him to.' 'I'll hang on,' said the old man in extreme nervousness. 'Have you ever felt it before?' 'No never,' said the old man. 'You're trembling Mm . . . Mmister Rockingham. Are you cold now?' 'No love.' The old man kept his hand where she bade him, and sure enough, just before the sun came up, he felt the baby kick.

Chapter 4

FRIDAY morning. The sun had risen. In the woods the trees were green and shining.

'Being a clergyman you could not escape from the past even if you wanted to.' Hannah Calvin shivered as she walked, drew her collar closer to her neck. 'Our vicarage is old but below it is an older. And below that no doubt, another. This path across these fields to your church must have been padded down by hundreds of years of parsons. In one of the registers in the chest in your vestry there's a baptism for an Elizabeth Pearce in the year of the Gunpowder Plot.'

'Aye. It's a grand morning.'

'I find it cold,' said Mrs Calvin.

Although apparently calm Calvin was excited at the sight of the church standing so strong in the dawn. Enshrined in the dawn. And because of this excitement, although managing to pay some attention to his wife, words of the days were tolling in his head like a tune from the bell tower ahead. 'I assent to the Thirty-Nine Articles of Religion and to the Book of Common Prayer and of the Ordering of Bishops, Priests and Deacons. I believe in the Doctrine of the Church of England as therein set forth to be agreeable to the Word of God, and in Public Prayer and Administration of the Sacraments I will use the Form in the said Book prescribed and none other, except so far as shall be ordered by lawful authority.' Was it really true at last? 'Instituted. Instituted and inducted,' tolled the East-wold bells: Calvin shook his head.

Mrs Calvin said: 'It is a long way. In future I shall bicycle.'

'Can I carry your bag?'

'I've already said no. It's not heavy. You'd look silly with it.'

'I'd look very nice,' said Calvin smiling. He took the bag. 'Thank you,' said Mrs Calvin.

76

The path narrowed, continued through briars. They had to walk single file: Mrs Calvin led.

Between these briars, young ferns, ragwort and thistles the Vicar of Eastwold heard the whispering of the Oaths of Allegiance and Obedience. He knelt before the Bishop, together they held the seal: 'We do by these presents commit unto you the Cure of the Souls of the Parishioners of Eastwold ... and authorize you to preach the Word of God in the Parish Church of Eastwold.'

Mrs Calvin said: 'A cold air is blowing in from the sea. It gets around my legs.'

Under the ferns, under the briars, spilling out of the earth, like the words into his brain, were thousands and thousands of little wild flowers, blue and violet and white.

'Aye, they're extras,' said Calvin.

'What?' asked his wife.

'Flowers,' said Calvin.

'It is not only goodness which gives extras,' said Mrs Calvin, following quite the train of her husband's thought.

Without turning her head, increasing her pace, Mrs Calvin said: 'I know I'm a trial. I shall get used to Eastwold of course like anything else. Naturally I'm disappointed. I have to say what I think. You're always telling me not to bottle myself up. The trouble with Eastwold is it is neither a village nor a town. It's not one or the other. There's no one else except that pathetic little chapel. And yet you won't have a proper congregation. You're not a theologian who needs the time and yet you won't have time to know everyone. I wish we could have gone to Bournemouth or London. That is what I would have liked. Not that there was ever any chance of it. This kind of parish can never be stimulated, *that* I know. Oh I can see *that* all right. You wouldn't get an able or an ambitious man coming here, that's obvious. That's why she got you.'

Looking ahead, past his wife's left shoulder, Calvin felt the Archdeacon's hand laying his own on the door and now the bells began to chime. 'By virtue of this mandate I do induct you into the real actual and corporeal possession of this Church

77

of Eastwold with all the rights, profits and appurtenances thereto belonging.' Then he himself was once again tolling the bell of possession. 'How many have done that twice,' wondered Vicar Calvin. 'And the same number too. How many have rung in twice.'

Mrs Calvin said: 'You are going to feel very isolated. You won't get regular visits from the Bishop and the Archdeacon here. They're only concerned with the unemployed in the cities.'

'Perhaps I won't want too many visits.'

'Ah,' said Mrs Calvin, triumphantly as if she had meant to provoke her husband's remark, 'don't you get arrogant. Just you remember you're not your own master. You're a servant of your Church.'

Calvin was not drawn.

Mrs Calvin said: 'I hope you're not going to stir up trouble and make it embarrassing for me and the children and just try to show off all on your own because you've got a place of your own at last.'

'Well that is what I am going to do,' announced Calvin, mildly.

Since they had crossed the field and reached the first stile Mrs Calvin climbed up and over holding on to her skirt. When they set off again, past the lilac, Mrs Calvin said: 'Don't think I don't know what's going on. Everyone in the place comes up to speak to me. I hear it all. They delight in it. You've got one advantage anyway!'

'What's that?'

'None of them liked your predecessor.'

'Richards did,' said Calvin dryly.

'The coal owner?'

'Aye.'

'Don't think I don't know who's who. I know who Richards is. And I can see why he liked Vicar Jones what's more. And why he won't like you. They didn't like Jones because they say he just wrote books. Books they couldn't understand I expect. At least he had dignity.'

78

On they walked across the green, green field.

'He would have been no trouble to the rich. Of course it wasn't Lady Cleeve who appointed him. It was her stupid husband. She only married him for the title they say. And he only went to Africa because he was so bored with her. Jones was a Welshman and naturally they were prejudiced from the start. I can't think why they all dislike the Welsh so much. They were glad he died.'

But Calvin was already inside the church, visiting the font, the place of prayer, the place of lessons, the pulpit and the altar, and in each he was replying: 'I will do so the Lord being my helper.'

'Hannah dear I shall be reading the Thirty-Nine Articles and the Declaration before the people myself next Sunday.'

'Of course none of the old vicars want to come to the country any more,' continued Mrs Calvin as if her husband had not spoken. 'Bishop Thomas remarked: "When you've one foot in the grave you want the other on a bus stop." '

'Did he say that?'

'Imagine that gouty old fool doing this walk every day. Anyway you're not going to get much change here. Farmers are the stupidest, most conservative people in the country—Father always said that.'

'They're not all farmers.'

'I know who there is. There's farmers, there's fishermen, there's the canning girls, there's those painters and people across the river, there's the shops, and the tourists in the summer.'

'Hannah, a lot of the labourers around here are badly housed, underpaid, isolated and exploited.'

Mrs Calvin stopped so abruptly that he almost bumped into her. 'If you're going to stir up trouble here I shall leave you.'

'Come on or we'll be late for prayers.'

'And I'll take the children too!'

'No you won't,' he answered with such anger that for a moment she was vanquished and resumed her way shaken and white.

Now *he* was walking ahead.

'Whatever you say John I know you won't really like it here. Please don't walk so fast John. It's only because of you that I'm saying all this. You're not used to the country. It's too quiet at the vicarage for you. You're used to bright lights and noises and all the people, and your friends. Please don't go so fast.'

'I'm not a spinning top, Hannah.'

'What do you mean?'

'I don't topple over when I stop.'

She seemed to ignore this statement. 'It won't be long before you think you're rotting away here. Nothing ever happens in the country.'

A string of wild duck flew into the orange sky from the south, wheeled away to the west as they approached the Calvins, straightened, and skittered into fen water.

'I didn't really mean it about the children.'

'I know that,' he replied. 'I lost my temper and I'm sorry for it.'

'But surely John,' she said in a gentler tone, 'from what I notice myself aren't the problems here just little and . . . personal ones . . .' And she laughed in a curious self deprecatory manner, 'like my own. Yes, like my own. They're not the sort to call *you* to arms. *You* want to be called to arms.'

'Yes, yours,' he thought, ironically.

'You're full of ideas but they won't want them. Even if you do find some interesting people here there can't be many and you know John, you're not what you'd call a man of patience.'

'No. No I'm not.'

Mrs Calvin sighed. 'Everybody knows everybody's business here. I really can't see you preaching to the same handful of people Sunday after Sunday.'

'There's more than I can do here, Hannah.'

'Look. D'you know what I read in the paper? "The country parson hangs on to his job although much of what he says about the gravest matters that engross the human mind is untrue and he knows it." It's from a book. They were reviewing a book!'

'What book?'

'*England's Green and Pleasant Land,*' she answered, pleased. 'It's just coming out.'

As they reached the churchyard wall he stopped and said in a grateful tone: 'Well, Hannah, for all your old grumbling I'll tell you one thing . . .'

'What?' she asked grudgingly but wanting to know.

'You've made me realize how I've got to study this place . . . I've been that excited I haven't thought about the place enough . . . not the place. I'll have to get to know all these trees and fields and hedgerows . . . and what the flowers are and where they bloom . . . and this church and churchyard, every corner and stone . . . and I'd best get to know about animals and birds. I'd best start walking, and listen and watch. I'd best have a principle of it. And then it'll grow.'

'Well at least I've done something,' she said. But she was pleased. And then she couldn't resist adding: 'Of course you won't have the patience.'

'Richard says we should keep bees.'

'Oh yes. More work. Where did he get that idea from?'

'A book. Aye you're right you see. And I ought to work at the soil with the men and go on the boats.'

'Oh well,' said Mrs Calvin, 'no doubt you'll become an authority on pigs and fish meal.'

She turned away from her husband and climbed over the stile into the churchyard as carefully as she had the one in the fields.

'I'm not going to come to prayer. I'm just going to polish some brass in the vestry. Give me my bag.'

He did so, and whether she expected it or not, he made no further reply. Together, they entered Eastwold Church.

When the clock struck eight Calvin ceased pulling on the bell rope, left the tower and entered the body of the church. He was pleased to see that there were at least twenty people waiting to pray with him, including Lady Cleeve. As he knelt he thought of arranging a parish breakfast.

'Let us pray.'

And peeping in at the bowed heads from the vestry door

with her duster and brass, Mrs Calvin saw that the matting they kneeled on was damp and mouldy and nothing the sun could do, now shining through the stained glass windows, was good enough to dry it out. Mrs Calvin sighed. 'Another bill,' thought Mrs Calvin.

After Calvin had spoken to the worshippers and made arrangements to visit each, he saw that Lady Cleeve still waited patiently at the back. She rose and approached him.

'Good morning,' said Calvin. 'Shall we go to the vestry? Hannah's there.'

But when they got to the vestry Hannah had gone.

'I don't wish to presume . . .' Lady Cleeve began nervously, looking as if she needed a cigarette.

'Presume,' said Calvin.

'There are so many things—advice, opinions, information . . . I have been wondering . . . we have not really spoken . . . we have understood each other rather than spoken. So there may be misunderstandings. I knew the sort of man you were. And I *heard* you. I heard you preach. I wanted you here. So . . . so what next?'

'Well what first?'

'The services. Yes, the services. What sort of services will you hold?'

'Well I'm not an Anglo-Catholic,' said Calvin smiling.

'No incense then?'

'No.'

'No incense then,' repeated Lady Cleeve, disappointed. 'Do you like it very much?'

'I do like incense,' said Lady Cleeve. 'I do.'

He considered. Then: 'Let's go into our church,' he said.

They left the vestry and re-entered the church.

'If it's all cleaned up and the dust's gone and the wind blows through and the mouldy matting and the mouldy curtains are all stripped out and Hannah gets all her flowers up . . . what price incense?'

'Oh I agree. I agree. A whole army of cleaners. But . . .'

'But you still like incense.'

'I do. I do like incense. And candles you see. I love candles. Now look at that altar with those dreadful fretwork tiers of shelves and those ghastly Birmingham candlesticks and yet the candles are never lit.'

'They should be lit,' he said. 'We'll light them now.' They did so. 'These shelves *will* have to go,' he said.

'But what about the incense?'

'I'll tell you what. I'll tell you what's in my mind. I propose to call a meeting here in the church on Saturday afternoon and discuss all those matters and suchlike . . . and to tell you the truth . . .' he smiled at her, 'there's some things I care about and some I don't and one of them's incense. You see I don't think it's a symbol—to me it's just incense.' He laughed.

'I'm not sure you understand.'

'I assure you I do.'

Lady Cleeve looked down at the altar cloth.

'Perhaps we'll have it first Sunday every month.'

'Are you serious?' asked Lady Cleeve.

'Never more,' said Calvin, smiling again.

'Well,' said Lady Cleeve, doubtfully, looking down as before, 'well, that would be nice.'

'Come,' said Calvin. 'Let's go and look at these Bible boxes.'

They walked from the altar to the front pews and stood over the padded boxes.

'That's mine,' said Lady Cleeve, pointing out her own, with pride.

'Yes,' said Calvin. 'I know. I know the treasures of the people who count.'

'Oh,' said Lady Cleeve.

'You see,' said Calvin, 'you're pushing the labourers to the back of the church and the side aisles, these boxes'll have to be removed to some other place.'

'Oh dear,' said Lady Cleeve.

'I mean they're not even paid for,' said Calvin and banged the nearest one with his hand : up shot a cloud of dust. 'Mouldy and disgusting,' said Calvin. 'You couldn't keep 'em clean if you wanted to. Not if you were in here every day of the week.

But that's not so much the point – I am going to suggest at the meeting that we start off by adopting the rule current in pew-rented churches of the seats being considered free, three minutes before the service.'

'They will reject the proposal.'

'Who will?' asked Calvin. 'I'm going to put it to a whole vote.'

'They'll still reject it. You'll see.'

'Well we will see,' said Calvin. 'I'm not having no over-aweing . . . and if they don't reject it and the poor get here first I'm not having the poor turned out.'

There was a pause.

'You can hardly expect us to line up,' said Lady Cleeve. Calvin laughed.

'Oh dear, I do like my little place,' said Lady Cleeve.

Into the arcades between the tall piers shone the rising sun. It shone upon the Angel figures, the Instruments of the Passion. It shone upon the Sedilia. It shone upon the Maltese Cross, it shone upon the Stalls. It shone upon the circular Communion table. It shone upon the Pulpit and it shone upon the Flags.

'Now Vicar,' said Lady Cleeve, 'I don't know how to put this . . . I . . . may I . . . may I tell you something . . . explain something of the nature of our congregation?' Calvin nodded, Lady Cleeve proceeded, and as she proceeded she seemed to find explanation easier if she walked, and so together they began a perambulation of the church. 'One would presume that whereas a city might know almost nothing of its church congregations, here everyone knows precisely who the church-goers are, and who are not. So . . . so, in a way, seeing that we do know exactly who is who, and who is what, it is much easier for our church to influence the whole tight community. The late vicar unfortunately did not choose to influence the community at all. But he could have. For he influenced them if only by neglect. During a feeble ministry such as his, when the church congregation falls off in its numbers, the affairs of the church are left to the management of those few faithful,

84

whom nothing and no one can drive away. Now, now, Vicar . . .' They had arrived beneath the Flags and looking up at them, and noting that he would have to get a ladder to shake out their dust, Calvin was surprised to see hanging beside the ancient ensign of Saint George, was the orange, white, and green tricolour of Ireland. Observing his surprise and anxious to regain his attention, Lady Cleeve ceased perambulating, tapped her foot imperiously upon the stone, and continued: 'It is very easy for some of the faithful I have been speaking of, to become so jealous of their positions of authority in the church, that while outwardly they may deplore the poor attendances at our services, their very attitude prevents the new vicar, you Calvin, from raising the size of his congregation.' And tapping her excited foot again at the startled Calvin she added: 'Such a man is Richards, whose money is in coal, and whose estate borders on my own.'

There was a pause of consideration from the Vicar. 'Excuse me,' said he. 'I know something of Richards. It's best I decide on Richards myself.'

'He's as far on the Right as is possible,' said Lady Cleeve.

'And are you as far on the Left as is possible?' asked Calvin.

'You mean in my position?'

'Well you're making a start,' said Calvin, smiling.

There was another pause. 'He has charm,' thought Lady Cleeve. 'He certainly has charm.'

'Vicar,' she demanded with sudden forthrightness, 'do you agree that our church in Eastwold will best influence this community if the lay members look up and out, and join in the secular activities around, and make *every* effort in their power to bring new members to the services?'

'As a matter of fact,' said Calvin, still smiling, 'you're my nomination.'

'For what?'

'For the new churchwarden?'

'But we have two.' Another pause. 'You mean Richards will be resigning?'

'Well don't you think he will?' asked Calvin.

After a moment Lady Cleeve nodded her head.

'You'll think about it please,' said Calvin.

'I'll pray,' said Lady Cleeve.

'Please,' said Calvin.

At the door they paused and blinked in the bright morning. Calvin was about to re-enter the church when he remembered and asked: 'How is it that we have the Irish flag hanging up?'

'Oh,' said Lady Cleeve, 'that was my late husband's mother's doing. She was Irish you know. It was during the war. Vicar Jones never bothered about it. I don't suppose he noticed. Perhaps no one has ever noticed. It certainly gave my old mother-in-law some satisfaction. How she got it up there I'm not quite clear. I think it belonged to some of the Irish who trained here. They trained on the cliffs you know. On the beaches and on the cliffs. And I believe they always said that *that* was the flag *they* were fighting for. They were a jolly lot. I can remember one of them kissing me . . . yes . . . my first kiss was from an Irishman . . . yes it was.'

'They've never come back?'

'No. None of them has ever come back. Why? Are you thinking . . . do you want to pull it down?'

'No,' said Calvin, 'I'm very glad of it there. It balances out Saint George.'

Returned to his study, chewing his tobacco at the window over the ivy, gazing across to the great tower, before he should answer the letters, Calvin could hear his wife interviewing prospective maids in her parlour on the floor below. Although he could not make out the words the pattern of sound was always the same—a halting series of questions from Hannah, slow replies, then a sudden and impassioned speech from Hannah which seemingly left the candidate bemused, and after a moment or two of silence the door would open and close, as that girl left and another entered.

Calvin went to his desk, took up the letters, read and answered each in turn: to Arthur Lewis, aged seven on the

86

burying of his bird, Oliver; to the Matron of the Hospital on the old people's ward; to the Disabled Servicemen's Association in Lowestoft; to the Headmistress of the Infants' School, and teach there on Wednesdays he would; to the Editor of the *Eastwold Times* with the announcement of his lunch-time services and a request for the loan of a suitable hall near the peoples' work; to the New Guinea Missionary; to the Rural Dean; to the Bishop; to Lady Cleeve; to the local Dramatic Society requesting the use of the Church Hall; to Catkin and Palm, the clerical tailor; to the BBC with thanks for their circular; to various charities; to various personal requests for money; to friends in Houghton; to friends in Jarrow; to friends in Flanders; a questionnaire to the County Council for the music and dancing licence for the parish hall; the money for 'Readings in St John'; the signing of Jean Dawlish's passport photograph; acceptances of twenty invitations . . .

And when he took up the last the clocks struck eleven.

Lady Cleeve had written:

'Eastwold Manor.

Thursday morning, May 7th.

Dear Vicar,

Confidentially I must inform you that my late father, Edward Hughes, left some monies which obtain a yearly income, and this income is to be used, at my discretion, for the children of the incumbent of Eastwold, up to the ages of twenty-five in each case, and whatever their sex. My father always said that "one's education did not cease when one left the University" and that "in the years immediately after one often felt the need for certain sums". These sums are at my discretion of course. But the money is there.

Furthermore there is an annual income of one hundred pounds for yourself which my father wished to be spent in meeting those financial embarrassments the ablest and most practical of vicars may encounter when his accustomed and limited stipend is all spent and has not proved sufficient.

Thus wrote my dear father.

I propose to implement this money forthwith and would be pleased to discuss the financial aspects of the further education of your children at your convenience. My father wrote also: "Should the incumbent wish no interference in the matter let the money accumulate to the benefit of an incumbent that does."

I trust I have your confidence in respect of this letter as for some unspecified reason my father was anxious his bequest remain "private as is possible in such a parish".

I am well and looking forward to seeing you.

Cynthia Cleeve

P.S.

There is also some money of my own I would wish to go towards the greatly overdue doing-up of our church interior. I really cannot stand the smell of that prayer matting any longer!'

Resting his bicycle against the kerb of the pavement outside the Eastwold Conservative Club so that he might put his letters into the pillar box, Calvin saw through the great bay window Churchwarden Richards and Boilerman Pearce engaged in close conversation. He thought for a moment of entering the Club to speak to the coal owner of his Bible box, then deciding that this was not a suitable place, nor a suitable time, he waved into the Tea Shoppe where the Eastwold ladies sat at their ritualistic morning coffee, sat at the poising, sat at the measuring of the spoons, and began to cross the road to enter Stephens' the Butchers, to see the new baby and to arrange the christening.

He was only half-way across when he was hailed. He turned in the road to note Boilerman Pearce standing on the pavement outside the door of the Conservative Club. Waiting for a horse and cart to pass Calvin returned to the side of the street he had just left. 'Good morning, Mr Pearce,' said Calvin.

'I shall have to give my notice.'

'Oh.'

'You moved my coke box from its place.'

Looking at the Club Calvin saw with interest that the positions inside it had become reversed – the worthies were now gathered at the window. Coal owner Richards sat at the bar alone with his back to the proceedings outside, apparently uninterested in them.

'From the porch?'

'Yes from the porch.'

Calvin sighed. Although he could not precisely hear he was sure that the ladies in the Tea Shoppe and the gentlemen in the Conservative Club also sighed.

There was a pause–rather a hush of expectancy. 'Was Richards sitting thus for calculated effect?' wondered Calvin. 'Could they hear behind those windows?'

'It spoils the look of the porch,' said Calvin.

'I shall have to give my notice then.'

'I accept it,' said Calvin, holding out his hand.

Since Pearce made no move to take his hand, Calvin was forced to put it in his pocket.

'Who's going to fill the boiler then?'

'I don't know.'

'It's not going to be easy to find.'

'I'll do it myself then. It'll be a good job for me.'

'You can't do everything yourself.' This time Pearce did turn about and move off.

Making an effort not to appear disconcerted Calvin waved to the ladies for the second time and once again set off across the street to the butchers.

Passing over the sawdust to the back of the shop he was greeted by the elder Stephens, Grandfather Stephens, with the words: 'Morning Vicar. Good to see you. Spare us a moment. Thank the Lord for a Low Churcher prepared to do the dirty work.' 'How are you then?' Calvin shook him by the hand. 'I say this,' said the senior Butcher picking up his cleaver and bringing it down upon a loin of veal to split it into chops for old Mrs Fisher, with the purple port-stained nose, 'I say your dated-out High flying Anglicanism to which Vicar Jones so stubbornly clung–being Welsh he wouldn't have Low you see reminding him of the chapel, being Welsh he wouldn't have *that*–I say that that High sniffing adenoidal Anglicanism is the sort to annoy all parties in a parish equally well. That's what I contend. Vicar, you've got to be Anglo-Catholic with incense and vestments and the whole of the trap-clap, not a word understood and all lovely like, or you've got to go real Low like yourself and announce there's no Hell, and comfort us all, and say all religions are good and one and the same and true. Now that's definite, Vicar.' Stephens gathered up the splitted veal to demand: 'What do you say little Mrs Fisher?' 'Not too much bone.' 'Eh?' 'There's too much bone there. I don't want that bottom bit.' Turning to Calvin she observed: 'You've got to watch Mr Stephens. You've got to you know.' Winking at Calvin Stephens raked away some of the offending bone, and seizing this moment to pass on, Calvin made his way through the shop.

Having baptized a dying child; having taken old Mr Williams his tobacco; having promised his vote to Socialist candidate, Smith; having joined the library; having listened to Mrs Ainley's complaint; having listened to Mrs Mill's complaint; having listened to Mr Mill's complaint; having given old Mr Thompson a massage; Calvin was walking down the High Street to collect his bicycle and ride home for a very late lunch when he heard a little patter behind him and felt a touch at his elbow. 'Vicar, dear Vicar,' murmured a gentle voice, 'when are you coming to tea?' 'When I'm asked of course,' said Calvin, smiling and turning. 'Tomorrow at four.' 'No, not tomorrow, we're having a meeting in the church.' 'Of course. Of course. Monday at four.' 'Delighted,' said Calvin, smiling again at the beautiful woman before him. 'I'm Miss Harris,' said she, 'Miss Dorothea Harris. I live at the Limes. Before you go . . . before you go,' she laid her hand on his arm, 'I've something really ghastly to tell you . . . so ghastly I hardly have the courage to mention it.' Continuing to smile, dropping her voice to an even lower murmur, looking about her to see that she was not heard, Dorothea Harris continued: 'Do you know Barbara Lewis?' 'The Sexton's wife?' 'Yes that is she. Well last night she and Frank Wilson, the assistant librarian, had intercourse in her sitting-room while her husband watched.' Taking his silence for something other than it was, Dorothea repeated: 'While her husband watched.' And observing that Calvin remained silent she dded: 'It was my sense of duty that compelled me to speak. This is a most dreadfully wicked and filthy place.'

Since Calvin yet remained silent, since his face had grown stern, Miss Harris began to lose a little of her confidence, murmuring: 'Nothing hurts me more than to have to inform you of such a thing.'

Still Calvin did not speak.

'I knew I had to speak out,' faltered Miss Harris, 'this is such a corrupt, such a filthy place.'

'Let us pray,' said Calvin.

'For the Lewises?'

'For us,' said Calvin. And he got down on his knees.

'What?' whispered Miss Harris, looking around. 'What here?' whispered Dorothea Harris looking at the pavement and then at her stockings and her knees.

Calvin made no answer. Calvin prayed.

To the wonder of the onlookers of Eastwold High Street Miss Dorothea Harris, who was known to them each and everyone, lifted a scarlet face from gazing at her Vicar's bowed head, cried out in pain and in mortification, and scuttled along the pavement in the direction of her house as fast as her legs could carry her.

It was some time before Calvin rose.

Friday afternoon in the metropolis, the Stephens' already closed in the High Street, rolled up their awnings, washed down their boards. By the Swan the first coach load from Lowestoft, behind the lead light windows the black-and-white waitresses laying out their teas. At the north side of the Sceptre, before the Greek Doric porch, the General and his nephew waiting to cross, while Herbert, the General's chauffeur, Herbert, the General's batman, spat and polished in the market place, polished the pride of Eastwold, a pre-war Silver Ghost.

'I do not,' said the General, seeing Miner Calvin crossing the South Green (the largest of Eastwold's many), 'I do not perceive how the fellow will last.' 'Mm,' said Robert Andrews, and laughed. 'What are you laughing for?' 'Herbert's put hi dusters on the pump.' 'Built in eighteen seventy-three,' sai the General. 'I do not know how the fellow will last. Whe are you returning to school, sir? Endurance is godlike. Hav you conversed?' 'We have not.' 'He tried to make me jump, said the General. 'I like him.' 'I go back soon,' said Andrews 'a week today. Why are we waiting to cross?' 'A Friday ? 'Correct.' 'It's a lively little town,' said the General. 'Not building that's a visual abomination.' 'Uncle . . .' 'I can se from here,' said the General. 'Have you spoken? He's no used to these trim gardens or these kept fresh flowers. Ver healing for him. I find them very healing. He's not used t them do you see.' 'How d'you know that?' 'He told me so Have you spoken?' 'We have not.' 'Ah,' said the General, 'yo should.' Nodding his head to confirm this last remark, noddin it in such a manner as to suggest that it was what he had bee leading up to all along, the General looked away at Calvi with even greater appreciation and interest. A processio turned the corner into the High street. 'Pony traps enterin the borough. We can't cross *now*,' said the General. 'Of cours we can, Uncle.' 'Yes he tried to make me jump,' said th General, 'there are no outstanding buildings in Eastwold bu the attraction of the many minor ones beggars description. 'Apparently so,' said Andrews and stepped off the pavement Anchoring his nephew with a firm grasp on the elbow, an slipping in a series of compliments before proceeding to grave matters, the General said: 'Your moustache is coming alon very well my boy, your moustache is coming along ver nicely. I cannot recall that mine grew as fast.' This please Robert and the General saw it. Pressing home his advantag he drew his nephew back on to the pavement beside him, an continued his investigation of the true object of his interest 'There he goes my boy. Look! See how he conducts himself He moves as a commander inspecting his forces, he singles ou his allies, he plans his campaign.' So Andrews looked agai and indeed it was true that as Calvin made his way over th Green he stopped and he talked with those who appeared t have time or inclination to listen. 'What I ask myself,' said the General, 'what I demand to know, is how intelligent is the fellow. He's been at it for days. He knocks 'em up in the night.' 'I don't believe you,' said Andrews. 'Well in a manner of speaking,' said the General, 'don't accuse me of exaggeration for you know very well what I mean. I ain't senile you know. I ain't daft. I've seen things you haven't. Oh yes.' Knowing his uncle would demand what he *did* think Calvin resembled, Andrews said in his most provocative, his most Etonian manner: 'He doesn't look much like a commander to me.' The General blew his nose in his handkerchief, mumbled something, peered about him, but in the end was forced to demand: 'And what do *you* think he looks like?' 'Like a Parliamentary candidate,' said Andrews, 'canvassing the electorate and counting his votes.' 'I think my analogy's the better,' said the General and stepped off into the road between two pony traps.

When he reached the other side the General had to turn back to wait for Andrews to join him and he shouted as if it were of the utmost importance: 'The way to engage men's loyalty is to fill their hearts with affection, with trust, and with respect.' 'People will think you drunk, Uncle,' said Andrews, still in the roadway. 'And on the contrary,' he continued as he gained the pavement, 'what you have to do to get men's loyalty is to make them afraid of you and satisfy their needs. Persecute Jews for example.' 'Jews?' 'Yes.' 'Ah,' said the General after a moment's reflection, 'that's very true. And it's beginning again they say. I do see that answers a need. Mind you I can't say I like them.' 'You don't know any,' said Andrews. 'You're right,' said the General, 'you've been right twice, I don't know any Jews, and my statement on loyalty was a naïve over-simplification.' He blew his nose again. 'I can't think how either of those remarks came out. It must be the weather. They just came out as I stepped on to the pavement.' 'They didn't,' said Andrews severely. 'They didn't, Uncle!' 'Very well I take your point,' said the General, 'don't press me too hard. It *is* the weather.'

Now realizing just how beautiful a spring afternoon it was they looked about them: the red and white curtains were blowing in and out of the one-storeyed cottages in the most abandoned fashion; the several young ladies of Eastwold were parading their friendliest faces, were laughing a great deal, were showing themselves in bright new frocks. 'Have you any feelings towards the women yet?' 'What?' 'Have you any feelings towards the women yet?' 'Uncle there's no need to shout.' 'But you didn't hear me.' 'Compromise, Uncle.' 'A boy of your age should be ashamed of that word. Have you any feelings towards the women yet?' 'Other things occupy me more.' 'As I thought,' said the General, 'as I thought. Who cannot give good counsel? All men are liable to error.' A smirk had come over his face. 'How long are we standing here?' asked Andrews with apprehension. 'As I thought,' said the General. 'Slow and steady. Hubert won't mind: I find the place congenial and so must he. Look at that lady now. Ain't she a picture? Love is stirring.' 'Don't be embarrassing, Uncle.' 'Can I embarrass you then?' asked the General smirking again. 'You know very well you can. *You* could embarrass anyone.' 'Women and oysters always seem to go together,' said the General triumphantly. '*Poverty* and oysters, Uncle.' 'No, women and oysters is better,' said the General with authority and Andrews laughed. Unexpectedly, a shadow crossed the General's face. He drew close to his nephew, he whispered with solemnity: 'Robert I must tell you something . . . something you must not forget . . . . whatever it is . . . *whatever* it is the sexual act is intimate.' Andrews was so surprised he was only able to realize his apprehensions had been fulfilled. 'I don't wish to be pompous,' whispered the General, 'one day you will understand exactly what I mean. And you may remember I told you.' In spite of the incongruousness of this private advice in this public place Andrews was able to say: 'Thank you,' and for some reason found himself touched. 'What is sad,' whispered the General, 'what is sad, is that when a woman can give you everything you need, *knows* how to give you everything you need, she is

94

no longer in a position to do so.' For several reasons Andrews too adopted a conspiratorial murmur: 'I don't understand.' 'You will, Robert,' whispered the General, 'you will.' Reverting to his normal tone he added: 'No other emotion has the power of a sexual one. The thing I have learned about women is that you must never . . . never . . .' Casting about for succour Andrews was relieved to be able to interrupt: 'Look the Vicar's coming to speak to us!' And indeed Calvin was bearing down with a purpose. 'What a tough,' said the General, 'bloody good sergeant you know. If I had had that fellow I . . .' 'Don't forget to introduce me, Uncle,' said Andrews. 'Of course I won't,' said the General. 'You're my brother's son. *You're* my brother's son! What a little toughy.' And whether he heard that remark or not, Calvin came straight to the point: 'General, how do. How do Mister Robert. We've not met but I've been told of you by my son. Lovely day isn't it? General have you got a moment for a serious chat about your Bible box?'

Lady Cleeve was surprised to hear her Aunt Beatrice announced from the terrace. 'Pour me a cup of tea with your own fair hand,' said Mrs Mellor descending the steps on to the flat lawn. 'What a place for a pageant.' She sat herself down in the sunlight not removing her hat, her coat, or her gloves. 'Aren't you warm, Aunt?' 'Yes but I'm tired and anxious to get on with it. *Your* cup will do—not too much sugar—and then I'll go up and bath myself. The trains are filthy these days.' 'Nancy will be bringing you a cup and besides I want some more myself.' 'Oh do please pour me something immediately,' said Mrs Mellor, 'I'm parched.' So Lady Cleeve did as she was bidden. 'Why didn't you let me know you were arriving?' 'I only thought of it this morning. My intentions matured upon the journey.'

The old lady swallowed her tea like a glass of water, sighed, and looked fixedly at her niece. 'You're fearsome, Aunt,' said Lady Cleeve, 'what ever have I done?' Beneath the huge brimmed hat there was silence: Lady Cleeve looked into the shadows there at the white hair cut so short and swept so severely back from such a high forehead and noted, deeper than ever, those numerous broad lines curving down past the corners of the pale eyes into the pools above the cheek bones. She noted too the scavenging nose protruding far but not so far as the chin. She lowered her gaze into the lapels of the coat with its turned up collar, and stared at the enormous, gleaming and jewelled brooch knotting the rough grey scarf. 'That's new,' said Lady Cleeve.

Without looking at it Mrs Mellor took the exquisite cup from the arm of her chair and placed it on the tea tray: Lady Cleeve refilled it and handed it back. Mrs Mellor drank it as quickly as before. 'They think I am going out of politics but I am not. They say I am too emotional.' Nancy entered into the perfect spring afternoon carrying a single cup, saucer and spoon on a silver tray. 'Thank you, Nancy,' said Lady Cleeve. 'You, Cynthia, are to come out of mourning,' said Mrs Mellor, 'take yourself to London and run my house. I want things done, I don't care what or who gets the approbation—if it comes to a fight I know the arts of war as well as my enemies. I perceive that for far too long I have neglected to advance our cause by diplomacy.'

'But what has this to do with me, Aunt?' Lady Cleeve was pleased to be sipping tea.

'It would seem to me,' said Mrs Mellor opening her handbag and taking out her meerschaum pipe, that we should undertake a salon for the social cultivation of the Socialist Party in Parliament. That is your task.'

'No,' said Lady Cleeve.

Mrs Mellor opened her tobacco pouch. 'The wives are lonely . . . when the husbands come home they are too exhausted to talk of their work or public affairs . . . since these wives of party and union officials can talk politics as well as anyone else they grow frustrated and resentful and in consequence many are becoming hostile to the whole Labour movement.'

'No,' said Lady Cleeve.

Mrs Mellor pressed in the last of the expensive tobacco with her square thumb. 'If nothing is done not only will the young wives become unpresentable in superior social circles but they will be left behind to stew in kitchens as their husbands rise.

'True.'

'The risk is real both to politics and family life.' Mrs Mellor pulled open a box of French matches and lit her pipe with practised skill in the faint summer breeze. 'Therefore . . . therefore we must harness their energies and turn these same energies to our interest. I am going to send out a letter to Labour women to meet at my house and you are to be hostess. We shall call it the Half-Moon Club. I call it "half" because although it is at first intended for the benefit of our sex only, its principal objects cannot be achieved until men properly enter into the gatherings.'

'I see that, Aunt.' Lady Cleeve was smiling. 'But why "moon"?'

'I don't know,' answered Mrs Mellor. 'It's a word I rather like. You are the jewel of the piece don't you see.'

'Like the jewel on your grey scarf.'

'Quite. Quite.'

Lady Cleeve took her ivory holder, inserted a cigarette, lit it and together the two women puffed away in silence apparently lost now in serious contemplation. A cart came grinding down the stone road to their left, vanished beneath the great red wall. Beyond the flat lawn, between the soft green trees, between the purple and white lilacs, lay a dishful of blue water. A whole sea bay spread out like a lady's apron. To the right falling, fading and pleated ran the emerald dunes with their wild shivering grasses. On and on and on. Out and out of sight. Mrs Mellor could not help but exclaim: 'How glorious. How truly glorious. This is the view my father loved.'

'Aunt,' said Lady Cleeve, 'you have a deep voice and think like a man . . . now I never think like a man.'

'Rubbish on both counts.' Mrs Mellor threw up her head as if reined in.

'Don't interrupt, Aunt. Not all your genius for organizing,

not all my charm, will make the wives of the Labour men leave their houses and hob-nob both with domineering female organizers and . . . and . . .' she puffed again in her schoolboy manner, 'such well to do women as ourselves.'

'Why don't you learn to smoke properly.' Mrs Mellor was irritated. 'What is the point of smoking a cigarette if you don't inhale.'

'The action comforts me,' said Lady Cleeve. 'What is certain is that there will not be lacking among those wives who are class-conscious a definite resentment of our intentions which they will find to be both patronizing and Machiavellian. In fact "offensive".'

'Don't you know I see that! However you said "our".'

'A slip of the tongue, I meant "your".'

'Thirty years later,' said Mrs Mellor, 'these very women will remember our salon with affection and with thanks.'

'I am only concerned with the present, Aunt.'

'Rubbish,' said Mrs Mellor. 'Pour me another cup of tea and for goodness' sakes don't be so selfish and short-sighted. My dear girl I do have your happiness in mind also – you can't stick up here all your life.'

'I don't intend to but . . . but it's interesting at the moment.'

'Yes, we'll come to that later. You are a woman of character and intelligence. You look like a duchess and indeed you almost are one . . . I won't have you wasted. You read with point, you know what you are about, you delight in music. There is not the smallest reason why you and your ladies should not become the real leaders of society under a Labour government. First the salon and then the nursery.'

'The what?' asked Lady Cleeve, astonished.

'Call it what you will,' said Mrs Mellor, 'we will enrol two hundred members and draw up a constitution. We will lay out a credit scheme . . . what you will . . . if they act we shall train them . . . if they sing they shall sing . . . if they write we want a revue. And indeed . . . indeed we will sing and we will give revues and we will present our musicals. We shall have Easter schools on the Continent . . . we shall paint in the Carmargue

. . . we shall ramble in the Lake District . . . and we shall decorate our Hall with our own bare hands.'

'And camp in the meadows at Oxford no doubt,' said Lady Cleeve laughing out loud.

'That is a much better idea than you think,' said Mrs Mellor. 'I want study groups, I want debates, I want publications.'

'Well, Aunt,' said Lady Cleeve, 'you are certainly inspired. Shall we see you then in the front row of the chorus?'

'No more mocking,' said Mrs Mellor. 'Let us get on with it. There is a real need. Is that our parson I see in the back?' She pointed up to where the General's open Silver Ghost gleamed and rose up the incline beyond the great red wall.

'Looks like it.'

'Has he been to the factories yet?'

'What?'

'If the man is going to stir them up in Eastwold he must get down among the canning girls and the seamstresses.'

'You must tell him.'

'I intend to,' said Mrs Mellor. 'Has he mentioned me ever?'

'No.'

'But he's been to see you?'

'He tells me the rich must give up their Bible boxes or put them at the back of the church.'

'Did he not make an exception in your case?'

'No.'

'Good,' said Mrs Mellor.

'But I like it at the front.'

'Oh stuff,' said Mrs Mellor, 'you're selfish. Has he got a policy yet?'

'Intentions I think.'

'Radical ones?'

'It would seem so . . . but I don't really know. I've rather been waiting to see . . .'

'Do I detect something secretive in your tone?' interrupted Mrs Mellor.

'Secretive?'

'Yes. Even guarded.'

'Well I don't know. It's early days yet,' said Lady Cleeve looking away from her aunt to the hawthorn.

Mrs Mellor regarded her with interest. 'It's early days yet,' repeated Lady Cleeve.

'True,' said Mrs Mellor thoughtfully, 'of course what the man needs . . . what that man needs is an emblem.' Mrs Mellor stood up, and banging both her fists on her knees as if she had strapped a pair of tambourines there, she shouted: 'Cynth let's nip up to the General's and we'll all have a damned good chat.'

Chapter 5

'THIS isn't no place for hiking, Mister Rockingham. Everything looks so near, yet it stays so far and takes so long to get to.'

'That's the flatness.'

'Ah I know.'

'We're not used to it you see.'

Though they had rested when the day was warmest they were weary again.

'We're not used to it you see.'

'What are all these yellow flowers?'

'I don't know lass.'

'Are they a crop or a weed?'

'I don't know.'

'These waterways do they have boats on them sometimes?'

'Must do. Must do.'

'Then why is there none now?'

'I don't know lass. It's late perhaps.'

'Perhaps it's the wrong time of the year.'

'Yes perhaps.'

The dyke beside them grew broader, the water stiller and more brown—on the sides fat clumps of sedge.

'I don't suppose they use them so much now,' said the old man sighing. 'How's your foot?'

'All right.'

'Shall we stop to bind it?'

'No it's all right thank you.'

'It's been a long time since we did.'

'No it's all right Mister Rockingham, really.'

Although the day had been fine the wind was growing cold. Because of a pale ribbon glowing in the east ahead of them where the sea was, it looked rather that the sun was rising and not about to set.

'Whoever heard of a starving ffarmer?'

'You don't stammer nearly so much now you know me.'

'It's always been like that.'

Although neither had spoken of it seriously for fear of discouraging the other they were ill at ease in this corner of England; unsettled by its flatness they felt like foreigners.

'It is rural isn't it?'

'Aye lass, rural. Rural it is.'

'Rural's a good word but bucolic is a funny one . . . I'm not ignorant.'

'I didn't say you were.'

'It always makes me think of beer . . . bucolic.'

'Yes, I can see that.'

'Do you like beer?'

'Aye.'

'I've never had a taste but I've had . . .'

'Wine in Paris,' said Rockingham.

'How did you know I was going to say that?'

Rockingham laughed. Then added: 'Drink's a great enemy of our class.'

'I do hope Eastwold's not going to be like this,' said Jean.

Over the flat open plain they trudged on a road as straight as a bridge. Few trees could be seen against the sky—just a poplar here and there by the dykes, and by the bridges.

'That farm house is big enough for a public building.'

'They're so square,' said Rockingham.

'They're red, but they don't look red.'

'That's the light,' said the old man changing his flag to the other shoulder and rubbing at the place where it had rested.

'Why am I doing this journey?' Jean asked herself again. 'What ever made me, what will I find?' And Rockingham was thinking: 'No wonder the sailors said the world was flat.' They walked another mile and could only have told they had moved by looking behind.

'Is that what they call a mm . . . mirage Mister Rockingham?'

He looked up, lifted in eyes and heart. After mile upon mile of this plain on which nothing had been raised over their heads for more than thirty feet the massive silhouette rising up in the sky might indeed have been a mirage, it stood above like some prehistoric rock worn away from the land by the wind and the sea.

'Would that be the ocean beyond?'

'I can't tell.' She shaded her eyes with her hand. 'I've never seen the ocean . . . that place is Boston and that church tower dropping from heaven is what they call the Boston "stump".'

'It's as . . . astonishing Mister Rockingham.'

'It is,' said Rockingham with pleasure. 'It is. What these people have done, what these people have done you see, what they've done is they've said to themselves we live down here on the flat in front of the flat ocean and by God if our Maker don't give us no heights to lift our eyes to we'll lift one up to him.'

'Yes.' Jean was smiling.

'Yes,' said the old man. 'Yes. That town was a great port once, now it's filled in and that stump's been light-house and watch-tower in its day.'

'Gg . . . God could hang his hat up there.'

'Mister Rockingham . . .' looking shy, Jean hesitated, 'Mister Rockingham . . .' Hadn't he heard? 'Mister Rockingham what is your flag for?'

Rockingham didn't answer.

'I don't mean to be rude Mm . . . Mmister Rockingham.' She was so unnerved she could hardly get the sentence out, 'but what's your flag for? And why is it covered up?'

Rockingham didn't answer.

Jean took a deep breath and asked as firmly as she could: 'Mm . . . Mmister Rockingham what's your flag for and what kind of flag is it?'

The old miner was still staring at the church. One hand held the flag, the other fingered his moustache, and Jean simply could not make out if he was deliberately declining to answer her questions, or absorbed. They stood in silence for what seemed to her an age. Not wanting to intrude upon him any more she too stared straight ahead at the rock of God.

On her left where he stood she heard a strange sound and although at first she could not make it out—the wind was blowing stronger—she gradually realized he was whistling through his teeth. Engrossed, smiling like a boy, he was whistling 'Jerusalem' and beginning to tap with his clogged foot on the road. 'I hope he's not what they call a religious maniac,' she thought.

The whistling and the tapping swelled and now he began to bang on the road with the end of his flag and to sing out the words at the top of his voice. She did not join in: the truth was that she had not seen this side of him before and did not know what to make of it. He went on singing.

When at last he ceased he turned to her, took her arm with his free hand and said, 'Alleluia. Yes lass, yes, yes, yes. I'm refreshed. How about you?' 'Yes,' she answered, 'Yes thank you Mister Rockingham.' 'We mustn't forget what a family we are, "a family of wondrous beings", and no one and nothing can stop us standing around the throne of God. Let us get up there before the dark.'

'Up on the tower?'

'Aye up there.'

So they continued their way into Boston past huge fields and the market gardens, past corn, sugar beet and the potatoes, with Jean's questions on the flag unanswered, and although the sun dropped, the straight grey road grew colder, and the windmills worked harder, both for different reasons, lost something of their weariness.

'What do you think of "Ian" Mister Rockingham?'

'That's a Scottish name.'

'Is it . . . but what do you think of it?'

'I like John.'

'No I like Ian. I think I'm certain to have a boy. We *are* getting closer. When you get closer it doesn't look like a stump Mister Rockingham.'

'It's fine and so's the House of the Lord beneath it.'

'You're very religious aren't you?'

'In my own way,' said the old man. 'Very. Yes, yes, yes, I'm religious.'

'But won't you be too tired to go up there tonight?'

'Not when I've bedded you down.'

'No I'll come with you.'

'Well we'll see,' he said. 'It'll be a long climb. All right I accept that.' He smiled again.

Although it was evident that they were gaining on it in the evening light the town of Boston seemed to be on the march.

The saw-toothed clouds over the 'stump' disappeared but the faint yellow and gold still trailed in the east. Not understanding this they climbed an old wall. Even so they could make out no reason for it. 'I thought we'd see the ocean from up here,' said Rockingham. 'I've never seen the ocean. Not the ocean itself. My lord it's retreated a long way off.' 'England's bigger and smaller then isn't it Mister Rockingham?' 'It is.' 'Time does alter things, Mister Rockingham.'

Rockingham gazed at Botolph's town, then at Botolph's church, and then he lifted his eyes into the very centre of the sky. The ribbon of yellow and gold had no apparent source up there: he could only think that from somewhere above, unseen, perhaps to the left, light streamed through where the cloud was thin. Unless of course this yellow light was being sucked up. To Jean, Rockingham seemed to be imploring or 'seeking guidance' as he might say. Too wise now to interrupt or question she let him gaze above, and did not move. 'At first,' said the old man, 'in that bit of blackness I could not make out a single star but now I see them all plainly, and there's three parallel, and there is what must be a planet.' Rockingham shivered with awe and she thought he was cold. 'Come on my dear,' she said.

'Ah,' said the old man. So Jean helped him down from the crumbling wall, took his hand, and led him right into Boston like a little boy. 'Alleluia, Mr Rockingham,' she said laughing. 'Yes, yes, yes.'

In Boston it had been a very busy day and was now a busy

evening—a sellers' and buyers' day. They had to push and dodge on the bridge and to walk in the gutter as they passed up the street: the public houses and the commercial hotels were surrounded by red-faced farming men still sealing their bargains over their pints of ale. 'Bastard covered 'em up for a year, sold 'em as home grown,' remarked one. 'What did he mean by that Mister Rockingham?' 'Common practice,' answered the old man, 'German potatoes you see . . . buy 'em cheap . . . very cheap . . . stack 'em a while . . . sell 'em dear . . . very dear.' 'You know a lot . . . and I like the way you say things.' 'I know things like *that*.' 'They use the word bbb . . .' 'Bastard?' 'Yes. They use the word bbastard as friendly around here then.' 'It would appear so,' said Rockingham. 'Who taught you to read by the way?' 'School.' 'Oh you went to school then. Aye well . . . yes, well you see.' 'Didn't you go then?' 'No. No time for it you see.' 'And you taught yourself then?' 'Well I had to didn't I,' answered Rockingham.

They walked on towards St Botolph. 'You know what I do,' said Rockingham, 'I mispronounce words. I've only read 'em you see . . . not heard them.' 'But I do that myself,' said Jean.

At the corner of the street leading into the square, before they turned right to go to the church, a little crowd watched a pavement artist. There was something hostile in the attitude of this crowd and something defiant in that of the kneeling man. Realizing such a man must be a strange sight in Boston, wondering why he had come there, they were skirting around him when he must have looked up and noticed and they heard him call out at them in a thin flat Welsh voice: '*You're* out of place in these parts.' So they paused. Immediately he saw this the screever grinned malevolently and pleased and stimulated, rubbed out the drawing he was working on, began a new one, and without looking up again shouted: 'You're out of place you with the white face and the baby coming and the black hair, and you the old man with the moustache who've been down the mines like I have.'

Embarrassed by the stares of the Bostoners, knowing that they were about to be used, Jean wanted to draw away but

Rockingham held on to her with his free hand and would not move. Although he continued drawing with quick strokes the Welshman saw all this and kept up his oration, varying his tone between that which was flat, biting and hard, and that which was a kind of mock, effeminate wheedling: 'He's got nystagmus this old chap you farming gentry . . . he's been down the bloody mines in the dark . . . all man-made with none of the Lord's light . . . he's had on his only overcoat in the cold, cold, cold, cold downshafts . . . oh yes up here in the fresh with you farmers—the diversions of traffic, the morning newspapers, the sunshine, the wind and the rain—down there with the old chap you're buried . . . they knock you up at half past four . . . down you go there and you're buried . . . there the runaway trams, screaming ponies, explosions, the fires and there the drownings . . . and when you get to your home you fall asleep on your dinner and when you wake up it's not night yet but it's cold and your evening's gone . . . Christ there's nothing to think about then . . . your wife's cold and gone asleep to bed so she has . . . he's got nystagmus you farming gentry but you rich buggers wouldn't know that.' Seized by a fit of coughing the Welshman was forced to spit and to stop speaking for a moment but he went on with his chalking in spite of his quivering shoulders and as soon as he had recovered he resumed: 'It's me lungs you know . . . they're killing my time . . . no tramps in the mines, that must prove something . . . hey what about putting a penny in his cap? For God's sakes don't be shy I'm telling you he's been down the bloody mines in the darkness . . . don't you see the bloody blue scars on his nose . . . don't you see that involuntary oscillation of the eye-ball? Don't you recognize that lateral oscillation?' There was a pause. All looked at Rockingham. And indeed the old man did feel his involuntary oscillation. 'Give him a penny for Christ's sake. Put a penny in his cap.' Since no one moved to do so, or for that matter was able—Rockingham leaving his cap on his head—the screever appealed to the old man directly: 'Hey mister . . . hey mister miner . . . hey mister penny miner . . . don't you know I need a nobber? Won't you take your cap around for me?' 'Come away,' said Jean. 'Come away,' repeated the screever, 'come away where? Nor you nor me won't get nothing off this lot less we catch 'em between two fires.' 'I don't want nothing thank you,' said Rockingham and might have been about to move off. 'Don't want nothing,' shouted the screever, 'are you religious then?' 'Incurably,' said Rockingham with unexpected humour. The Welshman laughed. The crowd laughed. Incomprehensibly to Jean, since she knew how little he had, Rockingham stepped forward and dropped a coin into the screever's hat. This gesture immediately provoked the Welshman into further energy and he cried out as in triumph: 'You see you never get a drop off toffs and farmers . . . it's only working men and foreigners give you a penny. You know why I come to Boston . . . because you're such a bloody challenge . . . you appeal to my perversity do you see . . . I'm a bloody catalyst do you see . . . that's what God made *me* . . . I've had a sixpence off a bloody Chinaman and a sixpence off a bloody blackie but never a ha'penny off a toff or a farmer.' He rose from his knees. Stood, pointed down. 'Look at that then.' And they all did and they pushed this way and that.

'Who's swearing? Who's swearing here then?' The crowd fell back, the policeman advanced. 'There's been complaints,' he said like a caricature in *Punch*. He looked down at the pavement. Silence. Then: 'Scrub that one out.' 'What?' 'That one. Scrub it out.' 'What one?' 'Don't you "what one" me. *That* one.' There was another pause. 'No I can't have anything in favour of Socialism can I?' 'Don't give me any more back answers,' said the policeman. 'Quick or you'll be loitering. No more lip.' So the screever was forced to rub out his little drawing with the sleeve of his jacket and as he did so the screever muttered:

'*Rest, comrade, rest:*
Cull we sad flowers to lay on your sad breast:
There till the world awakes to love, we leave you:
Rest, comrade, rest.'

108

Since a peculiarity of the wind in these parts is its dustiness they were rubbing their eyes as they left the square and went past the black door of the doctor's house towards the South Porch. 'I know I'm going to have a boy.' 'But you'll be pleased whatever.' 'Why did you give the chalker your money?' 'Oh . . . just because.' 'Because he said he was a miner? What does catalyst mean?' 'I don't know . . . I intend to look it up; I've an idea it's somebody who gets you into trouble.'

Relieved to find the South Porch open and the light still strong enough to see by they entered St Botolph through the dovetailed oak, passed a little chapel on their left, went straight towards the entrances to the tower. Their clogs so echoed on the stone that Jean thought her baby would be woken. Believing them to be alone she jumped when she saw the black-frocked figure in the shadows. 'Do not let me startle you. I often sit here after time. Did you wish to ascend for the tower is long closed?' 'Aye . . . we did.' Now Jean's baby did begin to kick which made her smile, and feeling no doubt that the smile was intended for him, the verger gave utterance to a sort of mirthless hissing laugh: 'I am a legend in these parts. They call me Silly Tilly.' 'Indeed,' said Rockingham and bowed. Not for the first time Jean was impressed by the old man's poise. 'Indeed to goodness,' hissed the black man in the shadows, 'it will cost you a sixpence each.' 'But you said it was . . .' 'A sixpence each don't you know,' said the verger. 'Ah now I can't afford *that*,' answered Rockingham. 'Then go your ways.' 'I hadn't thought 'twould be so much you see. I'll say a prayer for your lovely church.' 'You may but it makes no difference . . .'

Rockingham rolled away north-east into the body of the church and knelt; awkwardly, Jean stood where she was. 'The church needs your shilling,' said Silly Tilly, 'it is falling down,' and to Jean's extreme astonishment without a hint of a breath or a pause he began to whistle like a blackbird.

After he had rubbed his eyes with his long sleeve she asked: 'Why do they call you Tilly?' 'T. E. Tilly. Lost my wife. Once I stuck my head in the railings of a bridge and once in the gas.

What's he got there that man?' 'A flag.' 'I went to Oxford. I was there many years. You could be then. I was an eccentric. You could be then. What kind of flag?' 'I don't know. He always keeps it covered.' 'A house flag?' 'I don't know what that is.' 'It is your own but you have to pay. Are you not his daughter?' 'No.' 'Nor his wife?' 'No.' 'Do you note his hands on the flag . . . even at prayer . . . do you note that. I should not have married . . . not married . . . not suited. Where is your husband?' 'Eating mint sauce in Paris,' said Jean with one of her unexpected bits of humour, surprising even herself and noting with satisfaction that she'd didn't stammer with Silly Tilly. 'It don't matter about me but he's longing to go up tower. We're on our way to Eastwold to see the Vicar Calvin.' 'Are you so,' said Tilly, and hissed and this information appeared to satisfy him for he was silent.

The faint yellow mist from the fens and the waters, seeped in through the great oak doors, gathered in the high vault over the grey praying head. The moonlight shining through the coloured windows turned the dim carved decorated world into a cave. Jean allowed her mind to wander, she rested her brow against the cold wall. Her spirit floated into the cool mist like a leaf and there in the arches it swirled with her mother, her father; and her lover, the father of her child. She floated a leaf among leaves.

The clock bells above struck an end to her dreaming; Rockingham rose to collect her. Silly Tilly put his hands to his head until the reverberations had ceased, and then one of them into his pocket. This hand came out with a gleaming coin, which Tilly dropped into a hollow collection box. 'I have done, I have done it for you,' said Tilly. 'Ascend.' He took out a key from the folds of his dress, he unlocked a creaking door. 'Up and down the same way,' he said, 'ascend and descend. I have battled.' 'Thank you,' said Rockingham. Enchanted at this unexpected generosity, feeling some credit for it, and content to stay awhile with Silly Tilly in the vault, Jean had to pull herself together, say 'thank you' also, and begin the ascent of the western lantern. All two hundred and seventy-two and a half feet of it.

She had not ascended thirty steps when she doubted that she could reach the top. Growing narrower and growing darker the staircase seemed to be swaying from right to left, holding for a moment, and then positively collapsing back again. The cold, gusty wind blew so hard into her face that she thought it might blow her down into the church. Rockingham was already out of sight and must have been forced to drag his flag by the confine for she could hear its tap tap tap on the stones— the tapping growing fainter. She would have shouted: 'For God's sake wait for me Mister Rockingham' but she didn't think that he would hear, and indeed she was too frightened by the place to be irreverent in it. Comforting herself, she began to talk to her baby: 'Now little Ian or is it Elizabeth, your mother's in as dark a place as you are but she's colder. Don't start crying in there please or your mam will too. Your mam's up to heaven after your mad religious grandfather and why she's doing it or what she'll find there she's sure she doesn't know. If your grandad starts dancing up there in his clogs God knows but the tower'll fall down. Your mam's talking like this to cheer herself up. You've got no dad but you've got a grandad. I hope you don't get no ss . . . stigma . . . that's the first time I've stammered when I've talked to myself . . . I won't stammer with you. When I've got you out and on my knee . . . I hope you don't get no stigma being a bastard. Oh lord now I can't see at all. I hope this place isn't haunted. Could a church be haunted? Well if anyone could I'll bet it's this one. I'm absolutely exhausted.'

'Are you all right lass?' she heard from above. 'Is it too much for you?'

'It is much Mister Rockingham.'

'I'm sitting here to wait for you. Can you see?'

'No Mister Rockingham.'

'I can see you coming up. You'll be here in a minute.'

'Will I?'

'Aye. You'll need a sit. We'll rest and then go on.'

Presently she felt his guiding hand and sat in the darkness two steps below him. When she had recovered her breath she said: 'I'm aching all over.'

'It's my arse that's worst,' said Rockingham.

This statement and the way in which it was uttered—and in the place it was uttered—threw Jean into a fit of laughter.

'I must be bloody daft taking you up here and all,' said Rockingham, laughing with her. 'I wish we had a bottle of Scotch whisky.'

'So do I Mister Rockingham.'

'But bad for the babby I suppose,' said the old man.

They rested. Jean wondered how long Silly Tilly would wait and what if he were to shut them up in the tower. Rockingham held on to his flag, with his free hand he squeezed her shoulder. 'What's that long word for being closed in?' she asked.

'Claustrophobia.'

'Yes. Yes claustrophobia.'

'Do you feel it?'

'Yes. Do you?'

'No. Used to the mines you see.'

'It was funny that man knew you were a miner.'

'It shows you see.'

'How . . . how many more steps?'

'How many d'you think we've done?'

'I didn't count.'

'Perhaps a hundred?'

'Yes, perhaps.'

'Well they say there's one for every day of the year.'

'Never.'

'They do say so.'

'I don't think I can do it then, Mister Rockingham.'

He didn't answer this and knowing he must be disappointed she added: 'unless we take it very slow.'

'We will lass, we will,' he said, reassured and reassuring.

As they rose to continue he said: 'Hang on to flag and I'll give you a pull.'

'No, it's too narrow for that.'

'Then I'll go behind and give you a push.'

In spite of her protestations the old man squeezed down past her with his flag, she faced upward, delicately he placed his hand in the small of her back, and in this odd fashion with the flag tapping away like a drum calling up a wind that needed no calling, they resumed the climb. 'I do believe there's a platform before the very top,' said Rockingham.

They did not speak again until they reached this platform— Jean could not have spoken. When they went outside into the night she was so terrified she had to cling to the main wall of the tower and could not possibly look over the ramparts. She closed her eyes sure that this whole swaying structure was about to fall. She pressed her face against the wall, and she moaned.

'Easy now, easy lass,' she heard him say, 'you'll be all right in a minute. It's just a matter of getting used to. You'll get used to it you see.'

'Oh Mister Rockingham I'll never get used to it . . . it's awful . . . whatever kind of people have built this . . . and what did they do it for?'

'But we're not much more than half up you know.'

'It's quite up enough for me Mister Rockingham . . . oh take me down please . . . please take me down.'

'Just open one eye at a time,' said Rockingham. 'I do assure you you'll get used to it. It's quite as safe as any house.'

The wind continued to rage. Keeping her eyes closed she sat down resting the back of her head against the main tower, as if that at least were some kind of comfort. When she opened one eye she saw that the old man was leaning out over the middle of the rampart holding up his furled flag. She saw him turn and gaze up at the top of the tower with a joyful expression on his face. 'My goodness,' she thought opening both eyes, 'what's going on in his head now?' It was only then that she realized she was biting her lip and clenching her hands: so she stopped.

The old man may have sensed her movement: in any event he looked at her and putting down his flag for the first time since they had eaten with the lorry driver in the café in

Lincoln, he came forward, knelt, and taking both her cold hands in his, smiling gently, said: 'It's all right here lass, it's stood for a thousand years and will stand for a thousand more.'

'You sound like one of those poets,' she said, attempting a smile back. 'Not if we have an earthquake.'

'We never have them big enough in England,' he answered seriously. 'Do you feel inclined to go right on to the top?'

'You're crying Mister Rockingham.'

'Ah that's the wind. The tears are protective you see. To tell the truth . . . to tell the truth I never felt more joyful . . . Do you feel inclined?'

'Why are you so joyful?'

'Well . . . well I've seen something of what's to be done.'

'What? What's to be done?'

'Rather what may be done.'

'But what Mister Rockingham?'

'Well it's just a kind of . . . of picture of it.' And she knew him well enough to see that for the moment he would tell her no more.

She raised her head and looked up. 'Oh I can't,' she said. 'Why must we?'

'I shall have to go,' said Rockingham. 'Perhaps you'll stay here. We can descend together.' She did not answer. 'Having come so far I need go. Will you stay inside and rest. We mustn't put no strain on your baby.'

'I don't want to stay by myself,' was all she could reply. The pause that followed was awkward. Rockingham broke it. 'Your answer doesn't help me,' he said, embarrassed.

Jean stood, and with one hand still holding on to the buttress took a short step.

At first she flinched but eventually, as the old man had predicted, she was able to look out and down over the parapet. Frightened, giddy, as she was, blurred by the 'protective' tears, what she saw began to calm her. It was a Dutch doll's town that was set at her feet. The little brown river which had once met the open sea had got lost and wandered after it through green fields, mile after mile after mile. Although there were lights, new houses, and cars and people crossing the square, although there was bargaining in the market, she thought this the ghost of a place.

'You're easier,' said Rockingham. 'Shall we go on up?' 'He said it was falling.' 'Who?' 'Mister Tilly. He said so.' 'Oh he's mad daft,' said Rockingham. 'He's mad daft is Tilly.' Once more she looked above.

'It's so thin.'

'No it's solid. He meant the roof of the nave you see.'

'Our weight might over-balance it.'

'Never,' he said. 'Never. Trust me for that.'

'Then I will.' She was decisive at last. 'Yes I will, then.'

This staircase was longer, narrower, steeper and darker; at every second turn the light disappeared until an uncharitable slot of a window on the fifth showed and disappeared again; her legs ached, the wind raged like a sick wolf. Yet her decision on the platform below had given her indifference to the danger, she was becoming conscious that this was not after all to be missed, and most of all she was growing increasingly curious at what the old man behind her, pushing so strongly against her back, was up to. For now she was able to think clearer she could see he was certainly up to something. 'Oh yes,' she thought, 'he's up to something, is Mister Rockingham.'

At last, gasping, exhausted, they entered the light again and tottered out on to the next platform. The moon had risen higher but was not yet casting any significant light as far up as this. No, it was still dusk and the wind still raging. While she clung to the main tower the old man pushed past with his flag and she saw that he was upset when he realized that they had not yet reached the top. A step in front of them, to the left of where they had emerged, was a wooden door leading to another winding stairway and on this door was written: 'Dangerous to proceed further.' 'Well damn,' shouted Rockingham into the wind and went to try this door. It was locked. 'Well damn,' he shouted. He shook it. He kicked it. 'Don't be mad daft,' shouted Jean. The old man looked up at the main tower as if somehow or other he would climb that stone with his bare hands. 'What a bloody shame!' 'But what does it matter? What are you after?' she cried. 'I wanted to try it out. Just to try it. Not fix it you understand. Not here.' 'Your flag?' 'Aye my flag.' 'But can't you try it here?' 'No.' 'It's surely high enough.' 'It's got to be the top,' cried Rockingham. 'Well there's no way for you,' she said looking up herself. The wind blew and blew and blew. 'Why not give it just a little airing,' she shouted, consumed with curiosity, 'it won't spoil it *all* will it?' Rockingham shook his head. 'It's been unfurled before hasn't it?' 'No I made it new . . . I made it myself.' 'But just to give it an airing. It may have got damp. It'll dry like.' 'No.' 'But just to see. It may have got faded.' 'No, it's not faded.' 'Mister Rockingham I'm sure it won't spoil everything. Not everything.' 'You don't think so?' 'No of course not Mister Rockingham. Of course not.' 'You don't think so eh?' Catching her enthusiasm entirely he shouted out so loudly that the words were hurtled right over the ramparts 'I do believe I will.'

He drew back with her into the side of the main tower.

'Be careful this wind don't tear it out of your arms.' She was jumping up and down. 'It'll have to cast me off too,' he answered.

He knelt. She knelt beside him. Tenderly he undid the cord, removed the sacking. He spat on his old bruised hands, he brushed back his grey hair, he stood, he advanced, he braced his clogged feet against the ramparts, he held his flag high, and with a whip and a crack, there streamed out over the heads of the people of Boston, there streamed out into the dusk from their church, a great red flag, the flag of the Workers of the World.

Chapter 6

A CLOUD slid between him and the moon. He opened the door in the wall to enter the dark garden, touched the pump, trailed his hand along the side of the potting shed, came slowly across the damp lawn to the lighted house. As he passed the uncurtained room with the French windows he saw his mother inside dusting her father's bookcase. He was going to call when he realized he would frighten her. Something about her attitude interested him and in his new-found awareness he stayed where he was.

> '*The room stood quiet watching my mother*
> *Through the warm window I watched too.*'

Mrs Calvin finished dusting the books, took a chamois leather, sprinkled a drop of vinegar upon it, began to polish the glass. Over her head the gas lamp flickered and was steady. At the bottom of the panel she seemed to see her own reflection for she stopped, looked into the glass closely and tidied her hair.

> '*But not a hair was out of place mother*
> *And when you'd done you still kept staring.*'

She seemed to be asking something of the image in her father's bookcase. She put a hand to her head. He heard her then make a faint moan. She left the bookcase, went over to the closed desk, unlocked it, took a letter from a drawer. Stared at the letter, rather than read it, trembled over it, put it back in the drawer, took it out again. Put it back again, opened a bottle of aspirins, swallowed four without water, put the bottle into her coat pocket, re-locked the desk.

She seemed to keep asking a question. Her mouth hung open, hung slack. It was the same question, but he couldn't make it out.

She picked up her leather, went back to the glass, didn't polish. She sought her image, found it, stared into it as before. The hand went to the head.

She started as if she had heard a sound, looked at the door. She turned hopefully to the window. Richard stood still and felt frightened. When she realized she had heard nothing her body slumped. All poetry went out of the boy's head.

She was listening again. She went to the door, listened, closed it. An expression came over her face that her son had never seen. She must have been cold in spite of her winter coat for again she shivered. The expression on her face was as if she were about to do something that she shouldn't. *This* listening had been to make sure she was alone and would not be disturbed. She went back to her desk, did not unlock it, drummed her fingers upon it—confidentially.

She began to smile faintly like someone trying to hang on to a shred of humour in order to keep sane. He, whose mind had begun to be more and more occupied with literary allusions, thought she must look like Hedda Gabler, about to burn the manuscript.

Richard wondered if he should go in and whether there was something dishonest in his standing in the shadows. But he didn't go in. 'After all I am a poet,' he said to himself, blushing.

Mrs Calvin went to the mantelshelf to look at the family photographs she had arrayed. She picked one of them up, and then, as if pretending to herself that it was an accident, she knocked the one at the end on to the stone hearth. He heard the glass break. Still clutching the photograph she had picked up, she fled from the room.

Surprisingly the coming down had been more painful than the going up. They had said their goodbyes to Verger Tilly, they had eaten bread and margarine, they had drunk tea. As they walked along the misty river bank looking for somewhere to sleep the aching in their legs persisted, and was unpleasant.

'What sort of a man is Miner Calvin exactly Mister Rockingham?'

'Loves the Lord.'

'Yes?'

'Always helps his own class but would help any other. Wants everybody to have the same chances.'

'Ah well he may want.'

'He's no snob. He's determined. Very kind. Give you his shirt if you needed it. Not big but strong. He's for the people . . . that's what he's for.'

'But what's he like?'

'How d'you mean?'

'In himself.'

Rockingham pursed his lips. He took out his handkerchief, he blew his nose. 'Well he fought in the war . . . as stretcher-bearer you realize . . . no I don't suppose he killed anyone. No I don't think that.' He stopped where he could reach the river water, put down his banner, knelt and began to wash the handkerchief. 'When he come out the Labour party in Houghton backed him. I don't think nobody would have him as parson . . . not before that. They sent him to college properly . . . miner before that you see. Oh he's well scarred, well scarred.' Rockingham waited for the current, rinsed his handkerchief in a fresh patch of the brown silted waters. Doubtfully he held the handkerchief up to the moon. 'I suppose it *is* cleaner,' he said. He stood to wring it out. 'Went down the colliery at twelve you see . . . worked with myself . . . could have stayed there of course but went off to war . . . a conchie you see, sort of conchie . . . just sort of. I'm not too sure he's one now.' Rockingham finished his wringing, lifted his banner, tied the handkerchief loosely around its pole, lifted Jean from where she sat, with his free hand, and they continued.

'He was taking home twelve shilling a week. Give it all to his mother. It was he drove me to reading. She give him tuppence for comics, tuppence for chocolate, tuppence for a piece of good cake. We used to go to Institute. He seized on everything

… he wrote poems … mother was a Baptist but he liked things a bit prettier … don't think he writes poems now … well there's no evidence of it.' The old man adjusted his hand over the wet handkerchief on the banner-pole so that the water should cease running up his arm. 'Mind you he's Low … he's Low Church. He was evolutionist you see … yes he was that all right … he give talks.' Rockingham looked at Jean almost aggressively—as if in fact he was Calvin addressing one of those unresponsive audiences in Houghton long ago: 'He used to talk on it.' Rockingham sighed. 'Of course there was a lot of politics in the Sunday schools in those days.' His forehead wrinkled. 'Would his mother have known that I wonder? Would she have known?' He looked at Jean in such a way she felt called on to answer. 'I've no idea.' 'He was in one group made contact with the Independents.' 'What are they?' 'Independent Labour party … that's what they are … yes. that's how he got his backing you see.'

Now there was a pause while the old man sniffed. They came to a bridge, they crossed it, they passed some little chandlers' shops with their windows full of great jars of pickle and piccalilli. They stopped to look.

'Better than a hot meal that pickle.'

'Well as good as,' said Jean.

'I'll bet you're looking to the day you cook me a hot dinner,' said Rockingham.

'Dinner and supper too.'

They turned from the windows. They continued their way on the road by the river that was now leading them south and out of the town. They passed two or three groups of young people on their way to the pictures.

'The girls don't walk arm in arm like we do home,' said Jean.

'No,' said Rockingham adjusting his banner, once again furled and private.

'And their voices are higher,' said Jean. 'They're much higher. And they're all trying to dress like film stars.'

'Aye.'

'It's silly. It don't suit them at all.'

'There's always been a struggle for him you see,' said Rockingham. 'Cheating and roughness in the pit . . . conchie and not conchie . . . dying and killing and nursing in the war . . . starving in his home . . . Father was bad you see . . . took bad . . . lingered you know . . . lingered dreadful. And then his brother died . . . tubercular or something worse . . . of course his mother's gone . . . she was the Baptist. All gone now.'

'But what's he like?'

'Well . . . well he's an arguer. He's a striver.'

'Yes but what's he like?'

'How d'you mean?'

'In himself.'

'Well . . . well he's not at rest yet.'

'I know that,' she said, laughing.

Rockingham did not laugh. He was still puzzling how to answer her question, and no doubt to satisfy himself as to the true nature of his friend, Calvin.

'No he's not at rest yet,' he repeated in a worried tone.

'What gives him pleasure then?' asked Jean.

'Billiards,' answered Rockingham, lighting up at once. 'Billiards. He loves a game of billiards. And pretty girls . . . he loves a pretty girl.'

'What's his wife like?'

'Ah . . . ah well he married above him do you see.'

'Why did he do that?'

'Well I don't know,' Rockingham scratched his ear. 'I don't know everything. You want to know a lot. What a questioning lass you are.'

'I never seen the wife. Is *she* pretty then?'

'I wouldn't say that.'

'I'm sure she is pretty.' Jean sounded wistful.

'No. I can't say that,' said Rockingham. 'I'll tell you one thing . . .' He stopped to stamp his cold feet. 'She's not as pretty as you.'

'Well . . . well I never,' said Jean.

'She certainly is not,' said the old man. And they continued—Jean pleased and smiling.

They were now almost out of the shrunk, the remote little town. They had left the chandlers, the corn merchants, the farmers, the bullocks and the beer. 'Wherever are we going to sleep?' wondered Jean.

'He loved her father you see,' said Rockingham. 'I think he felt sorry for her. She was pretty then . . . then. She was younger then. She was happier then.'

'Isn't she happy now?'

'She don't look it.'

'Isn't that his fault?'

'No I don't think that . . . mind you I don't know.'

'It must be some of his fault.'

'I don't think it.' Rockingham shook his head. 'She seemed to take life bad after her last baby. She had that badly I believe . . . I have heard that.'

'How awful,' said Jean. 'Oh how sad Mister Rockingham.'

'Yes.' And then: 'But I don't know exactly,' he added.

'He never speaks of it?'

'Well not to me. And I never *heard* he speaks of it.'

'Perhaps he's not so good to her when they're alone.'

'No. No I don't think that.' But Rockingham was puzzled and was worried. 'No I *can't* think that.' He sniffed again. He pulled at his moustache. 'Yes from what I know she's a brooder . . . a natural sufferer you see. Who's to tell what happens between man and wife when they're alone.'

'Who *is* to tell Mister Rockingham!'

'You've found that then?'

'I have. I have indeed Mister Rockingham.'

They walked past the last house of the town proper on this road that was leading them south to Norfolk.

'Lies are awful things aren't they Mister Rockingham.'

'They are lass. They're crippling things.'

'They're awful!'

'They're the most crippling things in the world.'

'I mean with some people you just never know where you are.'

'You don't lass, you don't,' said Rockingham with sympathy. 'You don't *ever* know with some people.'

'They're like trying to peel an onion Mister Rockingham.'

They were both getting very very weary. They were walking slower. It may have been this weariness that made Jean say: 'I hope I don't have a bad time with my baby.'

'I prayed you wouldn't that.'

'Did you Mister Rockingham?'

'Aye.'

'In the church?'

'Aye. Back there.'

She was so touched that she stopped, caught his arm, and kissed him on his cheek. He put his free arm around her. Just for a moment they both turned back for a last lingering look at the Boston stump.

He hesitated, afraid, knelt down to pick up the broken photograph, stood before turning it over, realized that he was trembling. When he did look he was so relieved that the face smiling formally up at him through the shattered glass was not his own, that he blinked. 'Well, trust me to think that it must have been mine.'

With the allaying of his own fears he became perturbed: why had his mother done such a thing? If it had been her own image she had destroyed he would have understood—he supposed himself to be capable of such an action—but Betty's, little Betty's! Why on earth had his mother destroyed his sister's photograph? Of the deliberation of his mother's action he was not in any doubt.

He picked the glass out of the frame, dropped the pieces into the empty fireplace, added those that were in the hearth, put back the photograph on to the mantelshelf, precisely where it rested before. He was looking at it when he heard his mother re-enter the room.

'Have you seen your father? Supper's nearly ready.'

123

'No, I haven't.' He couldn't turn.

'I don't know where he is. I never know where he is. He wasn't in for tea. None of you were. Only Betty.'

'Only Betty,' said Richard, and now he did turn.

'None of you were.'

'Well . . . well it's such a change here, I expect we just forgot.'

'Where is Eileen now?'

'Just coming. We thought we'd walk back different ways.'

'You're not to leave her alone this time of night. There's all sorts of strange people in places like this.'

'None worse than oneself,' said Richard smiling.

'You're not to joke at me,' said Mrs Calvin fiercely. 'Don't you leave her alone again. There are wicked people about. Do you understand that?'

'Yes.'

'There are always people worse than oneself. The world is full of people worse than oneself. There are men who would . . .' She paused. 'It's simply not safe for a young girl.'

'Well I just ran ahead,' declared Richard and then intuitively, without knowing why, he added: 'I wanted to see *you*.'

Mrs Calvin frowned—the expression signifying both hope and disbelief. 'Did you?' she asked. 'Why?'

'I don't know,' answered Richard, not used to guile, 'I just did.'

'Well, one shouldn't have to explain love I suppose,' said his mother with irony, 'but did you?'

'I thought you might be a bit lonely.'

He expected her to speak and she seemed about to and then she didn't.

'You know . . . here . . . in a strange house . . . and your not being used to it. Everything being so big.'

He waited but still she said nothing.

'I mean I know we've all been out all the time and you have to do all the work.' He found himself putting out his arms to her and declaring: 'I do love you Mother.'

Perhaps he expected his mother to come to him and hug him —something of the kind at any rate—he was surprised when she stayed where she was, surprised when she stated without embarrassment, without accusation, without self-pity: 'Yes, but not as much as I love you.' And she added as if it were of the utmost concern: 'You should know that.'

Once again a spasm of pain seemed to bite its way into Mrs Calvin's head: once again her hands went to her temples.

'Have you got your migraine?'

'Yes.'

'Can I get you anything?'

'No.'

'Sit down Mother.'

'Yes. I'll sit down.'

'Is there nothing I can get you?' He knew she had taken her aspirins.

'No thank you, I'll be all right in a minute.'

'A glass of water?'

'No thank you.'

They sat silent. Outside the dusk turned into night. No one passed their windows. 'Then both of us sat home,' thought Richard.

> '*Then both of us sat home*
> *Sought to forget our sadness*
> *Some need brandy, some need lies.*'

Mrs Calvin sighed. 'It's gone.'

'Oh I'm so glad,' said Richard.

'Is that glass broken on Betty's photo?'

'Yes.'

'Did it fall down or did you knock it off?'

'It must have fallen down.'

'But you picked it up?'

'Yes. Yes I did.'

'I didn't notice it before,' said Mrs Calvin. 'That's another bill I suppose.'

Richard looked away from his mother to the mantelshelf

and it was only then that he noticed that the missing photograph, the one she had run from the room with, must be that photograph of her father on his wedding day. Richard dropped his eyes to the floor to think. He was entering the unknown and he knew it. The telephone rang.

The telephone rang and it kept on ringing. Neither moved. 'Please answer,' begged Mrs Calvin. 'I hate it.'

'You'll have to get used to it Mother,' declared Richard, who didn't like it either.

'I'll never get used to it. I hate it. *Please* answer Richard.'

Richard went to the hall but before he could reach the phone standing on his Great-Uncle Arthur three-cornered table, Betty had run down the stairs, and picked it up.

'Are you all deaf in this house then? Hello, who's that? Who's that then? Oh that's you then Dad. Are you Dad? All right then Dad. Yes, all right then Dad. I'll tell her then. Yes Dad. Enjoy yourself Dad. Yes I'm writing another poem. I'll tell you it in the morning. Yes, well then Dad, you have a good time.' Betty put down the phone. 'Hello face-ache. I'm writing another poem. Where's Mam?'

'In there,' answered Richard and pointed.

'Don't point, it's rude,' said Betty running to the door. 'Mam, Dad's up at the General's. He'll stay for supper he says, as they're having a chat but he won't be late. Not to wait for him he says. Mam, I'm writing a good poem. Will you shout when supper's ready.' Without waiting for an answer she turned from the door, shouted 'Goodbye funny face,' to Richard as she passed him, and ran away somewhere upstairs, calling from above, 'And keep your mouth closed when you're eating. Keep your mouth closed while you're eating.'

Ordinarily Richard would have laughed—on this occasion he went back to his mother's parlour and sat down in silence. She too was silent. They heard Eileen walk up one of the garden paths, they heard the back door slam, they heard her climb the back stairs. But neither of them spoke.

'How long, how very long ago it does seem.' The library was

126

not one of those that are mentioned in guide books but, like its owner, was homely, warm, spacious and old. 'Our fortieth birthday don't you know.' As if to confirm the memory, sighing nostalgically, Mrs Mellor gazed down into her great brooch that gleamed in the firelight. 'Sidney was received with musical honours at the dinner. How touched, how proud, he was. I see him now.' In the shadows of the bay window, Andrews turned up one of the oil lamps and smiled; abandoned on a cushioned floor with the General's cat, Lady Cleeve smiled also. 'Two hundred and thirty members, presided over, managed, superintended by Tawney—the modest Tawney whose historical study has overshadowed his service. Oh yes. We all felt then, don't you know, that even a minority Labour Government was a suitable laurel for our effort, a fitting crown.'

'Laurel is green for a season,' muttered the host. Sunk in the chintz-covered chair with the old Labrador at his feet, who looked even in sleep, even in death, to be guarding his commander, the General repeated: 'Laurel is green for a season, and love is sweet for a day; but love grows bitter with treason, and laurel outlives not May.'

'Yes. Yes indeed,' agreed Mrs Mellor. 'How long ago it does seem. How very long.'

'March 14th, 1924.' Andrews spoke briskly, without irony. 'Not so long surely.' Pushing his forefinger and thumb into his inconsiderable moustache he asked with all the irony he could muster: 'What was the nature of the music Mrs Mellor?'

'Regrettably not recorded: I remember it was loud.'

'Fled is that music.' The General rose, his dog awoke, rose also. They went to the butler's tray, the General poured himself another whisky. 'Fled. And now 'tis buried deep.'

'Mrs Mellor,' declared Miner Calvin biting on his tobacco, 'it doesn't appear that your Society concerns itself with Labour or Socialist policy these days.'

'Oh. Really. Don't you feel that "Labour and the Social Order" is enough to be going on with?'

'I don't.'

Lady Cleeve stretched herself. 'Aunt Ethel seeks new allies, Vicar, seeks changes of direction. Some of her friends think her too emotional for politics.'

'Your laugh is as thin and as sinister as a beggar's violin,' asserted Mrs Mellor, annoyed at what she considered a breach of confidence.

'What changes of direction?' asked Robert Andrews.

'One moment,' said Mrs Mellor, 'let me deal with one thing at a time . . . let's not rush our fences. I will admit, Vicar, that a certain amount of re-vamping is both necessary and called for. We cannot work miracles.'

'As I understand it,' protested Calvin, chewing on a fresh piece of tobacco, and to everyone's surprise leaving his leather chair to adopt his miner's crouch beside Lady Cleeve and the cat, before the huge log fire: 'Unemployment remains at the cheerless dead-level of a million and a half souls year after year after year . . . in fact now looks to rise . . . must rise . . . and you Fabians don't do nothing more practical than you did in your ancient declaratory resolution to the International Bureau in the war—which I do say you put well when you said: "the recurrence of any extensive or lasting unemployment in any country is now as much a disgrace to its government as the occurrence of cholera".'

'You like that phrase.'

'Oh aye I like it well enough but where are the doctors for this cholera.'

'There was,' remarked Mrs Mellor thoughtfully, gazing down at her brooch again, 'there was a reference in the Executive minutes to an appeal from the Longsight Unemployed Committee for some spare pamphlets.'

'The sole reference?' asked Andrews.

'I believe so.' Mrs Mellor was irritated.

'Well now that might in itself be regarded as unfeeling,' announced Calvin. 'Is it not true that there is no discussion whatsoever of principle at national level?'

'I suppose there isn't,' answered Mrs Mellor.

'You must wake them up.'

'I will,' cried Mrs Mellor. 'We will form a committee.'

Andrews laughed.

'What are you laughing at? Don't you believe in committees?' Andrews was silent but apparently not put out. 'Do you find me amusing young man? What do you think of our Society?'

'Truthfully?' asked Andrews calmly, feeling Calvin's interested gaze upon him.

'Of course.'

'I think you're a lot of intelligent idiots.'

There was a pause.

'You mean well,' added Andrews.

It was doubtful if anyone of his age had ever spoken to Mrs Mellor in such a manner—she was so astonished she was heard to gasp. Lady Cleeve giggled, Calvin simply nodded his head in serious agreement, and the General sat down again.

'Why?' demanded Mrs Mellor.

'Why? Oh well I don't exactly know why . . . I mean to find out, Mrs Mellor.'

'But what is the reason for your . . . your sentiment?'

'Statement?'

'Yes. Statement.'

'You've too many opinions, you show off to each other, you've no consistent properly worked out policies, no real attitude and when there's trouble you play safe.'

'Safe!'

'Yes. Of course I don't know what's better. Perhaps you're too democratic.'

'Ah,' agreed Calvin. 'Like the boy says . . . why for example doesn't your *News* carry word of the struggle over communist affiliation in the Labour party? Isn't that something to be discussed?'

'Now look here, my man,' protested Mrs Mellor. 'I agree we need a dynamic. When have I not said as much myself? There is indeed something in what you state . . . *something* . . . but when you say "perhaps you're too democratic" I spit.'

'*I* said that,' laughed Andrews.

'I know,' pronounced Mrs Mellor, 'there are cynics and fools and cowards among us but when you say "perhaps you're too democratic" I spit, and I add also thank God for it.'

'After you have spat I hope Aunt,' said Lady Cleeve. 'Spat or spitted?'

'Please,' said Mrs Mellor. 'Please no poor jokes for this is serious. No frivolity please.'

'But what exactly have you got to be democratic about?' demanded Andrews. 'Isn't it your job to organize, isn't *that* your work, so that one day other people, later generations, will have time and work, and money enough, to be democratic?'

'Young man you want a dictator.'

'Why not?' asked Andrews after a pause.

'Ah,' sighed Calvin. 'There we have it.'

'Before I answer your question . . .' Mrs Mellor took off her hat for the first time and pinned it carefully to the arm of her chair, 'let me tell you something of our struggle, and I mean struggle, because there has been nothing else. There has certainly been no dogma. Principles of action? We despise them. Fabians are *never* compelled. Dictators you say? If you want to know what we have achieved and are achieving then it is to our invididual members that we must turn, it is to their lives, it is they we must examine. Let us for instance take Sidney . . . what has Sidney *done*? *Done* do you see. What has Sidney *done*?'

Whatever Sydney had done, was not now to be disclosed by Mrs Mellor because the General, who seemingly had caught the word 'struggle' and brooded over it ever since, rose to his feet and in a voice of inexorable authority, hardly above a whisper, muttered: 'Struggle. Yes you see . . . the struggle . . . I can speak of that . . . I can speak of the struggle.' He rose again, the dog woke, they went to the empty bay window behind the sofa and with his back to his listeners the General began: 'Plumer's hair went white during those two dreadful years. All responsibility. No chance for glory. Pink face went sallow. Pot belly dropped back in his belt.'

Now the old man turned into the room so that his eyes gleamed out of the shadows, and gazing down upon them as he was with the dark bay behind he stood over all like some martyr on a cathedral wall.

'Deep mining offensive . . . hundred feet below . . . that's what we planned . . . colonel in the Engineers, I had my say . . . blue clay and water, January, 1916, six tunnels started . . . blow them all to bloody hell.' At his feet the old dog whimpered. 'Heel,' bawled the General, 'heel; well you may moan.' They watched as the Labrador sidled away and hid himself behind his master's desk. 'Heel,' cried the General in a hollow voice, 'come out of there you black bastard.' But the dog would not move. The General shook his head, blew out his cheeks, and bellowed again in his most commanding: 'Heel George, heel.' Back came the Labrador, cringing. 'You bad dog,' grumbled the General, knelt, and patted him on the head. 'Did I frighten you George?'

'Into the very bowels of the earth . . .' The General rose: the dog went to heel. 'Pumping engines . . .' He straddled his feet, the dog flopped between. 'Ten thousand men coughing picking and shovelling fifteen feet forward a day . . . electric lamps . . . ammonal ninety-five thousand pound . . . half a mile some of those buggering tunnels. *Five*, five miles of galleries and one million pound of T.N.T. And what did the enemy know?' He paused to give his question full effect. The dog whimpered. 'What did the enemy know? Why didn't they withdraw? Did they know and had plans? Were they burrowing like moles in the bowels below us? *Below us?*' He rubbed at his forehead. 'You see . . . you see one British prisoner could have given us away . . . think of that . . . and never did, never did.' He grinned sardonically: his dog cowered. His dog seemed to draw its great flap ears closer to its head. 'Was the Lord on our side? Was the Lord on our side Vicar? Couldn't they bloody well hear us Vicar? Was the Lord on our side two years?'

'Sometimes they did hear,' answered Calvin.

A pause. 'You *know*?' The General was surprised.

'A little,' answered Calvin.

'Ah,' said the General, still surprised. As if it knew what was to follow, the General's dog opened its eyes even wider, gazed directly up at his master and covered its face with its ears.

'Yes, yes, sometimes they did hear,' said the General, 'and when they did and broke into our forward tunnels from theirs they took us by the throats, and we clawed each other to death with our picks, and we smashed each other to death with our shovels.'

There was a sigh from the ladies.

'But the Germans didn't know the half of it did they,' said Calvin sadly.

'No,' said the General, wearily, almost bitterly, 'they didn't know the half of it. They didn't know how deep and how vast and how many.'

'The Newcastle shaft, the Snout, the Sydney,' muttered Calvin.

'The Perth, the Hobart and the Brisbane,' whispered the General. 'Were you there then boy?'

'I was.'

'Did you dig?'

'No I never dug. Not even a grave.'

The General walked away to the darkest part of the room; his dog followed. 'And the Berlin,' said the General. 'The Berlin Sap. Right up into the Kaiser's palace we said.' Lady Cleeve dabbed at her eyes, Mrs Mellor sniffed. Only Andrews was composed.

'Do you remember Sneddon?' asked the General, and burst into tears. Seeking to control himself the General knelt beside his dog who strove to nuzzle and lick at the old man's face. 'It's the drink that's done it,' said the General, 'it's this cheap bloody Scotch. I knew it was inferior. I got it from a friend. What rotten stuff it is.'

'I never knew him,' said Calvin.

132

'Lovely children,' said the General.

Silence. Emptiness. The General's head like a shell, singing of pain.

'That gas,' muttered Calvin.

'Yes,' said the General. 'Yes. My idea that. Make the enemy put their masks on and lose sleep you see. Doubled the bombardment. False alarms. Many of them.' He came forward to one of the oil lamps, turned up the wick. 'I wish I could draw you a map,' he said. 'Up there.' He pointed to the white plastered ceiling. 'Warm that night. Fog blanket. No wind. Then lightning and a clap or two of thunder. Ideal conditions. God on our side. Midnight, a shower of rain. After the shower a three-quarter moon. Half an hour before Zero: stop firing Plumer said.'

'We heard the nightingales singing in the woods.'

'We did,' said the General. 'Several of them round there.' The General went to Calvin and rested his hand on his shoulder where he still crouched by the fire, 'Zero hour: 3.10. 2.52: enemy flares. 2.57: enemy shrapnel. 3.5: the first streaks of dawn.'

'Cocks began to crow,' said Calvin.

'On Mount Kemmel,' confirmed the General. 'I looked there through my glasses. 3.6: another flare. 3.9: the Germans silent. Wondered what it meant. One minute's complete silence.'

'Aye complete. I timed it on my watch.'

'So did I,' said the General. '3.10,' said the General.

'3.10,' said Calvin, 'nineteen land mines went off.'

The General straightened up. 'Nineteen land mines went off together. And every man jack of us stood as the whole great ghastly German ridge, which had fired down on us so much and so long, blew itself into the sky, and nineteen flames reached up after and burned the pieces of men and earth, and when all the noise gathered up together it turned us deaf and blind, and it thundered over Flanders and the whole of the north there, and it rocked and rolled across the channel, and they say that Lloyd George was waiting for it in his study in

10 Downing Street and when he heard it he put out the light and he went to his bed.'

'And when we got on the ridge,' said Calvin, 'we threw Mills bombs at men too paralysed to surrender.'

'We did,' said the General. 'We did. Men too dazed to give in. Did you throw?'

'No.'

'And some kept trying to kiss us. Mad. Gone mad you see. Gone rotten mad.'

'The seventh of June.'

'A triumph for the Engineers,' said the General.

Silence.

'And thus,' remarked Andrews, 'did Sir Douglas Haig gain his first necessary triumph.'

'Robert,' said the General, 'Robert, I don't think you understand. Shall we dine, ladies and gentlemen?'

'Do I have to eat the crust?' asked Betty. 'You certainly do.' 'All of it?' 'All of it. And take your elbows off the table.'

'It's so funny to hear the farm horses plodding home and not the clogs and not the trams,' Eileen said happily. 'I still can't believe it. I never thought it would be like this. It's so quiet. The people here really seem to sleep. I never thought they did in Houghton. I thought they just went upstairs and lay there with their eyes open. But here they put out the lights properly and they go upstairs and take their clothes off and put on white nightdresses and they really sleep. This afternoon the clouds sort of left money in the water . . . pennies and gold. If you take off your shoes and just push one foot after another through the grass it's lovely.'

'The cows do that,' said Betty.

'I know. That's what gave me the idea.'

'Mind you don't catch cold. You're not to do it when the grass is damp.'

'No Mother I won't.'

'Damp feet don't give you a cold anyway,' said Betty, 'not

134

when you're young. I read that. It's all in the mind this book says.'

'If you contradict me Betty you'll go straight to bed.'

'Yes Mother.'

Silence except for the eating.

'Can I read my poem now?' asked Betty pushing her plate away. 'Go on then,' said Eileen. 'Mother's not listening,' said Betty.

Richard blushed. Feeling his mother's anxious eyes upon him he looked down at his empty plate.

'More dear?'

'No thank you.'

'Can I say my poem now Mam?'

'You should have sat in your father's place, Richard,' said Mrs Calvin.

'Why?'

Mrs Calvin did not answer.

'Why should he have?' asked Eileen.

'Well if his father's not here he should.'

'Why doesn't she look at us properly,' wondered Eileen, and Betty made a face.

Once again Betty asked with exaggerated calmness: 'Can I read my poem now Mam?'

'There *is* a word.'

'Please, Mam.'

'Yes "please". Very well.'

Betty took a breath and began. ' "The deep green sea." '

> 'Down, down in the deep green sea
> Jewels of cool freshness waiting for me.
> Would I watch the fish go slinking by?
> Watching and staring with glassy eye.
> Would I watch the eel with the slender head?
> Under the rock on the green sea bed.
> Would I watch the crab waiting for night?
> Not daring to feed in the bright day-light.

135

Would I rise to the top and see the sea-shore?
And never look in the depths of the ocean any more.'

'Well?' asked the author. 'Well I like it,' said Eileen smiling.
'Very nice dear,' said Mrs Calvin. 'Why doesn't the crab dare
to eat in the bright daylight?' asked Richard.

'It doesn't like the daylight.'

'I saw crabs eating today,' said Eileen.

'Oh.'

'And it wouldn't be daylight down there would it,' said
Eileen.

'No. I suppose not. Where did you see the crabs eating?'

'In the pools on the beach.'

'But these are deep-sea crabs. It says that.'

'Oh.' Eileen smiled again.

'Nobody knows what they feel. So it's all right.'

'But it still wouldn't be daylight down there,' said Mrs
Calvin.

Betty gripped the end of the table with both of her fat little
hands.

'It would near the top,' said Richard; the tone had something of an edge.

'Would it dear?' Mrs Calvin turned to her son, smiled
briefly, looked away up at the ceiling.

Silence.

Betty stood. 'By the way I'm going to write a book about a
young boy in Spain. Bags wash.'

'Bags dry,' said Eileen.

'I'll put away,' said Mrs Calvin.

'Mother that's my job.' Richard was irritated. 'You go and
sit down. We'll bring you some tea.'

'Will you dear?'

'Oh Mother don't be so suffering,' said Richard and regretted it immediately. Mrs Calvin opened her mouth, but did
not speak, and left the kitchen. The girls pretended not to
notice, picked up the dishes, went into the scullery. Richard

decided to apologize to his mother, got as far as the hall, felt he couldn't apologize, turned back.

'You know Leen,' he heard Betty saying, 'our Mam don't like me.' Eileen made no comment. 'Do you think she likes me Leeny?' 'Oh she's just moody.' 'You know what she makes me feel Leeny?' Again no answer. 'Leeny do you know what she makes me feel?' 'No.' 'Like I'm one of those step children. Like in books.' 'Oh don't say that.' 'But she does.' 'Well . . . well you shouldn't take any notice of it.' 'I can't help taking notice can I . . . I'm like one of her step children in a book.' 'You're too sensitive.' 'I'm not sensitive at all . . . if I was there'd be trouble.' 'Well don't let it get you down.' 'I won't,' said Betty, who sounded tearful to Richard now, 'it's always been like this. I won't let it get me down because my dad makes up for it do you see.'

Richard waited for a moment and was just about to enter the scullery to help when Eileen said: 'I could see Ricky quite liked your poem.' 'D'you think he did?' 'Well he wouldn't have been so serious else.' 'Oh he's always serious. Why isn't he here helping?' 'Speaking to Mam I expect. Trying to cheer her up.'

'*I* liked your poem,' said Eileen. 'It made me think of the pool on the sea-shore the first day. I found a lovely pool.' 'Well,' said Betty, giggling, 'it's not all that good, I know that really, but I am going to be a marvellous writer, I am you know. I'm going to be better than Richard.'

Richard was about to step forward, when 'crash' went a plate on to the stone scullery floor. 'Oh Lord,' whispered Betty, 'shall we throw it in the dustbin?' 'She'll still notice.' 'Shall I say I did it?' 'Oh. Oh. Would you?' 'Yes.' 'Oh you are kind. I love you.' And Richard heard Betty hugging his eldest sister. 'Watch out,' said Eileen, 'or we'll break another.'

He had actually taken a step when Eileen said: 'Mam's not happy you know.'

'Why isn't she?'

'I don't know exactly.'

'Is it Dad?'

'Well . . . well there's something between them isn't there. When I get married I'm going to marry a man who loves me all the time whatever I'm like.'

'Me too,' said Betty.

'Otherwise I won't get married.'

'That's right. Nor will I.' Another pause. 'Leeny do I speak more Lancashire than you?'

'Perhaps because you're younger.'

'Leeny are you trying not to?'

'Yes,' admitted Eileen.

'But what do *you* think it is between Mum and Dad, Bet?'

'I don't know,' said Betty.

'I think it's sex.'

'Do you?'

'It must be.'

'What is sex exactly?'

Richard didn't want to hear any more so he tiptoed away.

When the laughter died Mrs Mellor returned to the attack. 'I would say,' she glanced from Calvin to Andrews, 'you two are a positively unholy alliance.'

'Eyes of most unholy blue,' affirmed the General. 'More coffee my dear Mellor?'

'No thank you.'

'Cleeve?'

'Thank you General.'

'Cigar?'

'No thank you.'

'Mellor?'

'I have my pipe. And well you know it.'

'Calvin?'

'I prefer to chew,' said the Vicar, looking somewhat bemused.

'Shall we adjourn?'

'No General.' Mrs Mellor took up her bag and from it her tobacco and pipe. 'Not for the moment. I'm winning here.' She fished for matches, found none, and was passed a box by her host—who seemed to be amused at this. 'Thank you General. Now Vicar, do you think that my idea for the Half-moon Club is a good one and do you think that Lady Cleeve is the right and proper person for it?'

Calvin smiled. 'Why not?'

'There was once,' said Andrews, 'a murderer who killed seven people, including his wife, with an axe—a Frenchman I believe—and when the judge asked him why he did it—a French judge—he replied: "Why not?" '

'You are an infuriating young man!' However there was admiration in Mrs Mellor's tone. 'I suppose Eton is responsible. Must you go there?'

'It seems so.'

'To tell the truth aren't you a bit of an outcast? A bit of a misfit?'

There was a pause and then Andrews answered, frowning: 'Don't let's talk about Eton.'

'Eton boys grown heavy. That's what we are. Just Eton boys grown heavy.' The General was gazing into his brandy.

'Would you tell me a little about it?' asked Calvin.

Andrews hesitated, then reassured by Calvin's intense and respectful interest he began: 'I'm a scholarship boy you see Mr Calvin . . . my father's in India . . . I came home when I was four . . . at my prep I longed to go to Eton . . . you know . . . privacy . . . the libraries . . . a room of your own, even a fire. Getting out of all those games. I'm popular at Eton. I'm not bad at games but I refuse to play them now.' He paused. 'Could I have a glass of wine, Uncle?' 'Why not?' Andrews smiled, poured himself half a glass of wine, studied it, and continued: 'I do stand out at Eton. I know that. The point is it has made me a most ghastly snob. I notice the way you eat you see Mr Calvin. Can't avoid things like that. I do hope so much to get over that in time. We think ourselves very enlightened in my lot. We don't believe in God, we do believe in Lenin. Naturally we're against all authority . . . my friends that is. And yet we're not you see . . . that's what's horrible. Most of us will conform in the end . . . probably sooner than later, and it's quite frightening. We read Shaw and Wells most of the time . . . my group that is. But you see *I* hate it because really I don't work there, and I learn so very little, and yet, and yet it's forming my character in a way I despise.' He paused again, then added ironically: 'Oh yes there'll always be an Eton.' He sighed. 'It's going to take me so long to get over. I'm not going to Oxford. I've told Uncle.'

'It was Oxford made Beerbohm insufferable,' said the General.

'Bit of a come down after Eton my Bill always used to say,' Lady Cleeve took out her ivory holder.

'To resume,' Mrs Mellor puffed away at her pipe: 'You mustn't forget Calvin that the Society has established a Local Government Information Bureau to co-operate with your Labour party—with no less gifted a person than Robson as part-time secretary.'

'Yes that is doing some good.'

'And they have started a most awfully good penny journal don't you know—the *Local Government News*—it appears ten times in the year. Some excellent articles . . . you should read G.B.S. on the Public Libraries. So stimulating. Oh there've been so many. I do enjoy them: conduct of elections, behaviour of the district auditor, that marvellous attack on Lord Eustace Percy for his education acts . . . awful man . . . and, and that brilliant, brilliant essay on the design of petrol stations . . . so informed you see. Well now look here you must admit that that at least is a great guide and policy-maker in municipal affairs.'

'I do read it,' said Calvin.

'And I,' said Andrews.

'What a pair you are! Poles apart and incorrigible. Unfortunately the financial support for the journal doesn't measure up to its worth.'

'That's often true is it not,' Andrews smiled.

'Boy you're a cynic. Boy you're positively malevolent.

Whatever is his father like General?'

'Dull,' said the General. 'The boy don't know him. He's my boy really. Or so I like to think.'

Andrews laughed very pleasantly.

'Gets his brains from his mother but she'd never admit to that.'

'*I* would.' Andrews was ironic. 'I would. I hardly know my father.'

'You're rather attractive you know,' murmured Lady Cleeve. 'You grow on acquaintance. Yes, you're rather grow-onnable.' She paused. 'Are you get-attable also?' This astonished Calvin, and reduced Andrews to confusion and silence. Embarrassed by their embarrassment, seeking to cover it up, Mrs Mellor announced: 'I shall conclude. First, *we* broke the reign of Marx, *we* showed that all his words are not divine, *we* showed that he could be wrong, very wrong, and *we* showed that one might be a Socialist without being a . . . a Marxian parrot. And finally, finally *we* showed that the State is not always the enemy of the working class— that the State can be used by the working class. And to its advantage.'

'I wonder,' said Calvin.

'So do I,' said Andrews, still blushing a little, and not raising his eyes from his wineglass in case Lady Cleeve should smile at him in a provocative manner.

'Oh now, now, now, come now,' cried Mrs Mellor, 'the State is not merely the *gendarmerie* of the middle class. It is more than that. Concessions may be obtained by all and for all.'

'Wrung perhaps,' said Calvin. 'And I still think your Society has emptied out the baby with the bath water.'

'A fine phrase but what does it mean?'

'It means you're all milk. That you've saved yourself from dispute but lost consistency and drive. You've no political philosophy worth speaking of, and that's why you put off lots of possible members, and most of the Labour movement. I mean if you look at it, when do you state fundamentals?'

'Oh dear,' shouted Mrs Mellor, 'Oh dear how unjust! And

141

as for the leaders of the British Labour Party they're so very stupid and so very dull.'

'You prefer the Continentals?' Calvin was sarcastic.

'I do indeed. Far more cultured and far more intellectual. How I prefer them!'

'And when have you discussed political theory with them?' Calvin sounded angry. 'I'll bet never. And if you did you'd get a shock. The truth is Mrs Mellor you Fabians regard abstract economics as a waste of time. You're all a bit "pukka" you know—that's what you are.'

Silence.

'Aunt,' asked Lady Cleeve in her slyest tone, 'what original ideas has the Society had?'

'I beg your pardon! Pukka indeed!'

'What ideas has the Society had of its own, Aunt?'

'Ideas,' said the General, 'they've not got any ideas. That was the main trouble.' He rose, he refilled his brandy glass: 'None of the commanders had any ideas . . . that was the whole damned trouble. Couldn't find any way around it do you see. It's all very well to talk now.' He returned to his place at the head of the table, he drank, he rested on his elbows. 'Oh where are the bravest gone?' In the dining-room fireplace a damp log started singing: the General looked toward it as though it might answer his question. 'A quarter of a million men gone . . . in a place as big as Hyde Park. Forty shells a minute. It's done Colonel, pass on, nothing lives there any more.' He finished his brandy. 'When the grenades ran out the froggy *chasseurs* threw stones. Small shell blew off the Captain's right hand—Sergeant Major Wright used his boot-lace as a tourniquet. D'you know one day . . . there . . . after two days of it . . . I suddenly noticed . . . the damned sun was shining . . . must have been shining all along . . . it was . . . I read it later in the gazette . . . and in dead letters: "Dear Mother . . . the sun is shining here today." I saw with my glasses German Pioneers cleaning out with their flame throwers a trench still occupied by one of my forward companies . . . I saw that myself . . . methodically. I saw a young blond man, excellent health, glowing with it, well shaven, clean uniform, and drawing on a cigar. Probably a Dutch cigar. None of the Generals had any ideas you see.'

'Vicar,' Mrs Mellor began to knock the ashes out of her pipe, 'you mustn't overstate your case.'

'You lost your fellow there didn't you?' asked the General abruptly.

'Hill 60,' said Mrs Mellor.

'That's what I mean,' said the General. 'That's *where* I mean. Do you still miss him?'

'I've learned not to.'

'Ah. But you do miss him. *I* see you do.'

'I've learned not to,' said Mrs Mellor firmly.

'So you say,' muttered the General. 'So you would have us believe.' He rose again with his glass. 'Bled the nations to death.' Without warning he hurled his brandy glass into the fireplace. 'That's what we used to do,' he said. 'In the chateaux. Human lives were . . . corpuscles. But what else? Couldn't see any other way. Here. Let's go to the library. Break the bloody spell. Coffee!' He turned and pointed at Calvin. '*You!*' he said. 'You understand. You understand because you were there. By the way . . .' his voice became wheedling, 'by the way did you ever kill a man yourself . . . face to face . . . you know what I mean?'

There was a long pause.

'Yes,' said Calvin.

'Ah . . . ah. I never did you see. Never in my life. Not in my whole . . . career.'

'Well . . . I had to,' said Calvin. 'Only once. One of ours.'

'Come in,' he said sitting up on the bed.

'You were lying down.'

'Just for a minute.'

She went towards the open window, he noticed how thin she was.

'Don't shut it.'

'You'll catch cold. It's damp here.'

'Mother I like it open.'

'I must get your curtains up tomorrow. People can see in.'

'Only if they're in the garden.'

'Well they might be.' Richard laughed. 'People are very strange you know,' she said fiercely. 'Peeping Toms are everywhere.' She held her oil lamp close to the wall by his dressing table: 'There you see, there, it is damp.'

'I hate this wall-paper. Can I paint it over?'

'What colour?'

'White.'

'Why do you hate it?'

'But it's so hideous.'

'Oh I see. You couldn't paint it over. It would have to be stripped.' She came towards the bed. 'I've got a carpet in mind for you.'

'You look like Florence Nightingale with that lamp.'

'After night duty no doubt.' And she smiled. 'You didn't bring me my tea.' The smile vanished as briefly as it had come.

'I'm sorry I forgot. Shall I get it now?'

'No. I made some myself. You didn't put the dishes away.'

'I'll do it now.'

'I've done it for you.' She went to his mirror, she straightened it. 'I was a very beautiful woman once.'

Quiet, but not for long: a board creaked in the uncarpeted floor; an owl hooted; somewhere Eileen began to sing and then, stopped. Looking up into his mother's face—framed though it was by soft light—he felt again that he was being drawn into the unknown—there was an avidity in her gaze. She came closer and it was then that he realized she had been drinking. Apart from funerals, birthdays, marriages, he did not think that she had ever taken a drink in her life.

'Eileen told me she'd broken a plate but I knew who it was and I told them so. I knew immediately from her tone.'

'How clever of you Mother.'

144

'There's no need to be unkind.'

'Well I don't usually say things like that.'

'Tonight I make you?'

'Yes,' he answered, surprised.

'I've lit a fire in my parlour and I've got us some tea there. Will you have some with me? Please.'

'Yes, I'd like to.'

She nodded her head in relief. 'I sent them both to bed.' She turned and went to the door. It was at the door, with her back towards him that he thought he heard her whisper: 'She's not my child.'

'What?' he asked. She neither turned back nor answered. He got up and followed and all the way along the bare corridor he wondered if he could have heard right.

Going down the stairs he was conscious of the size and strangeness of the house. 'Will we ever be able to afford carpets?' he thought. Below him, as if in answer, Mrs Calvin said: 'We'll never be able to afford proper carpets.'

At the top of the stairs he saw that she had placed a vase of flowers on a chair, and that the lamp she carried so unsteadily, having a discoloured glass, threw out patterns of light which eddied and washed down the hall like a wave and when they reached the front door seemed to be blown back by the draught.

Letting him pass, as they entered the warm parlour, she closed the door behind them. 'Sit down, Richard.' She went to her desk, took a key from her apron pocket, unlocked the desk, opened a drawer, pulled out a silver cigarette case and offering the case, asked: 'Would you like to smoke?'

He looked at her in astonishment: 'You know I never smoke.'

'You're old enough. Don't you smoke on your own?'

'No.'

'Not at school?'

'No.'

'I'm sure the other boys at Bolton did.'

'Of course some of them did. I didn't. You know that.'

'I don't know what I know,' she said. 'I'm not sure I know anything.' She laughed.

'She's so strange,' thought Richard, 'she must be drunk I suppose.'

'This was your grandfather's,' she said, holding the cigarette-case up to the light. 'He was a wonderful man—but you know *that*.'

There was a long, long pause. She made no move to pour him some tea, which he now supposed to be cold. He would have loved to have gone to his bed.

She lit herself a cigarette, and stared into the fire. Silence. She turned to him, half smiled, turned away again. Silence.

He sat up in his chair as if to go: 'Mother,' he began, 'I . . .'

'I've always wanted to talk freely to someone,' she interrupted. 'I never have. You're the only one. I might manage it with you. If I keep trying.' Again she glanced at him, again she looked back at the fire. 'If it were possible I would talk to you entirely freely . . . I don't suppose it is. If I could, I would present my life, I would say take this, throw it away, leave it, or . . . or restore it, yes, restore it . . . as you please. But take it. For you love me. You could be the Judge. Take my life for it is yours to judge. But I can't do that.'

Not only had he never heard his mother speak like this before, he had never supposed that she could.

'Unfortunately I do not believe in God like your father. Not even in a life force. I don't believe in anything. Not *believe*. I like some things. Some people. I love some people . . . in a way. There is no purpose to life, I know that. I have known it for a long time. People who believe otherwise deceive themselves. That is natural. I've kept this from your father for his sake, and from you children for your sakes. I've hidden this like an illness. I put flowers in your father's church . . . that's just because of him. I did believe in God once. It faded.'

'Life is good though,' said the boy.

'You know nothing of it. Naturally it can be pleasant. On the whole it is too cruel for the ordinary person. And too difficult. At least we have enough to eat. And when you're old it is horrible. I am very ambitious for you. Should I have brought you into the world—I often ask myself that.' Richard resented this remark.

'But you're not old Mother,' was what he said.

'Don't you think so? I do. I know I am. If you don't care whether you live or die you're old. I don't even feel *that* strongly.'

'I expect you're just a bit tired.'

'Have you been into the town?'

'Yes.'

'Have you noticed how dull it is? Those porches, those lace curtains in the windows, those clothes, those stupid women shopping with their stupid faces, those stupid old men wandering all over the pavements but so carefully crossing the road . . .'

'Yes?'

'And any moment a brick could fall on to their heads or a car drive right up the pavement and run them down?'

'Would you like that?' he asked curiously.

'Yes. I think I would,' she answered. She turned to him and her eyes gleamed. 'Yes, I know I would.'

'Oh, you're just in a mood, Mother.' He was shocked. 'It's better than Houghton.'

'What could be worse! They're not people there. They're animals. Think of Houghton on a Saturday night.'

'But where would you like to live?'

'Somewhere hot. In Italy. Yes Italy.'

'But Mother, if you think all these things are drab like you say why do you furnish our house like you do and dress like you do?'

'If I didn't it wouldn't be furnished at all.'

'If you had a lot of money would you change it?'

'Of course I would.'

'Is it money that worries you then?'

'Of course.' She shrugged her shoulders, added: 'And everything else.'

'What else?'

'We can't turn over a picture book like we used to and point to cows and horses.'

Somewhere above the sound of Eileen singing again, then bath-water running away.

'I hope she hasn't used all the hot water,' said Mrs Calvin. 'In the beginning there was a nursery . . . everything else has been an . . .'

'Illusion?'

'If you like. Worse than that. Yes. You see me thin, tired, grey, middle-aged, wasted. You see me get the meals. Hear me rebuke you. I come in, I go out. You don't know at all what I was.'

'Or might have been,' he suggested, bravely.

'Oh who knows about that,' she said with indifference. 'I can't even tell you what I was. I don't know anything about it. Nobody knows. Your father doesn't know. The doctors don't know.'

'Doctors?'

'I'm always asking doctors. Doctors don't know anything.'

'Asking them what though?'

'Don't you understand?'

'No.'

'Your father just pities me or desires me . . . nothing in between. Asking them why I'm so unhappy I suppose.'

'And what do they say?' he managed.

'They say they don't know.'

Tears had come into the boy's eyes.

'They always say they don't know . . . whether they're young or old. One of them told me to have a drink now and again. I never have.'

He made a move to go to her. She turned and said with authority: 'No, sit where you are.'

A large white moth fluttered on to the window, beat in vain trying to enter, then stayed where it was, peering in at them. 'A spy,' smiled Mrs Calvin. 'One of God's creatures. All mothers want to be queens. Naturally. I would tie you to me if I could. After all I appeal to your conscience . . . will you

148

abandon me who have suffered so much?' She smiled again. 'Poor little white moth,' she said, 'who will soon be dead. If only I could offer, could stand for some ideal, for you.'

The moth slid down the pane, fluttered up it, slid down again on to the wood. Richard longed for it to disappear. 'Isn't it pathetic,' smiled Mrs Calvin, 'it has only itself to blame—or is that unfair?'

'Unfair,' said the boy, irritated.

'You must not think that it's your father's fault. Your father's very good to me. He's not often . . . difficult. Not now. I've been like this with *him* for years.'

'Like what Mother?'

'Like I am with you.'

'What!'

'Well don't you know what I mean?'

'Of course I don't.'

'I know you do.'

'But I don't Mother!' He had almost shouted. 'I don't know what on earth you're talking about.'

Exhausted, the moth dropped out of sight.

'I'm mad you see,' she said smiling. 'There, the moth's gone. I'm mad but no one will admit it. There's a lot of mental illness in England . . . I've seen it everywhere. Even before I was married. Especially women of my age. But nobody admits it. Least of all the doctors. They don't understand women you see.' Carefully she carried her cigarette to the hearth and shook the ash into the fire. 'I've no other reason to be like this. Your father loves me you know. I can't let him . . . your father . . .'

'Oh God,' prayed the boy, 'please don't let her tell me any more.' He wanted to put his hands over his ears. He wanted to be alone.

'The other day in his church,' she said, 'it was morning, the first morning, the sun was shining in at all the windows, all of them . . . imagine that . . . and even there, even there . . .' her face contorted with pain. 'He ran down the aisle to me and he kissed me . . . he held me so hard . . . he's so strong . . . he doesn't seem to know how strong . . . so rough . . . do you think . . . do you think?'

'What?'

'He'll ever give up worrying over me?'

The boy gasped with relief. 'No,' he said. Then, 'No I'm sure he won't,' he added. He took a breath: 'Mother, why are you telling me all this tonight?'

'It's this place,' she answered straightaway, 'I'm going to lose him here.'

'Why?'

'I wish we'd never come.'

'Why?'

'You're going to lose him too.'

She came back from the fire.

'You'll never lose *me*,' said the boy.

'Thank you very much,' she said. 'Thank you my son.'

Silence.

'I hated Houghton,' said Mrs Calvin. 'I wish I could explain. Everything I've said is lies—I mean I make it too important.'

Perhaps she *is* mad, thought the boy.

'I do wish my father wasn't dead.'

'What was *your* mother like?'

'I can't remember her.' Mrs Calvin was irritated. 'I can't have any more children. I can't.'

The boy sighed. 'We're beginning again,' he thought.

'Does Dad want to then?'

'Oh he'd have a house full. It's easy for him.'

'Aren't we enough for him?' Richard sounded wistful.

'Nothing's enough for your father. He'd . . . he'd like . . . he doesn't know what we women go through. Your father would . . .'

When she paused he was grateful because he knew that he didn't want to hear what she was going to say.

'Would you like another drink Mother?'

'What do you mean "another" drink?'

'What I say.'

'I haven't been drinking.'

150

'Don't be silly Mother, I know you have.' He pointed to the sherry bottle and the glass on the desk.

'Don't speak to me like that. I never drink.'

'As you please, Mother.'

'You can ask anyone.'

'And now,' thought Richard, 'she's like a child.'

The boy began to nerve himself to the question that had been driven from his head and which he wanted most to ask. He didn't know if he should. He got up and he walked to the fireplace—her father's photograph was still missing.

'Where's Grandad's wedding photo?'

'In my room.'

Then he frowned and almost without his determining it, out came the question: 'Did you have a bad time when Betty was born?'

'Terrible. It is terrible. A man can't understand. No man ever feels pain like that.'

'How do you know,' said the boy suddenly going white and angry, 'how do you know what a man feels? Did you ever have a bayonet in your guts in the war?'

Mrs Calvin was taken aback. Silence.

'Was it bad with me too?' the boy asked quietly.

'Yes.'

'And Leeny?'

'Yes. I had no anaesthetic. They wouldn't give me anything.'

'But it was the worst with Betty?'

She did not reply.

'But Mother it was worst with Betty?' he insisted. Still no answer. 'Mother!' he shouted.

'She's not my child,' she screamed at him. 'Don't you understand. She's not my child.'

He was so shocked he felt as if she had slapped him. He stood trying to recover himself, and understand, when she screamed at him again. 'And shut that drawer!' 'What?' he asked stupidly. 'Shut that drawer!' Confused he looked down at the desk beside him, where indeed a little drawer was open.

Vaguely he noticed that in this little drawer was a single folded piece of paper, perhaps a letter. 'Shut it quickly!' He did so. Then the desk itself. He was looking at her, mystified and frightened, when she did what she had refrained from doing all evening, she ran to him and embraced him crying out: 'My son, my son.'

Chapter 7

THE needle fell back from the regulator; up the rise the lorry strained, grumbled and shook. The vibration from the tank sent pins and needles into her bones, she changed position, rested her left arm on the old man's shoulder. In his sleep in the passenger seat the old man smiled but did not let go of his flag—one end poking out of the window. The driver glanced at her sympathetically, pulled his muffler higher on his neck.

'I wonder you never doze off having to gg . . . go along so slowly and always the same. All alone too.'

'Ah.'

'It's like being in a ship. In the dark it is. And the headlights searching everything out. It's awful when you rr . . . run over a rrabbit. I didn't know you could do that. You mm . . . mmust have seen some ff . . . ff . . . funny sights on your journeys.'

'What!'

'You must have seen some ff . . . ffunny sights.'

'I've seen a dead man,' said the driver.

The draught from the open window blew stronger on her neck as they left the rise and descended. 'Really,' she thought, 'Mister Rockingham might have put the flag in the back, it would have been safe enough.' 'You must like a bit of company.' 'What?' 'You must like a bb . . . bit of company.'

'Ah.'

'He thinks I'm a chatter-box,' she decided.

'You notice I'm driving in the middle of the road . . . giving the branches a wide berth . . . because of the flag you know.'

'That's very good of you,' she said brightening up.

'It wouldn't do for the flag to catch a branch.'

'No I see that.'

'It might break it you know. Or break the window glass.'

'Yes.'

'It would give him a start if it caught a branch.'

'Yes.'

'It would wake him up, the old man.'

'Yes.'

'If anything big comes toward us and there are branches that side I'll slow down.'

'Yes.'

'Or a hedge.'

'Yes.'

'If it caught in a hedge this end might come back and crack you across your head you know.'

'Yes I *do* know that.' And she looked nervously down at the furled end between the old man's knees.

The moon broke through cloud, shone into the valley below. Solid, heavy and framed by stone hedges the little forest looked to Jean like the painting of an old landscape artist she'd seen in the museum in Bolton. It lay there dark, enclosed, primitive —as forbidding as her past. She wished that the road would turn aside, and not enter, but it did. In the forest it sounded as if all the trees were ticking like clocks.

'This was where I saw the starving dead man,' said the driver.

'Oh,' gasped Jean. 'Oh. Well I'm not surprised.'

'Just joking,' said the driver. 'Here,' he said, handing over a paper bag, 'eat this.'

'Oh I can't,' she exclaimed when she saw the sandwich inside.

'I've no call for it,' the driver assured her. 'I'd be pleased. Eat it or it'll only waste.'

She didn't believe him but she was so hungry she couldn't refuse. 'You are kind,' she said.

They left the forest, rolled on through fields. The fields disappeared, the beams of light, contained by tall hedges, became one. They passed through a stone village. They entered a pool of mist. More fields, more mist.

'That was good,' she said, folding up the paper bag neatly.

'Here,' said the driver. He took the bag, threw it out of the window.

They passed through another village with laughing and singing in a public house. 'The Red Lion,' said the driver. 'Good beer.'

'The countryside's not so interesting now.'

'What is that flag of your father's?'

'The Union Jack.'

'Ah. The Union Jack. He carries it with him does he?'

'Everywhere. Everywhere he goes.'

'He hangs on to it tight.'

'He does.'

'He must have been a flag bearer in the war.'

'No he was too old for that.'

'Well he must have been a flag bearer in something,' said the driver with certainty.

The regulated lorry groaned on and on and on. Confined, and so slowly moving, aching all over from that climb, her past slipped out of the window and fled down the dark road in front: she felt her dead mother's power. Supposing she were to walk through the back door with her baby boy, her Ian, and there would be her dead father in his tub by the fire, and her mother would come out of the scullery and say: 'Hello Jeanny, home for Christmas are we, and whose bab is that you're minding then?' 'It's mine,' cried Jean with a start, her hands going to her stomach.

'Ah,' said the driver, 'so it is. There's no denying that. You've been dreaming you know. Your mam's dead then?'

'Yes.'

'And your dad?'

'Yes.'

'Ah. I've got four wee ones myself and another in the oven.'

'Have you?' Jean was delighted. 'Tell me about them.'

And he did. All the way to Norwich.

A mile or so out of the city the driver asked Jean to wake Mister Rockingham. 'I shall be going off presently to Diss and to Stowmarket,' he said, 'that isn't your way. It's best you find somewhere to kip in here. It's a big town with good sensible folk . . . you'll find that.'

155

'Thank you,' said Rockingham. 'Did I drift off?'

'Drift off! You sank Mister Rockingham.'

'Well you've got to take advantage at my age. Oh I'm stiff now though. Is your behind cold on the tank?'

'It is a bit.'

'Have you been having a good chat?'

'We have.'

'She is chatty isn't she?' Rockingham spoke to the driver.

'No worse than the wife.'

They came to traffic lights, passed a shop. At a cross-road Rockingham started and shouted out: 'Hey thank you, could you stop here.'

The driver looked into his mirror, pulled up.

'I've seen a face I know do you see driver. Here's a fellow will tell us exactly where to kip.'

The old man opened the door, held out his flag and descended. Mystified, Jean followed. Looking back up the road she realized that the 'face' was the screever's.

'Oh let's not ask him,' she said with alarm.

'But he'll know.'

'Oh let's not have anything to do with him.'

'No?'

'He gives me a prem . . . a premonition, Mister Rockingham.'

Recognizing his benefactor under the lamp the screever cried in delight and came hurrying towards them: 'Hello there you the generous old chap with the moustache and you the young missis. Here I am. And what can we do for each other on a cold dark night?'

'Drive on then,' said Jean, resigned and embarrassed, 'drive on and thank you.'

'Thanks very much,' said Rockingham, worried now.

'Ah,' the driver shut the door. 'Good luck. And good luck with your baby.'

The driver wound up the window; the screever was almost upon them. As the lorry rolled off Jean turned her back to the screever and watched it and waved: although she knew this gesture was a useless one in the darkness, she made it because she felt so stranded, so 'turned out on the street'.

But the screever was on them, holding out both hands in greeting, grinning all over his face: 'Well, well, well.'

'Do you know where we might spend the night?'

'The very place. We're almost at it. What a stroke of luck for you you met me. I'll take you there at once.'

'I saw you from the lorry.' Rockingham spoke apologetically.

'Did you? Did you? You've got sharp eyes in your old grey head. And how's the lovely young missis.' He put his hand on Jean's wrist to turn her round. She did turn. She turned. 'Take your hand off me,' she whispered in a voice the old man had not heard. 'Take your hand off me,' she whispered, 'and never, never touch me again. Not as long as you live.'

The old man saw that the screever smiled.

A minute later they still stood there. The screever kept smiling. He was slighted, he implied, but he was enduring. He did not seem to wish to proceed. He simply stood there smiling.

When Jean shivered, dropped her gaze, and turned her head from the screever—as if he slipped out from underneath stones—the old man tucked his arm into hers, placed himself between the pair of them, and demanded: 'Where to Welshman?'

'Is it best?'

'I believe when the ladies are with child they are often frail,' said Rockingham. 'I have heard that. Don't be a dog. Forgive the lass. Come.'

'Am I not worthy?'

'How do I know!' Rockingham laughed so naturally that the screever laughed also, and even Jean was forced to a smile.

'I remember a church,' said the screever, 'it is a church I have in mind. I'll lay on but it's a way yet. It's almost supper. You said you were a religious. It's soup for supper and sing to the Lord for it. Shall I carry your pole?'

'That's no pole.'

'A flag is it?'

'Aye.'

'Shall I carry your flag?'

'No. No you may not.'

'Am I not worthy?'

'That's to be seen,' said the old man but this time there wasn't the ghost of a smile. They set off.

They walked in silence, at a good pace—the screever slightly ahead—towards the centre of the city. They walked in silence for a quarter of a mile.

A damp mist gathered about their bare heads. Their hair silvered, was picked out by lamplight as they passed beneath. Lamplight, silver and darkness. Gloom, dejection and muffled echoes.

'Welshman what do you mean by a church exactly?'

'You'll see if you wait the turn.'

'He'd cut our throats for a sixpence,' thought Jean.

Occasionally, where the mist was thicker, someone, going away, on the other side, passed them like a boat.

'It's his fault,' thought Jean. 'I know it is.' And Rockingham thought, 'Ah well, women, they do lack tolerance.' And the screever thought 'I'll do that bloody girl one day and I hope I can find this fucking church.'

Here the mist was a fog. No one passed them on their side . . . only the other. The light here shone up and not down, the posts twisted. They peered and strained. They felt their way through a battlefield. All was scarred. Shells had fallen here. 'What part of Norwich is this?' wondered Jean.

Here it was lighter because of the windows. Now they walked in ancient and narrow places with houses as cracked as walnuts. Not so much mist. Not so much fog. Nothing was open here. Nothing. All was confined. Jean had to push out her arms to ward off these baleful little houses wanting to fall in upon her like tombs. But here it was surprisingly mild. She sweated. Only her feet were cold.

In the alleyway Jean went second. She didn't like that.

From the alleyway they crossed a tiny square built by madmen, and all present, behind the shutters, ready to spring. So

Jean had to speak: 'I think this walk is awful. I think they're all going to fly out and set our clothes alight.'

'It's not up to much,' agreed Rockingham.

'It's not far, it's not far now,' reassured the screever. And Jean *was* reassured at the sounds of their voices. 'It is different in the light,' said the screever. 'It ain't so bad in the light. It's curious here tonight.'

More squares. Occasionally, very occasionally, an old clerk remained at work behind uncurtained windows and he would straighten and look out and listen as they passed and seemed to Jean to be making a plan. 'They'll be telling of us, they'll be beating drums beneath those cabinets. Please speak,' said Jean.

The screever said: 'We go between the black cathedral and the black castle and we're there. This is not, you will have seen, a place to make your fortune, oh no. This place is bloody ancient. This is an old hole. This isn't no parvenu upstart nouveau rich of a place. This is bloody dignified. This thinks it's a bloody capital—the capital of the east. East bloody Anglia—this thinks the sun shines out of its ancient eastern arsehole.'

'Have we seen the best of it?' asked the old man.

'Course we bloody have.'

'You know Welshman,' said Rockingham seriously, 'some can swear and some can't.'

'I beg your bloody pardon.'

'Some can take a word and make you sick,' said the old man, 'with themselves, with their tone alone they can do it. Yourself for instance.'

'So?'

'I just say that . . . as a warning.'

'Like "fucking",' exclaimed the screever, grinning in the darkness.

Whack went the end of the flag pole across the screever's ear: he staggered, he knelt down howling.

'Pick yourself up,' said Rockingham, 'or I'll do it for you.'

'You meant to do that,' cried the screever, 'you were ready for it.'

'I meant and you meant,' said the old man. 'And I was ready.'

'Come now,' said Rockingham. 'We'll proceed.'

Much comforted by this incident Jean walked to the church with lighter steps. Rockingham was thinking 'If he's no coward he must be waiting his turn.' The screever, for the moment, was too pained, too surprised, to think at all.

'Now just you get into bed and I'll go down and get us some tea.' He looked away from her father's photograph.

'Yes, that'll be nice.'

'You'll sleep better then.'

'Oh I won't sleep. Not till your father comes home.'

She sat herself on the bed. Taking his hand from her shoulder Richard went to the door.

'You wouldn't ever abandon me would you? I know children do. One suffers so much for one's children.'

'And then they suffer for theirs,' answered the boy, reaching for the door handle.

'You are part of my body,' said Mrs Calvin in a dazed tone.

'You're tired Mam. Make ready for your bed. Why not have a hot bath while I'm getting the tea.'

'I'll hate it when you go away. I'll hate that.'

'Perhaps I'm going to hate growing up,' he replied, sounding as tired as his mother.

'You look exhausted. You're exhausted.'

'Mother I must get the tea.' Richard nerved himself, and went out.

He had descended those creaking stairs into the kitchen and was putting the kettle on the stove when he felt hands over his eyes and he jumped.

'Don't do that again. I nearly punched you.'

'I've got bare feet,' laughed Eileen. 'Hey Ricky, hey she's having a bath!'

'Mother?'

'Yes. And I heard it all.'

'All?' he asked, disbelieving.

'All Ricky.'

'Were you outside the door?'

'No, no, no. In my bedroom. You can't help hearing up there. You can hear everything!'

'Really?'

'Yes. Everything. There's no carpets you see and it comes up by the water pipe.'

'Well. You shouldn't have listened.'

'I couldn't help it you fool.'

'You shouldn't have listened,' he repeated. But he almost smiled. Then he did smile, and warming his back against the stove, he asked: 'Hey Leeny what do you make of it?'

'Well,' she said, 'well, well, well.'

'Be serious Leeny, it's no joke.'

Eileen giggled.

'She's our mam Leeny. Please.'

'She's mad,' said Eileen. 'That's what my old boy. She's a case. She's a Doctor Crippen.'

'Please Leeny.'

'Well,' said Eileen. 'what did she mean when she said "she's not my child"?'

'I don't know.' He frowned. 'I just don't know. Bet looks just like her don't you think?'

'I think she looks more like Mam than either of us,' said Eileen, 'that's what I think.'

'Keep your voice down Leeny.'

They both looked up.

'I think we're all right here,' whispered Eileen, 'it's just that pipe.'

'Well just in case.' There was a pause while they looked at each other.

'You'll have to tell her.'

'What!'

'I mean you'll have to tell her you can hear things up there.'

'I shall not. Not in this world.' She burst out laughing. 'My son, my son,' she cried and hugged him.

'Get off me,' said Richard. 'You're cruel. Don't mock or I'll give you a jolly good punch.'

'Just you try it.'

'Well don't mock, it's not fair.'

'You punch me and you'll get one right back. Still . . . still you're quite right,' she agreed. 'I mustn't mock.'

Again they looked at each other in silence, and Richard was comforted.

'But it's awful for Bet you know.'

'I do know,' agreed Richard, not liking to add that he too had been eavesdropping. 'Yes I do know.'

'She feels it. She told me.'

'Richard! Richard!'

The children froze.

'Richard dear I'm ready for my tea.'

'For God's sake say something,' whispered Eileen.

'Just coming Mother,' the boy shouted, 'the kettle's on the boil.'

They had almost reached their church. The climb had so tired them that they paused for a moment at the top of the steps, and turned to look down at the lights.

The screever said : 'Well they sicken me these people, they want their own stinking parliament.'

'Do they?' asked the old man, 'why not, if they're solid? Aren't you for the people then?'

'I'm in favour of centralization.'

'Centralization.'

'That's what I'm in favour of.'

'Why?'

The screever waved out his arms over the city : 'I don't trust such fools as these.'

'I don't suppose they're worse fools,' said the old man mildly. 'I can't say as I'm in favour of centralization myself. I do believe the evils outweigh the advantage. They've too much to do in the bloody Commons as it is.'

'No swearing,' said the screever, delighted.

'Oh I don't mind "bloody",' said the old man. 'That's fair enough. It's only Catholics don't like that. And we're not Catholic are we—so that doesn't offend.'

'No, we're not bloody Catholic,' said the screever after a pause.

'I mean you understood me didn't you?' asked the old man.

'Only too well,' answered the screever. They breathed deep, they sighed, they set off once again—through the graveyard.

It was only when they had turned the corner by the newest of white marbles that Jean saw with surprise that there was a large queue—a clothes line of a queue; Rockingham too gave a start: a thin, a grotesque, a noisy file of bearded hungry men. And so pallid and stinking. Old boots and foot-rags.

'Did I smell like that when I first met Mister Rockingham,' Jean asked herself. 'Oh dear, did I?'

'Take your place,' said the screever, all smiles and left them to look for allies or friends or acquaintances. But he soon returned, shaking his head. 'There is none I am met with,' he told Rockingham, 'that is rare. Of course I'm not travelled in these parts. It's my second trip and last. It's lucky I remembered Friday night,' he grinned again, 'yes I remember it all right—doors open nine fifty-five.'

Now Jean could *see* that all were dirty and she the only woman. 'Why so late?' she inquired nervously.

'A whim of the Vicar's,' said the little Londoner in front of her, touching his forehead and smirking. 'He preaches better late.'

Rockingham asked: 'You know this place?'

'Supper and then the service.'

'Yes it's the service you'll *like*,' said the screever, grinning again.

'Will he?' the little tramp looked surprised.

'No beds?' asked Rockingham.

163

'There's a shed with a stove. Nothing for the judy though,' said the cockney.

'There isn't!' Jean was dismayed.

'None I know of.'

'Well supper first and then we'll ask Vicar,' said Rockingham.

'That'd be best. He won't allow her to skipper. Not when he sees her in the light. Oh he'll give her a deaner . . . no doubt of it.'

She was now so tired she went to sit on a gravestone while Rockingham and the screever kept her place in the queue. Although her head bowed forward on her knees, she did not sleep—her thoughts, her fears, the place and the smell were too much for that. She saw that the old man leaned against the wall of the church as if in support, and that the screever turned away from him, and constantly scanned the queue with quick furtive glances and smiles, as if in some kind of cheerful anticipation. Then her baby moved and she forgot the screever.

The clock struck the half hour; it struck the quarter. She rocked the cradle, she sang her son to his sleep.

Abstractedly the tramps laughed, whined, told stories, swore, stamped their feet, waved their arms, picked up pebbles from the path and threw them at the graves.

The doors opened, Rockingham called, she raised her head, rose stiffly and re-joined the queue.

A tall thin vicar with a pince-nez on the end of his nose, and three maiden daughters behind, ushered them up a stairway to the balcony at the top of the church. The warmth was truly a gift from God.

They crowded into the pews, they sat and waited their turn.

And in their turn the three daughters averted their eyes (but looked at Jean boldly), and served each with a one pound jam jar of tea, a half pound jam jar of soup, and a half a dozen slices of bread and margarine.

'Oh it is good Mmister Rockingham.'

'It is lass, it is.'

It was only after she had gulped down the soup, and felt it descend, and warm up her son, that she was able to relax, stretch and take notice. What she noticed first was that the screever had sat himself at the end of the row behind them and seemed to have worked himself into an even greater state of happiness; the screever kept rubbing his swollen ear—kept rubbing it like a charm. She forced herself to look away from the screever.

The church was no treasure house, no temple of eternal artistries, no cathedral of the beautiful. It was a depository of doctrine. Psalms bleated everywhere from its walls; so did texts of hell-fire and damnation. This church threatened and warned; it was a slaughterhouse for souls.

And its hymn book, thicker than the Bible itself, too heavy for a single hand, contained three and a half thousand— all of the worst. The largest collection on earth.

Jean shuddered: 'I expect this is the sort of church you like Mister Rockingham. You know that Welshman keeps looking funny at you.' 'Does he?' replied the old man serenely. 'No I can't say that this is one of my favourite spots. It's a bit plain.' 'It *is* plain Mister Rockingham. It's positively thread-bare.' 'Except for the exhortations.' 'Yes except for them.' 'It don't give sinners much of a chance.' 'It don't Mister Rockingham.' 'Now drink your tea my dear before it gets cold,' said the old man.

As she drank she surveyed the congregation in the well below. They reminded her of a gathering of turkeys unfit for the table. There were few men, and the vicar the only young one, and as they waited for the supper to be over and the service to begin the ancient women would kneel in prayer and peer upwards through their rheumatic fingers in apprehension, in curiosity and in disgust. And sometimes they stood and stared boldly, stretching their necks, eyeballs popping, clucking their disapproval, gobbling the sight.

The moment the organ gave its first painful blast those who had stationed themselves near the gallery door ran through it.

And Jean was surprised that those also who had looked meekest, most reverent, and most grateful, disappeared. There were left what one might call 'the hard core'. Glancing from the door to the screever she saw that his eyes gleamed at their unholiest as he watched Mister Rockingham gazing down at the minister; and when he realized that Jean had noticed this delight the screever grinned at her. She was afraid.

The minister mounted his pulpit: the congregation stood. 'The Lord Will Provide.'

At the first words of the revivalist hymn, as if at a cue, the tramps in the gallery around her began a concert of their own. She who was not religious was shocked. They sniggered, they whispered blasphemies, they muttered obscenities.

When she turned to the old man he was gazing down as serenely as before. 'Well he can't be in a vision this time . . . no surely not,' she thought. And yet Mister Rockingham remained unperturbed.

Not unaware of the opposition from above, the worshippers sang louder. So did the tramps. They lit cigarettes, they shrieked out their blasphemies, they leaned over the balcony, threw pellets of paper, a toilet roll, a pair of underpants, and the rags from their feet.

Dismayed at Rockingham's composure the screever worked himself along to the seat behind and tapped the old man on the shoulder. As if he knew who it was Rockingham did not turn. Disconcerted the screever sat back in his pew. 'What does he want?' thought Jean, appalled. The screever leaned forward again: 'I thought you called yourself a religious,' he taunted. Rockingham did not turn.

The minister with the pince-nez was brave—he could not have been so deaf not to have heard the celebration above—the tramps were now making more noise than the organ—and when the organ ceased and the congregation sat and feebly cried: 'Hush' he looked straight up at the gallery and called: 'I shall pray for you up there, you the unrepentant, the unsaved sinners.' He had just begun: 'Brothers and Sisters . . .' when the screever scuttled along to the corner of his pew, stood up on the end of it, and screamed: 'This is Saint and Sister Agnes up here, is it true about you and the fucking organist?'

Such was the applause and jeering from above that the congregation ran into a huddle like hens and riding high on his triumph the Welshman pointed at Rockingham and cried: 'Hey he's a bloody religious, aren't you—taking our bread as can pay.' Silence in the gallery; in the well the minister calling for prayer. The screever said: 'Will you deny me thrice?'

Rockingham stood, above; below, they prayed.

Rockingham said: 'Gentlemen.' Then: 'Come here Welshman.'

Whether it was the look of him, or what he had said, or the way Mister Rockingham had said it, Jean didn't know but she did see those around the screever fall away and there the screever stood, cornered and still.

'Put down your bloody flag,' he screamed. 'And I'll give you one as'll bounce you into a pot full of piss.'

Rockingham put down the flag. 'Right,' said Rockingham.

Rockingham stood; the screever made little rushes along the pew, spat, screamed, abused, spat, retreated. He jumped up on the seat, advanced along that, spat, screamed, abused, spat and retreated. He kept on trying to nerve himself to get close enough to fight.

Below, they prayed. 'You're a cunt,' shouted the screever. 'I'll kick your balls in. You're the son of a fucking prostitute. You're a fucking bolshevik bastard.'

And then he was pushed.

There was a choice for the old man and he took his choice. He didn't flinch, and he didn't turn the other cheek. When the screever jabbed at him with the knife that had been thrust into the screever's hand, Rockingham took that jab on his left forearm, brought his clenched right fist down on top of the screever's head, put his knee into the screever's stomach as he fell forward, and surveyed him as he lay there.

Then Rockingham staggered, and fell back, held his arm, and picked up his flag—perhaps for support. The flag was raised with both hands. And he who had pushed and handed the screever the knife was stunned by the flag.

Rockingham said: 'I'll carry out my friend, you carry out yours. Let them below have quiet.'

Chapter 8

IN THE dark her room was fragrant with hawthorn blossom. She put her elbows on to the window-sill.

She felt very sorry for her mother but what could one make of such a person. She wondered if she should love her mother more and then dismissed the thought as meaningless.

Why did she say: 'She's not my child'? Could that possibly be so? Was Betty her father's child by another woman? 'No,' said Eileen aloud. 'Ridiculous.' Her mother must mean something else. What did her mother mean? All she had was her mother's incontrovertible statement: 'She's not my child.'

A breath of wind blew on her cheek. The fragrance of the hawthorn was carried into the room behind her and down the bare corridors to the rest of the house. Her eyes followed the slope of the garden to the tree. The tree, the wall, and the sky were indistinguishable but she knew how the tree stood there in its holiday dress. She had never seen anything lovelier than that pink hawthorn in bloom. She knelt above it thinking how much better she could see it because she could not see it, closing her eyes in darkness so as to have only the hawthorn before them, breathing deep, floating across the garden to perch in the blossom. In her mind there was not a single branch, not a part of one, uncovered with flowers.

There shone out on to the tool house a light from her mother's room. She can't sleep, Eileen realized, poor mother. She wondered whether her mother had ever said to her father: 'She's not my child.' She frowned. Of course she couldn't say that if Betty wasn't, because her father would know it, she would only say it if Betty *was*. She brooded over this paradoxical conclusion, which somehow she knew to be correct.

The light from her mother's room growing stronger—her mother must have turned up the oil lamp, or lit another candle—Eileen was allowed a glimpse of the white hawthorn beyond the shed and in this soft light it did not look real—it looked as if it were swaddled in paper lace. She gazed back again into the darkness at the pink.

It was now she remembered the insistence of her mother's tone when her mother had shouted at Richard to shut the desk. Eileen took her elbows off the sill. It had occurred to her also that her mother always kept that desk locked. Was there anything private in that desk? 'She's not my child.'

She got down off her bed, tiptoed to her door, opened it to see if Richard's light was on—it wasn't. She could hardly wake him up. She would have to wait till morning.

She thought: 'Surely he would have said if there was anything hidden there'—but then it wouldn't have occurred to him, not Richard. Besides, this wasn't the point . . . because the way her mother had shouted, there must be *something* in that desk.

She knew where the key was. The key was in the pocket of her mother's apron, with all the new keys, and the apron was hanging, where her mother had left it after putting the supper dishes away, on the back of the kitchen door.

But did she dare? And was it right?

Eileen smiled: she had appreciated how furious she would have been if anyone had looked inside her private desk. 'I wouldn't lock a desk though,' she said to herself by way of justification. 'I wouldn't have a private desk.'

'I can't resist it,' whispered Eileen.

On the landing by her mother's room she stopped: was her mother just lying there, or reading, or what? Would it be wisest to go and knock on her mother's door, tell her mother she couldn't sleep, ask her mother's permission to make a cup of Horlicks, ask whether her mother would care for a cup herself? And then of course when she was down there she'd take a good quick look.

She decided against this because she didn't want to face her mother.

Slowly, carefully, patiently she began to tiptoe down the landing towards her mother's door. Several times she was forced to stop and test the squeaking boards, and very soon she knew that she couldn't succeed. She thought, smiled, tip-toed back to the bathroom and pulled the lavatory chain.

Before the noisy old cistern had half-filled Eileen had flitted like a little moth across the landing, down the stairs, and was warming herself by the kitchen stove.

She warmed her bottom by the stove and foresaw the impossibility of lighting the gas in the parlour. A candle? Blow out a candle and it smells; and the smell lingers.

She went to the back door, unlocked it, went out into the yard, pulled the front battery lamp off her father's bicycle, re-turned, re-locked the door, realized that should her father return he would be entering through the front and therefore she should hear him in good time, took the bunch of keys from her mother's apron, shone the lamp, picked out the key that mattered, crossed the downstairs hall, entered her mother's parlour. She stood there for at least a minute in the open door, listening. Satisfied, she shut the door and went to the desk.

Here she hesitated. 'If people won't tell us how things really are,' she said to herself, 'then we have to find out don't we.' And yet she could not proceed.

The clock on the mantel struck the half hour and she jumped. As soon as she had recovered she looked at the desk.

She knew that the lower drawers of the desk were full of bills, receipts, business letters, church letters, and family photo-graphs. Therefore if 'anything' was to be found, it would be found in the top. 'Shut that drawer', her mother had shouted 'shut that drawer'—the drawer she was referring to must be one of those little ones, one of those pigeon-hole-sort-of-ones in the top.

She unlocked the top of the desk, pulled out the slots below, lowered the lid on to the slots.

She went back to the closed door, opened it, listened, closed it again, came back to the unlocked desk.

She switched on the bicycle lamp, sat herself down in her mother's writing chair and pulled out the top left-hand drawer. It contained lavender and a ribboned package of letters, addressed in her father's hand to Miss Hannah Duckworth, The School House, The Avenue, Houghton. She put down the lighted lamp on the desk and lifted out the package with both of her hands—she weighed the package in her hands. She held the package forward in the lamp-light. She sighed. The package was so neatly tied, it smelled so sweet, and the letters were so frail and so old and so often read.

'I always found sex very difficult Vicar . . . particularly abroad . . . naturally it's better there, in the heat. Some years I positively lusted after women . . . yes lusted . . . especially abroad . . . though I am fondest of English women . . . English and Scottish. Some years not at all! That's what puzzled me. Some years I didn't lust at all! Down by this lake on my chestnut . . . George here, my dog, bounding behind . . . bounding? More waddling really . . . inspired waddling . . . on the move, and when he's on the move I don't call him George I call him Dog.

'Dog on the move and me on the move and the chestnut really stretching . . . You know there were two cavalry charges in 1918 . . . two! People don't know that . . . both successful .. practised six weeks you see, saw it myself . . . galloped very fast, jumped right over the enemy trenches, threw back grenades from the other side . . . or in the air going over . . . infantry followed up quick of course. They didn't carry sabres you know Vicar . . . carried revolvers, rifles and grenades. Only trouble was some of them went into their haunches, into their stomachs . . . old shell holes . . . mud and that . . . some tripped on the wire . . . barbed wire. Down by this lake in the park with Dog and the chestnut and the vista. I thought of that . . . yes thought of it . . . that vista there . . . those beeches, those oaks, and that cedar and I said, galloping, I said: "This is our country Dog, this is England, and there's nothing like it!" ' The General uttered the most deprecating of laughs. 'I said aloud: "Dog there's nowhere like it." ' The General averted his eyes, leaned forward and patted his Labrador: the General had made his statement.

Calvin thought, but did not reply, 'General, that is not England and you are not England, or only a little little part of it, and you live on an unearned income, and what you stand for is rather smug.' He did not say it because he liked the General, because the General was an old man, and because he had hopes for the General—he had many hopes. There would be a better time for replying to the General.

Calvin looked at the clock on the mantelpiece: he wondered how Hannah was getting on; he ought to get back to Hannah. She had been so tired by the move; and then that first morning in the church when he had kissed her! 'I can't see anyone till I've got the house straight,' she had said. Surely people didn't mind if a house wasn't 'straight'; and so many ladies of the parish had expressed their desire to call. She hadn't decided on the daily help. 'Still that's up to Hannah,' thought Calvin, 'I'd best keep out of all that or it'll be worse. Dear Hannah, dear Hannah. It was awful when . . . when things . . . went wrong.'

Mrs Mellor cried, as though it were tea-time: 'Now Vicar you have escaped us too long. Let us bend our gaze upon you. Let us scrutinize you, dear Vicar.'

'Yes,' agreed Robert Andrews, enthusiastically. 'Let us.'

'You're welcome,' said Calvin quietly, still thinking of his wife.

'Ask him a question or two.' Lady Cleeve smiled at Robert Andrews.

'May I?' asked Andrews, not this time discomfited by Lady Cleeve.

But Calvin laughed at Lady Cleeve: 'It's quite good how you manage to vamp a young chap without being offensive.' And he winked at Robert Andrews to show his sympathy.

'She goes far,' said the General, peacefully. 'She'll catch a Tartar. If I sleep now take no notice. If I snore give me a dig and if my dog snores give him one. I believe he snores when I snore. I've been told that.' The General looked at his nephew.

'Perhaps we should all go home,' said Calvin, looking again at the clock.

'You're *always* misquoting, Uncle,' said Andrews.

'Can't go home until the fire goes out,' protested the General.

'Oh no indeed you can't Vicar,' agreed Mrs Mellor. 'We haven't scrutinized you. The night is yet young.' 'It's what we came for in the first place—your scrutinizing,' murmured Lady Cleeve.

'I beg you to stay until the fire goes out.' The General sank deeper into his chair. 'I'm closing my eyes but I'm listening.'

Everyone laughed, because they thought that in a moment the General would be fast asleep; they were wrong.

Robert Andrews said: 'I hope you will rebuke me if I am impertinent. I know I can sound offensive, not meaning to, and on this occasion I certainly do not.'

'Go on boy,' said Calvin, smiling, still thinking of Hannah.

'It's when I get excited . . . I expect you've been asked this many times: what is a vicar for?'

'Can I first say what I'm not for?'

'Yes of course if you will then say what you are for.'

'It's to give me time to clarify.' Calvin leaned forward, towards the boy. 'As a matter of fact I've never been asked before—not in so few words.' Abruptly the General sat up, waking his dog. 'Too interesting for sleep,' said the General. Lady Cleeve put down the cat; Mrs Mellor tapped out the ash from her pipe.

Calvin said: 'I am not a man without religious doubt. I am not a man preserved from temptation of the flesh—though, in fact, food and drink don't mean much to me.'

The General sighed. 'Would it not be true,' asked Mrs Mellor re-furbishing her pipe, eyes gleaming like her brooch, 'that while you contend with nearly every temptation we all of us meet, there are also reserved for you vicars, singled out, yes reserved I say, peculiar, devastating and insidious temptations as subtle as the Devil himself?'

'I think that's true,' answered Calvin.

'Ah,' murmured the General.

'Yes indeed,' exclaimed Robert Andrews.

'You'd like to investigate *that*, wouldn't you boy?' smiled Lady Cleeve.

'Do you believe in the Devil?' asked Andrews, not put out by Lady Cleeve—even perhaps flattered.

'Not exactly,' Calvin answered, 'not in two words. Let me answer your first question.'

'What do you mean: "not exactly"?'

'First questions first Robby,' barked the General.

'More of the Devil after. What's a parson for?'

'A parson,' said Calvin, 'like all, is a sinner. It is not his business to find fault. It is his business to find good.'

'If he finds good, isn't he finding fault?' Andrews frowned.

'I see distinction between "finding" and pointing out.'

'I take that,' agreed Andrews, relaxing again.

'He's not a man ordained from high to punish and rebuke into the continuing of what's traditional, he's not a man to enforce what he considers truth, but he is a man who wishes you to consider what he considers. He should offer what he has to offer respectfully. Offer it to those who feel like him that man . . .'

'Cannot live by bread alone,' interrupted Mrs Mellor triumphantly.

'Aye that's right,' said Calvin.

'Nor woman neither.' This from Lady Cleeve.

The General rose, re-filled all glasses, except Calvin's, who had waved his hand in refusal.

Calvin continued: 'A parson should not tell people they ought to come to his church, he should do his best to keep his church alive and make them want to come. He should keep his church alive for the people, and for himself. He should keep himself alive . . . alive to God. And he should get down on his knees every day and he should long to give men something good.'

'There are a few paradoxes here,' declared Robert Andrews.

'Paradoxes, old fond comforting paradoxes, paradoxes embodied,' said the General.

'But I hadn't finished.' Calvin bit on his tobacco. 'And I always find there are paradoxes.'

'You're one yourself dear Robert,' stated Lady Cleeve.

Calvin said: 'In the naval regulations it says my job is "to be the friend and adviser of all on board". I can't do it always —I'm not always asked to—I think it's much the best to be asked. Still I think that is a good definition of a parson. Whatever a man's work or anything else about him, outlook or belief a priest should want to stand by and lend hand and head.'

'What do men most want to hear at the end?' asked the General.

'Usually whatever gives them most comfort.'

'Ah.' The General sighed again. 'I see that. If a fellow's really evil Calvin—someone you wouldn't like at all . . .' the General grinned. 'Say a Fascist persecuting Mussolinean Eyetie Capitalist . . . say that . . . would you help such a fellow?'

'I'd love to.'

'Help or correct?' demanded Andrews. 'Or comfort?'

'Well *that* is the point,' answered Calvin seriously. 'I would mean to help.' He paused. 'You can draw a line.'

'But would you?' Andrews again.

'Maybe the fellow wouldn't be too bad on his own,' said the General.

'They're always better on their own,' agreed Calvin.

'Always?' asked Andrews.

'Well nearly always,' said Calvin.

Mrs Mellor demanded, puffing at her pipe: 'Have you finished with this question because I . . .'

'Excuse me, no I haven't,' said Calvin, 'I want to say more of what I am for—as Mr Andrews requested—I feel this: there's no job anywhere, at any time, a Vicar can't do for someone if he wants to serve as Christ served—it might be emptying a lavatory or digging a garden for an old man. A Vicar should warm up cold places. He should always be hopeful. He's part of crowds . . . not outside them. He's not a guide, he's a pilgrim. He's got to think and learn about Jesus every day—for his own sake and everyone else's. He should have the social evils around him on his conscience the whole time—he should shout out against them all the time. And not, never, compromise.'

'Even if no one comes to his church?' asked Lady Cleeve with a glint in her eye.

'Even then, even so,' said Calvin. 'It is better for a vicar to be called Bolshie than be mere upholder of Church and States. He must be unshockable, he must hate sin. He must love. He must remember how hard it is to be a Christian. He's not here to stop people being free. He must pray every day but there's no need to tell the world about it. He should be a good listener, he should find out about other people's jobs.' There was a pause. 'Well I don't know if I've answered your question Mr Andrews . . . I wouldn't do anything else. I wouldn't be anything else.'

'You're a militant Christian,' announced Mrs Mellor.

Calvin said: 'I respect theology—you've got to give reasons for your faith—but we in our Church are suffering from the academic. I don't think you've got to make obeisance to mere intellect. I don't look to theologians who don't move amongst people. And who always leave out Jesus Christ.' He paused. 'I hope,' he said. 'I myself hope to be a revolutionary priest . . . in the proper sense of the words.' He stood, and looking away from them all, added in the gravest of tones: 'The revolutions of the Rich over the Poor were very peaceable . . . not too much bloodshed . . . what was necessary . . . in the seventeenth and eighteenth centuries I mean. In the dictionary it doesn't say "revolution" means bloodshed, it says it means complete change. Reform means shoring up the capitalist system, revolution means having a new one. If a system is based on justice and generosity revolution is madness, if a system is based on injustice and greed revolution is necessary and is wise and proper.' He paused again, looked directly at each in turn as if expecting an interruption, and hearing none, continued: 'Even the Archbishop's report on industrial problems . . .

even his report, concludes that our present system is based on principles fundamentally opposed to those of Jesus Christ. We are not therefore to be reformists, we are to be revolutionaries.'

'You're a communist sir,' said the General slowly, 'I knew it . . . and I didn't know it, you're a Bolshie sir.'

'I knew it,' said Lady Cleeve, 'it is why I asked him to Eastwold.'

'I knew it,' said Mrs Mellor with a pleased look at her niece, 'what I don't know is where it will lead us in Eastwold.'

'You do not know where it will lead,' said the General, pointing at Lady Cleeve.

'She knows more than you think,' said Calvin.

'Does she,' snorted the General.

'I do,' replied Lady Cleeve with unexpected firmness and lack of affectation. 'I have thought about it a very great deal.'

'By yourself?'

'By myself. Who else is one to think with? He is a Christian Socialist.'

'He's a Red.'

'He is a Christian Socialist, General.'

'Terms,' said the General, 'terms! He's a Red.'

'The late Bishop of Oxford,' said Calvin, 'Charles Gore, speaking at Caxton Hall on February 1st, 1912 . . . did you know him General?'

'No,' answered the General, surprised, and therefore attentive.

'Gore,' said Calvin, 'Bishop of Oxford, General, quoted Christ's denouncing of the rich and blessing of the poor and stated: "I dare any one of you to say that this was not a revolutionary doctrine. It is only because we are so used to the sound of words that they can be uttered in any one of our congregations . . ." '

'How true,' murmured Robert Andrews appreciatively. 'How very very true.'

' "That they can be uttered in any one of our congregations," ' Calvin continued, smiling, ' "and not seem revolutionary doctrine, which we have got again to digest and make our own." ' Calvin walked towards the General and, surprising the others as before, fell into his crouch: 'General, there'll have to be a revolution and it can only be brought about peaceably if the vested interests will allow it. If blood is to flow you may take it the responsibility will rest with those who cry: "Shoot the miners; shoot the Irish; shoot the strikers." We don't want blood to flow. Do they? Do you?'

'We?' muttered the General.

'We. Are you rich, General?'

'No.'

'No invested capital?'

'Nothing to speak of.'

Robert Andrews laughed. So did Lady Cleeve.

'I have,' said Lady Cleeve. 'Or I couldn't support our Vicar'—Andrews laughed again.

'We'll come to that in time,' said Calvin, and though he smiled at Lady Cleeve he seemed to Andrews to mean it. 'Are you a Christian, General?'

'I begin to wonder.'

Robert Andrews laughed again for the third time, enjoying himself to his utmost.

'May I,' asked Calvin, rising and walking to the fire beside Lady Cleeve, 'quote you the Magnificat?'

She had not untied the love-letters from John Calvin to Hannah Duckworth. What had finally decided her against undoing that faded ribbon was the realization that the clue would not lie there—in fact could not lie there: she had seen by the light of her father's bicycle lamp that the postmark on the bottom and last-written letter—the letters being placed in chronological order—was January the seventh, nineteen hundred and eight, which was exactly one week before her parents' marriage.

Eileen's hands went to her head in the darkness—raised in bewilderment. She had sat here at this desk for a long time. She was still trying to puzzle out the implications of the information contained in the four documents enclosed in the

179

blank envelope in the centre drawer—the four documents
that were given a drawer all of their own.

Once again she switched on the bicycle lamp to shine it on
the contents of the blank envelope; once again she read.

'My dear dear, wife,
    I love you Hannah.

It is a beautiful summer night here and there is no breath
of wind. The night is spoilt only by the German gunfire
which has raged all day. Our guns have not fired so much
and are quiet just now.

Hannah I have made up my mind that when this dreadful
war ends I want to stay in the Church. I have thought about
this so long and so much. I am sure it will be managed
somehow. I have prayed and prayed for it. I only wish I
could have been a Chaplain out here. Hannah . . . I
stopped writing for a moment—all the German guns have
gone quiet. It is extraordinary, quite extraordinary, there
is silence, complete silence. It is frightening.

Hannah the silence is frightening.

I'll go on writing because I feel so frightened. Everyone
in the shelter is looking at each other. The soldiers are
fixing their bayonets.

I do wish I was with you for the baby. I hope and pray
so much it will not be as hard as it was with Ricky and
Leeny. I wish the doctors were able to make child birth
easier for women. Perhaps it is because they are men that
they haven't. Surely they could invent something that
would help.

It is still quiet.

I wish I could be with you throughout the birth but
doubtless this would not be permitted and perhaps you
yourself would rather be alone at such a time. Would you?
For a father it would be wonderful I think. At least I feel
it would for me. I wonder if it will be a boy or a girl. If it
is a girl what about your own name? What about Hannah?

Now our guns have begun battering. We cannot understand it—the German guns do not answer.

I can see out of the door of the shelter.

The Germans have not fired for five minutes.

The men around me are keeping looking at each other—
the officers seem very suspicious. Is it some sort of trap?

Oh Hannah I love you so much. Why does God permit this terrible war? Why? I am going to pray.

Hannah there is the strangest of sounds above—it is like flocks and flocks of birds coming from the East. Millions and millions of birds. I am going to have a look.

Hannah thousands of shells are passing overhead that don't burst. I am sorry I cannot write more about the children—I was going to—I think I'd better stop now. At first we thought the shells were duds but they are gas.

Your husband, John

P.S. I finished the letter later. Do not worry for me. I am all right. Everybody thought the shells were duds but it was gas. It was awful, Hannah, awful, awful. Hannah why couldn't these gas-makers just have made something to help you properly with your baby? Kiss our children for me. Oh Hannah, after this war.'

The girl sighed to herself, switched off the light and sat in the darkness, listening. The house was quiet but she could feel her heart beating. She had once overheard her father telling her grandfather about that gas: how the corpses had turned green, how he had lived for weeks in a smell that was a mixture of putrefaction and old vinegar. Yet she knew she herself could hardly imagine it. She wondered whether she would have wanted a husband to write to her at all, or like her father had done, write with some restraint. 'I would want to share it all,' she decided. 'Yes everything. A wife should share all.'

Eileen switched on the lamp again and picked up the second of her father's letters from France.

'My dear Hannah,

I cannot just understand Doctor Pullar's attitude—to refuse to give you an anaesthetic "in any circumstances"—did he *really say* that—strikes me as quite monstrous. As for his remark—which I have heard made before—that he opposes it on "moral grounds" because "we must not rob God of the deep earnest cries of women in labour" I have never felt so angry. Will you say to him that he is a healer not a moralist? It is not his profession to make those kind of judgements—nor anyone else's. I wish I could be there

181

to argue with him and help you. I expect though from what you write he is such a stubborn man he will not change. Please tell your father to take you to someone else immediately and find a younger doctor to give you a second opinion. Oh Hannah how upsetting that visit must have been—no wonder you felt so ill. Thank God you did not miscarry.

I have just spoken at length to a young doctor from Guy's Hospital who has just come into the line to help with the gassed survivors. He told me that soon there will be much more help for women in labour but that many general practitioners are still very unsure of giving drugs and are frightened to handle them. And he says many are against them altogether. He assures me that in your case, after such difficult births as you had before, that while your labour pains cannot safely be entirely eased there is a state that can be brought about for you called "twilight sleep"—I think the patient is injected with morphia in a syringe, and something else which I cannot spell. Please tell your father about this and seek out a new doctor. *Go to Manchester. This must not be a question of expense.*

Hannah this is not as you say, "God's fault". Hannah it cannot be. I know how upset you are. God knows, I know. Try to have faith. Please, please try. I find it so difficult to write about this—if only I could get leave. But I shall not desert. I will pray for you constantly. My dear think of our new child . . . please think of that. I know you didn't want to have another child but . . .'

Here Eileen shook her head and brushed back the hair that fell over her eyes—her father's handwriting had ceased as if he had grown desperate and no longer knew what comfort to offer. Further down the page he had begun again.

'If only I was with you to help.'

There was yet another space as if this time he had been called away for when the letter continued it was in pencil, faded and difficult to decipher.

'We have retreated and advanced, retreated and advanced. The guns were the biggest yet after the gas. The gas I wrote to you about killed everything. It killed the flowers, and the leaves on the trees all died. Even the snails and slugs and insects on the ground died. The only good thing was the flies died. Some of my friends carrying the stretchers just clutched at their throats and fell down.

I myself have been terribly lucky. It has been the worst yet. I won't write too much about it. I know how it upsets you. What was so terrible was that this gas they sent was too strong for most of the gas-masks and even those that worked like mine you could hardly do anything in, or breathe in right. It's called Green Cross Gas because of its shell markings. It's not right all this, Hannah.

I won't write any more now.

Good, good luck with our baby.

I love you Hannah.

God bless you.

Your husband, John'

As before the girl shook her head and sighed, put out the lamp to listen, switched it on again, and picked up the last letter.

'July the Seventh,
The School House,
Houghton.

My dear husband John,

I am still in the hospital but will be home at the School House when you receive this letter.

Your third child is a daughter. I have called her Elizabeth because I do not wish her to have my own name. The doctors refused to give me any anaesthetic. Doctor Pullar told me I was not a woman who needed one. Elizabeth's birth was the worst of all. The pain I suffered was indescribable.

I have not been able to write before. Elizabeth was born on June the 22nd. Aunt Alice brought Richard and Eileen to see me. Richard didn't like the hospital. Father was too poorly to bring them. I am too tired to write any more. There are several bills I cannot pay.

Your loving wife,
Hannah'

Eileen put down her mother's letter: she did remember going in on the train to Manchester; she remembered the smell of the hospital, the long corridors, her mother crying and talking all funny. She remembered the little Elizabeth like a tiny seal and so ugly. She remembered Aunt Alice who kept lifting her veil to make her kiss her. Eileen shivered.

'There are several bills I cannot pay,' whispered Eileen. And yet there was one bill her mother had paid. Eileen shone the lamp upon it. It was not a piece of fiction this faded receipt, this frail and folded piece of paper so carefully preserved, gazed on it seemed as often as the letters. This receipt read:

'127 Waterloo Place,
Manchester, 1915.
July 30th.

To Doctor Bernard Goldsmith
Anaesthetist
For Professional Services
Rendered to Mrs John Calvin
Fifteen Guineas
Received with thanks
With compliments
Anaesthesia given on June 22nd.'

Wearily, pensively, sadly, but carefully, Eileen put everything back into its accustomed place in her mother's desk. She locked the desk. She crept out of her mother's parlour, crossed the hall, the kitchen, and the scullery, re-fastened her father's bicycle lamp outside the back door, returned to warm herself by the kitchen fire. 'She's not my child,' she muttered again. Eileen was unable to understand. 'Should I say something to Dad somehow?' she wondered.

And then she yawned and had to start puzzling out how on earth she was going to get upstairs and safe into her bed again without her mother finding her out.

Lady Cleeve had left the fire and reclined now in an armchair facing the centre of the room. Dominate such a company she could not, enhance it she did. Lost in a haze of cigarette smoke, her dark blue dress spreading over the carpet like a cape, she sat there as serenely as the portrait of herself over the mantelshelf in her drawing-room at home in Eastwold

Manor. 'That Basque would make much of you, Lady Cleeve,' thought Robert Andrews, 'he would paint your bones.'

Looking at her closely while she listened to Calvin speaking of the Thirty Nine Articles, Robert Andrews received the impression that she was gathering herself for a serious speech—yes she seemed to him to be preparing some personal statement. 'How handsome she is,' thought Robert Andrews.

Sensing his regard Lady Cleeve inclined her proud head and gave him a quiet, a solemn, a quizzical glance. The boy half-smiled in return, returned his attention to his uncle.

The General said, 'Calvin if you will commit yourself to such a way of living, call it what you will . . . Christian, Christian Socialist, Bolshie or Red . . . and this mode of living you base on noble and generous behaviour you will find in the end that human nature does not alter, or alters so little as to be of no moment, and that the rules, the laws it obeys are evolutionary. These laws, these rules are not influenced by exhortation, even less by precept and example.' In his profound melancholy the General sniffed. 'Should you become Archbishop, John Calvin, you will find it impossible to make all your good ideals practical and workable. And what I fear for you sir is that when you realize this, *know* it rather than realize it, when you *know* this sir, you will not be the man you are now—for there will not be so much for you to live for. You see young Calvin . . . you see you are a man who needs a pattern.'

'You speak of the end of my life.'

'I do. The flame of life must have something fine to burn on.'

'But isn't the great thing to go on even when you've lost it? And anyway just to go on?'

'You're impossible, Calvin,' said the General.

Turning away from Calvin, shaking his head, sensing something of Lady Cleeve's moment of purpose, the General barked at her: 'Young woman what are *you* up to?'

Unmoved, Lady Cleeve sat as she was.

'I command you to tell me something of your thoughts.'

'General,' answered Lady Cleeve. 'I will.'

She sat a little more upright in her chair, she extended her white arms further along the black leather, she looked first at the ceiling, then down at the floor.

'What are you seeking?' barked the General.

'I am seeking the right tone. I find it so difficult to be humble. You see I have my house and all that and so forth . . . quite by chance . . . I began to read my Bible. You see I have no children.' Here Lady Cleeve paused, and glancing down at herself without embarrassment, continued: 'I must have children if I can, and yet . . .' she shrugged her shoulders, 'it may be that I never will. I *feel* I never will. I tried you know. I saw . . . I submitted myself to doctors. I don't think I am the right shape for it . . . or something . . . one never knows . . . there may be a miracle . . . I shall endeavour again . . . someone may oblige, can oblige. And so, so the truth is I am becoming a Christian.'

'Sidney always said "marriage is the waste paper basket of the emotions",' remarked Mrs Mellor. 'Of course,' she added thoughtfully, 'I do believe Beatrice has the ideas and Sidney does the work.'

As if she had not spoken Lady Cleeve continued: 'So I intend to support our Vicar in every possible way, and if it is the right word "grow" . . . yes "grow" with him.'

Calvin said: 'Thank you.'

'Extraordinary!' exclaimed the General.

'I expect my dear you will become addicted to fasting,' said Mrs Mellor seriously, and was surprised when Calvin and Robert Andrews laughed.

'You see,' continued Lady Cleeve, 'you see I am too vain, too orderly, too insecure and too lonely not to believe in my God.'

'In other words,' said Robert Andrews, 'you are a coward Lady Cleeve.'

'Only in certain respects,' said Lady Cleeve. 'I am found to be resolute in others.'

'With your Faith as your prop?'

'I hope so yes. How could it be otherwise?'

Then Calvin stood. Frowning, he said to Andrews: 'I was

oing home to the wife, now I can't. I have to challenge you
Mr Andrews.' He shook his head slowly from side to side as if
had begun to ache and added: 'It's more for me than for
ou I expect.'

Apparently, having anticipated this, or something like it,
Andrews nodded in acceptance and replied: 'You will under-
tand that statements I make, answers I give, are necessarily
ased on observation, usually historical observation, not on
ersonal experience.'

Calvin approached the boy and standing over him, seeking
ather to draw him out than over-bear, asked: 'Have you ever
een religious?'

'Yes. When younger. At Eton at first I was particularly
eligious . . . needing a refuge. "Let me hide myself in Thee"
muttered, and I did hide, I certainly hid. Indeed I was more
bsorbed in religion than anything else—except perhaps
istory.

'It was quite apparent that God, after-life, and free will,
vere the prime considerations of man on this earth—I used to
it in my study and consider them for hours, days . . . in fact
I've never been given to such a consideration since . . . so . . .
o after examining each in turn I decided that none were
ikely.'

'Not likely?'

'No. Not likely. At first I found this conclusion very depress-
ng. It doesn't upset me now.'

'My dear boy,' exclaimed Mrs Mellor. 'My dear, dear
oy.'

Calvin asked: 'How did you manage to conclude this?'

'Well of course it is, and only is, a matter of personal
opinion, is it not? I don't wish to break into confession.'

'No, no more confessing,' agreed Lady Cleeve. 'We've had
enough of confessing . . . I have done that. In any event, confession is not revealing. It is one's actions that reveal.'

'Come on,' said Calvin, 'how did you decide all that?'

'As to God's existence I merely examined all the arguments
I could lay my hands on in favour of it and do you know I did

not come across one that would have convinced a child unless they had wanted, wanted beforehand, to believe the conclusion.'

'Well of course,' said Calvin slowly, 'you do come to the point where you go down on your knees or you don't. There is a place where reason ends and faith begins.'

'Reason ends,' cried Mrs Mellor. 'Oh how sad.'

'Human reason is so weak,' said the General.

'Well Mr Calvin,' said Andrews. 'I just think God's silly you see. And about immortality . . . well it's quite clear that the line between body and mind being such a hair's breadth of a line, how can one go on without the other? I can't accept that. How can the mind fly off somewhere? What would it be doing all day? What would it be doing? Naturally I can't prove God doesn't exist—I just don't think God's any more likely than Neptune.'

'This word "coward",' deliberated Calvin, 'a moment on that. Are you saying that Lady Cleeve's showing cowardice if she wants the prop of God—if she feels she must have Christ to live?'

'Oh yes indeed,' answered Andrews, 'oh dear me yes.' He looked up at his questioner with great reproach. 'If her faith was anything other than a religious one everyone would sneer at it. It's only the word "Christian" that keeps it respectable. Whatever does she want props for? She ought to be able to live life. That's the glory of life surely . . . helping oneself. You don't want to ask some mythical being to help you. Life is to be lived. By yourself . . . a man ought to be able to live life.'

Lady Cleeve looked sad, Mrs Mellor nodded; the General had closed his eyes.

Calvin frowned again: 'It takes a lot of confidence that . . . even to begin. Does it matter if it's God's prop or self-help?'

'Terms,' said the General, with his eyes closed. 'Terms.'

'On the contrary,' said Robert Andrews with irritation, 'it is not at all a matter of terms! It signifies enormously how you define it. These descriptions are of worlds apart.'

After a pause Calvin said, 'Aye you're quite right.' He paused again, added: 'Of course you're not attempting to explain the universe.'

'I don't think I'm attempting to explain anything.'

'But isn't it rather,' asked Calvin, 'that the prop, the faith, God, is sought because that . . . what is sought is bigger than oneself and bigger in such a way that it's not only cowardice because . . . because you see you want to *do* it for the greater . . . the greater being? Do you follow me?'

'Oh entirely,' said Andrews taking out his handkerchief and politely, almost elegantly, blowing his nose. 'But are there not many things greater than oneself and outside oneself? Life is so hard, seemingly more miserable than pleasant for most, everyone wants something to hope for. Understandable but not excusable. All an illusion. I do not mean to sound presumptuous when I say that I agree with much you have said . . . but for myself I would not be an illusionist, would not be a perpetuator of illusion and myth . . . I would rather be a moralist . . . a preacher without vision . . . except social vision. No mystical vision! That I detest. Since life *is* so hard, so ghastly, as my uncle has testified . . .' And now at last the General refrained from comment because the General was asleep. Undeterred, and smiling at Calvin, Andrews went on: 'If life is so hard it is simply wisest to help each other all we can . . . to our fellow travellers it behoves us to be kind.'

'Not always,' said Mrs Mellor.

'Oh yes always,' said Andrews, 'in the long run that is. We must contribute our lives to each other's liberty. There are other courses to take but that is the wisest. I am awfully sorry to orate, but naturally one does. There is one's family, one's village, one's . . . one's parish, one's country and one's world. I mean *these* are all outside oneself and greater. I'm afraid Vicar if your sort of organized religion is to go on, it will only go on because wars and miseries and earthquakes go on.' He paused. 'Perhaps,' he murmured, 'that is why God causes disasters, perhaps He needs them.'

'If He's there to need them,' said Lady Cleeve, subtly.

'Oh quite,' agreed Andrews, not put out. 'Anyway it seems to me that it is when you are unhappy you turn to God. Or so I've noticed. When communities have solved their social problems they don't turn to God. In the seventeen hundreds when things were quiet they were all free-thinkers—after the French Revolution naturally they all went religious again. Don't you think Mr Calvin that since the Russian Revolution the English bourgeoisie . . . or whatever one calls them . . . has been so terrified by *that* sequence of events that that is why they—those of them who do—go to church. They're frightened they'll lose what they've got if they don't pray to God to keep it. And so on. Oh they're a mean lot!'

'Aye,' said Calvin. 'Aye.'

'Look here sir,' said Andrews, rising from his chair and standing over Calvin to emphasize his argument: 'When we die the mind rots like the body and another thing is that your tawdry old Christian religion has done more harm than good! I won't descend to blaming the Faith for the inadequacy of its individual members, laity or priests. I won't even speak of its tortures, its torturers, its persecutions, its wars and its cowardice . . . no I won't speak of that.'

'What will you speak of?' asked Calvin.

'Of its greatest crime.'

'And what crime is that?' thundered Mrs Mellor, triumphant, as if she had made the accusation herself.

'The crime of making the people of the world believe something without *reasonable* evidence. And therefore corrupting thought and education. And therefore establishing a dreadful morality . . . a morality that states it is *good* to believe certain things and *bad* to believe others. And truth . . . truth is not allowed to come into *that*. Sir, the amount of intolerance that has gone to preserve the Christian faith is overwhelming. It is beyond comprehension.'

'Yes,' said Calvin. 'Yes,' said Calvin slowly, 'you speak of true evil. And what is worst you see it in our schools . . . in our schools now. Where they take a little child and they don't present to him the other side. Yes Mister Andrews I know religion helps fear . . . and fear helps religion. Yes much of what you say is right. I agree that what you hear in nearly every church stops you thinking . . . stops you thinking honestly. I agree that our sermonizers are making important all the wrong things. I agree with so much except . . . except I'm a Believer and you're not.'

Calvin turned away from Andrews and over the sleeping General he made the sign of the Cross. Surprised as she was at this gesture and the suddenness of it, Mrs Mellor was still able to demand: 'Do answer the boy though Vicar.' 'Yes do,' murmured Lady Cleeve. 'He's put me down.'

'Don't be silly,' said Calvin. 'This boy'd never put anybody down.' Then: 'I will answer you Mr Andrews but not now.'

'When?' cried Mrs Mellor.

'Yes when?' cried Lady Cleeve.

'Mr Andrews I shall answer you on Sunday morning in my church.'

'Oh dear. It's still so early. Why not now?' cried Mrs Mellor.

'Because,' said Calvin, 'I really must go home and see the wife. Will you thank your uncle for me and remind him about the meeting tomorrow.'

'In the church hall?'

'Oh no,' said Calvin. 'In the church.'

The church was immense. Very, very cold with the smell of ether, candle-wax, and dust. It was too large for its congregation, the stairways were like castles.

The echo of the footfalls was lost in the enormous avenues. Sometimes she was left alone in the middle of the narrow island of pews that stretched up the nave.

Beyond the island on the great deserts of bare stone, over the inscriptions over the ancient graves, stood the nurses crying out: 'Push.'

'Repeat after me,' said the priest; 'Repeat after me,' said

the doctor. Looking at him she repeated in an ascetic, an obedient and gloomy tone:

> *'What is life? Life is madness.*
> *What is life? Life's what seems*
> *A mirror gleams*
> *Sometimes joy, sometimes sleep*
> *Life's a dream, weep.*
> *Even dreams are dreams.'*

The priest looked down at her from the corner of his eye, put away the needle into the box with the others, went away without turning his head.

'Repeat the second part with emphasis,' said the Sister of Mercy. 'Push woman, push.'

'Repeat the second part with clarity, repeat the second part with belief.'

Down into her eyes flew the death-watch beetles, on to her head fell the roof of the chancel. Through the beams, even in the twilight she could see the dropping sky. She could see the pale sky. She cried out not to God but to the cypresses. 'A depression in the child's breathing,' someone said. 'I wanted to write, I had to write,' she said herself. Delirium. Delirium. Delirium.

'I cannot remember,' she said. 'I cannot remember. She cannot be mine because I cannot remember.'

Sweating and weeping she threw off the beams and ran towards the pulpit. He was there, calling to her, trying to get off his gas-mask. The nurses pulled her back and tied her to the beams. 'Push,' they cried, 'push.'

They tied her hands, they tied her feet, they tied her arms, they tied her legs. They crucified her with the needle. She felt the needle but she had no pain. She submitted. The graves opened. Her father disappeared. She bled.

The bell stopped ringing. The service began. The only sound in the church was her husband praying. In a practised voice, in a bored voice, she read the lesson. She could see the whole judging congregation. 'She is not my child,' she read without pain. 'She is a pathetic little thing, I will do my best for her but she is not my child. I have no memory of her. I am responsible no doubt but she is not my child. There was no pain. There was no labour. Someone brought her to me. Let us pray. She is not my child.' And she kept on intoning with other fragments, from other worries, with other fragments, from other dreams: 'She is not my child. Someone brought her. Someone brought her. She's not my child.'

Exploding into her brain like the bell of an alarm clock burst the closing of the back door of Lady Cleeve's Bentley and her husband's tread upon the drive: wrenched from the depths she woke with a cry, and lay on her back trembling, and looking at the oil lamp, in extreme exhaustion.

The tread continued remorselessly up the drive like an alarm clock she could not 'stop or bury'. She covered her ears with her hands. She struggled against screaming, and though she won she could not stop trembling.

She sat up.

When she heard the front door slam with hurried movements she got off the bed and undid her dressing-gown. Her headache raged. She was burning hot. She threw the dressing-gown on to the floor.

She took her comb from the dressing table and combed her hair down with fierce quick pulls. She shook her hair loose about her face.

She tugged off her nightdress, seemed to try and smooth down her body with the palms of her hands, snatched back the nightdress from the chair, put it under her pillow, got back into bed.

When Calvin entered the room she was looking fixedly at the door with the sheet pulled up to her chin.

'Hello dear,' he said. 'I'm sorry to be so late. I thought you'd be asleep.'

'You know I can't sleep without you.'

'What?'

'You know I can't sleep without you.'

'Aye,' he said. 'Well I've missed you dear.'

'I want you,' she whispered, turning her head, and lying on her side away from him, but letting the sheet go so that he could see her bare shoulders.

'What?'

'I want you.'

Very, very slowly he came to the bed, sat, put out his hand and gripped her shoulder.

He felt her body stiffen, then she whispered again.

'What?'

She did not seem to be able to answer.

'What Hannah?'

'Give me another baby.'

Under his hand her body stiffened and tensed so that he thought she might have some kind of seizure. Neither of them knew how hard he was gripping her shoulder. 'Never you mind,' he said.

There was nothing for him to do but wait. Finally she broke, and sobbed.

He was able to weep with her.

Chapter 9

THE black pond had water-lilies growing around the edge. When they set down the litter she did not get off, remaining on the grass and the knotted rope, cradling her head on her knees, watching them undo their boots and push their feet into the pool, each foot making a dry rustling sound before it disappeared.

In some places the black water bubbled.

'A storm brews up like a jar of tea,' said the cripple glancing east. All the men sighed.

When they rose and were ready to pick her up again she protested but they would not hear; in their different ways they maintained that they would bear her till dusk.

The litter was not comfortable. It consisted only of two poles and rope. It was curious how they always took the same positions. It was the cripple who noticed this and suggested changing. It was Mr Lambert, the cripple, who had thought of the litter.

She found it easier to lie back and watch the storm clouds. She closed her eyes. She dozed. She slept. 'Sh,' said the cripple.

'Don't you think I'd best walk through the village?' she questioned waking up suddenly. But none of them answered her.

By the time they were crossing the green in the centre of the village small boys were running after and shouting out.

Windows were thrown open above; doorways crowded.

But none of them answered.

Only when they were on the open road and even the cyclists, wheeling and swooping like crows, had abandoned them, did the cripple call from behind: 'I should have taken advantage and nipped round the back.'

'Not with the flag,' said Mr Brander.

'You carry the flag,' said Mr Johnson.

'You bear the old flag,' said Mr Slattery.

'You're joking aren't you Mr Lambert?' asked the old man.

'Of course he's joking,' she said from the litter.

'I'm the first one to nip round the back though,' said the cripple, in his hoarse voice.

'Are you still light-headed my dear?' asked Mr Johnson.

'I am, Mr Johnson,' she confessed.

The procession moved on. The westerly wind dropped a little. The rain and the thunder did not come.

They reached the main road again. Lorries began to pass. None of them stopped; none of them were asked to.

The setting sun shone down upon the Suffolk border. In the distance they could see the four square independent tower of Saint Michael. Again their pace quickened.

Jean smiled at Mr Rockingham sniffing the air like a pointer—she knew what he was thinking as he gazed. Every now and again he would glance back at Mr Lambert to see his flag was safe. What trust reposes there, thought Jean. She wondered if they all knew what the flag was and decided to ask after they had eaten—if they ate, that was.

'That summit up there,' said Rockingham gazing at Saint Michael, 'is so square and unrelieved I think the congregation must have run out of money—before they could add battlements, parapets and pinnacles that is.'

'You'd like to be up there Mister Rockingham.'

'I would Jean. I would like to be up there. What height would you think that tower is?'

Mr Slattery said: 'One hundred feet.'

'Ah! a hundred feet,' sighed Rockingham.

'It doesn't compare does it Mister Rockingham,' said Jean shyly.

'No lass it don't. But it's different to Stump.'

Mr Slattery said: 'They used to call me Buck. I never swear in front of women anyway. I never have. Not even with he pints inside of me! Not at my stoniest. It's not the done thing. Now the French do it. They do that. And the French women do that. Anyway ... at any rate ... present company are and excepted ... I don't never have no women to swear before.'

'I wonder why they called him "Buck",' thought Jean, 'can't be his teeth.'

Mr Slattery said: 'There aren't what you call women tramps—not women of the road. There isn't no stream of lady love plying the highways.'

'I've seen one,' said Mr Johnson.

'Yes I've seen one,' said Mr Brander.

Mr Slattery said: 'One, you seed one. That's not many. And I'll bet you a guinea she didn't pick up her skirts and sit herself down beside you all smiles.'

'She didn't,' said Mr Brander.

'No she wouldn't,' said Mr Johnson.

Then Mr Slattery said: 'Below a certain low there's only men.'

'That's true,' agreed Mr Johnson and Mr Brander.

'That is true,' agreed the cripple. 'Below a certain level there's only men.'

Mr Slattery said: 'So you never hold a woman in your arms. Not never. If you can't find a woman in the low level you can't reach up and touch the white moon. You can't catch 'em above now can you. Women don't reach down. No. Not to the dirt. No, we don't do a roaring trade in women down here. No. Women never reach down poorer. Not this poor any old road. Love me, love my dirty shirt. No you're on your own as regards that on the road.' Mr Slattery sighed. 'No there's no hope of wife nor lover down here. No hope of any woman at all unless you steal a shilling for an old tart right out of the hospital door.'

The procession moved mournfully on.

Mr Slattery said, rubbing his eyes—which had begun to run in the setting sun: 'And that's a crying shame for a start ... I mean you couldn't call me an old maid or a prude?'

No one answered.

'Could you?' inquired Mr Slattery.

'No you couldn't,' said Jean.

'Well then,' said Slattery, 'they ought to put a stop instante
to women unlicensed and not inspected by the proper author
ties. Now whoever ventilates that matter will confer a lastin
boon on all concerned.'

'Some man is always responsible,' said the cripple with
certain sadness.

Mr Slattery understood the responsibility Mr Lambert wa
referring to but chose to ignore it. Mr Slattery said: 'That
why you have this raping and so much of the other. Althoug
the raping's only occasional. Tramps don't have a lot fo
that.'

'They've not the strength,' stated Mr Johnson.

'No well that's right,' said Slattery. 'We're not the sort a
rapes. That's big healthy farmers and labourers. But that'
why there's so much of the other in our life. We can't take ou
grist to any other mill. No, that's why there's so much of th
other in the spikes. Only last night but one there was a gagge
touched me up twice. I had to speak to him severe. I had t
inform him—so he cried. Yes he was pitiable. No, I don't lik
it. I never liked it.'

'I don't know what they do,' said Mr Johnson sadly.

'Nor do I,' thought Jean.

'You're joking,' said the cripple.

'No he's not been approached,' said Mr Brander. 'He's ofte
told me that.'

'It's not precisely that I don't know,' said Mr Johnson
'I've been told but I still don't know it . . . if you understanc
me. It is . . . it is beyond my imagination . . . shall we say be
yond my ken.'

This piece of explanation gave them all food for thought-
even Slattery was quiet until they were almost at the outskirt
of Beccles.

Mr Slattery said: 'Ah. Ah. It bows me very heavy to be cu
off from the world of women entire for the rest of my natura

life. That is what is dispiriting. It's this physical rotting off all by meself – that does me up.'

'You're not young Mr Slattery,' said Mr Johnson.

'Sex is fundamental,' said Slattery.

'I've got it both ways,' said the cripple. 'No women and a shot leg. That's twice over. That's double. Women don't like dirt you know.'

'They don't,' said Jean. 'Not in others.'

'No one likes it so much in others,' said Mr Johnson. 'I've often puzzled over that.'

Mr Johnson continued: 'Mind you there's dirt and dirt. I must point out myself that to my mind the true sin imposed on us, on *us*, is the idleness, the imposed idleness. The law of the land being such if we're not walking we are lying in a cell. And if we are not ensconced in a cell we are lying outside it waiting for it to open. This gentlemen is dispiriting enough for such as myself but how much more dismal for the uneducated.'

Mr Brander said: 'But I think the worst is the starving. Sometimes I've cried with weakness. I just have to sit down when I am and I just stare. I'm not so fitted for it as some. If it wasn't for Mr Johnson I would have . . .' here Mr Brander paused in search of a suitable word, and finding it continued: ' "retired", yes "retired", a long time ago. I didn't expect this do you see. I wasn't brought up to it. Do you know I was at my best in the war. I was an excellent batman.'

'Batman Brander,' said Mr Slattery with joy. 'Batman Brander. Batman Brander and Father Rockingham.'

'Sometimes,' said Mr Brander, with dignity. 'I cry because these are my only rags. When I think of the suits I have worn.'

'And the tailors you have known,' said the Irishman, grinning.

'No mockery,' said the old man. 'Laughter must be in the correct spirit.'

'Laughter must be in the correct spirit,' cried the cripple.

'That's hard,' said Mr Slattery.

'But just,' said Mr Johnson.

Mr Brander continued in his quaver: 'What is more my

199

boots don't fit. They pain me these boots—they have always
pained me. It has been a year and they have never worn
in.'

'They've not become adjusted to the shape of your foot,'
cried Slattery. 'That's what they've not done you see.'

The cripple said darkly: 'There's fifty thousand of us in
England alone.' He spat. 'And most of us fought for King
and Country.'

'*I* volunteered,' said the Irishman. '*I* volunteered. I should
have stayed home and saved me strength for the Tans.'

'Fifty thousand,' muttered the old man.

'God damn those rotting Tans to hell,' said the Irishman.
And this time no one rebuked him for swearing.

'I should get meself back home and sort it out,' said the
Irishman.

'No you cannot do that Mr Slattery,' said Mr Johnson, 'for
you haven't the strength nor the resources. Yes Miss Jean and
Mr Rockingham, fifty thousand. Round and round and
round we go but not merrily.'

'Is that a joke?' asked the Irishman, his sad thoughts in
Ireland.

'It was intended as such,' claimed Mr Johnson. 'Mr
Brander laughed.'

'I did,' confirmed Mr Brander.

Mr Slattery said: 'Ah well you're no humorist, you haven't
got the trick of it. But you're right though. On and on and on.
And this is what we fought for. Hey Father Rockingham do
you suppose there's a thousand on us would tramp for enjoy-
ment?'

'Not for choice,' said the old man. 'I've seen it and I know it.'

'That Welsh would,' said the cripple.

Mr Johnson said: 'Here you are, there you are, turned out
and on to the next. On the move. Kept on the move. Eternally.
It is no use and it is meant to be of no use.'

'Work is the only answer,' said the old man. 'Work and
Jesus. Work you enjoy.'

'All change,' cried the cripple.

When they had resumed their way Mr Slattery said: 'But we all know that about work.'

'Sing us an Irish song, Mr Slattery,' asked Jean.

Without more ado Mr Slattery sang:

> *'Here's a health to Slattery's Aunt*
> *And the reason I'll tell you why*
> *She always kept things decent in*
> *The Slattery famileye.'*

'I was hoping for a love song,' said Jean after the laughter.

'To tell you the truth,' stated Slattery, 'I hadn't the strength for it. Not for a love song. I'll maybe sing one later.'

The procession was almost at Beccles.

'They used to let us break stones in the spikey,' said Mr Brander nostalgically.

'It wasn't good for your hands, Gerald,' said Mr Johnson.

'We put the quarry men out of work,' said the cripple. 'That's what stopped it. Oh we're a dead loss.'

Mr Johnson said: 'It's the constant moving that's so bad.'

Mr Slattery asked: 'Father Rockingham why can't we just grow our own food? Why can't we just do that now?'

'In the spikes you mean?' questioned Mr Lambert, the cripple, as hoarsely as ever.

'Because those who could manage it, could organize it, could start it, don't care to,' said the old man. 'They're not bothered,' said the old man.

'Ah,' they all said. And nodded their heads. 'Ah yes. That's it.'

Mr Johnson said: 'On further consideration I put these facts: Fourteen hours a day in the spikey, the other ten walking and dodging the police. Five years on the public charge for want of a desk . . . that is me and Mr Brander.'

'For want of a few tools, that's me,' said Mr Slattery.

'For want of everything but my brains,' said Mr Lambert, the cripple.

At last they were in the outskirts of Beccles. Jean was about to demand to be set down when Mr Slattery said: 'Before we repeat our rules I think we might consider this: if we're parasites we're paying for it. Here we all are in our buck's cast-offs. And we're paying.' His gaze brooded on his gaping brown boots. 'Other feet once nested there warm. We're paying for it in varicose veins alone.' He sighed, looked heavenwards. 'Lord I don't know what we're despised for but the dirt and there's reasons for that. Give me a place to wash meself Oh Lord. We're not wicked are we Lord. We're bloody harmless.'

'No swearing,' cried the cripple.

'That was blasphemy,' said Mr Johnson.

'Mr Rockingham doesn't mind bloody,' said Jean, laughing.

'No exceptions,' said Mr Brander.

'Right,' said Father Rockingham.

'You'll have to watch your own tongue Mm ... Mmister Rockingham.'

'I will lass, I will.'

As they were setting her down Buck Slattery demanded: 'Anyway what is meant by that word?'

'What word?'

'Work.' Mr Slattery said: 'It's a word I'd like to hear defined. I know this! I know this! I earn my pitiable living.'

Realizing that victory was his, since so few had decided to abstain, Calvin smiled and began to count. Heads turned, as Coal owner Richards left the church.

'Forty-seven *against* then and one hundred and fifteen, one hundred and sixteen ... no.' Calvin's voice was filled with delight when the General's hand rose slowly into the air .... 'one hundred and seventeen *for* the removal of the Bible boxes.'

No one quite knowing what to do next there was an uneasy silence.

It was the elder Stephens who resolved this silence.

'May I speak, Vicar?'

'Of course.'

It was noticeable how hushed the Butcher's voice had become—how different from its usual commanding bellow.

'Could we adjourn to the vestry?'

'Why?'

Looking around him reverently as the last of the sun shone through the stained glass, palpably awed by his surroundings, Stephens continued in a whisper: 'Vicar I make out your idea for us all to meet in the church first and see you here and take a fresh look at it like . . . now we're getting on to contentious matters I don't feel it's right to argue in here like. I definitely don't feel free to argue with you so much in here as I might in the vestry.'

'Is that the general feeling?' asked Calvin after a long look at his sheep.

It seemed that it was.

'Let us just keep the church for services and such like,' begged Mr Stephens.

'No,' said Calvin firmly. 'I need the House on my side.'

'Vicar,' requested Lady Cleeve.

'Yes.'

'Could we not remove those screens obstructing the high altar?'

'We could replace them with old open-work railings,' said slim Mrs Partridge with the Eton crop and the earrings, who owned the new bookshop.

'I'd paint 'em for ye,' offered a man in a beard and a cape.

'Splendid,' cried Mrs Mellor, wishing she could smoke her pipe. 'I wonder I hadn't thought of it. Well done.'

And even in the church everybody laughed out loud, but coal owner Richards' secretary.

Cutting through the merriment a prim but determined voice was heard to ask: 'Vicar are you of the opinion that the ladies of the Women's Institute should go over to the Mothers' Union en bloc?'

Everyone knew this to be a thorny question.

Calvin answered: 'It has always been my opinion that both are indispensable and balance up.'

203

Since this answer seemed to be meant, everyone was satisfied, and now there were some claps. Then as if the whole congregation had long wanted to applaud, there was an outburst of clapping.

Sitting at the back with her brother, Eileen clapped as loud as any, and when her eyes began to shine several present noticed the Vicar's daughter. But where was the Vicar's wife?

'It is leadership that we require,' barked the General. 'Then we can act.'

'I have prayed to God it is leadership you will get,' said Calvin. 'You know some tension is bound to exist between parson and people in the best of parishes.'

'Tension can be creative,' cried Mrs Mellor.

'Indeed,' said Calvin. 'So let it be in Eastwold.'

And Mrs Fisher said: 'He works at church all day, Vicar does . . . we only have spare moments . . . spare moments . . . that's how arguments come.'

'As I said before,' Calvin scratched thoughtfully at his ear, 'my first requirement is for you to get to know me. I'm isolated being Vicar. I can't get nothing done except by persuading and since I'm always around and you're always having to listen, I may get to be boring you.'

Some of the ladies demurred.

'I may very well get to bore you,' said Calvin smiling, 'so you've got to help me. And perhaps the best way is practical. First, the churchyard's overgrown and untidy—there's grass in the gutters—we could have evenings on that first and then some "church ale".'

'I'll be there,' said Mr Stephens.

'Yes he'll be there if there's ale,' said Mrs Fisher. 'You've got to watch him Vicar.' And she added. 'But it is a disgrace those gutters. It is.'

Calvin said: 'Now I'm very anxious to go into the question of the music—couldn't we have a mixed choir?'

'What no surplices?'

'What the ladies in it?'

'The ladies in it!'

'The ladies in it,' said Calvin.

'We'll have to think about that won't we,' drawled an assured voice from the back.

'Who spoke?' asked Calvin.

'I spoke,' answered Mr Barrow—coal owner Richards' private secretary—rising, stroking his nose, and calmly adjusting his spectacles.

'Why not think of it now?'

'How can we,' answered Barrow with studied arrogance, 'the organist's not here, Calvin.'

This indeed caused a stir.

'He should be here,' cried Mrs Mellor. 'Where is the fellow?'

'I expect I know where he is Mr Barrow,' said Calvin. 'I expect he's having tea with your man Richards.'

'You're not one to mince words are you, Calvin,' said Barrow as insolently as possible.

'No I'm one as'll punch a nose,' said Calvin, to everybody's consternation, except the General's, who barked: 'And he would. He's no pacifist. He may be Red but he's a leader. He was there you know. At the front. Flanders field. He was there. Were you there, sir?'

'I was not,' replied Barrow, shortly.

'Ah. I thought not. I could tell from your tone. What a funny voice you've got sir. Yes I think he'd punch your nose. And if he did . . . if he did it might help your catarrh, sir.'

Worsted by the General, who was so much his social superior, the private secretary sat down. Lady Cleeve asked: 'What of Mr Lewis, the organist?'

'Well,' said Calvin, 'we had a chat and from what he told me I must say I don't too much like the sound of those accompanying versicles and responses by the organ. I'm not High as you know . . . it's *musically* I don't approve. I just don't like the sound of it.'

'No you're not High,' cried Mrs Mellor, longing for her pipe, 'you're not High, you're Low.'

'Mrs Mellor I'm not Low.'

'What are you then?'

'I'm Broad.'

After the laughter Calvin continued: 'You see the men don't turn up for the choir practices anyway so as a consequence the standard's very, very poor—why can't we have everyone who sings well and would like to? Boys, men, women and girls.'

'I shall leave the choir,' stated Mr Brown, 'if there's women and girls.'

The ladies disapproved: 'What prejudice!' said Mrs Mellor. 'Good riddance then,' cried Mrs Pepper. 'Pompous ass,' muttered Lady Cleeve. 'Get out of it,' said little Mrs Fisher. 'Get out of it then.'

'Ladies, calm yourselves,' said Calvin. 'Mr Brown this isn't Canterbury Cathedral.'

'*I* shall not calm myself,' said Brown. And he left the church straightway.

'And even so shall we need a new organist also?' asked the insolent Mr Barrow, adding to the confusion.

'And what shall we do with the surplices?' cried the thrifty little Mrs Fisher. 'Can we get a price for 'em?'

'Are we . . . are we to have a musical . . . a musical service?' The question was asked in a thick foreign accent by a little bald man who sat beside Mr Farthingale—who was bearded and wore the cape. 'Are we to have a truly musical service?'

'That's what I would like,' answered Calvin slowly, trying to puzzle out who the questioner was.

'In that case,' said the little Swede, 'I shall be pleased to play the organ for three months' trial and undertake the practices for the choir. I am better at writing for female voices.' He sat down abruptly, rose, added: 'I do not promise miracles with your hoarse Suffolk throats.' And sat down again.

Calvin judged it best to accept straight away and inquire into it more fully later. 'After all he did say three months' trial,' thought Calvin.

Immediately, Mr Brown re-appeared in the doorway and

leaning against it like a man with a wound he shouted: 'And I say this, what's more. Patience is what a country parson should have. It's wrong to tamper with local loyalties. Local customs. Established customs. Care is needed. I've been here man and boy. And what's he! He's a foreigner.'

Almost in tears Brown continued: 'If you don't like the service in a town you can go elsewhere . . .'

'You've got a car,' interrupted Mrs Fisher.

'Yes I have,' said Mr Brown with dignity, 'and I shall use it. And what is more . . .' Here he paused and looked meaningly at some of the men, 'I shall resign from the cricket and go and play for Loddon.'

And so, Mr Brown disappeared for the second time.

Miss Winifred Orwell asked: 'If Mr Anders is to play the organ, train the choir, and honour us with his musical arrangements, might I revive the Morris dancing?'

'Yes, yes. Let's do that,' agreed several.

'We're still doing the broom dance at the Arms,' said Mr Winchilsea. 'Miss Orwell can have the hand-bells and use the yard.'

'I could start with some of the easier but traditional dances —Bean Setting, How d'ye do, Sir, Rigs O' Mallow—and the songs are so very very lovely: Raggle Taggle Gypsies, The Two Magicians, Mowing the Barley.'

The octogenarian, Mr Robinson of Manor Farm, now stood, and sang in a quavering tone:

> *There were three gipsies acome to my door,*
> *And downstairs ran this alady, O!*
> *One sang high and another sang low*
> *And the other sang bonny, bonny Biscay, O!*

At the end of the verse he inclined his head, announced, 'Last verse,' and continued:

> *What care I for a goose-feather bed*
> *With the sheet turn'd down so bravely, O!*
> *For tonight I shall sleep in a cold open field,*—
> *Along with the raggle-taggle gipsies, O!*

The ancient sat down without another word and such had been the pathos of his singing, that the meeting sat silent with him. Finally it was the General who was resolute enough to proceed: 'Could I?' asked the General, 'revive the Scouts? I'd treat them as soldiers you see. They'd like that. I know they would.' 'Permission granted?' said Calvin.

Having been given the required permission and informed the meeting that when he inspected the lads he would wear his full dress uniform and his primrose kid gloves, the General suggested that one of the sidesmen should keep a Good Samaritan register for the men of the parish with a note of their special skills. 'I am sure in my own mind,' said the General, 'there are many good chaps who will come to the Sunday services if they're doing something with their bare hands for the church in the week.'

'Yes, yes, he's so right,' boomed Mrs Mellor. 'What we ought to do ... what we ought to do is to have a "demonstration" night. We should invite all those who have already volunteered in this and that, and all those who are interested in volunteering. Invite the Press you see—that is essential. Even the un-Churchy papers. Photographers must be invited. That is particularly essential. And to be quite certain we are on the right lines the Vicar must pray for half an hour in the morning.'

Robert Andrews was pleased to note that the comicality, unintentional no doubt, of Mrs Mellor's last remark, had not escaped Calvin and that Calvin smiled as he glanced away from Mrs Mellor and announced proudly to the assembly: 'Why our church can shine top to bottom like a new pin. Our church and churchyard can be full of flowers.'

But Mr Barrow, the secretary, rose for the second time to announce that he would just like to read his employer's considered statement before the meeting adjourned. Mr Barrow read:

'To my fellow congregationalists of Eastwold.
Our new incumbent is a member of the Church Socialist

League. I protested at his appointment before he gained it. I protest against it now. I shall go on protesting.

To my mind what strikes me most about him is that he has what the great Charles Dickens described as "the ruling passion". He has his little hammer under his pillow and he chips away at all our countenances. And yet I am certain that this man has no definite theological beliefs. I am equally certain that this man would put the class war before his country.

The people who join the Church Socialist League have always been able to believe anything or nothing so long as they are members of the Church of England and economic Socialists. Many of its members are pacifists. This man is not that. Perhaps it would be better if he were.

In essence this man is a self seeker who wants most to propagate the class war. He is a hazard to this Parish. He is a trouble-maker. He is a malcontent. He is crassly stupid. Unaware. Intolerant. And a self-righteous bore.

I do not intend to resign as Church Warden—an office I have held for twenty-three years until after the election of the new Parish Church Council on May the eighteenth. When the results of that election are known I hope I may not be required to resign at all. By that time many of you may have come to your senses and other and saner voices may have prevailed. By that time many of you may have come better to understand the true nature of the Pastor who seeks to lead you. To lead you to God knows where. To destroy our happy community. To destroy our tradition!

I am writing to the Bishop to communicate these views.

I hope and pray that the new council will be returned with a majority who think as I do.

I remain,
Your Church Warden,
I. T. Richards'

There was a long pause.

'Finished?' asked Calvin.

'Yes indeed,' said Mr Barrow.

'Nothing to add on your own account?'

'No,' said Mr Barrow.

'War. War has been declared,' said the General.

'Let us pray,' said Calvin.

The parishioners of Eastwold were about to kneel, when in a passionate voice, Robert Andrews leapt to his feet and stammered: 'Look now. Ddon't . . . ddon't be put down by such a man whatever happens. Ddon't be put down by such a hypocrite. I mean Richards. He doesn't care for any of you. He just doesn't. I mean . . . I mean I'm an atheist . . . I really am . . . but if . . . if you're going to give yourself to God's cause, for what your souls are worth, maintain God's quarrel properly as if it's the whole business of your life. Fight for Him and not for yourselves. Mr Calvin's trying to do that. He may be misguided but he's trying. You can see that. If you're doing your best you won't mind losing. If you're defeated then you won't be ashamed, or thwarted, or even surprised. I expect you'll get to expect it. Success isn't your business if you believe—it'll be your God's. Your part is to follow the Vicar and not care about the result. It's going to be very exciting if you follow him because . . . because there's plenty of people who . . . who'll try to knock you about. Listen . . . listen don't give a damn for such as Richards. Well that's all . . . that's all I can think of. That's what I . . . Of course all preachers are bores. At least that's what I . . . that's what I . . .'

Faltering, stopping, feeling he *had* made his point, Robert Andrews hurried from the church.

Rising to his feet, gazing after him, the General cried: 'Well said, lad, well done.' Turning and beaming at those around him the General cried: 'He's my boy you know. That's who he is!'

'I thank him for his sentiments,' said Calvin. 'Shall we pray?'

The parishioners of Eastwold got on to their knees.

The wind of the sea rose up in the quiet, and came to the church, making the candles flicker. The sound of the waves mingled with Calvin's prayer as if they were all in a ship, bound for a distant shore.

'I think,' said Mr Slattery, 'I've convinced myself entirely, it's time for our supper.'

'You're right,' said the old man.

'I'm off here then,' said Mr Slattery, 'follow me.'

They followed him off the road into a spinney.

'I'll start the fire up,' whispered the cripple beginning to root under the hedge for dry sticks.

'We'll help,' said Mr Johnson, and Mr Brander.

'You were lucky in Beccles Mm . . . Mmister Rockingham.'

'I was.'

Together they laid out the provisions, the old man and the young girl.

'Mmister Slattery was right about one at a time.'

'They call it "mooching",' said the old man. 'I had a good "mooching", I had.'

The rain and the thunder had not come yet but they knew the storm *was* coming.

When they had got the fire going, and gathered a pile of wood, and sat themselves down, and the tea was brewing up in the cans, Jean asked: 'If it rains tonight how are we going to manage?'

'It will rain,' said the cripple.

'Then how are we going to mmanage?'

'That depends,' replied the cripple.

'On what?'

'On Mr Rockingham. Are we going further tonight or kipping here?'

'It's not a bad place,' murmured Rockingham, looking through the trees towards the falling light.

'It's a clean place,' said Mr Johnson.

'We've done a good stint, Father,' said Mr Slattery.

'I don't think we could presume to bear the litter in the dark, Mr Rockingham,' said Mr Brander, 'should we stumble the lady might come to harm.'

'I'm walking from now on,' protested Jean. 'All the time.'

'No I don't think we could bear the litter in the dark,' muttered the cripple.

'The thing is,' said the old man, slowly, 'I fancied being at his morning service.'

'What, matins?'

'Aye that's it.'

'Not vespers?' asked the Irishman.

'No, matins.'

They were now able to drink their tea and eat their gifts and watch the boiling potatoes.

'Speaking as a man of practicality,' said Slattery, 'by my considered calculations of the distance concerned, and the capabilities involved, I think it hardly likely we could offer ourselves at the matins.'

'Too much for the lady,' said Mr Johnson.

'If we stay here tonight and rest up proper,' said the cripple, 'we could fix the litter on top of that wall there and peg this sack I've got and these newspapers I've got and that'll keep off the rain, or some of it any road. Otherwise if we're in the dark we're on to God knows where.'

'True,' said Rockingham.

'We'd be drowned,' said Slattery gazing towards the storm-clouds.

'We've got to think on babby,' said Rockingham following Slattery's gaze. 'It's a night we ought to be in.'

'We'll never get in now,' said the cripple. 'Not in these parts. Not except by chance.'

'Someone might take *her* in,' said Mr Johnson.

'No I don't want to be separated again,' cried Jean anxiously, 'I just don't. I couldn't sleep last night. I was that lonely.'

'I believe as I can fix us a shelter will serve,' said the cripple. 'What with branches and this sack and these newspapers. It'll serve her turn.'

''Tis always cold after midnight in this country,' said the Irishman. 'Hey there's a find.'

And he pointed to what looked like a piece of old galvanized iron.

'Yes I can make use of that,' said the cripple.

'Mr Rockingham,' said Mr Johnson, 'as to your wishes— since tomorrow is Miner Calvin's first proper Sunday I imagine he will read the thirty-nine articles in the morning to his congregation, and that it will be in the evening, that the full benefit of his powers of sermonizing will be enjoyed by his congregation. I believe that to be likely.'

'So I would assume also,' said Mr Brander.

'I wanted to be there for his inauguration. Still it's most interesting what you say.'

'Then it's vespers,' cried Slattery.

'Mind you we'll have to start first thing.'

'With the dawn,' cried Slattery.

'Yes we mustn't dawdle,' said the cripple.

'Oh I shall walk all the way tomorrow,' said Jean.

The potatoes being ready, they took them out, warmed their hands, and were grateful indeed to eat what was hot.

'I've had tay from Convents, Baptists, Church of England, and all sorts,' said Mr Slattery. 'A convent's always good for a cup of tay.'

'Are you a Catholic then Mmister Slattery.'

'Was,' replied Slattery shortly. 'Strong Protestant now.'

No one pursued this.

'To see a tramp as he really is,' said Mr Johnson, 'you should see him naked. That would give you a very good idea of his ... his "depredations". Were one to line up a dozen naked tramps by a wall you would have a doctor's delight.'

'I don't know about delight, Arthur,' said Mr Brander mildly.

'You'd have an executioner's delight,' said Slattery with relish. 'Now what you say is true, Mr Johnson. Very, very true. I'm comparatively healthy meself but I've got eczema, I'm short-sighted but I've got no glasses, I've got chronic bronchitis, catarrh, varicose veins, fallen arches, chilblains, toe-rot, indigestion, unspecified pains in me back, and on top of all that I've got to wear a truss.'

'A truss,' cried Jean.

'Oh I've got to wear a truss,' affirmed Mr Slattery.

'He's not joking you know,' whispered the cripple.

'Indeed I am not,' said Slattery. 'I tell the doctors my

symptoms and they tell me what it is. I'm only lucky I've not yet been received of the dreaded haemorrhoid.' There was a pause. 'But I doubt I will,' he added sadly.

'I don't know how you've escaped it,' said Mr Brander 'I really don't.'

After yet another pause the cripple said: 'I think we'd best be getting our shelter up afore the light goes.'

'Isn't there time for Mr Slattery's love song?' implored Jean.

'Have you the strength for it Mr Slattery?' asked Mr Johnson.

'I believe I have,' said Mr Slattery. 'You know I haven't sung a love song since the war. By the way it's me own tune.'

'One moment,' said the cripple. The cripple opened his tin and handed around the cigarette ends he had picked up from the pavements in Beccles. 'Right,' whispered the cripple. And Mr Slattery sang:

> *'Shy one, shy one,*
> *Shy one of my heart,*
> *She moves in the firelight*
> *Pensively apart.*
>
> *She carries in the dishes*
> *And lays them in a row.*
> *To an isle in the water*
> *With her would I go.*
>
> *She carries in the candles,*
> *And lights the curtained room,*
> *Shy in the doorway*
> *And shy in the gloom;*
>
> *And shy as a rabbit*
> *Helpful and shy.*
> *To an isle in the water*
> *With her would I fly.'*

There was silence in the spinney long after Mr Slattery had finished his song. Sighing Jean said: 'That was lovely Mr

Slattery, thank you very much.' Sighing Mr Johnson said: 'Thank you very much Mr Slattery.' And sighing Buck Slattery said: 'Yeats you know. William Butler. To a tune of me own composition. Me own musical arrangements. No I haven't sung that since the war.'

Splitting the shadows, that unmistakable, that terrifyingly flat Welsh voice demanded: 'Did you think you'd got rid of me then? Singing are you now. Singing are you. That's not tea you're drinking, that's piss.'

On the top of the dyke, just out of stone's throw, he danced up and down. 'Did you think you'd got rid of me you bloody bastards? I was on to you. I was on to you ever since Beccles. Don't think I've gone hungry. I've got a cold chicken and a chop.' Here the screever waved something into the air. 'What do you think of my new jacket?' Holding up his arms like a scare-crow he pirouetted: 'What do you think of my Norfolk jacket? You haven't got nothing like that. Shit faces!'

The tramps, Rockingham and the girl, sat where they were.

'I've not finished with you yet,' shouted the screever. 'I've not done. You didn't think that did you. Old grey faces. Old bread and margarine.'

'I'll see him off,' whispered the cripple, picking up the flag like a spear and rising with it.

'That cripple's a bloody dago,' shouted the screever, 'he's a scrounging pimp, a mother fucker, and a whore-master.'

Muttering ferocious imprecations of his own, forgetting quite the 'rules', the cripple advanced turning back only to announce: 'He's done it now. That's what he's done.'

Mr Slattery rose also and joined the advance.

'I'm an artist,' shouted the screever, 'you're all below me. You're bastard beggars, that's what you are. You've never had more than half a crown in a day. You're starved. You're bastard Nancies. I've got an idea for you. Get up the trees with the flatties in Hyde Park. That's your sort. Go nobber for the flatties. Earn yourselves a deaner. Stick some mouse-traps up your arseholes and climb up the trees and wait for custom. You'd enjoy that, bastard Nancies. Wait for custom and turn 'em all in. After. After mind. That's what you're good for. Scum. I'm an artist. You're a load of bastard beggars. I'm a cartoonist. That's what I am. I'm no chalk dauber. Hey old one-leg, got your balls twisted? Can't you come on faster than that.'

Enraged Mr Lambert did his best to come on faster than that, holding the flag-pole higher over his head as if he might hurl it when he got the distance. Mr Slattery had almost caught Mr Lambert.

'All right you Irish ponce. Come on and I'll do you. Bastard foreigner. Is your truss weighing you down? Come on you bastard Irish tripper. Fancy yourself don't you. Come on prick face. Come on shit pot.'

Now that Mr Slattery and Mr Lambert were within range, the screever bent down to a pile of stones at his feet—the pile that only now they realized he had so carefully prepared—and picking these stones up began to hurl them with such vicious energy, that after Slattery had been hit on his ear, had clutched at it with a howl, and the cripple had been hit on his good knee-cap, they retreated to the protection of the trees and called: 'Mister Rockingham.'

Dancing up and down like a jack-in-the-box he bawled, he whooped, he howled: 'Ah. Ah. Ah. Ah. I done you haven't I you bastards. I done you up. I told you I would.'

Crash went another rock into the branches beside Mr Lambert.

'I'll have your good leg off you yet you bloody dago.'

Crash went a rock into the branches above Mr Slattery.

'I'll have your bastard ear off you bastard Irish pimp. Hey, Rockingham! You know these two fellows next you are Nancies. You know they're Minnies. You know that don't you? The police are after them. You know that. Always exposing themselves that's what they are. Sister Johnson and Sister Brander. Done prison for it. They're a bastard pantomime. The hairy sisters. They'll entertain you all right.'

This was too much for Mr Brander and for Mr Johnson: without a word to Rockingham, or to each other, they rose

216

and positively fled towards the screever, and though he hit Mr Johnson in the chest, the screever wasn't able to hit the flying Mr Brander at all, and so when like two avenging arrows coming at him in the fast fading light from two such different, two such cunning angles, the friends converged upon him, the screever gave a final derisive cry of: 'I'm careful of my appearance I am. You're a dirty lot,' jumped off the far side of the wall, and was gone.

Exhausted Mr Johnson and Mr Brander climbed up on to the wall; presently they were joined by the wounded Irishman and the wounded cripple.

But the screever had gone.

They looked, they sighed. They shook their heads.

Far away in the dusk, came the cry: 'Don't think you've done with me yet.'

Around the hill the assertion was taken up and repeated, all around the plain it rolled until at last it returned and died. 'Don't . . . think . . . . you've . . . done . . . with . . . me . . . yet. Don't . . . think . . . you've . . . . done . . . with . . . me . . . yet.'

'Mr Lambert,' called the old man, 'since the jackal's about you'd best bring me my flag.'

'Do they know what your flag is Mmister Rockingham?' whispered Jean at the fire.

'Aye lass they know.'

'It's just as well the Welsh don't know Mister Rockingham.'

'Yes perhaps it is, lass.'

Rockingham threw more wood on to the fire. Slowly the others returned.

'What do you think of that then Mr Rockingham?' asked the cripple, hoarser than ever, and still rubbing at his knee.

'Yes what do you think of that?' asked Mr Slattery, gasping for breath, and still rubbing at his swelling ear.

'I don't,' said the old man. 'I don't think anything on it at all.'

The flag was handed over.

'It'll be safer,' said the old man.

Then it was night.

'I don't think nothing on it at all,' repeated the old man, 'and neither should you.'

'My but that was a warm jacket he had,' sighed Mr Slattery.

It was after midnight that the thunder sounded and the first rain fell. Jean huddled herself on the lee-side, close to the hedge, and the men stood and pressed their backs against her best as they could to keep her warm.

For a time the cripple's roof worked well enough, then such was the rain the water leaked on them everywhere. 'That's finished the picture of Churchill, on the *Express*,' said Mr Slattery. 'Churchill swims the channel, Churchill swims the channel,' cried Mr Slattery, like a paper-boy. And they all tried to laugh. Then Jean began to cry. When they tried to comfort her she could only answer: 'It's nothing. It's just that I'm tired I expect.'

'I'll boil up for you,' said the cripple, and went out. But try as he would Mr Lambert was unable to light the fire and returned.

'I've never not been able to do that before,' the cripple said. 'No matter how wet. I've never failed before.'

'It's all right, dear,' said Jean.

The rain fell, fell, fell. Fell with the unceasing sound of a fountain. They stood in water.

Jean felt that she was going to drown.

'Last night out lass,' said the old man.

'What if he don't like us Mister Rockingham?'

'Your last night out,' repeated the old man.

As suddenly as it had come the rain ceased. The night grew warmer. Like animals they huddled together in their crib, leaned on each other, and slept.

Jean was awakened by a fierce shout from the old man.

'Oh no. Oh no. No you don't.'

Was it a nightmare?

The old man fell back against the hedge, slid down it, still holding on to the flag, into the puddles.

'You're all Nancy boys. I caught you. I caught you **at it**. You stink of piss, that's what you do. You stink of piss.'

'He was after my flag,' said the old man. 'Thank the Lord **I** sleep light.'

'Well you could hardly sleep heavy here,' said the Irishman, helping him up. 'You'd have to be a genius for that. You'd have to be Rockingham Van Winkle.'

'My goodness Mmister Rockingham.'

'That was a close shave,' said Mr Johnson.

'Thank the Lord I had hold of the right end,' said Rockingham. 'The furled end. Or he might have torn it.'

'Do you think he's gone mad?' asked Mr Brander.

'Aye he's turned cretin,' said the Irishman. 'That's it.'

'That *was* a close shave,' said the old man. 'Now that *really* was.'

'Don't . . . think . . . you've . . . done . . . with . . . me . . . yet.'

'Let's get on. Let's get on the move,' whispered the cripple.

'Let's get on the road,' implored Mr Johnson and Mr Brander.

'At this rate I shall have to be offering up a prayer for the Welsh,' said Mister Rockingham.

At the top of the rise stood a blood red sun.

They stopped.

They were beginning to dry out.

In places the girl's legs had rubbed raw against her skirt.

In no more than a minute the sun rose, clearly, above and beyond a cedar and the birds that had slept in the tree flitted away in an orange light, like bats.

Then they could not look at the sun directly. Then not at all.

They bowed their heads, they rubbed their eyes.

They turned to look behind.

The long falling gleaming road was deserted. Not a rabbit. Not a bird. Not a weasel. Not a stoat.

'Thank God he's gone,' said gentle Mr Brander. 'I couldn't answer for the consequences else.'

'You'd do him an injury, Gerald,' said his friend.

Jean saw so clearly, almost as if for the first time, how all these men except Mr Rockingham were scare-crows. What struck her most about their faces in the dawn was that she couldn't see their eyes. Their faces as the screever had said, were grey, bread and margarine faces.

So she turned and she looked ahead.

Now there was no sun—simply a vast flowing out of pale light.

The men turned also.

They resumed the pilgrimage.

The pilgrims climbed on towards the top of the slope. They rounded a bend. And there he was.

He was enshrined. He was dazzling. He had framed himself in the light. He was ringing his bell. He was shrieking out in welcome. He was astride. He was inviting pursuit.

He had washed, he had shaved, he had slicked back his hair.

He began to sing. He began to sing in Welsh.

'Now where the hell did he get that from?' groaned the Irishman, aghast. 'I'll pray for a puncture.'

How the screever sang.

'He thinks,' said the disgusted Mr Slattery, 'I know what he thinks—he thinks he's the Holy Piper, the Holy Pied Piper of Hamelin. It's the sun. It's gone to his head. He thinks he's a bloody bard.'

'I don't intend to be one of his rats,' said Mr Brander with spirit.

'If I can pawn my mother's locket,' offered Mr Johnson. 'We'll get on a bus.'

Pivoting upon his bicycle, shining and clean, the screever put his weight upon the pedals, and slowly started to lead the pilgrims in the direction of Eastwold Town.

Chapter 10

THE Word had been made flesh, and dwelt among them; the Word had been passed, for the church was fuller than on Armistice Day. Girls from the cannery were there, fishermen, labourers, farmers, shop-keepers, and members of the 'professional classes'.

There were also some 'foreigners'—of these strange faces it had been whispered by several of the locals that they were 'communists' or 'Bolshies'.

Lady Cleeve had arrived early to sit in her habitual seat with her aunt. Coal owner Richards had arrived late but having been kept a seat by his highly salaried and effective secretary, Mr Barrow, he too sat at the front. The General also had arrived late with his nephew, Robert Andrews, and not having, or indeed wishing, anyone to keep a seat for them, these two were now at the back. Mrs Calvin sat with her children in the middle of the church and apparently was still pre-occupied with that damp and mouldy prayer matting for throughout the service she spent her time studying it.

'Psalm one hundred and thirty-eight.'

Upon the roof of the church a gentle rain began to fall. As they rose some of the congregation heard it and thoughtfully looked up. 'God's pity,' thought Richard. 'God's tears.' He did wish his mother would raise her head.

'This psalm is ascribed traditionally to David. At its end the plea is: lowly and frail as we are our Creator does not despise us. The gods referred to in the first verse are the false gods of the heathen.'

A gust of wind rose up over the cliff from the sea and approached the church carrying salt spray.

'I will give thanks unto thee,
O Lord, with my whole heart:

> *even before the gods will I sing*
> *praise unto thee.*
>
> *I will worship toward thy*
> *holy temple, and praise thy Name,*
> *because of they loving-kindness*
> *and truth : for thou hast magnified*
> *thy Name, and thy Word,*
> *above all things.'*

Passing over the graveyard the sea salt whitened the tombs.

> *'When I called upon thee,*
> *thou heardest me : and enduedst*
> *my soul with much strength.*
>
> *All the kings of the earth*
> *shall praise thee, O Lord : for*
> *they have heard the words of my*
> *mouth.*
>
> *Yea, they shall sing in the*
> *ways of the Lord : that great is*
> *the glory of the Lord.'*

When the gust of wind struck the church, the church seemed to shiver, and in the tower, very faintly, one of the bells tolled. 'Tolling for some sailor,' thought Richard.

> *'For though the Lord be high,*
> *yet hath he respect unto the lowly :*
> *as for the proud, he beholdeth*
> *them afar off.'*

The wind entered the church itself, the curious turned their heads : a bent little man in an ill-fitting Norfolk jacket, looked nervously about, shut the side door behind him, and scuttled away into a corner for an empty place on a stone bench. Even in the shadow the sea spray shone on his black hair.

> *'Though I walk in the midst*
> *of trouble, yet shalt thou refresh*
> *me : thou shalt stretch forth they*
> *hand upon the furiousness of mine*
> *enemies, and thy right hand shall save me.*
>
> *The Lord shall make good his loving kindness*
> *toward me : yea, thy mercy, O Lord, endureth*
> *for ever ; despise not then the*
> *works of thine own hands.'*

'Amen,' sang the little man in the Norfolk jacket, as loud as any.

The congregation seated themselves; expectant was the hush that filled the church.

'My text,' said Calvin, in a resonant and unapologetic tone, 'comes not from the Bible but from Keir Hardie in the *Labour Leader*, nineteen o four.'

The great back door of the church swung open and the strongest gust of all ushered in the new entrants as if they had been blown from the depths of the grey North Sea. And they looked like Ancient Mariners this pilgrim band. Rockingham stood at their head, holding on to the flag with his bandaged forearm, and grasping Jean with the other. Rockingham stood at their head and gazed up at the pulpit with joy.

The heads that had turned, remained turned: although the congregation near by whispered and beckoned to them to sit down, the leader of the pilgrim mariners seemed unable to do so, and consequently, uneasy as his followers were, shifting as they did from foot to foot, none of them budged. The leader merely gazed up at Calvin with a rapt, a beatific smile, spreading across his face.

It was a moment before Calvin, studying his text, looked down from the pulpit. In that moment one of the sidesmen, thinking the tramps had mistaken the church for the workhouse, approached Rockingham, and gently taking the bandaged arm that held the flag, attempted to lead the old man away. He might as well have tried to move the church.

From the corner was heard a solitary, a triumphant laugh. But now Calvin saw.

'Why it's Mr Rockingham isn't it,' he exclaimed, peering down the aisle from light to shadow.

'That's who it is,' called Rockingham, 'that's who it is, John.'

Descending from the pulpit Calvin hurried down the long avenue with outstretched hands. It was only now that many of the congregation realized he was wearing clogs. Beside her son Mrs Calvin hung her head, the only person in the church who had not turned.

'I didn't see you at first Mr Rockingham. Welcome. Welcome to Eastwold.'

'Thank you. Thank you.'

There followed one of those series of human sounds which contained no recognizable words, but in which both men conveyed their unspeakable happiness. Coal owner Richards later described it as, 'yapping and moaning and pawing at each other like dogs.'

'These are my friends, John,' said Rockingham, after the embracing was over. 'This is Jean. This is Mr Lambert.'

'Pleased to meet you,' whispered the cripple, hanging his head on one side and raising an arm over it like a bird with its wing.

'This is Mr Johnson. This Mr Brander. And this Mr Slattery.'

'Delighted,' said Buck Slattery, bowing slightly from the waist.

'You're all cold and wet.'

'Aye somewhat.'

'And tired.'

'Aye. But you'll go on with your service. After, John. After.'

Looking at them doubtfully as if he should take them to a fire Calvin was asked: 'Please go on with your service John for that's what we've come for.'

'Will you make room there in that pew nearest the heater?' Calvin asked.

To the credit of the people on the bench, they moved over straightway. 'Oh,' sighed the screever. 'Oh.'

Re-entering the body of the church, on his way back to the pulpit Calvin glanced around, laughed, and called out: 'You can sit down now if you like Mr Richards'—and it was true that the coal owner was still on his feet staring in the direction of the tramps with such a suspicious expression on his face, that it appeared as if he thought Calvin had whistled up for arson, or for anarchy, these thin starving men and that pale, pregnant girl. Recovering, giving Calvin a malignant look, Richards did indeed sit down and only when the congregation had given its attention back to Calvin did the astute Mr Barrow tug at his employer's sleeve, and draw his attention, first to the dejected screever, and second to Mrs Calvin, sitting with her head bowed in her hands.

'My text,' said Calvin again, having ascended.

' "A great principle may be so overlain by dogmatic interpretation as to be unrecognizable; nay, the dogma may in course of time come to be considered of greater importance than the principle itself. It is well, therefore, to examine all formulas and phrases which we are told are not only part and parcel of the true doctrine, but the only real interpretation thereof."

'J. Keir Hardie in the *Labour Leader*, 1904. You'd think he was referring to the Christian religion wouldn't you?' Calvin paused. 'Mmm,' he said. 'There was another good thing Keir Hardie wrote. He wrote that when it comes down to it socialism's aquestion of morals. Socialism's mainly got to do with the relationships that exist between man and man. Mmm. If for five minutes a week you'll consider afresh what you take for granted, there's no knowing what can be done here. I hope you'll examine what I say and examine what my enemies say.

'When you go out into Eastwold what do you see? In the High Street wealthy people wasting money. Some of them lazy people. In Wellington Street at the back of the station there's some hard-working people jammed in a dirty place like rats. That's not all you see but you can see that. Numbers ten, twelve, fourteen, sixteen, eighteen, and twenty Wellington Street.

'Outside the Eastwold Conservative Club yesterday were six children begging, none of them had any shoes. They live numbers ten, twelve, and fourteen Wellington Street. They're Ramsays, Pearces, and Robarts. I believe they're related to some of you.

'Don't tell me there's much worse elsewhere. I know that.

'I'm going to get up a list of people in this parish over-worked and under-paid. I expect it'll be a long list. I've only got two on it tonight: Mr Farrell who's sixty-five and takes round the newspapers for Edwards, and Mr Blatchford who lost an arm in France and works part-time for the Council. If anyone wants to inquire into the facts I'll be glad to give 'em right after the service.

'In Eastwold parish there's the church, the Christian Religion, the Picture House, about seven Rolls-Royces, fourteen private tennis courts, race-horses, and so on and such like—as you say here—a lot of beautiful walks, and there's also, sickness, starving, poverty, exploitation and vice.

'If anyone would like to contradict me please do.'

He waited for 'contradiction', descended from the pulpit.

'Wrong and sadness is here in our parish, and it strangles the life out of just about half of us. Maybe not half here. I don't know yet. I'll get the figures.

'We're one family. Do you think that some are animals? I'm afraid you do.

'Most of you give a bit, here and there, every now and again. None of you give enough. Except perhaps one or two, like Mr Thompson, who's nothing but his war pension and spends his days pushing the sick about in their wheelchairs. Well, some would say he's not good enough for anything else! I say he's marvellous.

'I say that everyone of you here is responsible for the way things are. I say that some of you are responsible if only because you put up with it. How many care? Not many. Just for a bit. Talk a lot. Too busy on their own account. Hmm.'

Calvin walked forward down the aisle and into the midst of his congregation. 'I say that those of you who are doing well fob it all off. You talk about there having to be poor and there having to be rich, having to be servants and having to be masters, and give a poor man a wash bath and he'll put his coal in it. Rubbish. We can all be rich. Or rich enough. We can all be masters and all be servants. And we can all have a bath without coal in it. Let's give the lot baths and see!

'By the way I'm not afraid of generalizations. They're often necessary to start out with. They worry most those who want to qualify everything. Naturally some of them too . . . generalizations . . . are useless or rubbish. Naturally.

'It is your obligation to God and Jesus Christ to find an answer to the mess we're in. Every one of you. And I say that if you seek you will find something without much trouble. There's *somebody* you can help!

'As Mister Andrews there with his uncle, said yesterday, at the meeting: "Don't be put down."

'Look here you've only got to open your front doors.'

Calvin moved on, passed by a new vase of flowers. Stopped at it.

'The economic way in this country is all wrong and has to be replaced by another and totally different. Minor changes, minor reforms may be good, but what's needed is a *way* that won't have any victims at all. I tell you capitalism's got to go. Capitalism's got to be destroyed.'

Calvin turned about to look at the people behind him.

'I stopped just now by these flowers because the church looks so different already. Don't you think so?'

Since his parishioners seemed too reverent to answer Calvin repeated: 'Don't you think so?'

This time one or two murmured that they did think so.

'Mrs Partridge arranged this vase,' said Calvin. 'It's getting to look a happy church. Think what we can do with it. We must have some of those streamers, and perhaps turn that chapel over there into a children's chapel and put their drawings up. I do wish some of you ladies would wear bright handkerchiefs on your heads.'

He moved on down the aisle.

'Yes, minor reforms to ease the lot of the victims of capitalism are fine but we've got to have a system with no victims at all. That's the goal. No question! If you shake your heads in disbelief I'll tell you for certain, things *are* going to happen one day in this country that none of us here would credit. It's always been like that in history, mind. If it doesn't there'll be a lot of bloodshed. And then slowly it'll happen after. But anyway it'll happen. You can't stop history.

'The question is not, was Christ a failure, the question is are we failures?

'Hmm. Of course Jesus was always upsetting the ordinary good Jewish business man with calls to the life of service and self-denial.' Calvin laughed. 'I'm not quite in the position to make his demands but in his Name I'll make many.'

Stopping by yet another vase of fresh flowers he pulled it a little towards him, so that it might better catch the light. 'These are lovely aren't they? I never thought enough about flowers till I got down here.'

He moved on.

'On one point entirely do I agree with the defenders of the present social order – capitalism and socialism can't mix.

'Three questions: why should production be left in private hands? Why should there be a free market when it makes for inequalities? Is the only reason a man will *strive*, to put money in his purse?

'The capitalists don't understand that their own system will bring them down: free competition, as it's called, will make for more and bigger monopolies, and in answer the workers will form their own monopoly. The bigger an industry, the nearer it'll get to public ownership. These so-called adjustments "in the market" won't prevent deeper and deeper crises. There's no doubt socialism's inevitable. I want it sooner and better than later.

'Do the owners want it at the point of a gun?'

A great sigh ran round the church. When it had died Calvin wheeled and pointed at the effigy of the crucified man over the altar: 'I say He would have set His face against private enterprise, against the free market, and against the profit motive. I say Jesus would have set Himself against capitalism with all His militant strength.'

It was at this point that Mr Richards stood. Those close enough were able to note that he stood with the aid of his ceremonial staff, the staff surmounted with a small silver cross. He stood there as ominously as he was able but he did not speak until he was asked. He *was* asked.

'Yes Churchwarden?'

'I am a man of order.'

'Yes?'

'One of my duties is the keeping of order during divine service, and another the giving of offenders into custody.'

'Yes.'

'Naturally, therefore, I don't wish to offend. May I . . . *may* I ask a question?'

There was a pause.

'You did seem to invite a question or two earlier. Or it may have been you invited an answer.'

'Ask your question,' said Calvin.

'Yes,' said Churchwarden Richards, heavily. 'I will. Did you mean to say that if Christ were here now, and he couldn't get his way against the "owners", as you call them, he would, therefore, enforce his will at the point of a gun?'

'I don't know, if he would,' answered Calvin.

'You're hedging me. Did you mean to say that?'

'I think,' said Calvin slowly, 'Jesus would certainly get himself into the position where he would have to be shot.'

'That's not the same thing.'

'No, thank you for making it clearer,' said Calvin.

'Do you support the Russian Government?'

'Yes,' said Calvin, 'yes indeed I do! But I am worried at the signs it is showing of using the violence of other governments. I am worried and perplexed by that.'

229

'Thank you,' said Churchwarden Richards and sat down beside the excited Mr Barrow.

'I want,' said Calvin, turning back towards the pulpit, 'a living wage and a national minimum for a man no matter what his turns of fortune. That of course is only the start. I want equality. I don't mean uniformity. I mean equality. Don't say we can't afford it.'

Arriving at the pulpit Calvin sat himself down on the second step and now there were those close to who could see that not only was he wearing clogs, but that his feet within these clogs, were bare.

'Equality means fair shares. It doesn't mean uniformity and it doesn't mean the same income. To be equal isn't to be the same. To be equal isn't to be the same. We don't want the end of variety. The variety of man is what is most to be cherished. Most to be encouraged.

'It's not one ladder that's needed. It's millions. We want all kinds of ladders. Ladders for those who can't climb. Ladders for cripples—if you like.'

Calvin stood, looked thoughtfully down at Churchwarden Richards composing a sentence: 'My Lord Bishop, I will be frank with you for I am an unrelenting champion of private enterprise, the free market and the profit motive,' he looked at Mr Barrow, smiling; looked at Mr Stephens, the butcher, wondering how he might explain 'capitalism' to any who asked; looked at his children; looked at his bowed wife; looked at Mrs Mellor biting her thumb nail; looked at Lady Cleeve as enigmatic as her cat; looked at Robert Andrews, frowning; looked at Mr Rockingham who seemed to be gazing up at the flags, looked at the pale handsome girl resting on Mr Rockingham's shoulder; looked at the General; looked at them all.

'Equality of opportunity? Do you know what that phrase we used so often and so optimistically in nineteen hundred and nineteen should mean? It should mean that people with the same abilities should have the same chances, no matter what the difference in their circumstance or birth. People should get the education they need for the work they aspire to and get it on ability alone. Some of you can't even conceive such a thing happening, and yet it is nineteen hundred and twenty-five. Nineteen hundred and twenty-five years since Jesus was born.

'Equality of opportunity? The second thing it should mean is that people of unlike, of dissimilar and little ability, should also be given chances—and the chances must be such as allows them the possibility of fulfilling themselves . . . *themselves* . . . whoever, or whatever they are, or what that fulfilling may be.'

Calvin ascended the pulpit, leaned forward, looked down and said quietly: 'There will always be the weak and the strong, the fortunate and the unfortunate, the healthy and the sick. We can't change that. What we can change is social discrimination. What we can change is social injustice. Since nature doesn't care about equality, only man can redress the balance. And he should.'

Rubbing his temples with his hands as if in weariness, Calvin continued, 'You're going to hear a lot about this from me. Particularly in my church. But I'll argue it out anywhere. I shall always refer back to two things—socialism's a question of morals, and capitalism's got to go. Next Sunday we'll examine some of the other "isms".'

Bowing his head, some may have concluded that Calvin's sermon was over—they were wrong. Drawing himself up again Calvin said with *passion*: 'We here, in Eastwold, in nineteen hundred and twenty-five, live at the turning point. Men may say of us: "Their eyes could have seen the second coming of the Son of Man." Is the vision *already* fading into the darkness? Ours are the hands that must reach up and invite for there will be no imposition. Here now, in nineteen hundred and twenty-five, the Church has its choice: fulfilment or death.

'To fulfil itself the Christian Religion must carry over into socialism and communism—look, I use these words for want of better—I know what I call communism is taking on a whole lot of significances because of Russia—if you look up the *Oxford Dictionary* you'll find it says only of communism: "a theory of society according to which all property should be vested in the

231

community, and labour organized for the common benefit" —
so that's what I mean by it. To fulfil itself, the Christian
religion must carry over into these systems, and fuse them, with
the divine ideal of honouring every single individual, holy, and
sacred. If this is not done I tell you the whole Church and the
Christian religion will be cast out into darkness and depart
from the face of this earth. It will dwindle. It may take a
thousand years dwindling, but it will perish just the same. And
it'll dwindle very fast! Just as the Jews . . . the Judaists,
crucified Christ, so will we have crucified him too. And much
more painfully. You will see our mass a black mass, prayer
will be a sort of . . . sort of psychological disease, spirituality
will be just a shutting off, an evasion, and moral idealism will
be moral evasion.

'Of course there'll be crusades. Mr Richards there will be
riding out. There'll be whole hosts of reactionaries dressed up
in Bishop's robes. You won't be able to get a horse for Bishops!
They'll all be riding: the owners, the reactionaries, and the
Fascists. And there'll be a lot of hangers on . . . of every description. Cowards, hypocrites, torturers, fools, intriguers, sadists,
masochists, the selfish and the plain wicked. They'll have a lot
of banners but however they disguise the slogans you can be
sure that "on behalf of private property" will be writ very large
underneath. And of course as usual the men who make the guns
and own the horses will get very fat, and all the generals on
both sides'll be very bad, so there'll be a lot of blood letting.
Oh yes for a short time some'll grow rich. Consider I say, their
children, and their children's children.

'The more the Church evades the true conflict, the more it
tries to keep the dreadful pattern we've got, to the accepted
order we've got, to the so-called traditions we've got, the more
it denies the progress of the people, then the more it becomes a
death cult, a perversion, a denial, a . . . a spiritualization of
despair.

'Look here you people, isn't it true that in our day the Church
is exerting less and less moral power, offering less and less
enlightenment. I'm not sure it's offering any, in fact! It sees

before it a society desperately ill, diseased, and it closes its pious eyes, smug eyes, holier than thou eyes, *blind* eyes, and it resolutely and steadfastly refuses to help to the cure.

'Jesus Christ would condemn our Church. He would condemn it for this very missing of the only flood of spirit in our time – the flood of spirit in socialism and communism. How He would open the flood gates.

'And Jesus would join in world movements. The place He'd be ill at ease in would be our churches. He'd be a stranger there but He'd be at home in the "class war"—as Mr Richards calls it. And in that very war is the world's growing point—I know it is—its growing point and its storm centre.

'God above, when religion's alive it don't belong to the backwaters and the harbours, it belongs to the open sea.

'The test of a religion is how much it's secular. The test of a religion is how much it's pertaining to the world.

'I say again our Church stands on the threshold of its most important choice: to involve itself with communism or to evade it. We crucified Christ when He stood before us—who and what are we crucifying now? Ourselves?

'Of course the reactionaries will argue that communism and socialism are not religions. That's the whole point. I never said they were. What I say is Christianity needs communism. And I say communism needs Christianity. Don't tell me that it's special pleading that the Church should enter into social reform! Try and tell Christ that!

'If the Church of England . . . if the Church Catholic . . . is no longer to stand for . . . and . . . and *be* the observing of what is holy in the advancing purpose of history, if it is not to be the tidings of the Kingdom, the revelatory informer of the Kingdom, the dispenser of the Kingdom, if it is not to be the gospeller, then it is indeed "the opiate of the people", it is indeed a deluder, and a denier. It is indeed a false refuge. A corruptor. It is indeed Death.

'If that is what the Church is to become I would rather it dissolve like a dream, and leave not one trace, one ruin, one robe, one ornament behind.

233

'If that is what the Church is to become may it perish.
'Amen.'

The rain misted and fell. Speeding resolutely into this mist
Mrs Calvin and her children.

Watching her go, bidding his employer goodbye for the
present, Mr Barrow closed the door of the Rolls-Royce, and
gestured to the chauffeur to drive off. He noted Calvin on the
porch with the last leavers, he noted those in the churchyard
excitedly conversing, then he raised his umbrella and crossed
the road to where the little man in the Norfolk jacket, and with
the lady's bicycle, stood like a snake with darting head, watching all exits to the church. 'Good evening,' said suave Mr
Barrow, 'I think your friends remain inside.'

'Piss off,' said the screever.

'What?' said Barrow, taken aback.

'Didn't you hear me the first time. Piss off.'

When Mr Barrow made as if to do so the screever demanded: 'What are they up to in there?'

'I don't know,' replied Barrow, 'I was hoping you did.'

'I don't take nothing from religiouses,' said the screever
bitterly, 'I've learned my lesson on that, but I'll find out what's
on in there.'

'Who is the leader?'

'The leader?'

'Yes; the old man?'

'He's a bastard religious. He don't like me. I was good to
him.'

'You find out what's going on in there and keep me informed
and this guinea's yours,' said Barrow, not really able to believe
that the screever wouldn't take the money.

'I was good to him,' said the screever. 'But I didn't know he
was a bastard religious. I had a drawing outside St Paul's.
Outside St Paul's on the steps. Outside St Paul's on the flag-
stones. Beautiful. Beautiful. Best thing I ever done and the
bastard vicar in a black coat came out and danced up and
down on it like it was hopscotch. Danced up and down and set

234

the police on to me. On the ground. Outside St Paul's. Do you know what it was? He kept shouting out "Filthy, filthy. Lewd, lewd, lewd. Obscene," he cried: "Obscene. Obscene." Know what it was?'

'No,' said Barrow. 'What was it?'

'A copy of the Venus de Milo with her arms drawed in.' There was a pause. 'It was a copy of the Venus de Milo with her arms drawed in,' said the screever. 'I did it from an art book.' The screever jerked and spat into the air. 'There's no God,' he said. 'I should have pissed on him.'

'You're fond of that word,' said Barrow, amused now.

'Don't you mock me. I should have pissed on that vicar. Got on the step above and pissed down on him. I should have got up on the dome, up on the bastard dome.'

'You really do have an obsession you know,' said Barrow laughing out loud.

'That dago's only fit to lick up fag ends. I done him you know.'

'How do you mean you "done him"?'

'I've took six pounds Cup Final Day. Eight Boat Race! You have to have a good nobber though or you're done. There's not one of that lot draws better than a horse. They don't think of nothing but their bread and marg. They all discussed it you know. I heard that. Later I heard it. I was insensible. I know it's something to do with that bastard flag.'

'What?'

'How do I know "what". I was insensible. Come up from behind and hit me on the head.'

'I see.'

'When I was ready for 'em they were gone.'

'Where was all this?'

'They was gone when I waked. Are you a religious?'

'What?'

'Are you a religious?'

'No.'

'You were in church.'

235

'Ah well only as a part of my duties,' said Mr Barrow with a certain amount of inspired cunning.

'Life's not going to get any better. I can tell you that. They all think it is. Bastard fools. They told me it was that flag! That Vicar's insane. That's what he is. I'm so much smarter than them it's pathetic.'

'What flag do you keep talking about?'

'Hey!' The screever pointed. 'He's going in now, that looney.'

And sure enough Calvin had given his last handshake and was re-entering the church.

'He's going into them you see.'

'Why do you dislike them so much?'

'I've got to see what's going on,' said the screever in a frenzy. 'I should never come out. I should never have come out of the church. That's where I made my error. They'll see me if I go in there now. They'll turn on me like jackals. That's what they are. And he'll set on to me that Vicar. He'll try to rend me. He's a bastard Bolshie and a centralizator. That's what he is.'

'You're right,' said Barrow.

'I am. I know I am. I'll bet it's something to do with that bastard flag or why are they in there then?'

'What flag?' cried Mr Barrow, in desperation.

'Is there a side door?'

'What?'

'A side door to the church?'

'I expect the vestry door will be open.'

'Which side?'

'That.'

The screever turned and scuttled, dropping his bicycle just where it was.

'I'll come with you,' called Barrow.

'You will not. I don't want your bastard guinea. Piss off. You're a religious.'

At the corner of the church the screever paused, shouted: 'I do things on my own.'

236

And with that he disappeared.

Looking after him, Mr Barrow could see nothing for it at this moment but to make his way home to Mr Richards. He did not feel equal to entering the church. 'And in any case,' he decided, 'I mustn't let my imagination run away with me—there's probably nothing enough here for me to make capital of. What an extraordinary little man.'

So Barrow started home to his employer. As he did so the misting rain fell slower. Fog rolled in from the east and muffled the waves below. Muffled the uneasy bell in the tower.

'So you see,' said Calvin, 'we'll have to make proper, more permanent arrangements tomorrow. I'll think on it tonight. Now . . . now if Hannah's short . . . you're not to notice. She's a woman who thinks in a certain way and sometimes it's difficult for her to adapt herself. You understand she's my wife and I love her . . . I'll not be being disloyal to her . . . I'll be fair.'

'We understand I'm sure,' said Mr Slattery with dignity and with tact.

'Shall we go to the vicarage then? The thing is if you want . . . I know there's a lot you can do.'

There was silence while each thought on this with gratitude and relief, and in some cases they couldn't believe that there really was the possibility of a change in fortune after all this time.

'Come,' said Calvin.

'Before we go will I show you my flag?'

'Aye,' said Calvin, surprised.

'You see,' said Rockingham, unfurling, 'you see, John.'

Deep was Calvin's sigh.

'It's the flag you see, John.'

'You made it yourself Mr Rockingham?'

'I did.'

'Ah.'

Everyone looked at the flag.

'Why was that?'

Silence.

237

'Why did you Mr Rockingham?'

Rockingham bowed his head.

'Why Mr Rockingham?'

Like a child who will not be pressed to an answer the old man took his flag and walked away to stand beneath the other flags in Eastwold Church, beneath the Tricolour of Ireland and beneath the Union Jack.

And there he remained with his head bowed as if in prayer.

'It's best not to force him on such matters,' whispered Jean.

'You've found that?'

'I have Mm . . . Vicar Calvin.'

'Miner Calvin.'

'Aye. Mm . . . Miner Calvin.'

'And perhaps . . . perhaps he doesn't want to force *me*,' said Calvin slowly.

'He tells its history,' said Mr Slattery. 'He's told that.'

'He told you its history?' said Jean.

'Yes he did.'

'But he never told me,' protested Jean.

'He told us that night,' said Mr Slattery. 'Told us all. He give us a long conversation on it.'

'All those tramps?'

'Aye that was it,' said Slattery. 'You was off, you see. You was with the pincer nez.'

'Well he never told me,' said Jean, upset.

'He said 'twas waved long before the Bolshies had it,' whispered the cripple.

'He said,' corroborated Mr Johnson, 'that he held no brief for or against the Bolshies . . . he said that the news from Russia was too confusing for him to make out what was going on there.'

'He said William Morris honoured it,' said Mr Brander. 'William Morris and the English poets. He said it was called the Oriflamme in Henry the First.'

'He said it was in the French Revolution,' whispered the cripple.

'Did he say it stood for the rights of man?'

'The rights of man?'

There was a pause.

'Well I don't know if he did,' said Mr Johnson.

'He might have,' said Mr Slattery, doubtfully.

'It stands for the rights of man,' said Calvin. 'Whatever they say, whatever they do, that's what it stands for.'

After another pause Jean whispered shyly: 'You know where he wants to hang it Mminer Calvin?'

'Aye.'

'In *your* church.'

'Aye.'

Once again they all looked over at the old man, silent and bowed. A draught made the candles on the High Altar flicker.

'I see,' said Mr Slattery, 'you have the old Sinn Feiner flying aloft up there beside the Union Jack.'

'Yes it's been there since the war,' answered Calvin without taking his eyes off the old man.

'Ah 'tis the flag of freedom and a United Ireland. 'Tis a flag that stands for self determination itself. For the very principle. Now there's been some deeds of horror been done under the other, under the Jack.'

'There have,' said Calvin, but still watching the old man. 'There should be an inscription on *his* flag.'

'But there is,' cried Jean. 'There is an inscription. "He hath made of one blood all nations." I saw it on the "Stump". I saw it fine.'

'Let us go to him,' cried Calvin.

Rockingham lifted his head.

'What if *your* flag was to hang up there?' said Calvin. 'What if that Mr Rockingham? Wouldn't it balance them out? The symbol of the One in Many and the Many in One.'

Over the old man's face came his look of joy.

'They'd complement each other out wouldn't they,' said Calvin quietly. 'You might say they stand for three different truths.'

'You should take down the Jack,' said Mr Slattery.

'No they'd be a trinity, like,' said Calvin. 'There's good in all of them you see. Eh Mr Rockingham?'

Rockingham was unable to answer.

'Where would you want yours Mr Rockingham?'

'In the middle,' muttered the old man at last. 'You mean it? You'll have my flag?'

'I will.'

'Well how . . . how shall I get it up?'

'There's a ladder in the vestry.'

'A ladder?'

'Aye.'

'In the vestry?'

'Aye.'

'Then I'll get it John.'

So Rockingham went to the vestry alone, fetched the ladder back, climbed the ladder himself, was handed up his banner, fixed it between the Tricolour and the Jack. Everyone clapped. Rockingham descended. The Red Flag was raised in Eastwold.

Chapter 11

'MILNER'S gone,' announced Mrs Mellor, not looking up from *The Times* as Lady Cleeve entered the breakfast room in her riding clothes. 'You smell of horse.'

'Don't you like horse?' asked Lady Cleeve going straight to the hot plate.

'Sleeping sickness,' said Mrs Mellor. 'I'll wager he got that in Africa. He was there only a few weeks ago don't you know.'

'That would seem logical then,' murmured Lady Cleeve helping herself liberally to ham and eggs. 'Is it contagious?'

'He would have got it in Africa do you see.'

'He would hardly have got it in Canterbury, Aunt.'

'He could if it's contagious,' boomed Mrs Mellor.

'Now don't be cantankerous, Aunt. Did you not sleep well? Did you not have a good journey from town? I was sorry not to have waited up for you, I felt so tired.'

'Tired!' Mrs Mellor sniffed.

'Yes,' said Lady Cleeve, ringing the hand-bell.

'Milner? Wrote a tribute to Arnold you know.'

'Arnold?'

'Arnold Toynbee dear. Toynbee Hall. You're so ignorant.'

'The historian?'

'No dear. No. Not Arnold the historian, his Uncle Arnold. Toynbee Hall Arnold. Striking man. Great lover of truth and so zealous for the public good. Author of those fragmentary but influential pieces published in 'eighty-four under the title of *The Industrial Revolution*? He was always down at the Whitechapel.'

'Nancy,' said Lady Cleeve, 'I would adore some fresh coffee.'

'Is she not swelling?' asked Mrs Mellor when Nancy had gone.

'It would appear so.'

'Have you spoken to her?'

'It is not a matter that I shall raise until she does,' answered Lady Cleeve firmly.

'Then I shall not raise it either,' said Mrs Mellor.

'I should hope not,' said Lady Cleeve. 'After all it is none of your business.'

'I believe it's a common occurrence here,' observed Mrs Mellor. 'I would like some statistics on Suffolk. Mind you it was worse when those Irishmen were about. No doubt the Vicar will have a word.'

'It suits her,' said Lady Cleeve. 'I wish it was me. I shouldn't think the Vicar will have a word.'

'No. No. In a way you know it's a pity you've become so devout. You might have followed Nancy. Think of the benefit of rearing a son of your own without some dull father about the place.'

'You'd like that.'

'I would,' said Mrs Mellor. 'I'd adore it. After all the General's reared no-nonsense-Andrews without a mother.'

Mrs Mellor lit her first pipe of the day, puffed three or four times, turned again to the paper. 'He should have gone on longer with Toynbee you know. Milner. Of course he was on the Inland Revenue for years. He got a First in Classics. He won the Hertford, the Craven, the Eldon and the Derby.'

'Horse-races?'

'Scholarships! He didn't want to let in those coolies you know. Those Chinese coolies. They don't say that here.'

'What's this! "The president bluntly informed the meeting that in India the Mahatma is a spent force"? Rubbish!' Mrs Mellor banged down *The Times* so hard upon the breakfast table that it spilt Lady Cleeve's cold coffee on to her toast.

'Aunt,' murmured Lady Cleeve slyly, 'if you would be quiet and stop reading me out titbits from my own newspaper I could tell you news of far greater import.'

'About Nancy?'

'No, not about Nancy.'

'About what then?'

'Lay down my newspaper, Aunt.'

Mrs Mellor did so: 'Well, Niece?'

'Calvin has hoisted the Red Flag.'

'The Red Flag!'

'The Red Flag.'

'Well! Well I did say he needed an emblem. Wasn't that my idea? Did I not say that?'

'You did, Aunt.'

'The Red Flag! Where has he hoisted it? Where? Over the vicarage?'

'No Aunt. Don't be silly. In the church.'

'Oh in the church. With the other flags?'

'Of course.'

'But you did say "hoisted"!'

'Well Aunt, hung, hoisted or draped—what does it matter?'

'It matters a great deal,' said Mrs Mellor severely. ' "To hang with others" and "to hoist alone" are very different things indeed.'

'Yes I do see that,' agreed Lady Cleeve after a pause. 'However . . .'

'I mean to say if it's draped,' cried Mrs Mellor, 'who has even *noticed*! who could have noticed! Nobody noticed the Tricolour except that enormous Irishman who used to embrace you under it like mistletoe.'

'He did not!'

'He did indeed.'

'Aunt don't be sacrilegious.'

'Why not?' inquired Mrs Mellor, laughing, 'I have always been aware of your deepest desires. Your secret wishes. But go on Niece. I'm all agog. Why has he draped it and what do you feel?'

'I don't feel anything, Aunt. It doesn't interest me a great deal. I don't know why he hoisted it.'

'Draped it Cynthia!'

'All right, draped it! But of course I shall support him.'

'Support?'

'Well there are complaints and those who wish it down.'

243

'Who?'

'Richards for one.'

'Ah! But how very ridiculous when you come to consider it. And fomented no doubt by certain other middle-class persons.'

'Of course. Greatly fomented.'

'Well, well. Well, well, well. It must *not* be lowered.'

'On Monday,' said Lady Cleeve, 'when you saw fit to depart upon your humdrum affairs . . .'

'Don't be rude, Niece. Don't be tart.'

'Calvin organized a petition supporting those locked-out miners in Wales and we all sent off some food . . . naturally this made Richards incensed and when on top of it he heard about the Flag also he . . .'

'But how did he hear about the Flag?'

'The screever, Aunt.'

'The what?'

'The screever.'

'What on earth is that? A mole?'

'The pavement artist.'

'Pavement artist.'

'He was arrested.'

'Arrested.'

'For striking a policeman. On Sunday night, after the service, he went to the police station and ordered the sergeant to arrest the Vicar and Mr Rockingham and those tramps.'

'Mr Rockingham?'

'The old man. Arrest them for hoisting . . .'

'Draping!'

'All right Aunt, draping! Draping the Red Flag in the church. Thinking he was drunk do you see . . .'

'Mr Rockingham?'

'No Aunt, the screever! Thinking the screever was drunk the police sergeant laughed at him and was about to shut him up for the night when the screever kicked the sergeant on the shin and ran off shrieking obscenities against the police force, the town, the Vicar, the other tramps, and yourself!'

244

'Myself!'

'No Aunt,' laughed Lady Cleeve. 'I was only joking. Not you. You were not included.'

'Well,' said Mrs Mellor. 'Well. Where is this fellow, this screever, now?'

'Oh locked up,' said Lady Cleeve. 'Waiting trial for assaulting the police. And accusing them of the most dreadful things.'

'Who will he come before?'

'Hamilton.'

'Ah,' sighed Mrs Mellor. 'Ah.'

'It has not been dull, Aunt. Not dull in Eastwold.'

'No. There's food for thought here,' said Mrs Mellor. 'Here already we have abounding results.'

In the vicarage garden that splendid Thursday morning while waiting for the tea to brew up on the brazier, the cripple was showing Betty his tricks with the pigeon, Mr Slattery was partitioning the tool-shed, Mr Rockingham was repairing the roof of the bothy, Mr Brander was practising on the battered typewriter, and Mr Johnson was trimming the circular flower-bed.

'Tea up in two minutes,' whispered the cripple, putting a handful of corn on his shoulder beside the pigeon.

'When its wing mends Mr Lambert will it fly away?'

'I hope not Miss Elizabeth.'

'So that's good.' Running beneath the study window she shouted: 'Tea'll be up down here in one minute our Dad.'

From somewhere inside: 'All right our Bet.'

Unseen at the window on the floor above the study, Mrs Calvin looked down into the garden, her finger-nails driving into the palms of her hands, telling herself that she must be fair. Hearing a gentle knock at the door of her room she started.

'Come in,' said Mrs Calvin.

'Would you like me to dust this room next Mmm ... Mrs Calvin?'

'Yes. Yes please.'

245

Entering the room Jean began to dust. Aware that Mrs Calvin's eyes were intent upon her Jean became self-conscious.

'Do you . . . do you think it is safe . . . *safe* for my youngest daughter to be with those men?'

'Yes,' answered Jean, 'I think it is.'

'What about that horrible little cripple?'

'He wouldn't harm her I'm sure.'

'I don't know how she can bear him . . . he makes me feel sick.'

'He's very nice really. Once you get used to his disabilities.'

'But they smell so much.'

'I don't think so much now.'

'Their skin is so horrible. Do you think she'll catch something from them?'

'I don't think so. Perhaps you could ask your doctor.'

'You didn't catch anything from them?'

'No,' said Jean. 'I didn't.'

'Nothing in your hair?'

'No.'

'But you were very careful, no doubt.'

'Yes.'

'Well *she* isn't,' said Mrs Calvin.

Mrs Calvin turned her back on Jean and resumed her appraisal from the window.

'They look starved you know. Would you . . . could you go through her . . . her . . .'

'Through her hair?'

'Yes.'

'Of course I will,' said Jean. 'Don't worry about it Mrs Calvin.'

'I couldn't do it,' said Mrs Calvin.

Down below Mr Slattery began to sing in the tool-shed.

'Did the Vicar mention anything to you of his permanent plans for you all?'

'No Mrs Calvin. I don't think he would without consulting you,' replied Jean in her straightforward manner.

'Oh.' Mrs Calvin was reassured.

246

'On the first night he said he'd have to ask you about everything.'

'I see.' Mrs Calvin was very pleased indeed.

'Jean.'

'Yes.'

'Jean—when is your baby due?'

'I don't know.'

'You don't know?'

'Well I haven't been to a doctor yet.'

There was a pause.

'I shall get one today,' said Mrs Calvin. 'Don't reveal anything about it to anyone else. It's just something between you and me.' Noting Jean's surprise Mrs Calvin added: 'Don't worry. I shall pay. I'm going to pay for it all . . . pay myself. From my own money.'

'Thank you Mrs Calvin.'

'Well I . . . I like you Jean.'

After another embarrassed pause and realizing that for some unknown reason Mrs Calvin was near to tears Jean replied: 'I'm so pleased.'

Speaking with a naturalness that had not been hers for some time, Mrs Calvin continued: 'I'll be honest, I didn't expect to . . . but I do. I don't like women very much. Then I've not known a woman of your generation. I think you find life easier than we do.'

'I don't know about that Mrs Calvin,' said Jean ruefully.

'Oh I think you do,' said Mrs Calvin. 'I'm sure of it.'

Turning away, staring down into the garden below, Mrs Calvin saw her husband come round the corner of the house and make his way towards the brazier, reading a letter as he walked.

'No. I don't like all those men. Jean, I am a very difficult woman . . . sometimes . . . I think . . . I think you can be a help to me. I don't know why. I'm glad you've come. But I couldn't have all those men in the house. Not anywhere. I just couldn't.'

Abruptly Mrs Calvin left the window and the room. Since

she was the last person on earth Jean herself had anticipated liking, Jean felt both very relieved and very touched. 'I do know how she feels,' thought Jean, 'oh I feel so sorry for her.'

The door opened: Mrs Calvin stood there, looking down at the floor: 'You're to have your baby here. In this house. I don't want you to strain yourself. On no account are you to do any lifting. You are to have an hour's rest every day after lunch.'

The door was closed for the second time, and Mrs Calvin was gone.

'Oh,' said the girl, 'there you are little Ian, in her own way she's very nice you see.'

In the garden Calvin reached his prepared seat, the throne by the brazier, waited for his mug of tea. Handing Mr Johnson the *Daily Express*, as was the custom, he continued to read his fistful of morning mail.

'When Mr Johnson's read out the news I've a poem to say.'

Sitting on the broken chair with his pigeon the cripple whispered: 'Yes. News first and then the poem, Miss Elizabeth.'

'Opposition to the budget becoming more vehement.'

'As usual,' said Mr Brander, stopping his typing.

Mr Buck Slattery had ceased his song and emerged from the tool-shed: 'You're getting quicker with the old machine.'

'I am,' agreed Mr Brander.

'All England basking in sunshine.'

'We're pleased to share it,' said Slattery. 'We don't mind a bit of sharing.'

'I hope you get your roof fixed before it ends Mr Rockingham,' said Betty in a practical tone. 'Else some of you'll have to come up and get in my bed.'

'Fifty-two car deaths a day. Appalling casualty rates in America.'

'I thought to go there but now that's put me off,' exclaimed Mr Slattery.

'Three trains in collision at Cannon Street.'

'That's not a good station for kipping,' whispered the cripple. 'Sh, now lovey, sh, and your dad'll give you another bit of corn.'

'I used to race 'em you know,' said the old man sitting down heavily.

'Angry Post Office workers—they won't discuss their wage claim.'

'Oh they never do,' said Mr Brander handing out the mugs of tea.

'Thank you Mr Brander,' said Betty, thrilled to get hers first.

'Look at this—ain't it a laugh,' said Mr Johnson passing round the picture of German troops on the back page goose-stepping in Berlin.

After all had laughed Betty asked: 'Shall I read my poem now?'

'Please,' they replied.

Glancing up at the house as if to make sure she wasn't observed from within and therefore could not later be rebuked for her immodesty Betty read:

> *'Have you ever thought!*
> *Have you ever thought as the years go by*
> *When it's your turn to die*
> *They put you in a coffin deep*
> *And down you fall about twenty feet*
> *One week goes well, but then your coffin begins to leak*
> *Worms crawl in thin, worms crawl out stout*
> *Your blood it turns a disgusting colour, and falls out like*
> *   clotted cream,*
> *Your eyes fall in, your teeth fall out*
> *And that's the end of you know what.'*

'Well now that's the most frightening lyric I ever heard in all my born days,' commented Mr Slattery, and meant it. 'Whatever inspired that?'

'It's remarkable,' agreed Mr Brander.

'And it's got double rhymes and all,' cried Mr Slattery.

'It's very morbid Miss Elizabeth,' said Mr Johnson. 'Have you been reading other poets?'

'No it's all mine,' said Betty indignantly. 'What's morbid mean? I didn't steal it.'

'I think,' said the old man, 'when you're younger it's natural. I think that's a natural thought. Not that I consider it myself in that manner. I don't think we should read too much into it.'

'I don't understand you,' said Betty. 'What did you think Dad? I didn't steal it.'

But Calvin seemed utterly involved with a letter.

'What did you think my Dad?'

'What?'

'Oh Dad! Dad you weren't listening.'

'What, pet?'

'I read a poem Dad and you weren't listening.'

Looking up Calvin was astonished to see how near his youngest daughter was to tears.

'Oh I'm sorry Bet. I'll hear it later. It's this letter. You'll come up to my study and I'll hear it later.'

'Well you *must* hear it.'

'All right pet. How am I going to answer this?'

'What?' asked the old man.

'Well I'll read out some of the bits,' said Calvin, 'and we can hear how it sounds in God's fresh air. It's from my Bishop. I'll leave the compliments.'

Sipping his tea between extracts, with the sun warming his back, and shining on the massive letter, Calvin read:

'Let me begin by saying a few words on the parson's freehold and why it is that I, your Bishop, must ask rather than demand, must persuade rather than enforce.

The incumbent of an English parish obtains a freedom in the conduct of his ministry which is unequalled, which is unprecedented. Not Dissenting Minister, not Roman Priest is so little ordered by authority as is the Anglican parson, for the first answers to his Congregation, the second to his Bishop, while the third, our parson, within the vast bound of the law, which sees his cure of souls as his personal property, may answer to neither. How awful then should such unique freedom be misused. How awful if freedom become defiance.'

Calvin glanced up from the Bishop's missive. 'Awful indeed,' said Calvin dryly.

'What next?' asked Rockingham.

'Whether foolish, unteachable and tactless, whether clever, teachable and tactful, the incumbent will be unusually free from official interference; whether industrious and loved, whether lazy and reviled, his position is secure so long as he avoids behaviour which scandalizes the public conscience and forces episcopal action. He determines the hours of service, he determines his pastoral duties. His parochial church council may grumble, protest, denounce —nothing more. His Rural Dean, his Archdeacon, his Bishop can report, visit and direct. That is all. Can they remedy neglect, laziness, and secularity? They cannot. What is more, the laws against the parson's neglects are barely workable in hard practice.'

'Does he get to the point?' asked Rockingham.

'He's making the position clear,' Calvin answered smiling. 'His and mine. He knows I know all this.'

Mr Slattery agreed: 'He is that, getting to the point. I follow it all. Oh he's subtle. He's very subtle.'

'Removal from the living is the only solution to proven pastoral inefficiency and this a remedy of such harshness that it can only be fairly taken when the rights of the parson have been properly assured. It is worth bearing in mind that the generosity of parishioners always considers the parson's wife and children when the question of expulsion arises, for expulsion may bring poverty. In fact it is rarely the Bishop's lothness to use his lawful powers that allows the continuance of rank ill-conduct, rather it is the reluctance of the parishioners to come forward and attest to those "crimes" on which they so vociferously remark.

Yes, in theory, my powers of discipline as Bishop are vast, in practice they are minute; I am sure we would both agree that a Bishop's powers cannot be increased without destroying the standards of equity which Church and public properly hold in awe. And it is a fact, I think, that while in certain cases a Bishop might manage to bring enough force to make the incumbent resign, in other cases he cannot.'

Calvin looked up again and smiled.

'This then is your position as I see it. A position not to be abused. A position to be honoured with all your heart, and mind, and soul. I say that, while it is your bounden duty to preach Christian truth, however unpopular that may be, I say that, while it is your bounden duty to champion moral and social righteousness, it is your equal duty to maintain and set forth as much as lieth in you quietness, peace, and *love* among all Christian people. May I therefore now ask you soberly to consider what purpose the Red Flag serves in your Church? May I ask you to ask yourself why you were so ready to raise it there? May I ask you upon reflection to take it down?'

There was a sigh from the little audience. Rockingham bowed his head.

'I do not think I need quote you here many of the letters I have received from your parishioners—some are ill-judged, some childlike, some abusive, some fair—I will despatch them to you if you so desire.

I say to you John Calvin that in my eyes there is a difference between championing social righteousness and meddling in mere party politics. Does your Flag advance the cause of the Church? I say to you that a refusal to remove the Red Flag will surely cause dissension and strife in your parish, will rouse ill-will, will produce sorrow and anxiety even in the minds of some of the real saints of God in England today. On the high ground of Christian charity I therefore beg you once more to remove the Flag and to cease to use provocative language.'

Calvin put down the letter.

'Is that all Dad?' asked Betty.

'No lass,' answered Calvin. 'The Bishop reflects at some length how a parson may put himself and his love of a cause before his parish. He reflects on the desire for publicity. He reflects how a parson may want to run before he can walk. He reflects on the true function of a country priest. He considers the nature of vanity. He considers the soul. He considers the after-life. And he considers what's best for Eastwold.' There was a pause. 'It's a long letter,' said Calvin. There was another pause. 'Perhaps I am vain,' said Calvin.

'I think,' said the Irishman, 'a man must have a proper conceit of himself. My own fault is I never did. I never have enough conceit you know.'

'He voices the opinion of the majority within my church.'

Mr Slattery said: 'What I've noticed is 'tis only the rich who say the poor are bad on the whole except for that Welsh, and except for the poor who've got rich. 'Tis only the rich who speak so much of the life to come. And 'tis only the poor who take any comfort from the thought of it. From the thought of Heaven. Unless a rich has lost a loved one—or something like that. Well if supporting the poor turns you into a party man, you're a party man. If the Conservatives was to do for the poor you'd vote for them now wouldn't you? Wouldn't you vote for them if they was to do for the poor?'

'I would.'

'Well there you are then. Mind you that's not likely to be put to the test. That piece of voting. No.'

Mr Rockingham rose.

Vicar Calvin looked hard at Mr Rockingham.

'Mr Rockingham, we'll leave the Flag in peace.'

'It's fair if you put it to your whole congregation,' deliberated the old man. 'That is what's fair. Or your Church Council.'

Calvin appeared to consider this statement at length and then to choose not to answer it for he took up another letter and announced: 'By the way our Mr Richards writes to inform me that he has written to the War Office to ask them to remove the Flag and the Sinn Feiner too.'

'The War Office,' cried Mr Slattery.

'Aye.'

'That's a damned piece of a thing of foolishness. Being familiar as I am with the snail-going ways and the tape-red methods of the War Office they'll not get 'em down in ten years, nor he an answer.'

'And a question put to the House of Commons also,' said Calvin.

'And what's more about the War Office,' said Slattery, 'it's twice daft for we're not under martial law. House of Commons is it now!'

'Desperate measures,' whispered the cripple.

'The Bishop was correct when he spoke of publicity,' interposed Mr Johnson.

'And is not that a good thing?' asked Mr Brander.

'Doesn't every little help,' queried Mr Johnson. 'Every piece of attention?'

Slowly Calvin nodded his head.

'Will they write about it in the papers, Dad?'

'Aye. No doubt.'

'Will they write about you Dad?'

'No doubt.'

'Do you want them to, Dad?

And now Mr Rockingham left.

'Where are you off to?'

Rockingham did not reply.

'Please tell,' whispered the cripple.

'Just to see the Flag's all right.' The old man continued on his way.

'I thought that,' whispered the cripple.

'Should we have a guard on the Flag?' asked Mr Johnson. 'For it becomes a cause.'

'I think,' said Calvin, almost to himself, 'there's some things a bishop can demand but a parson shouldn't give. I'm a fellow-servant not an underling. He wants me to live at peace among my Christians but who are they in this parish? Those like Richards who'd have a few locked-out miners shot for an example? Those who put country before Christ? Those who put their private property and their income before Christ? Is it my private vanity or my public zeal that forces this quarrel?'

254

'But why do you want that Flag so much Dad?'

'Because it stands for a principle, Bet. It stands for equality and it stands for the federation of all the nations. The togetherness of all the nations.'

As was his habit at this time Calvin got down on his knees. When he rose he said: 'Mr Brander, you'll be helping me get out a pamphlet on the Flag this afternoon and answering some letters.'

'Yes.'

'Mr Johnson go up to the General's—show him this letter from Mr Richards—tell him I'm still for the Flag. And ask him which side he's on. And if on mine, what he proposes to do about it.'

'Yes.'

'Mr Lambert it's your turn for a bath while Mrs Calvin's shopping.'

'Yes. We've drawn up a rota.'

'Bet, go in and help Jean.'

'Yes Dad. And what will you do Dad?'

'I'm off to speak to the *known* socialists,' said Calvin, 'to call a meeting on the Flag and to find out how we'll best get all the votes we can for the Church Council election. And I'll be going down to the cannery and the Young Farmers' place. We've got to get down to serious business now. I've . . . I've got to justify leaving Houghton. Aye. Aye I have. You're right about the Flag Mr Johnson. You're right. It becomes a cause.'

Chapter 12

SUNDAY, May the seventeenth, nineteen twenty-five. The screever woke banging on the door of his cell. Robert Andrews postponed his return to Eton; Mrs Mellor her re-entry into politics.

The rain fell behind Mr Barrow driving from Cambridge, fell upon the young man driving from Oxford.

Down the hill into Saxmundham the young man from Oxford passed Barrow's car so fast that Barrow couldn't see him at the next turn.

This was the Sunday Miss Dorothea Harris woke to the knowledge of the father of Jean's child.

Betty Calvin had a lovely morning; excused church, because of her cold, she wrote 'The Swallow'.

> *'Gracefully, carefully, flies the Swallow*
> *In and out the trees with sorrow*
>
> *Never thinking unless he worried*
> *What his mother would say.'*

On May the seventeenth, nineteen twenty-five, many in Eastwold realized their importance.

When the young man from Oxford entered Eastwold Square his motor-bike back-fired. He parked it. Holding his umbrella, he climbed on to the pump. No one came to listen; he drove to the church.

The argument had passed from sleep to breakfast table, to coffee-cup, to prayer, to pulpit.

Taking Calvin's arm as they emerged from the vestry, glancing up at the sky, smiling at the onlookers, winking at a child, the Bishop murmured: 'The rain has stopped for us. A remarkable sermon. Full of fire. Let's take a turn around the graveyard.' Ascending the weeded path to a round of applause, reaching the quiet, the Bishop disengaged his arm, continued: 'You have excited your several admirers. A well-meant sermon. Excellent in intention. Full of brimstone. A great case for the Flag. But riddled with self-justification, so let's take a turn.'

'Politics isn't a dirty word. It shouldn't be separated from morals.'

'Calvin, do you know your greatest fault?'

'Pride?'

'Over-simplification. You are a man of virtue. Is that enough?'

'The appeal to keep Christ out of politics is wicked. It's the voter's fault politicians behave as they do because the voters don't act responsibly.'

'I don't disagree. Please do not think me a fool. You mean well — is that enough? The dilemma for the Church is this: when one arrives at a political decision, one has almost certainly compromised a principle to reach it.'

'If the Church is to keep out of every bit of life where principles might be compromised it may as well bed itself down in this cemetery.'

'A negative attitude can have a positive significance.'

'Of course it can. By refusing to vote we're ensuring continuance. We're the Tory party at prayer. That's what we are.'

'Do you want the Church itself to become a political party? Think on past evils. When *that* has historically occurred, torture and bloodshed have followed. I resist *that* with all my heart. Christianity in politics I approve, the Church in politics I abhor. Terrible it is indeed for a country when the Church enters the struggle for power. Power makes the demands of expediency, self-interest, ruthlessness and deceit. Power makes the demand of terror.'

'Your attitude is denying Christ, for you're assisting all political reactionaries. "He that is not with me is against me." '

The Bishop scratched his nose. ' "He that would save his life must lose it",' said the Bishop. 'What the Church must concern itself with is conversion. If Christ finds enough disciples, society will change its laws.'

'It is downright wrong for a Christian only to cast his vote, pray, and leave the rest to the politicians. It's wrong.'

About to reply, the Bishop heard the young man from Oxford, who had climbed on to the wall at the front of the church, begin *his* address: 'Communism despises the Christian religion: Because one: It is the way of those who cannot alter or comprehend the human environment. Because two: The organized Church is a political movement which has never been able to stop a war, which has never been able to change economics—even when those economics were contrary to its own. The organized Church has always supported the status quo. The organized Church has always supported the forces of reaction while shouting out the need for settlement by talk. Trees must be judged by their fruits. Eh?'

'Trees *must* be judged by their fruits,' said Calvin.

'I know his argument,' said the Bishop. 'He has a loud voice. Let us continue our own.' Exerting the gentlest of pressure upon Calvin's arm the Bishop led Calvin deeper into the graveyard.

Descending the slope into Eastwold from the south, in Mr Barrow's car, the young men did not appear to be interested in their surroundings, although none of them had seen the town before. Staring straight ahead, Mr Butterworth in the front passenger seat, beside Mr Barrow, repeated for the third time that morning: 'The world is divided into the stupid and the intelligent. The responsibility of the intelligent is to make the world better for the stupid.'

'Quite,' agreed Barrow, looking tired.

'All mediation and compromise I oppose. Those are the signs of the decadence of the bourgeoisie. Is that the church tower?'

'Yes indeed,' answered Barrow, relieved to see it.

'The nation is the one supreme duty. The whole nation must be militarized.'

Barrow sat up, trying to straighten his narrow shoulders.

'Order must be restored. Power must be gained by violence, retained by violence. Fighting spirit, military discipline, ruthlessness and action must be exalted, ethical motives must be rejected.'

'All?'

'All.'

'Why exactly is that?' murmured Mr Barrow.

'Because they weaken the resoluteness of the will,' said Butterworth with contempt.

Gazing up at the square tower, not once glancing at the driver, Butterworth stated: 'All theoretical considerations are subservient to the inexorable dynamics of the factual situation. Ultimately everything depends upon the fluid decisions of the leader. Decisions cannot be discussed. Decisions must be obeyed.'

'We insist upon the iron logic of nature, Barrow,' said Montague in the back.

'Shut up!' said Butterworth.

As they passed through the square Barrow murmured: 'Mr Richards is most anxious that his name is not brought into . . . this.'

Butterworth did not reply.

'I should have mentioned that before,' Barrow said nervously.

'His contribution has been generous.' The tone reassured Barrow, somewhat.

At the corner of Church Road Barrow was forced to brake sharply when Mr Lambert the cripple stepped off the pavement to retrieve his pigeon: Barrow swore.

'That revolting old man should have been shot,' said Butterworth, who had banged himself on the windscreen. When the car accelerated again, Butterworth said, rubbing his forehead: 'We must get rid of lice like that before we can even begin.'

In spite of his irritation with Mr Lambert, this time Barrow did not answer. Looking in his driving mirror Barrow was relieved when he saw the pigeon was unharmed. Such relief was noticed.

'Drop us here,' said Butterworth abruptly. 'No need for you to go any further. This'll do.'

Mr Barrow did as he was told.

Testing the moisture in the soil with his finger, the Bishop said: 'But we all have our hobby-horses you know. I have some of my own. Much in the Bible, taken literally, is rubbish. Its history is often inaccurate, events are out of context, prophecies are not fulfilled. My dear boy, St Paul's idea of a second-coming with the bodies of the living transformed into the spirit bodies of the dead, and returning on the clouds of Heaven with Christ, is rubbish.' Rising to look into Calvin's face with something like affection on his own, the Bishop continued: 'I know it is the *whole* Christ you wish to follow, but you are not Christ.'

'It is the whole Christ I wish to follow. In Christ there is gentleness and anger. His teaching by mouth and by symbol provoked them to murder him.'

'Others have done that,' said the Bishop, as kindly as before.

'Do we not promise in our ordination to "use both public and private monitions" to those who need them?'

'To try to reform the world without even desiring, by the grace of the Good God, to re-create oneself, is to become a nuisance to one's neighbours, and to fail in the very object of one's desires.'

'To try to save my soul without loving my neighbours, and without battling for God's world, is the surest way to lose my soul.'

Resting his hand on a tombstone the Bishop remarked as mildly as before: 'No Christian has the right to be a party man. You do not live spiritual moments and then material moments—you live both at once. When you eat you can listen to Mozart. You can't appease your own hunger by feeding a

riend. Physically, you are frightened of pain, spiritually you
re frightened of the unknown. The Christian faith should let
 man come to terms. Eh?' Taking Calvin's arm again, resum-
ng the walk, the Bishop said: 'I repeat that where practical
nds are a man's concern, efficiency is vital, and *such* efficiency
lemands force. On the other hand my dear, dear, boy, there is
ove. Love! When spiritual ends are our concern, good rela-
ionships between man and man are what matter, and such
elationships can only be forged by love. John, the Church
imply must not, cannot, set man against man, be the causer
f bloodshed, coerce man into chaos, impose its gospel on the
unwilling. You are caught in a trap.'

'Without politics there is no salvation. The weapon is not a
sword. It is a cross.'

'*There* we are agreed. *There* we are agreed,' said the Bishop.
'Let us go deeper.' The Bishop continued to exert his gentle
pressure upon Calvin's arm, continued to walk Calvin between the tombs.

Proceeding towards the poor box the three young men from
Cambridge did not take any notice of the grey-haired old man,
with the moustache, seated on a stone bench in the corner of
the church nearest the sea.

Going down the aisle Butterworth kicked over vases of
flowers.

'How much shall I put in?' asked Montague.

'Four and sixpence,' said Butterworth, pinning his note.
Addressed to the Vicar of Eastwold, the note read: 'Red
Flag removed as symbol of Antichrist. Equivalent value placed
in poor box.'

'That'll be the vestry there,' said Wiseman.

As they went to the vestry to fetch the ladder Montague saw
the old man, and pointed him out, but the young men
supposed him to be asleep.

'It is lovely here,' said the Bishop. 'You're a lucky chap you
know.'

'Aye.'

'Yes we all have our hobby-horses. Now I . . . I believe many of our Christian teachers put the Bible to such ill use as to render it the greatest barrier to human friendship on earth.' The Bishop smiled at Calvin's surprise. 'Oh indeed I do,' said the Bishop. 'I believe *that*. And is this surprising from a church whose gospellers are demeaned into recording like gramophones the most worthless part of their heritage, who positively and relentlessly enshrine the least valuable part of their culture day after day after day? Who insist upon a provincial view of the universe? Who preach what is pre-Christian, who affirm for the uncritical?' The Bishop laid his friendly hand on Calvin's shoulder. 'My dear John,' said the Bishop, 'I have arrived at the ghastly realization that the so-called Christianity of most of our parishioners is a naïve psychological mish-mash which has been formed by the child, and buttresses the adult, in whatever special way that that adult demands. This gluey mish-mash is so vast that truth discovered by the intellect, or imposed by the reality of living, is sucked into it as if it were a swamp. Not well expressed John, but you follow me, no doubt.'

'Into the swamp I expect,' said Calvin smiling for the first time since they had entered the graveyard.

'But John why are you *so* keen on this Flag? That is a bit beyond me you know. Just because it's a symbol?'

'Aye,' said Calvin. 'Because it's for a fundamental, without recognition of which, men would perish.'

'I'm not sure you and I *can* resolve it,' said the Bishop. 'Perhaps it were better it were taken out of our hands. It's only a thought.'

'How do you mean?'

'Well . . . well perhaps a judge. Then again, perhaps not.'

'You mean the law courts?'

But before the Bishop could answer Calvin started to run.

Butterworth had actually ascended and touched the Flag when he felt the ladder sway and heard the commotion break

262

ut on the floor below. He had time only to glance down at he old man, kicking and flailing, before the ladder was pushed ut of its true.

Grasping for support Butterworth stretched upwards. Such vas the angle of his fall that it was not the Flag in the centre he briefly caught, it was the Union Jack on the left.

Butterworth, ladder, and Union Jack, crashed to the floor. Before he fainted Butterworth felt a kick.

When Calvin and the Bishop arrived in the church from the vestry, and others arrived through the main door, they found Butterworth groaning with his broken arm, and Rockingham till kicking and kicked.

Faced with this audience Montague and Wiseman drew back.

The old man seized his advantage: he pulled the Union Jack from underneath Butterworth, picked up the ladder also; he staggered for the great west door.

'Where are you going with all that Mister Rockingham?'

'I'm going to burn the damned things in the road,' said the old man. He did not look back.

Chapter *13*

THE day for the electing of the Parish Church Council was fine and warm.

Immediately after lunch the carriages and cars started bringing voters to the Guildhall, and the General's Scouts started helping the aged and the infirm across the dangerous streets.

All afternoon, into the evening, the haranguing of the crowd in the Square continued.

Union Jacks, placed in doors and windows, were torn down, were replaced. When Abbey and Son, the drapers, had their windows broken, all the shops shut and boarded up.

By six o'clock Mrs Mellor had accomplished fifteen 'missions' in the Rover, Lady Cleeve twenty-three in the Bentley.

Sitting on the balcony of the 'Sailor's Arms' with his deckchair, rug, and sandwiches, Robert Andrews wrote the first twenty pages of *Up and About in Eastwold and England*.

Although Mr Stephens was polling officer, both sides had watchers to scrutinize.

Dorothea Harris could not find enough quiet in the square to pass on her knowledge. Far away from the square, knitting baby clothes at the vicarage window, Mrs Calvin pointed out to Jean how the shadow of an iron rail fell on the lawn like a cross.

Hurrying out of the Guildhall, to finish building his new ladder, Farmer Chesterton was stopped by Richards: 'How's it going for us now?'

'Very favourably,' answered Chesterton, with satisfaction. 'A solid majority. There's no doubt of it.'

'It *is* a cross,' said Jean to Mrs Calvin, without the hint of a stammer.

'Yes, a solid majority it would seem, sir,' said Barrow, coming up to Richards from behind.

Growing hoarse at his bedroom window in the Swan the

young man from Oxford was not done yet: 'Man is the measure. As Engels says: "A really human morality which transcends class antagonisms and their legacies in thought becomes possible only at a stage of society which has not merely overcome class antagonisms but has even forgotten them in practical life." Anti-Dühring. Page one hundred and nine. At every stage of history men have had their standards of right and wrong but these standards have always been applied *within* the class. *Never* to dealings of that class with individuals outside its ranks. This is the double standard of morality. Gentlemen only raise their hats to "ladies".'

Accelerating to pass a bus Lady Cleeve considered for the first time, in practical terms, the seduction of Robert Andrews.

'Speaking to Clara Zetkin,' shouted the young man from Oxford, 'Lenin declared: "Although I am far from being a sombre ascetic, the so-called 'new sexual life' of the young people—and sometimes of the old— seems to me to be often enough wholly bourgeois, an extension of the good bourgeois brothel..." '

As he spoke the young man from Oxford continued to hurl pamphlets on to the crowd below.

'Look Mr Richards,' said Barrow re-lighting his employer's cigar, 'Calvin's mounting his cart again.'

Calvin was ascending, brandishing a letter with one hand, and holding a thermos-flask in the other.

'I've just got this by the afternoon post,' shouted Calvin. 'I'm going to read it out before I stick it up on the church board.

' "An impression seems to prevail that the demonstrations made during the past few weeks by a number of undergraduates from the university are representative of the general feeling of Cambridge. We wish to state that a considerable body of opinion in the university views these proceedings as an impertinent interference in matters which the inhabitants of Eastwold are quite able to settle for themselves, and is an insult to the intelligence of the inhabitants of Eastwold. We also feel that that which has taken place is, in effect, a regrettable recourse to the process known as 'direct action', a process which those who made the demonstration would be the first to condemn, if indulged in by another class of the community.

It is necessary, too, to point out, in view of possible misunderstanding, that these proceedings have not the support either of the whole university, or of the Cambridge Union Society.

(Signed) etcetera.

Calvin descended: there was applause, there were also shouts of: 'Liar, Forger, Lunatic, Pig, Blasphemer, Devil, and Antichrist.'

'Smash his windows,' shouted Montague.

'Smash the windows of all cottages not flying the Union Jack,' shouted Wiseman.

'He should be flogged.'

'He should be drowned.'

'He should be stoned.'

'Antichrist.'

Calvin climbed back on to his cart: 'Don't be bullied. Keep on affirming the Christian principle the Flag stands for. The Flag stands for equality . . .'

'What right have you got to burn the Jack?'

'Arsonist.'

'You should go to prison.'

'You should be burnt.'

'The Flag stands for equality,' shouted Calvin. 'The Flag stands for the brotherhood of the nations.'

This was the day Richard Calvin started his sonnet sequence: 'The House.' Reversing the normal form, he began each poem with the rhyming couplet, containing a statement, followed this with a generalized elaboration, followed that with a specific elaboration. There was no conclusion.

Enraged, Richards cried at Calvin from the steps of the Guildhall: 'The Bishop's going to evict the Flag by way of faculty—that's what he's going to do.'

'Oh no he's not. For he can't. Brothers! Brothers! The law as to faculties is very confused. Bishops'll be wanting a

266

faculty for hymn-books and hassocks next. If the Union Jack don't need a faculty what price a faculty for the Flag!'

'I'm getting up on that bloody cart,' said Richards to the astonished Barrow.

'Be careful of your heart, sir.'

Pushing his way through his own and Calvin's supporters Richards struggled towards the cart, crying all the time: 'Hear me out. Don't forget the horrible massacres that have enabled the Leninites to seize power. Hear me out friends.'

'Help the hypocrite up,' shouted Calvin. 'Don't kill him down there. Let's have the hypocrite up here in the light. By God he's gone purple.'

Panting and glaring, heaved up by many hands, Richards continued as soon as he was able: 'I have reported this man to the War Office. The Red Flag will soon be removed.'

'Their tape is as red as the Flag itself,' shouted Calvin. 'They'll never get it down.'

'Bolshie.'

'Capitalist.'

'Who are you to stand against the War Office?' shouted Barrow.

'We're not under martial law,' shouted Calvin.

'It's improper to have it in the House of God,' shouted the draper.

'It is not,' shouted the butcher. 'It's right.'

'I've had a question put in the House of Commons.'

'They'll have to pass an Act of Parliament.'

'I am applying to the Church Courts.'

'Mr Richards is applying to the Church Courts! Mr Richards is applying to the Church Courts.'

'The old idiot's applying to the Church Courts,' shouted the young man from Oxford, still throwing pamphlets out of his window in the Swan, in spite of the manager now banging on his locked door.

'Burn the Red Flag!'

'Burn the Jack.'

'Anyway when the poll's done,' shouted Richards, 'the new Church Council will have it down for good.'

'We'll win.'

'We'll win.'

'Burn the Red Flag!'

'Burn the Jack.'

In spite of the clamour no one moved from the square to act directly. No one lit a fire. Richards retired for brandy. The General's army at the church, and Rockingham's army at the church, sat peaceably with their commanders in the candle-light.

The voters kept coming and going. The crowd swelled.

At midnight the tellers appeared on the steps of the Guild-hall and Mr Lovelace cried in vexation: 'Calvin has done us! Calvin has done us! A remarkably heavy poll. Lady Cleeve leads with one hundred and seventy-five votes. Mrs Mellor is second. Total vote for our party, seven hundred and eighty-six. Total vote for the Reds, three thousand one hundred and sixty-six.'

Once again there was tumult in the square. Rockingham entered it to begin the hymn.

This was now the day that the screever was released from his prison cell.

Chapter 14

MAY the twenty-third was a good day for Calvin.

'No Action by the Government.

In the House of Commons yesterday the following
question and answer on the subject were given: Mr
Rupert Hogg (Co. U. Brighton) asked whether the Prime
Minister had received a resolution from the residents of
Eastwold, complaining that the Vicar permitted a Sinn
Fein flag of revolution and rebellion in their parish church
and preached sedition and disloyalty from the pulpit. Sir
J. Boyd (Under-Secretary, Home Office), answered: "The
Prime Minister has received the resolution mentioned and
he sympathizes with the resentment felt by the people of
Eastwold with regard to the conduct of their Vicar, but
since the latter appears to have confined himself to expres-
sions of opinion, and used no language calculated to incite
to violence, no action can be taken by the Government." '

This report in the *Post* was supported by a small letter with
a large heading:

'The Red Vicar.
To the Editor of the *Post*.
Sir —
In your issue of May 21st I see the account of a further
attempt to tear the Red and Sinn Fein Flags at Eastwold
Church by undergraduates from Cambridge. As I passed
the Church yesterday I saw Boy Scouts and old men tidying
up the scene. The flags still hang. Is there no law, either
ecclesiastical or civil, which can prevent the desecration of
our churches by their use for revolutionary purposes such
as these?

Yours etcetera
M. G. Bowley
M.P.
The Limes, Shawnbrook, Beds.'

Under the heading 'This Week' in *The Custodian*, there was

this paragraph: 'We have no doubt that Mr Calvin is greatly enjoying his notoriety but a church is not the kind of building in which to defy your enemies. Mr Calvin's proceedings are a trifle too reminiscent of those of Bombastes Furioso—"Who dares this pair of boots displace, must meet Bombastes face to face." We hope that the representations of the Bishop will induce Mr Calvin to behave with ordinary decency and bring him to see that neither religion nor the Social Revolution is advanced by using a church for the purpose of rabid politics. The fact that Mr Calvin is an entirely absurd person whose political opinions are of no importance cannot be allowed to stand in the way of calling him to order. He is entitled to preach any brand of politics that commends itself to him, and even to drape himself in red flags and Sinn Fein banners if he pleases, but he must not do these things to the annoyance of the parishioners whose views of the uses of churches are of a more old fashioned—perhaps he would say bourgeois—type.'

The *Daily Messenger* simply described the defeat of the 'extremists' by Alfred Rockingham and General Andrews: 'The emblems of Internationalism and self-determination still hang side by side in spite of yet another attempt to take them down.'

In the *Illustrated English News* the entire first page was taken by a drawing of Calvin, preaching from his pulpit, flowers on the church floor, and a female choir singing 'The Red Flag' behind him. The caption was: 'Bolshevism in a Suffolk church: The Red Vicar of Eastwold preaching.' On the next page was written: 'The Vicar of Eastwold, John Calvin, combines Bolshevism, for which he claims to find sanction in the Gospel, with ritual. He hangs the Red Flag and the Sinn Fein flag in his church and issues leaflets called "The Eastwold tracts". One of which contains an appeal "to help the Christian Socialist Crusade to shatter the British Empire and all other Empires to bits". In a recent sermon he said that the object of the Christian Socialists was a Workers' International. On May 21st a meeting of five hundred parishioners condemned the Vicar's actions as "outrageous, and an insult to sensible and law abiding citizens." The Bishop of Watermill wishes all Church people to know that "the deplorable affairs at East-wold are engaging his most earnest attentions". Describing the service there last Sunday, our artist says: "The choir is a mixed one and sits in the nave. The girls wear veils of different colours and materials. The congregation was largely com-posed of very young men and girls. The Union Jack has been banished from the church and burned by some old tramps." '

Mr Richards received the followed letter from the Bishop:

'Dear Sir,

I have received your letter, and also the resolution adopted by a meeting at Eastwold. I am not going to call attention to the number of persons attending the meeting, which you state to have been between two and three thousand, but I would point out that I do know the figure of the total population of Eastwold.

Still, no doubt you had a large gathering. But you fail altogether to give me any information as to why the in-habitants of Eastwold, if the resolution voices their opinion, cannot take the natural course.

I read of undergraduates from Cambridge, I read nothing of the inhabitants of Eastwold.

I can only repeat the proper procedure is to apply for a Faculty for the removal of the Flags in the Consistory Court. This has not been done. I do suggest to you Mr Richards that instead of meeting in the Public Square to pass resolutions calling on the Prime Minister to act, it would have been more consistent and practical if the meeting had decided to use the power which *they* themselves possess before appealing to others to exercise their power.

I need scarcely assure you how I deplore all these incidents. I have directed the Vicar to remove the Flags on more than one occasion. I have pointed out to him the pain and grief which his action is causing men and women not merely in the parish but throughout the country. I trust, I pray, that even now Mr Calvin may see his way to do that which is obvious.

In concluding I must point out once more that when you were church warden you failed in not protesting against the placing of the flags in the church without a faculty, and the people have failed in not applying for a faculty for their removal.

I am ever yours,
J. E. Watermill'

'God damn the bloody Bishop,' said Richards, crumpled up the letter, and threw it at Mr Barrow.

'I must forward it to the Archbishop of Canterbury,' said the frightened Mr Barrow.

Finally, this was the day the screever found lodgings in Eastwold, and the Vicar of Eastwold was able to issue the following statement: 'At a meeting of the Parochial Church Council of Eastwold held last night it was agreed as follows: "We re-affirm the Christian principles for which the Flags stand, namely the right to freedom for each nation, the community of nations, redeemed from avarice and its outcome in the capitalist system. We cannot therefore advise the Vicar to take down the Flags or to yield to hooliganism or violence. But we would make a further effort to persuade the more reasonable of our critics.

' "We wish to draw attention to the passage of Holy Scripture inscribed across our Flag: 'He hath made of one blood all nations'." '

Chapter 15

As before Eileen woke first, stared at the ceiling, raised her thin body, put her elbows on the window-sill. As before the star of Venus shone. Straight lines of light dropped in the sea. 'Empire Day,' said Eileen.

Above Eileen, on the west side, Jean rose, went to her window. 'The town's breathless this morning, little Ian. Very dignified you know. You wouldn't think there was a poor man in the place. No lights in the windows like Houghton. The houses are just catching the sun, the old bricks at the back have gone ruby. There goes Mr Slattery! I'll make Mrs C. a nice cup. I wonder if your grandad slept well.' Jean looked at the church.

Opening his eyes Rockingham saw that the guards were at their posts. 'Good morning Alfred,' said the General. 'Empire Day.' Taking off his coat, the General handed over a flask of tea. 'Fine and mild. Going to be hot.'

'No doubt of it. Thank you George,' said Rockingham, rising to stretch.

Singing as he walked by wild flowers Mr Slattery saw a flutter at a cottage window. When he ascended the stile he saw another. Across the town sprang a little army of Union Jacks. Mr Slattery quickened his pace towards the church.

In Wickham Market, acknowledging the leader, the two scouts saluted, adjusted their goggles, revved up, drew away at speed. Smiling, the leader was handed his morning coffee.

Putting down the letter and opening his egg, Calvin sighed. 'What's that for?' asked Hannah. 'It's from the Archbishop.' 'Yes?' 'He wants me to remove the flags, or in conscience to resign, as my action is in direct violation to my oath of allegiance to the King.'

273

'Can he make you Dad?'

'I don't think so, pet.'

Calvin was pleased to hear no remark from his wife.

'If the government, yielding to the clamour of the pluto-cratic press, attempts to make the Flag illegal, it will be necessary to discuss the exact nature of the oath of allegiance.'

Even to this Hannah made no comment.

In the bluebell wood Robert Andrews looked from Eileen to Richard: 'You know Dick, though the least amiable of the newspaper attacks have come from the *Morning Post*, *The Custodian*, *The Church Times* and *The Winning Post*, what is most serious is the attitude of the daily press, who finding they can't defeat your father by fair means, attempt foul.'

'Yes,' said Richard, looking at the sea.

'Yes,' said Eileen, looking at Robert.

'I mean they appear with such headlines as: "Vicar Surrenders." "Vicar Hauls Down Flags." I wrote to them but they refuse to insert a correction.'

'You'll have to write again,' said Eileen laughing.

'The *Daily Express* did insert a contradiction,' said Richard, mildly, still gazing at the sparkling sea.

'Yes. In an obscure corner. As one would expect the *Daily Herald*'s been the champion but I must admit I am astonished at the attitude of the National Union of Police and Prison Officers. England can be so odd. So unexpected. Now why on earth are the National Union of Police and Prison Officers doing us such good service?'

'You do sound funny,' said Eileen laughing again. 'You're always so serious, Rob.'

In the woods the birds sang.

'Look here John, as I informed Cynthia a moment ago, there are always busybodies attempting to secure convictions against workers singing "The Red Flag" – but the magistrates won't do it don't you know. Why they'd have to arrest the entire London boroughs of Bethnal Green, Edmonton and

274

Stepney! The Archbishop can't charge you with breaking the oath of allegiance when you do what the King's law allows.'

'I don't care if he does,' said Calvin.

'I mean,' said Mrs Mellor, 'the oath of allegiance was imposed when the King had authority. Wisely, or unwisely, he now has none. Don't you know he's got less initiative than the President of the United States! It is the financiers and speculators who have the power. It is the secret gang of interests that is destroying the King's honour.'

'Excuse me a moment,' said Calvin, putting his hand over the mouth-piece of the telephone. 'Are you going out dear?'

'I've got to do the shopping—we're eaten out of house and home these days.'

'Be careful in the town today.'

'Nobody had better lay a finger on me,' said Hannah. 'Nobody would dare.'

Calvin smiled.

When he saw one of his scouts coming back over the rise Butterworth ordered his driver to stop. Waving down the cars behind, the driver did so. Almost before the procession had halted the scout screeched up to Butterworth's window.

'Two huge charabancs stopped ahead.'

'Yes?'

'Having coffee.'

'Yes?'

'Union Jacks.'

'Yes?'

'Union Jacks run whole length of roof-tops.'

'Specially designed?'

'Yes. Ladder sections carried on roof.'

'Who are they?'

'Placards bearing emblems: "Engineers from Chatham"!'

'Patriots.'

'Shall we make contact?'

'No. No. Proceed as to plan.'

There was a hooting from behind—another large charabanc

with the passengers waving Union Jacks passed Butterworth's halted column.

'Excellent,' said Butterworth. 'Tourists. Patriots! Distraction and fodder. Proceed as to plan.'

The motor-cyclist below adjusted his black goggles, revved up his engine, saluted Butterworth, wheeled, and was gone.

'Right driver,' said Butterworth, smiling at his blonde mistress, in spite of the pain in his arm. 'Give me a kiss,' said Butterworth.

On the sides of houses, bare walls, and fronts, loomed his slogans, his emblems and his cartoons. Unceasingly he commented and he explained: 'Here's Calvin about to be possessed. Possessed by the Devil. Here's the cripple being possessed. Here's a pigeon bringing the cripple messages. Here's the Irishman being possessed. Here's the old man. They're all being possessed in different ways, you see. The old man's completely possessed. He's mad.'

The screever moved on.

'Here's the old man as the Devil. They're all Nancies you see.'

'What?'

'What's that?'

'Nancies. That's what they are. Nancies and Catholics. They're Jews you know. Here. Here they're going to be Jewish monks. Over there they're Red monks. Over there Black.'

'How is that then?'

'Yes, how is that?'

'They're all part of the same organization you see.'

Keeping his eye out for the Law—some of whom remained unsympathetic—the screever continued to parade his artistry around the square.

'I'm just about to start on the big one, the grand one. The Arrival. The Arrival of the Avengers. The Avenging Angels. The Angels take the Bolshies and cast them into the sea. Outer darkness and the sea.'

Proceeding to the huge blank space between the butcher's

276

and the draper's the screever called: 'Now watch this. Watch this. Here I'm about to begin my masterpiece. My piece of resistance.'

'Don't worry Mr Rockingham,' said Calvin. 'Remember my oath to the King of England is qualified by my oath to the King of Heaven.'

'It's those damned law courts I'm feared of, John.'

'That'd take months, Alfred.'

'Once you get in their hands you're never out, George.'

'We're not in them yet,' said Calvin.

'I hope I never live to see it,' said the old man.

'Alfred feels we might lock and bar for the day,' said the General. 'I'm against it myself.'

'Oh I don't ever want the church barred,' said Calvin.

'Only for today,' said the old man, 'should things get out of hand.'

There was a pause.

'You'd be keeper, Mr Rockingham?'

'Aye.'

'Shall I give you the keys then?'

There was another pause.

'Would you?' asked Rockingham.

Calvin handed over the keys of his church, moved, the General turned away to join Mr Slattery.

In spite of the engineer on the steps of the Guildhall, in spite of the screever by the pump, the schoolmaster continued his address from the cart: 'What did my son who died for it care for the Union Jack? What did he who died for it care for the British Empire?'

Seeing Mrs Calvin enter the baker's shop Dorothea Harris, spinster, began to push her way across the square. The sun got warmer.

'What my dead son cared for is England and its green fields. England and its country lanes. England and its laughter. Home! Thank God he's not here to see what's being made of it!'

277

Underneath her veil sweat formed on Dorothea's nose.

'My son didn't fight for Empire, he fought for country. He loved the Jack but he was deceived in it. He was deceived in it by the Imperialists.'

Jostled, Dorothea fought her way on with her veil awry. The throng seemed to her to grow thicker at every step.

'He was deceived by the financiers, politicians and newspaper proprietors who grow fat on Empire while they build an England fit for heroes to starve in.' The schoolmaster shaded his eyes from the sun.

Overtaken by Dorothea, on their way to the church with the General's binoculars, Mr Johnson and Mr Brander were crying: 'Hear, hear, schoolmaster.'

'Preserve the town of Eastwold,' came the cry from the Guildhall. 'We from Chatham come in friendship,' cried the engineer. 'We don't want violence. People of Eastwold let us this day remove the flags of anarchy and Sinn Fein from your beautiful church.'

Glancing at each other with pleasure, the scouts adjusted their black goggles, revved and were gone from the square.

'Burn the Flag,' shouted the screever. 'Stone the possessed. Cast out the evil spirits.'

'The Jack is not the old flag of this country. The Jack is the modern flag of brute-force dominion.'

'That man shouldn't be allowed to teach our children.'

Cheers and counter-cheers. The butcher stepped on Dorothea's foot. But Dorothea persisted.

'In its present form,' shouted the schoolmaster, 'the Jack was constructed to celebrate the triumph of a swollen and greedy Empire. The motto of old England and the true loyalists is: Right is might! The motto of the ex-Kaiser, the Prussian Empire, the British Empire, and all empires founded upon swank and grab, is "Might is Right!"'

'That schoolmaster's a Bolshie,' shouted the screever. 'He's a German sympathizer. He's a German spy. God save the King.'

'God save the King,' shouted the engineers. 'German spies.'

'They're Bolshies, they're Russian spies,' shouted the screever. 'God save the King.' The screever climbed up on to the pump. 'God save the King. The Anthem. The Anthem!'

Standing on the pump the screever sang:

> *'God save our gracious King*
> *Long live our noble King.'*

None of the policemen could get at the screever on the pump. The screever sang. When the crowd joined him in the Anthem, the screever cried: 'Knock off the hats of all those keeping them on. Take off your hats for the King. All those who keep their hats on are Bolshies and Russian spies.'

But the bereaved schoolmaster did not remove his hat, and in spite of the Anthem continued to orate—in spite of the blows and the imprecations there were several in the square who kept their heads covered. When Dorothea arrived at last on the pavement by the baker's, the baker had boarded up, and Hannah Calvin had gone. Dorothea Harris fought her way round to the back of the shop.

With a thousand flags flying, the sun directly overhead, the third train-load from Lowestoft arrived, and the roads into Eastwold jammed; with the General on the church tower training his binoculars at the square, Rockingham below by the gate; with Butterworth's party at the ready in the chara-banc and the cars, with the screever exhausted by the pump, with the engineers hoarse; with Mr Richards' and Mr Barrow's party on one balcony and Lady Cleeve's and Mrs Mellor's party upon another, Dorothea Harris found Mrs Calvin: Mrs Calvin emerged into the shadows of a side-street with her last purchases—a pair of slippers for Jean.

'Good morning, good morning,' murmured Dorothea. 'We haven't met but I know exactly who you are. I do hope we can be friends. I have long admired you at a distance. I so hope you will come to tea. My name is Dorothea Harris.'

'Thank you,' said Mrs Calvin.

'Isn't it noisy! I could hardly get out of the square. What a horrible crush. Horrible. All those sweating men. I hope you will call me Dorothea.'

'Are you feeling ill?' asked Mrs Calvin, seeing that Dorothea was trembling.

'The smell was unbearable,' said Dorothea. 'It almost choked me, and oh! this heat.'

'I believe that Miss Harris,' said Hannah. 'I have some smelling salts in my handbag. Why you're trembling all over! Perhaps you have sunstroke.'

Laying her hand on Hannah's arm, glancing about her, seeing that even the shoe-shop in the side-street had now closed its doors, Dorothea trembled even more violently, and whispered: 'Oh Mrs Calvin I'm so sorry . . . I'm so sorry but I must tell you . . . the wife is always the last to know . . . it is something really ghastly but I know . . . I *know* I must tell you . . . I *know* I must find the courage. And to think that a man of God . . . a servant of the Church . . . a Vicar . . . could . . . would . . .' Dorothea Harris drew back her veil, looked straight into Hannah's eyes and breathed, breathed: 'Oh Mrs Calvin, Hannah, may I call you Hannah? You see I do *know* it is my sense of duty that compels me to speak . . . my feeling, my sensibility as a woman . . . Hannah it is your own husband who is the father of the unborn child.'

Hannah turned grey.

'That you see my poor, poor dear is why the girl came to Eastwold.'

Hannah did not speak. Her handbag and her basket fell to the ground. 'I know . . . I simply *know* you will not be able to allow her in your house another moment,' panted Dorothea.

But Hannah Calvin was sick. She leaned against the wall of the shoe-shop and she retched.

'Oh my poor, poor dear,' cried Dorothea. 'What can I do to help? Oh my poor, poor dear.'

Moaning, blinded with tears, her skirt and blouse covered

with vomit, Hannah pushed herself away from the wall and ran from Dorothea Harris in the direction of the square.

Cheers and counter-cheers. In the hot square Calvin had finished his address from the balcony. Revived, the screever was turning his attention to Calvin, the young man from Oxford was quoting Marx on a rooftop, the engineers were raising their huge Union Jacks, and Mr Richards was calling so violently for a petition that once again Mr Barrow feared for his employer's life.

'Let us sing the hymn!'

Almost before Calvin had finished the demand, Mrs Mellor had begun in her deep contralto:

> *'The Son of God goes forth to war*
> *A Kingly crown to gain*
> *His blood red banner streams afar*
> *Who follows in his train?'*

Unheard, old Mr Robinson whispered up to Calvin's balcony: 'I believe in you Vicar Calvin. I believe in you.' Unseen, Mr Butterworth loaded both barrels of his shotgun, and climbed up the ladder to his charabanc roof.

Now the cannery girls, the fishermen, the workers and the 'foreigners' began 'The Red Flag'; now the engineers, the shopkeepers, the farmers and the patriots sang: 'God Save the King!'

Anthem upon anthem.

Blows were struck. Hats knocked off. Noses bled.

Firing both barrels of his shotgun into the air Butterworth stood up on his charabanc. Shocked, the young man from Oxford slid into the gutter; shocked, people screamed, fainted and spun as if they had been hit.

Piercing the confusion, through his megaphone, came Butterworth's order: 'Enough. No more. To the church. Down with the Red and up with the Jack.'

Irresistibly, like a tank, Butterworth's charabanc began to roll across the square. Behind followed Butterworth's cars. As if he had been their leader the engineers from Chatham fell in at the back. So did the patriots. They fell in at the sides. The Eastwold constabulary was swallowed. Swallowed the fishermen and the workers. Remorselessly that procession thrust from the square.

'They're hitting with sticks,' cried Mrs Mellor. 'That's not fair. Those terrible young men. Oh dear! Look at that!'

Darting like a lizard between the ranks of Butterworth's vicious army, the screever caught Butterworth's charabanc and climbed the ladder to the top. On the balcony Robert Andrews moistened his pencil; Richard and Eileen turned pale.

'To the church,' raved the megaphone. 'To the church.'

Bowing his head in deference, cackling, the screever sat himself beside Butterworth to repeat: 'The church. To the church.'

When a resolute young policeman made an attempt to reach up to Butterworth's leg the screever kicked him in the mouth.

Aghast, Lady Cleeve put her hands over her ears and looked to Calvin—Calvin was gone.

'They're coming Alfred,' called the General. 'They've won, Alfred. Those young bastards used sticks. The workers can't do anything more. They've been smashed, engulfed, and swallowed. The girls are crying.'

'What about the police?'

'Too few.'

'A lot of them then?'

'Yes. A lot of them Alfred. And organized. More than I dreamed of. They're out of the square now. Everyone's together now. They're all of a piece now.'

'Ah. Could we stop 'em?'

'Not without guns.'

'Who fired?'

'Only one. Butterworth. Only for effect.'

'They're inflamed then?'

'Yes Alfred. They're a mob.'

'Would the little boys stop 'em?'

282

'Might.'

'Best lock up eh?'

'Yes, Alfred. Alfred I don't think the little boys would stop 'em.'

'If they link hands.'

'I'm doubtful Alfred! Alfred I don't want the little boys to try.'

'The point is George they're already trying.'

Lowering his binoculars from the advance, the General raised himself above the ramparts to look directly below.

'You've trained them too well George.'

Mr Rockingham, Mr Slattery, Mr Johnson, Mr Brander, Mr Lambert, and other old men of Eastwold, stood within the churchyard wall—outside, in the lane, the thin line of Boy Scouts had linked their arms from hedge to hedge.

And their General could hear their whispering beneath the noise of the approaching crowd.

'Boys, fall out.'

They did not move.

'That's an order, Scouts.'

They did not move.

About to descend to enforce his order, moved and troubled, the General was halted by a sudden quiet. Raising his binoculars he looked back at the mob. At the head of Church Lane, in their path, a solitary figure knelt on the ground. Before he had re-focused his binoculars, the General knew who the figure must be.

The General heard the screever shriek. No one moved.

The General heard Butterworth shout: 'Drive on.' The bus remained where it was.

'Pull him out of the way!' No one did.

The crowd edged past and around the praying man but the buses and the cars were still.

The crowd dropped their voices. They began to whisper. Even those at the back.

The General thought the assault on the church had ended—there was no momentum.

Out of the crowd ran a woman—throwing her arms around the kneeling man, knocking him off balance. The General could hear her crying: 'I didn't believe her John, I didn't believe her. I promise you that. I promise.'

Over and over again she cried: 'I promise. I promise.'

Before the General had time to look at her face, the crowd swept over Calvin, and he and the woman were gone.

The buses and the cars proceeded.

Before the General reached the bottom of the tower, his boys in the lane had been punched and kicked aside. When he entered the body of the church, the crowd were banging on the doors.

'Vestry locked Alfred?'

'Of course.'

'Let 'em beat themselves out.'

'Aye, let them. On God's rock.'

Together they sat down in a pew.

'I hope to God my boys are all right.'

'I pray so.'

'Oh they'll have broke their hearts and maimed them but they won't be dead,' said Slattery.

'They punched them up,' whispered the cripple.

The General turned pale.

Outside the church the noise increased.

'I suppose the doors will hold,' said the General. 'Calvin was trampled over . . . I suppose they wouldn't dare a battering ram . . . Calvin tried to stop 'em.'

'We could see,' said Slattery.

'It was Mrs Calvin that did it,' whispered the cripple. 'They will use a battering ram.'

'Mrs Calvin was distraught about something,' said Mr Johnson. 'She was, she was,' said Mr Brander.

The banging and the shouting increased.

'We're not the Bastille,' said the General.

Then the first stone shattered a window.

'That's the Welsh,' whispered the cripple. 'I know that's the Welsh.'

284

In a moment stones flew in at all the windows—glass shattered on the stone.

'They've gone mad,' muttered the General.

'It's that Welsh,' cried the cripple.

And now something heavy was thrust against the great west door, and through the vestry they could hear a muffled thud, thud, thud.

'That vestry lock'll never hold,' said Slattery.

'Pile up against 'em,' said Rockingham, wrenching the first pew.

And the old men did. They uprooted the pews. They staggered. They fell. The old men piled the pews against all doors.

The old men looked up and saw the besiegers gazing in at the broken windows—on shoulders and ladders. They saw the screever. They saw Butterworth.

'They're all old,' cried Butterworth. 'There's only twenty. That vestry door'll never hold. Shove now, shove, shove, shove, shove.'

'I see the flags,' cried the screever. 'Shove now, shove,' cried Butterworth. 'They're almost down. Come now. Come now, let's get in.'

They kicked in the glass, they knocked in the glass with their elbows.

It was Robert Andrews who raised Calvin to his feet.

'I'm all right, lad,' said Calvin. 'Just winded. Kicked a bit. Just bruised.'

Calvin looked to where Hannah lay in a faint.

When he took her from her helpers to put his arms around her, she moaned.

'Any bones broken?' asked Robert.

Calvin felt.

'I don't think so,' said a man.

'No, I don't think so either,' Calvin agreed, in relief.

'Her nose is bleeding,' said the man.

The shouting, the screaming, and the banging at the church grew louder.

'I think they're almost in,' said Robert.

Now Richard and Eileen found their parents.

Hannah opened her eyes, looked into her husband's eyes. She was about to speak when she sensed those other anxious faces gazing down. She closed her lips. She reached up clasped her hands around her husband's neck, drew him down, buried her face. 'I love you,' they heard her whisper. 'I love you, I love you, I love you.'

Throwing a hymn-book and a Bible at the wriggling screever in the window, the General turned to Rockingham to agree the surrender before further damage was done, or any more human hurt. But the old man was no longer beside him. The old man was ascending a ladder.

With Slattery and the cripple supporting, the old man climbed to the Flag.

Rockingham seized the Flag; Rockingham descended.

The crowd entered the church through the vestry. The crowd ran for the Flag.

Laying the pole about him like a scythe Rockingham made for the tower.

Seeing what was to be done, scurrying down a side-aisle, the General reached the tower first and took out the key of the door. When Rockingham was able to enter, the General locked the door behind them.

Exhausted, the General knelt on the bottom step.

'Thank you,' said Rockingham and went up with the Flag.

Unable to move the General lay stranded. The General gasped. The General collapsed as Butterworth's men began to break through the tower door. Somewhere, somewhere above him the General heard Rockingham's clogs.

Supporting Hannah, the Calvins stopped when they heard the cry of joy.

Above them on the tower broke the Flag.

'He's wedged it in the battlements,' said Richard. 'He's singing,' said Hannah.

He was singing. They could not see him; but they heard.

' "Jerusalem"!' said Robert Andrews. ' "Jerusalem"!' said Eileen.

Inside the church there was still shouting. Outside all was quiet.

Outside the church the people looked up. The sun shone on the Flag. The wind came up from the sea.

Someone began to toll the bell.

They saw Rockingham stand on the battlement beside the Flag. Then there was shouting and he jumped back, out of sight. Below they saw nothing—they only heard. They heard Rockingham singing. They heard the screever. They heard the struggle.

Rockingham, Butterworth, and the screever, came over the edge of the tower.

As they fell Rockingham held Butterworth in his right arm, and the screever in his left. Even when they hit the stones he did not let them go.

Above, slowly, the Flag leaned out after in the wind. For a moment it grew out of the parapet like the branch of an oak tree; the pole seeming to bend and to be alive.

The Banner spread. They could read the inscription. Blood red it streamed in the sky. The Flag was enshrined. It exalted.

Then the dark wind came across the North Sea, swept up over the cliff, broke on the tower, took the Flag from behind. The Flag leaned out further, hung, fluttered, drooped and fell.

The bell tolled.

Calvin picked up the broken Flag from the stones, untangled it, and covered the bodies.

Then, as Robert Andrews wrote after: 'Calvin looked up at the church tower in anger, and he shook his fist.'